WENDY JAMES

THE STEELE DIARIES

fi

For Sam, Abi, Nell and Will: 90% inspiration;
10% perspiration (or thereabouts ...)

Now where should the effect of black on white, or white on black, begin, and where end? Where should separation appear and where merging?

Hans Alexander Mueller,
How I Make Woodcuts and Wood Engravings

Where have you gone? The tide is over you
The turn of midnight water's over you,
As time is over you, and mystery,
And memory, the flood that does not flow ...

Kenneth Slessor, 'Five Bells'

One's life is not a case
except of course it is.

Les Murray, 'Three Poems in Memory of my Mother
Miriam Murray née Arnall'

RUTH

2007

Douglas Grant calls me shortly after my father's funeral.

It's only my second day back at the surgery and I'm trying hard to get through the morning's list and leave for the hospital by midday. It's proving to be as impossible as ever; somehow every fifteen-minute consultation (old Mrs Hudson's arthritis, Jimmy Carver's asthma, Irene MacFarlane's ulcerated calf) stretches to twenty minutes, sometimes thirty. My patients' stories, which I would once have encouraged as part of a conscientiously holistic approach to their medical care, seem interminable, intolerably pointless, when all that's really needed is practical intervention: a renewed prescription, a clean dressing, a change of medication. It is already 11.45 and I still have three more patients to see before I can leave. Romana puts the call through just as Mrs MacFarlane limps out the door following an exhausting ten-minute diatribe detailing every particular of her daughter-in-law's criminal child-rearing practices.

'I've a Mr Grant for you, Dr Howatt. He says he's calling on urgent family business.'

There is precious little urgent family business to attend to now, but I think perhaps it is the real estate agent, or the builder I've just employed to tidy up Dad's house, and that Romana has somehow confused the name, so I take the call.

'Is this Ruth?' he asks. 'Ruth Howatt?' The voice, with its indeterminate accent, seems vaguely familiar.

'Yes. This is Ruth.'

'My name's Douglas Grant, Ruth. You may have heard of me. I was your grandmother's biographer. And I was a friend, long ago, of your mother.'

I know who he is, of course, but say nothing. Leave him to fill the silence.

'I read in the papers last week ... your father's obituary. I'm terribly sorry. It must be a difficult time for you.' I am surprised by the man's voice—he must be in his seventies, but it's not an old man's voice; it's full of purpose and enthusiasm and has none of the wavering I've come to associate with age.

He clears his throat. 'I knew him too—long ago when we were young. We were never friends, but he was a good man, I'm sure of that. I know he loved your mother.'

He was a good man; he loved my mother. All of a sudden I'm enraged. I'd like to tell this man, this Douglas Grant, that my father was more than the man who loved my mother. That he loved—and was loved by—his children, too; that he was a good husband to his second wife, my stepmother, Judy. That he was a good son, a good friend, a good doctor. That there was more to him than my mother. That there was more to all of us than my mother. But as always I am polite.

'Douglas Grant,' I say coolly. 'Yes, I've heard of you. Of course. It *is* a difficult time, yes. But why are you calling?'

'Look, there's no point beating around the bush,' he speaks in a rush, as if he wants to get something over and done with, eager to get off the phone, suddenly. 'I wanted to get to you. To get onto you before anyone else. Have you spoken to anyone else yet?'

'Anyone else? About what?'

'About the diaries. I'd like to see them. I'd like to have the opportunity to see them before anyone else. Perhaps we could edit them together. You know, don't you, that I'll look at them more sensitively than anyone else? After all, I knew her well during a critical period of her artistic development. Perhaps the most critical. I realise that my relationship with your mother—that there may be certain ... ethical ... difficulties. But you understand, this is so often the way in these situations. It's inherently a difficult process. It's my opinion that no one has yet managed to offer a proper critique of your mother's work—in the context of her life. But now—these diaries. They might give us the full picture. They might give us the opportunity to put the last few months of your mother's life, her final work, into a new perspective ...'

'Mr Grant,' I interrupt. 'There's been some kind of mistake. There are no diaries. My mother left no diaries.'

He is silent for a moment, then: 'Ah. I'd thought your father ... He hasn't left a parcel, perhaps, for you? A letter? There's nothing in his will? He did leave a will?'

'Mr Grant. It's a very busy time. I have a patient waiting ...'

'Perhaps I could ring you back? Or if you'd prefer, we could write. I can give you my email address. I think we really need to discuss this.'

'I don't think there's any reason for us to correspond, Mr Grant. My father is dead. My mother left no diaries. There's nothing for us to discuss.'

ZELDA

This is the diary of Zelda Caroline Steele
    Aged 14
    Holland House
    Avalon
    Sydney
    New South Wales
    Australia

**TOP SECRET
KEEP OUT
STRICTLY PRIVATE**

This diary will be a record of things that concern me, Zelda Caroline Steele. These things are nobody else's business, so if you are reading this and you are NOT Zelda Caroline Steele, then stop reading NOW. This diary is none of your business.

<u>List of New Year's resolutions:</u>
I will get up early
I will keep a sketchbook
I will keep this diary
I will clean my teeth without being asked
I will work hard at my studies
I will write to my father and mother regularly
I will not argue with Jules
I will not mope
I will help Jules in the garden
I will not eat so much cake and sweets

Jan 1, 1959

How should I begin? Should I write 'Dear Diary'? But that sounds quite silly as this is a book, not a letter, and I'm writing it to myself. Maybe then I should start 'Dear Me'? Paul has said that sometimes people give their diaries a name—but this seems even sillier. What name would you give a diary? Something cute and silly, a name you might give a cat—Fluffy or Soxy? Or maybe something very grand and serious-sounding like Aristotle? No, this is silly, just pointless rambling, and if I am to be serious about keeping this journal I should just leap in and write what it is to be me—Zelda Steele—as <u>this</u> is the point, surely, of a diary. So that I can read later just what it felt like to be me at this particular moment in time & remember events, because both are so easily forgotten. For instance I have scarcely any recollection of what it meant to be Zelda at 2 or Zelda at 6—there are some small things for example I'm sure I remember the cot I slept in when I was only a baby. Jules says that it's not possible, it must be from a photograph, but I can remember the white rungs and a flannel sheet with little brown bunnies and the feel of it wound around my finger quite distinctly.

Anyway, right now, on this first day of the year, 1959, this is me, Zelda. I live in Sydney with my adopted parents, Julia and Paul Holland, not far from Avalon Beach. Paul and Jules don't have any other children, but my real mother (Annie Swift) has two other daughters (Nesta and Eve) and has just had a baby boy (Troy), so I suppose I have three siblings though thankfully as they live up at The Entrance I don't have very much to do with them. I went to the local public school when I was 7, but only for a short while as this did not work out. I can't remember why exactly. I think I didn't fit in & Jules wasn't happy with the standard of the teaching or the other children there who were a pretty rough bunch. Mostly I recall being upset that I could not eat whenever I wanted to—or go to the toilet either—and once I even wet my pants which was a dreadful, shameful moment.

Jules tried to teach me for a few months, but that was a terrible disaster too, as she was very impatient. Since then I have had tutors for my studies. Some of them have been AWFUL, but the latest one, Jenny Barstock, is okay. Our lessons are generally pretty casual and I am allowed to follow my interests and also to read as much as I want as long as I write a 'report' afterwards, but this year I am leaving to go to Helicon, a boarding school in Springwood in the Blue Mountains. This is not something I am looking forward to particularly, though I will be very glad to get away from here—Jules is driving me completely crazy at the moment. She is always on at me about something or other that I am doing or <u>not</u> doing, which I suppose is normal at my age or so Paul keeps telling me, but still it is very hard to bear. Paul does not work at a proper job, both Paul and Jules inherited money and have investments, and though we do not live in any fancy way—in fact Jules is as mean as can be in some ways— we are very comfortable. Our house is quite a famous one, it is made of sandstone and was designed by the man who de- signed Canberra—Walter Burley-Griffin. It was photographed in a magazine just last year, which is quite amazing to me as it seems quite ordinary—in fact the house is quite small and uncomfortable in lots of ways. For instance we cannot get any television reception and there is no hot water tap in the kitchen and the stone is cold and the whole house has a damp under- ground cavey smell when it rains.

My <u>real</u> parents—Annie Swift and Ed Steele—are artists. Ed is very famous now, some people have said he is a genius, but after the war they were very poor and when my mother left my father neither of them could look after me, so Jules, who was my mother's best friend, as well as being Ed's 'patron', adopted me and I am, as they all like to tell me: lucky lucky lucky!! I have all the benefits of inherited 'genius' but do not have the suffering that usually comes with it as my parents very kindly gave me away to make sure that I had a privileged and settled life which they couldn't give me themselves. I think Ed has plenty of money these days but this does not mean he wants the responsibility of a kid—anyway he is always travelling and has a new wife Ynez who is from South America and can barely speak a word of English. Annie is married to Clive, who is an artist too, and though she is quite well-known in art circles she isn't very successful because she is 'before her time' (says Jules) and they are very very poor, as Clive hardly works because of a war injury.

We have 2 acres and as well an artist's cottage and studio here that is Jules's pride and joy—along with her kitchen garden which she tends as if it really mattered even though we are just a walk away from the greengrocer. There is always someone else living in the cottage—some painter who is an unrecognised genius and needs help and a place to stay. Sometimes a whole family will live here—the Bixes were here for almost the entire year last year—they had four kids, but all boys and too young to be company for me—and in the end Jules could not stand what she called Ilsa Bix's slovenly ways and they had to go— the house was filthy and unfit to live in and Jules spent a whole week scrubbing it out after they left—and as it turns out all the work was only second rate and George Bix has gone back to working in the bank. I thought some of Ilsa's wood block prints were quite beautiful, but Jules says they are old-fashioned sentimental rubbish.

I have what Jules calls a Raw Artistic Talent and <u>so I should</u> being the child as I have already mentioned of <u>two geniuses</u> and have been given <u>Every Opportunity</u>—especially as the artists who come here generally have to give me lessons as a condition of their stay. So I know a great deal about art which is useful as this is to be my vocation—or so Jules tells me constantly. This always causes a row between Jules and Paul who says that I must not be put under any pressure to perform— that art may not be my mettier (!?)—and that Jules should just relax about it. All the artists are kind, though mostly they just let me do my own thing—of course they're too busy themselves, and some are obviously tongue-tied around kids—and some of them—though I would never say this to J—are just plain lazy. The best art tutor of all was Max Klein—who is only second rate, maybe even third rate in Jules's opinion, or since they fell out, anyway—but he was good at explaining perspective and balance and how to mix colours properly. I like to draw and colour in pastels and last year made illustrations for all my favourite fairytale characters. Jules hates these though she tries hard to hide it—she always gives me this look and says that many artists' juvenilia is full of these fairytale themes and that eventually I'll grow out of it ...

I've also done some sculpting and pottery and most recently learned how to do wood block prints. Last year we sent a madonna & child wood block that I did with Ilsa Bix as our Christmas card. Jules thought it was a bit too religious, but Paul was impressed and insisted that we have it printed up properly. He said it had good clean lines.

I have a dog called Rip—he is a Bitser who we found when he was only a pup abandoned down at the beach—and I guess he is really my best friend. We spend a lot of our spare time at the beach—Rip is better at surfing than most people—he'll always go out just as far as me, anyway. There are three other dogs—King Charles Spaniels—that are Jules's 'darlings': Ophelia, Portia and Cordelia. They don't go to the beach, of course, they're spoilt rotten little lapdogs and do not have much to do with my ruffian Rip other than eat his food whenever they get the opportunity.

And this is me so far: I have lived here since I was around six months old and my life is not very exciting but I hope it will be one day.

This diary was a Christmas present from Ed, who came to Christmas this year—with Ynez—for the first time since I can remember. He writes in a diary too—but he told me that it's not some sort of literary exercise for him, as he always burns his at the end of each year, and never ever rereads. So his diaries are not a record, or an ade-memoir (?), but the one place where he can be brutally honest with himself. He laughed when he told me this and added that he doubted that real honesty was ever a possibility—but that it was well worth the attempt.

But I think that I won't burn my diary as he suggests—what a terrible waste of paper, and of effort too. Surely it would be better to reread all the entries one day in the future—or even to pass my words to someone else to read. But then, as Ed points out, perhaps the thought of that—of being judged by that imaginary reader—will stop me being completely honest, and make me self-conscious. Anyway, I can try.

As well for Christmas I received:

· One small sketchbook and another one, larger, from the Bixes.

· A new swimsuit—red with blue edges and buttons—from Jules.

· A tomato pincushion made by Nesta and Eve.

· 136 Derwent pencils from my Great Aunt Lucille.

· £5 from my Uncle Norman.

· A tin of Yardley body powder from Annie and Clive.

· A set of oils and brushes and a wooden box and easel that Paul had made especially. The box is cedar, with all sorts of dinky little compartments for this and that and it has a special space for the palette—which is cedar too.

· Three books: *Huckleberry Finn*, by Mark Twain, from Jenny Barstock; *The Good Earth*, by Pearl S. Buck and *The Harp in the South* by Ruth Park from Paul and Jules.

· An old Japanese print that is very beautiful: a woman is combing her hair and gazing at her reflection. It

is a meeji print by a well-known artist and very valuable and I must of course let Jules look after it until I
am older. This is from Jules.

Ed brought a present from his mother, too: a game of quoits
and a stack of comics which I <u>love</u>!! I had a great time playing
quoits with Ed who I beat every game; Paul was harder, but still
I won 4 out of the 6 games we played. The Robertses and their
children were here for Christmas too—but they are too little to
play yet—though the baby had some fun pushing the quoits
about and having a good chew when no one was watching. I
guess they were tastier than the mushed vegetables that he was
offered. The Fannings came with their daughter Marjory for
drinks on Boxing Day—she is just my age and is going to Helicon too—but she was far too stuck up to play quoits. Why, she
might have damaged one of her perfectly filed and buffed fingernails! I made sure Rip gave her one of his especially friendly greetings and he left a fine pair of muddy footprints on her
white capri pants.

So now you know all about me, Dear Diary, Dear Me, Dear
Unknown Future Reader—and I promise I will <u>write again very
very soon.</u>

January 3rd

Jules has just told me that I am to spend the next week with my
mother. This will be the second time I've stayed with her—I
was sent there one weekend last summer—though Annie visited a few times when I was younger, and then when Nesta was
born, but that was just for a few hours for dinner or lunch. Jules
thinks that such visits should be regular—that I should spend
a week or two with her at least once a year. It is necessary for
my healthy psychological development, Jules says, that I get to
know my biological mother and my siblings. According to Jules,
I need to know them in order to properly understand who I am.

I am <u>So Lucky</u>, she tells me, to have this opportunity—most children who are adopted have no idea of their real parents. I could not help saying that I would be just as happy not knowing and would rather not spend even a minute a year in their horrible filthy little shack. And it will be so much worse now with the baby—no doubt there will be even more filth. SHE will make me work as she did last time—I will be made to help wash and cook and to 'keep the girls occupied' which generally means trying to stop them from killing one another—and never ever a kind word from Her. Her eye—when she ever deigns to notice me—is as cold and hard as the Snow Queen's. And then there's Clive like a skeleton & him limping about the place, coughing and spluttering and gasping for air and everything is so cramped and dirty I cannot think why ANYONE would think it healthy to spend time in such an unhappy atmosphere. Perhaps I can persuade Jules to make it just the weekend—a whole week is <u>too</u> terrible to contemplate.

PS As there is no privacy at their place and as there is no one there who has any notion of privacy—they are just as likely to read this book as not—I think I WON'T take my diary with me.

Jan 8th

It was unbearable—and I am home already and in terrible trouble. I could not stand it and on the third afternoon when the baby was finally sleeping and She was having a lie-down with Clive—I was supposed to be looking after Nesta & Eve—I simply walked out and caught the train back to Sydney.

It really is quite hideous there—Clive so sick and useless and reeking of medicine and grog and old man, and the stink of the baby all puking and foul nappies—the whole place has such a terrible smell—a STENCH—even the ocean breeze doesn't get rid of it. It's sickening. And She is most sickening of all. I could never please her: if I was quiet and good I was just a shadow & why could I not make some effort to be part of the family? And then if I did join in there would be something else: it would be better if I were quiet, I shouldn't excite the children so; it could disturb Clive or wake the baby. If I ate not enough of the food that she made, I was being difficult—not good enough for you, Miss?—and if I ate it all, or asked for more, there would be a comment on how much I ate, how expensive it was to feed an extra mouth, didn't I know how difficult it was (though I know that Jules sent her a big fat cheque—and I heard her send Clive off to town to cash it), what a greedy child I was, I should beware of getting too fat ... She is not really much kinder to the other children—we are all a trial, it is easy to see that, and she is inclined to hit the other two when she is in a temper (which she would never do to me), but there is something else between them too— the girls will slide over to her, rub themselves against her and she will give them a brief hug or ruffle their hair, before sending them on their way—but there is none of that for me, even if I wanted it which I do not. Her touch makes my skin crawl.

Despite Jules's cheque there was barely any food—the money was used for paper and ink, and beer and gin so far as I could see—the first night we had only potatoes and what she likes to call a salad which is only a bit of old lettuce and tomato and if we are lucky perhaps tinned cucumber to have with it. I was starving the entire time I was there. And the house is so filthy it is barely fit for animals—the dishes are never done, there is washing piled high and the bathroom is black with mould. There were ants marching through the kitchen as if they owned the place and there are spider webs dangling from all the ceilings. Oh, and there were mice—even in the bedroom. Urg! She spends so much time at her work—it is all that matters to her I think, apart from Clive and the new baby. Nesta & Eve are terribly neglected—they are lucky to get one decent meal a day and as for making sure they are dressed or bathed ... It is a wonder that they do not have some terrible disease.

I do not see what it is that is so wonderful about her 'work', either. Why is it so important that she be given money to do her work? (For in that household it is her work and Clive's rest that come first—everyone else can just go ROT.) Her work is just inkblots and smudges that I could do better myself—in fact <u>any</u> child could do just as good, if not better. She has no real idea of perspective or proportion that I can see & when I asked her about it she looked at me utterly blankly for a moment and then raised her eyebrow & laughed! We didn't all have the benefit of an art tutor, Zel, she said.

There is never a single word of kindness to me in that house, only slights. I have heard her (my own mother! imagine!) refer to me as 'the princess' which is hardly fair as she is the one who sent me to live with Jules and Paul. I did not choose to leave her.

Anyway, I am in big trouble—especially because when they eventually woke up, she told Jules, the girls were nowhere to be seen & it took some time to find them as they had scarpered over to the beach on their own, and, says Annie, could have drowned or been abducted. Nesta was badly sunburned—though I do not know how anyone would notice as she is naked half the time and is practically black. I know for a fact that they are always at the beach on their own anyway—half the time sent there to get them out of Her hair—so this is just a way to get at me. Still, I do not think they will send me there again.

Paul is not so cross—he understands my distress, he says. Jules though has no understanding at all—she thinks I am exaggerating and being difficult. I overheard them arguing when they thought I'd gone out. Paul said that Jules should realise that there's no way back—that she is making things more difficult. That it had been agreed at the outset that the separation should be total, so why was she trying to change things now, at this time in my life especially? Jules said that it was about time that I got to know my real mother—to establish some sort of relationship with her—and that she felt that it was only fair and right that Annie should take some responsibility for her own flesh and blood. I heard Paul say that it was far too late for this—that there would only be resentment; that such meetings were probably quite dangerous psychologically, especially when Annie is just as reluctant as me. That perhaps they had done wrong not to make the split completely clean right from the outset, and that he could see every meeting between Annie and me had been thoroughly upsetting. Perhaps, said Paul, there are forces that none of us understand working here. And perhaps they did wrong by not properly taking on the mantle of parents—they had always made it so clear that they were NOT my parents that perhaps I feel distanced, confused, estranged from everyone. This all made Jules horrendously angry. What Paul was saying was utter nonsense, she said, everything had been provided, everything had been done for my advantage, what more could they have given me? Then: How unfair it is that SHE should have to cope with it all—especially in the teenage years and with her own health problems. She hadn't understood fully what it had meant when she took me on—she hadn't realised that she'd be signing away such a large portion of her own life. I did not hear what Paul said to her, he spoke very quietly, so no doubt he was comforting her as he always does, even when she is wrong or behaving badly. Jules has always claimed that she would have loved to have had her own children but surely it would have been just the same with them. How does she think she would have coped with her own? And what is so different right now, I wonder? What has changed? Anyway, I shall be off their hands for good in just another month—exiled to Helicon with the revolting Marjory. I just <u>can't</u> wait!

PM

<u>Now</u> they tell me they are sending me to spend <u>two weeks</u> with my father's family. Another experiment in family bonding. Jules said they made the arrangement with Ed at Christmas and it is too late to change it now. They might have thought to consult me. Oh, joy. His parents—my grand-parents—live on a cattle station in the middle of nowhere out west—100 miles

west of some Godforsaken town called Boolah. It is a 15-hour train trip there, but my father and his wife will bring me back. I cannot understand this fascination Jules has with me getting to know my real family all of a sudden. I certainly do not care about them—why should I? They have taken no interest in me.

Jan 15th, 'Comebella'

The trip here was hideous. The first train—what they called the 'through mail'—was not so bad. It left at 9 at night and I had a sleeper to myself and managed to sleep most of the way to Dubbo. But the train from Dubbo to Boolah was impossible—the heat especially. I felt like I had entered an oven and closed the door. To make matters worse there was absolutely nothing to look at from the window: for the whole 8 hours of the journey there was barely a tree—only low scrub and the shimmering hot red earth going on forever. It got so I could not bear looking out at it and so I pulled down the blinds. I had brought a sketchbook hoping to make some drawings of the landscape. Jules had said what a brilliant opportunity it was—so many Australians have never been further into the interior than the Great Dividing Range—and that I should make something of the experience, and it should be especially meaningful to me as it is my father who has done so much to make it so real for all the rest of us. In the end, as I could not be bothered with any more *Huckleberry Finn*, I drew the people around me—as animals. The ticket man—a funny little fat fellow who was not as cheerful as his appearance suggested—I drew as a pig in a too-tight uniform. A woman with her three little children who sat on the bench across from me I drew as a duck with ducklings—such well-behaved little children, they barely made a peep (or a quack!) the entire journey. The middle-aged lady next to me—very thin with a slight moustache, and who dribbled repulsively when she slept—I drew as a goat & then felt dreadful as she gave me piece of the most scrumptious apple pie I have ever tasted, when she woke up.

I managed to sleep some of the journey thank goodness & when the train arrived in Boolah I was picked up by Ed and my uncle Albert who lives out at 'Comebella'. The drive out was ANOTHER two hours (!!), and it was unimaginably hot with an even hotter dusty breeze coming in through the windows and I was crushed all the way between the two men and the ute stank like—well I am not sure what the smell was exactly, though I have my suspicions—but it was a mixture of all sorts of dreadful things that I would much rather NOT have to smell!! And the road was just dirt and full of what Ed said were corrugations that made the car shudder and shake and sometimes even slide all over the place. Ed and Al laughed at me squealing and clutching at the seat and said it would have been worse if my grandfather had come to get me—the drive takes him more than 4 hours as he refuses to go any faster than 30 miles an hour which just makes the ride seem even rougher. We made a stop for lemonade and sandwiches at Ford's Bridge which is just a pub in the middle of nowhere—they went into the public bar and let me go into the ladies' lounge on my own, which was quite fun. It was very bare and primitive, but the barmaid was friendly and the lemonade was icy cold.

My grandparents' house was a bit of a shock. I don't know what it was that I was expecting—I've heard all the stories of Ed's deprived childhood, so nothing grand—but from the outside it looked like a real shack—lopsided higgledy piggledy weatherboard. But inside it was not all that bad—very clean and really quite comfortable. My grandmother cooks on a wood-stove, but the kitchen is separate from the rest of the house, connected by what they call a 'breeze-way', which is a huge joke as there is NO breeze anywhere! My bed is on the old veranda out the back—the sleepout. I thought it was awful at first, but it seems better somehow to be outside than in, and it is on the southern side which is the coolest. I cannot get used to this heat—it is <u>so</u> hot you feel as if someone had pushed all the air out of your lungs.

The people: There is Ed's mother—the Caroline I was named for, or, as she says I must call her, Grandma Steele. She was quite scary at first as she seems impossibly ancient—she is <u>so</u> wrinkly and is bent almost double. But for all her frightening appearance she is actually good fun—she has a wicked sense of humour and makes me laugh with all her funny old sayings & is teaching me to play cards. She was appalled that I did not know how to play any game more serious than Fish.

When she first met me, she said she was 'real pleased' to meet me (she has such a broad Australian accent, that at first I thought she was joking), then glared at Ed and said it was a disgrace that a woman should have to wait almost 14 years between visits from her own flesh and blood—at which Ed looked very awkward. I did not know this, but evidently Annie and Ed brought me out when I was only a few months old. It was the first and only time my mother ever visited and from what I can gather it was not a great success.

My grandfather—Grandpa Steele—does not look quite as old as Grandma. He is big and strong looking, but has a very gruff way about him. He smokes a pipe and is very quiet and has barely said a word to me, but Ed said not to worry, he doesn't say much to anyone.

It is extremely odd to think that these strange old people are actually my grandparents!!! Their life is SO different to mine—we could be from different countries, different planets—and yet somehow I already feel quite comfortable with them. Almost as if I belong.

My Uncle Albert and his wife Jane live in the new house which is in the next 'paddock' (which is not what I imagined a paddock to be—just red dirt with a few spindly trees here and there). Their house is new and brick and unlike the old home-stead it has all the mod cons. Jane is youngish and friendly. She is a Boolah girl, but was nursing in Sydney and then Dubbo be-fore she married Albert. They have a four year old, Diana, and twins who are just a few months younger than me—Pamela and Penelope. They are friendly enough, but I think they are completely horse mad, as that is all they have talked about so far. They were quite excited to talk to me at first as they wanted to know about television but they lost interest when I told them that we don't have one (Jules says it is lowbrow rubbish) and that I have only ever seen them in the shops. They have a Breeze-Air in their house, and Jane said that if it gets too hot in the old place I'm welcome to come over and stay with them.

The dogs here are treated terribly—they are work dogs—cattle dogs and kelpies—and there are 8 of them kept chained in a little pen with just a tin roof for shelter. They all bark like mad whenever I pass them and Ed says I am on no account to go near them as they are not domestic animals, not pets—they're work animals and can be quite vicious to people they don't know. No wonder when they are treated so cruelly—any dog would be vicious.

There are also four men who work on the station. They came over to the house for tea yesterday, but only two actually sat at the table with us—the other two are Aboriginal men and ate out on the front porch, which seemed a bit rude. When I asked Ed about it later he just shrugged and said that was the way things were done here—there was no unkindness meant—and that the Abos would probably feel very uncomfortable sitting at the table with the rest of us, as they have their own ways of doing things. The meals here are very plain—tonight it was just lamb and baked potato and slices of a tomato that Grandma said was from the garden. I haven't seen any evidence of a garden here—I can't imagine anything being able to grow in this dirt, and in the heat—surely it would just wilt?—though I haven't had much of a look outside, yet. I had thought I couldn't possibly eat a hot meal, but it was quite delicious. The lamb had just been slaughtered, Albert said, and I should think myself lucky—as it was generally mutton that they 'et' out here.

I have to go now—Grandma Steele is calling. Do I want to learn how to play poker tonight? she asks. I wonder if I do?

LATER

I forgot to say that Ynez is here too—she's not coping with the heat at all and barely comes out of the bedroom, not even for meals. Whenever I walk past I can hear her moaning and muttering to herself in Spanish. Grandma Steele rolls her eyes whenever her name is mentioned.

Jan 17th

I have finished *Huck Finn* which was the only book I thought to bring and there is nothing much to do—and really it is far too hot to do anything. I am expected to help a little—I peeled the potatoes for Grandma this morning and went with the twins to collect eggs and water the vegetable garden, which does actually exist. It's nothing compared with Jules's, only cucumber and lettuce and tomatoes and some pumpkin at this time of year, but I think that it's a miracle that they manage to grow anything out here. The heat only seems to bother me and Ynez so it must be possible to get used to it. Pam & Pen are off on their horses again, boring girls. They are determined to teach me to ride—even though I said I was not really that keen. All the horses here are too wild, they say, so they are riding over to a neighbour's station to borrow a suitable 'pony' (not a horse!) for me. This neighbour—the nearest!—is more than 10 miles away and because the ride will take up most of the day, the girls will have to stay overnight. I said they shouldn't go to any trouble, but it seems that this is NO trouble, quite the opposite in fact. All the men are working—even Ed who is needed for some reason right now, though Jules told me that he'd come here to paint. I can't imagine they would view such an occupation too well here—especially when there's so much 'real' work to be done. They look at Ed very oddly and laugh about him being a city slicker, especially Albert, who is sometimes quite nasty. Grandma Steele seems slightly sour on him too—though with her it seems like an old habit, with not much real bite—anyway it doesn't seem to bother Ed a bit. She gets this terrible look on her face whenever she starts in on him, and Ed just laughs and tells her to be careful that the wind doesn't change. She is much nastier when it comes to Ynez, who I think she hates. Though I suppose Ynez gets what she deserves. Yesterday she refused point blank to help Gran with the lunch dishes as she had just painted her fingernails and did not want to damage them. She lays on her bed most of the day with a damp cloth over her head. I do not know how she is brave enough—though I must say I wouldn't mind doing that myself.

I got a huge surprise yesterday when I saw Ed up on a horse—he looked completely at home—quite expert. Jane must have noticed how surprised I was. He really <u>is</u> a country-boy! Jane says that he might be a bigwig international artist now, but when he was 16 he had half the girls in the district in love with him—and it wasn't because of his skill with a paintbrush. I wouldn't have believed it—in all the stories I've ever been told, Ed's upbringing was miserable and hard, but really he seems completely at home out here. And Grandma and Grandpa Steele are quite affectionate and proud of him too in their own strange way, I think.

I am already quite good at poker!—Last night I won three games!! I have a good poker face, said Grandpa Steele. He says I take after his mother, Bella, who was a real deep one, he says. No one ever really knew what it was that was going on in her head—but you could tell it was something big. She took off when he was 10: no word why, Grandpa said, and no word since. He says she was a 'blondie' too—just like me! I am not sure if being like Great Grandma Steele is actually a compliment—but it is quite an exciting thing to be told that you're like someone, as it isn't something I've had said to me much.

Gran says that tomorrow after the washing (which is a big event and I have been told that I'll be helping) she will get down her box of photographs for me to look at. She says that she can't see anything of my mother in me—which I did take as a compliment and I am sure was meant as one, too. Your father has an odd taste in women for such a smart fellow, she said, loud enough for Ed to hear. Then added—that sour look appearing on her face: Though I must say she's a loyal one, Lazy Ynez, to stay with him all this time. Most women wouldn't put up with the things she's had to stomach. I'm not sure what she's talking about—though perhaps it's something to do with that English girl he visited with once. Maybe they were having an affair?

January 18th

Ed drove Ynez into town to catch the train back—she's had enough, I guess, and you can hardly blame her—even if the heat wasn't so unbearable, it's not like she's been made welcome in any way. Even Ed has been too busy to take much notice of her. And now he's planning to go with the stockmen tomorrow—which would make things even harder for her. They have to take all the cattle up country for grazing which will be about a week of riding and camping out. Then he wants to spend a month or so 'getting it down'. Grandpa has agreed to let him clear out one of the sheds—or to let ME clear out the shed, as this is what I am to do while he's away.

I have found an old copy of Grimms' fairytales—I think it was probably Ed's—and have been reading that for lack of anything else. The stories have given me the strangest dreams. Last night I dreamt I was the witch & that Hansel and Gretel had the faces of Nesta & Eve & they were both pushing me into the oven—only they could not as my shoe was caught on something. And then I woke all wet from the heat and my foot was tangled up in my sheet—which just goes to show how close dreams can be to what is real.

The twins are back with the pony for me—it is a sweet animal called Nugget—quite small and a bright chestnut colour with big melting eyes and a snuffly warm nose and while I am

NOT up on his back I think he's quite ADORABLE. But somehow, once I climb up I feel quite differently, and then when he
actually moves I break out into a cold sweat. So my two riding
lessons so far haven't been much of a success. It would help if
they didn't all stand around laughing and making rude comments about my general lack of ability. I would like to see them
in the surf. Then who would be laughing?

Grandpa Steele is quite a sweetie—he is the only one who
has asked whether I am happy with my 'in-laws' as he keeps
calling Jules and Paul. I said it wasn't so bad, that they were very
good and generous to me—at which he gave a big snort and said
that money wasn't everything, though it did smooth over a few
rough edges, and though it might not look like it he was in fact
quite a rich man himself—he just didn't like to flash it about.
That he hadn't done bad, not bad at all for a young feller who
started out as a bullocky. Then he said how very sorry he is that
he didn't get to know me till now as I seem a good sensible sort
of a girl. And then after a bit of a pause (there are always lots of
pauses in Grandpa's conversation) he said that it is a bad thing
to be taken away from your own flesh and blood. A bad thing.
Another pause: And I am to take no notice of them laughing at
my riding—they don't mean nothing by it, he says. That's just
country ways, he says. You'll get used to it, eventually, girly.

January 20th

I have finally got the shed cleared out for Ed. He will be VERY
surprised to see the state I have got it into—it is almost unrecognisable. I explained to Grandpa that Ed really could use some
light inside the shed so that he can work away from the dust so
Grandpa had Albert cut in two windows. There is no glass but
some canvas blinds that can be let down in bad weather—more
likely to be wind than rain out here—which makes the space
as good as a proper artist's studio—and better than some. Gran
brought down some old blankets to cool the walls as it is un-

bearably hot—but it is like that everywhere except for in Jane's loungeroom when they have the Breeze-Air going. I asked Grandpa why he didn't get one too, but he says that the Breeze-Air is unnatural and bad for you—the air has a dirty smell and it's liable to bring on a cold. He said that you don't notice the heat after a while: after 70 years or so, anyway. I cannot imagine getting used to it if I lived here for 100 years ...

January 21st

Tonight I am staying over at Jane and Albert's. Their house is much more comfy—the Breeze-Air is a wonderful thing—and Jane has let me sleep out in the loungeroom, right under it. She has given me a blanket, but somehow I <u>don't</u> think I'll need it. They have an electric stove and electric lighting and a proper fridge instead of the old kerosene one that Gran uses—Jane says Grandma and Grandpa could have these too, there is a battery room that makes enough power for both the houses—but Grandma likes her place the way it is. Jane told me that when Albert and Ed and their sister Eileen were kids, if they really wanted to tease Grandma, they would rearrange the furniture, which was something she could not bear. None of that furniture has moved an inch since they built the place 50 years ago, she said. There'd be grooves underneath the kitchen table, and the lounge suite. And nothing's ever been replaced, either ... After tea Jane and Al listened to the radio while the twins and I played Monopoly. They are not such bad girls—but they really have no other conversation than horses horses horses. Jane says they will be going off to boarding school—in Orange—next year, so perhaps they will have some of the horsiness knocked out of them there. I beat them at Monopoly.

Jane told me that G & G Steele could never understand why, if Ed couldn't raise the baby—meaning me—he hadn't brought me to them. They were terribly hurt by the whole business. They stopped talking to Ed for ages because of it, but things were pretty much back to normal now, she says—and though it might not seem like it, Grandma was really pleased to have me here. 'She's a tough old bird, your Gran,' Jane said, 'but she's had a pretty hard life.' She didn't go into any details, but my experience of 'wash day' last week—which was a day of non-stop work as Gran refuses to use anything electric & still uses an ancient wood-fired copper—made me think that life out here must have been even tougher when they first started out.

January 24th

Ed arrived home today a bit earlier than expected. He says he is all done in, but has an odd look in his eye as if he is really excited. He'd forgotten, he said at dinner, just what it meant to be out west—not just the colours and the sights and the sounds, which he'd been painting from memory, really, all these years he's been away—but the whole 'essence': that out here you felt immensely tiny and insignificant, but somehow right at the centre of the universe. He has been all around the world, he says, and seen the works of the old masters and the new; and Roman and Greek buildings thousands of years old only to find that <u>real</u> history, <u>real</u> art was here all along—in Australia—in the earth, the trees, the sky, the wind. He'd spent three days at the wetlands, not so far from here—just sketching—and he was amazed at the things that he'd known so well as a kid, and that he'd forgotten all about, he said. Then he camped out a few nights with a couple of native stockmen who were heading back from Queensland—Jimmy and Shep—and they told him all sorts of Aboriginal stories—their sacred myths, he guessed—of the land and their connection to it that he'd never heard. He'd come to the conclusion that whites were fools not to listen to the natives, idiots not to try and understand the land that we lived on—always trying to make it into another place & not working with what we've got. Not even trying to understand.

Grandpa completely ignored his speech (he'd pulled out his

hearing aid at the beginning of dinner as he always does—he likes to masticate in peace, he says), clapped him on the back and said loudly that he was pleased to see him back, that he'd thought they'd have to send out a search party—but he'd obviously remembered some of the things he'd taught him as a boy. Then said that he was real glad to know that Ed's not such a pansy as he looks. Gran looked at Ed, too, and shook her head: 'You've always had a head full of rot, Ed—and that hasn't changed. You're a mystery to me, son.' But she was smiling as she said it—I get the feeling she's quite proud of Ed, deep down—even if he <u>is</u> a complete mystery to her.

There is to be a dinner dance in Boolah tomorrow night—after a tennis match in the afternoon—and we are all to go in and stay the night at one of the hotels there. Ed groaned and said dear God, not a tennis club dance, that he wasn't going, couldn't, he had to get started on the paintings—but Gran said what did he mean he wasn't going? He had to go—as he's the main attraction. They'd never be able to show their faces in town, if he didn't ...

I think it's quite exciting!! Anyway, it will make a change. Luckily I packed a decent dress. I wonder if Jane has an electric iron?

January 26th

The dance turned out to be a bit of fun.

We stayed at the Tattersalls' hotel which was once owned, Gran told me, by her father—he had come out from Ireland and went first to Broken Hill where he owned several hotels and then bought this one in Boolah—which was where she grew up. Henry Lawson stayed there, she said, when he was out west but she was only young and can't remember a thing about it. Gran's nephew Phil Heffernan owns the place now and after the tennis and before the dance there was a family dinner so there was a whole lot more family to meet. They are a pretty 'country' lot—the kind of outback yokels that you hear about but never really meet—with accents so broad and flat it is hard when they are all talking together to understand what they are saying sometimes. The dinner was meant to be in 'honour' of Ed who hasn't seen some of his cousins for more than 20 years, but they have a weird way of showing this 'honour'—it mostly consists of smart comments at his expense and rude remarks about him being a real city slicker and being all dressed up like a bloody poofter. I must have been looking a bit put out by it all because Grandfather said (again!) that I shouldn't take it seriously as none of it was unkindly meant—just a bit of a joke, country ways, straight speaking—but a few of the remarks were quite nasty and I noticed that Ed did not look at all pleased.

I got some funny looks myself—and a couple of comments about my dress. I overheard some woman saying that Grandma should have stopped me from showing everyone else up and then another woman saying what a tragedy, to be given away— that a mother's love was something money couldn't buy and that you only had to look at me to see what a poor lost creature I was ... nasty cow.

Still, the dance itself was fun. The band wasn't half as bad as I'd expected and I danced to a couple of numbers with the twins and then one with Grandpa which was very awkward as he has a strange stiff-backed way of dancing which I could not help laughing about and this of course was only made worse when Ed winked at me and I had to pretend to be having a coughing fit because I was practically choking with laughter.

I got talking to a REALLY nice boy. His name is Richard Howatt and he is almost three years older than me but he treated me like an equal which is a bit of a change from most of the boys I have ever met. His father is the doctor here, and he is going to boarding school in Sydney this year too—Cranburn— and is not looking forward to it at all as he is perfectly happy here, he says, but they don't do the Leaving at Boolah High and he wants to go on to uni. I said that at least he will only have to board for one year, unlike me—I will be at Helicon FOREVER.

He knew that my father was quite well known as an artist and had even heard of Annie as he has an aunt in Sydney who takes him to galleries when he visits. He is thinking of doing medicine like his father and seems very grown up and sensible for his age. He is quite nice looking and a very good dancer. He hates horses, too—he said his mother sent him off to pony club when he was about 5 and even bought him a pony, but he made a complete fool of himself—fell off and hurt himself and could never get back on. He says just being near horses makes him break into a cold sweat which is EXACTLY like me. He is a laughingstock with all his mates—who are all horse-mad—because of that—though it has got better lately as he has just got a motorbike and is a bit of a whiz on that. He still has his pony—it is called DEV-IL!!!—and is one thing he definitely WILL not miss.

Jane said later that half the girls in Boolah are sweet on Richard, but he's not interested, and that they were all looking daggers at me as he has never taken the slightest bit of notice of any of the others. His father is an excellent doctor, she said, a Sydney man who's been here since before the war, but the mother is a terrible snob and doesn't usually mix with the hoi-polloi or come to any town 'dos'. She had noticed Richard's mum talking to Ed, so perhaps he was the attraction …

Anyway, Richard and I exchanged addresses and said we would write.

January 27th

I was showing my sketchbook to Grandma Steele—who thought that my pictures were marvellous—when Ed came in and asked if he could look through it. Of course I said yes, and he went through the book quite slowly, spending some time on each page, but all the time unsmiling. I pretended not to watch but could not help noticing exactly which pictures he lingered over, or sucked in his teeth or frowned at. When he had gone all the way through, Grandma said something like, 'She's got a bit of a talent, don't you think? There are some wonderful like-nesses there—and those lovely fairytale pictures! A chip off the old block, eh, Ed?' but all Ed said was, 'Well, she certainly has a facility for copying ...' and then said that it showed a great deal of promise, but that I should try to put <u>myself</u> into the work a little bit more. 'But I haven't copied anything at all,' I said, as I rarely copy anything, but he had put on his work-hat and gone out by then and Grandma Steele shook her head and said he was a thoughtless man, he didn't mean to be unkind, but when a head is stuffed so full of its own thoughts and ideas as his is, there's not much left over for anyone else. Then she changed the subject and asked if I might make her a gift of one of my sketchings—she'd very much like to have the one of Cinderella and her fairy godmother. Of course I said yes, but really I feel like tearing the pages up, one by one ...

January 29th

I wanted badly to see the wetlands and the birds, but there was no way I could be brought to ride over as they have all suggested, as it would be a 3 or 4 hour ride at least, which is 3 or 4 hours of complete TERROR for me, but yesterday Ed finally talked Grandpa into giving him one of the trucks and we left in the late afternoon. The twins had gone earlier on horseback, but it was only two hours' drive—and then we were over the border & in Queensland. (I had expected to see some sort of sign—the earth suddenly changing colour between states, but there wasn't anything! Very disappointing!) The lake <u>was</u> amazing and beautiful—so unexpected out here. It was still full from the wet-season and there were just so many birds it was as if we'd landed in the middle of an aviary. I felt entirely ignorant. I can only recognise about half-a-dozen species of birds at home—kookaburra, sparrow, magpie, etc—but Pam & Pen knew not only the common names of half the birds, but their Latin names too, as well as bits and pieces about the mating habits, and eating habits and migratory habits of the stilts and cormorants and herons and ibises and all the zillion different types of ducks. And they even knew the names of the trees—what a city girl I am!! Anyhow, I had my first swim here—and though the water was disgustingly muddy it was still fun—and I was able to show those twins, who can hardly swim—only the most BASIC breaststroke, but they will NOT put their faces in the water—a thing or two, for once. We caught yabbies and boiled them in a billy for dinner. They tasted a little like mud—and nothing like prawns—but I was so hungry I didn't mind. We'd packed tents, but Ed and I ended up sleeping outside, under the stars.

We had such an interesting conversation once the twins had drifted off: Ed said that he had hated Comebella and Boolah and everything it stood for for years. He had thought it the most tragic irony that the property was called Bella as he had thought it ugly, vacant, barren, a version of hell with NOTHING beautiful about it at all other than the prospect of escape. And even though he's been painting his memories of the outback for years, he's only just now beginning to understand and appreciate what he calls its weird beauty. He's begun to wonder, he says, if his terror at the prospect of spending the rest of his life at Comebella, and his desperation to escape, somehow blinded him to all that was—that _is_—good about life out here. Anyway, he is able to see it more clearly now ...

It is true what Ed says—it is quite a different world out here— much bigger and much stranger. And it _is_ weird. You could believe in anything—I wouldn't have been at all surprised to see a Bunyip emerge from the lake, or some sort of angel coming down from the stars. I didn't sleep until late—but I slept very well. The city seems a long long way away.

It's odd how little I really miss Jules and Paul—I've barely thought of home at all since I've been here. Anyway, I don't suppose they will be missing me much either. Though sometimes I think Jules might actually _enjoy_ all the nag nag nagging ...

January 30th

I am going back on the train tomorrow. When I first arrived I couldn't imagine really enjoying myself—but I will miss Bella and everyone here. Grandma has said that she would like me to visit as often as I can and perhaps I can come in spring as it is a very different place, and there is the Bachelor & Spinster Ball in Boolah after the shearing which is a fun time to be here—everyone in such a good spirits, too, with their wool cheques in the bank. There's a real holiday feeling, better than Christmas, she says. It is around school holiday time so I should be able to arrange it. Grandpa said today that he had enjoyed having me—it was good for him and 'mother' as he calls Grandma to meet their granddaughter again after so many years, and that Ed had not really thought well into what he was doing—it being a very bad thing to split a family up like that—but that he supposed he didn't have much choice, not having a regular income and things still so uncertain with the war only just over, but that was all water under the bridge now and he hoped very much that I would keep in touch. It was a VERY long speech from Grandpa ... I asked them if they would like me to write and they said of course, that they would love to hear from me. So I have promised them one letter at least every month—though I don't know what I will write about as life at boarding school is bound to be very dull.

Gran has said I can take back the fairytales with me to read on the train—they were hers and not Ed's as I had thought and she would be pleased to see them go to a good home as she has no further use for them with her eyesight not what it used to be. I did not like to tell her that I probably have these same tales—in much more beautiful binding—and that I am really only reading them for want of something better to do ... but it is such a kind thought and I will treasure them because they belonged to her. She gave me a hug which is the first time she has touched me and we were both a bit awkward about it.

It was funny saying good-bye to Ed—he's to stay here another 6 weeks before he and Ynez go back to the UK on the steamer. We had had those conversations, & I had thought that perhaps we were getting 'close' in some way—like a real father and daughter. But at the station he was very matter-of-fact—he shook my hand, gave me a £5 note and told me to be a good girl for Jules and Paul. He is like a genial, friendly but distant uncle, who is perfectly happy to spend time with me, and to teach me this & show me that, but there is no special bond between us—he behaves no different really to Pam & Pen. Once I'm gone I am quite sure that in some way I no longer exist to him—other than someone to send a postcard to every now and then, or a present at Christmas. But then he wasn't exactly missing Ynez, either—she telephoned twice while he was there and he had Grandma tell her that he was out—so I think perhaps he is like this with everyone. Jules once said Ed was desperately in love with my mother, and that it took him years and years to recover when she left—so perhaps she has hurt him in ways that he can't ever recover from.

February 2nd

Home. That first glimpse of the ocean was wonderful—and the smell and feel of the air. I escaped to the beach with Rip as soon as I could. The feel of the surf after all the heat and dust of the train was like magic. I could feel myself expanding in the water like a great big sponge. I swam out past the breakers and just floated ... until some silly lifeguard whistled me in and gave me a lecture about the dangers of the deep. Still, it was worth it.

Hard to settle in again to our usual life—after being in that crowded little house our place seems quite lonely and empty with just Paul and Jules and me. Oh, and it's so cold compared to Bella. But they seem happy to see me and it is good to have my own bedroom, my comfy bed and all my things. I could not imagine missing Comebella, but I do.

Tomorrow Jules and I are going in to town for lunch. She has had my Helicon uniforms made and we are going to pick them up and then go for a big shop, and a visit to some galleries and then go somewhere swish for lunch.

February 3rd

Lunch was scrumptious and I ate far too many cakes, as always, and felt slightly sick (which was only, said Paul when I told him—my 'just desserts'—URG). After lunch we went to a gallery in Paddington where they are showing some of my mother's work. There were three 'seascapes' which were very odd I thought. Big blurry faces and bodies, with all the detail on the small things in the landscape: seaweed, shells, grains of sand. The exhibition programme notes—which were written by Jules—said that the works reveal Annie's fascination with childhood. All her paintings show the world—the world of the seaside in particular—from a child's eye. Evidently my mother's 'ability to render the world from the child's point of view' is unparalleled. I had to stop myself from having hysterics when I read this—Annie being the least likely person I know to EVER consider ANYTHING from a child's point of view!!! Anyway, I don't know WHAT to think of them and I cannot see why everyone is so admiring. It is not like my father's work where you can see—even if the figures are distorted—that he actually knows what he is doing, that he understands the principles of perspective, form, composition, etc. Annie's certainly are child's-eye drawings—they look to me as if they were done BY A CHILD. Her art is not at all remarkable or stunning as I keep hearing people say.

We collected my uniform. URG!! It is a brown sack. Absolutely HIDEOUS! It is impossible to imagine anything MORE ugly. And surely a school that values 'freedom of expression' and is concerned with the 'nurturing of a unique and individual creative soul' shouldn't force its students to wear a uniform?

(Jules says this is the sort of thing I should NOT say out loud when I get there—as she does not want me sent home in the first week!) There is also a special calico dress made to look like a Roman toga with a braided silk girdle that we wear for Eurythmics, which is some sort of weird group dance that we girls are made to do. If the outfit is anything to go by, Eurythmics is sure to be exceedingly goofy and embarrassing.

Paul had given me £5 to buy a book or something to take with me on the train: I bought a pile of *Beano* comics and two girls' annuals. Jules sighed loudly and rolled her eyes: 'Oh God, Zelda, what on earth do you want with all that rubbish? Surely you're too old? Why don't you buy this lovely little book on Rembrandt—?' but she could do nothing to stop me as it is my own money.

I'm beginning to think life at Helicon won't be SO bad. At least it will get me away from Jules. Lately just about everything I do is <u>wrong</u>: everything I wear looks dowdy, whatever I eat is too fattening, my opinions are SO ill-considered, my interests are so low-brow, the expression on my face is simply wrong wrong wrong. It is beginning to drive me mad!!

February 4th

Jules and Paul have been asking questions about the visit to Bella—Jules especially seems very interested to know what exactly it was I did out there and can't work out why I enjoyed myself so much. In fact she seems a bit put out by the fact, which is just batty when it was all her idea & I didn't even want to go!! It is hard to describe the experience and strange how everything that seemed so important becomes so very ordinary the minute I start to tell them about it. Jules seems to think that it is ALL deprivation. Perhaps she had expected—or hoped—that being with the Steeles would make me properly appreciate all that they have given me. All the privileges, comforts and opportunities that they're always telling me I'm so lucky to have.

Jules has never been out there, but evidently her one meeting with Grandma Steele was a terrible disaster—by her account anyway. Jules says that she had found Grandma a rude, ignorant, ill spoken hillbilly—like a caricature of a rural Australian—and that is why, she says, she had left contact with them until I was old enough to cope with such people; until I was a little self-reliant. There was no way, she says, that she would have sent me there when I was younger—as she would have feared for my physical safety. This made me so furious, but of course I just make things worse when I argue or try to defend them. Jules just rolls her eyes and says that my egalitarian instincts are admirable but that one day I'll understand her attitude. If I <u>ever</u> do I swear I'll jump off a cliff. She is SO insulting, such a SNOB!! I suppose she's heard so many of Ed's stories of his childhood—which are all bad and cast his family and Comebella in the most terrible light—that she thinks it quite remarkable that he actually survived. She says that though she admires his work enormously, she really can't imagine how this landscape inspires Ed, or how after growing up in such circumstances and in such a place he had any thought for Art or any other Higher Thing at all. It is nothing short of a miracle, she says.

I have told her that she might get an inkling shortly—that Ed is all set to paint that world from quite a new and very sympathetic perspective—and that anyway it is not quite what she imagines; that there is goodness and beauty and Higher Things!! just as much as here. But of course I could not put it properly into words. Paul does seem to have some understanding. He grew up in the countryside in Victoria—though not the outback—and says that if Ed's paintings succeed, if they can capture something of the beauty as a counter to his characteristic concern with the harshness of the interior, they will revolutionise Australian art. Jules of course said how nice that would be for Ed—though she didn't suppose there would be any acknowledgement of what they (meaning her and Paul) had done for him in the early years. Most likely <u>they</u> would only ever get to view the paintings in a gallery with the general public. Paul gave her a hard look which I know is because he does not want her to speak about my father like that in front of me. As if I care.

Even though she <u>says</u> that it's essential that I get to know my family, I don't think Jules really understands just how important my visit to Bella really was—it's as if she can't believe that getting to know the Steeles actually means a great deal more to me than 'developing my artistic potential'. Sometimes I think Jules never sees anything except in terms of what she calls Higher Things. But it seemed so satisfying somehow, being part of a family. I guess it's something most people, Jules included, just take for granted. It's hard to explain—it's not like they KNEW me better in a real sense, or I knew them, just that it felt comfortable somehow, right. I felt like I belonged. And then there were the physical things—like Grandpa saying I reminded him of his mother, and getting glimpses of my own features in photos of relations and ancestors. One time Jane commented on how I made just the same expression as my father, Albert, my grandmother, and the twins too: when I exert myself or am concentrating very hard, the tip of my tongue pokes out of the corner of my mouth ever so slightly. This is a habit that makes Jules <u>ropeable</u> and she is always picking at me about it—she says I look silly—so I've tried to be conscious of it to stop doing it, but it's different now, something precious, because I know it's something I've inherited. This is not something I could ever say to Jules as she would be terribly upset to know how distant I feel from her and Paul. I have lived with them all this time— nearly my entire life—yet they don't really feel like my family in the same way it felt like being with family out at Comebella.

February 8th

I start school tomorrow. Jules and Paul and I are to drive up to Springwood with Marjory Fanning and her mother. Paul and Jules have been arguing about the school all weekend—thinking

I cannot hear everything they say, as usual, though it is a bit late for that, surely. Jules is convinced that it will be a huge benefit—the principles of the school's founders are similar to hers, as they believe that Artistic Expression is of the utmost importance in education and moral development. She says that an education provided by dedicated, talented, honourable women—teaching the girls to use their God-given talents to the best of their ability—and in the most beautiful physical surroundings—cannot be faulted. It is not at all an academic school—which is what worries Paul—they do not expect high marks or university matriculation. Paul thinks that I would be better off at one of the good Sydney schools, as I am bright and should at least be given the opportunity for proper academic teaching. But Jules says why?—as I will never have to make a living, anyway—and that of course I will still be learning maths and science and history and can sit the final exams if I'm so inclined. Paul thinks that it might be difficult for me to make the transition to being in a large group and that I might be better off as a weekly boarder somewhere—that way I can at least come home for weekends, but Jules says I need to get used to being around other people. Paul pointed out that the woman who established the school is one of the Lindsay mob, and utterly opposed to Modern Art. 'They will have her painting wood-nymphs and satyrs,' he says, 'which is surely not the sort of artistic education we planned for Zel', but Jules says that my taste is already highly developed (!!!!) and that the emphasis on artistic expression at Helicon will make up for any minor differences of principle. I can't help wondering why, if she only wants my artistic talent nurtured, I don't just stay here …

I sometimes think that I am like Jules's PROJECT—I wonder if she would have been half as interested in me if it weren't for the fact of my parents, though this is a silly thought to have really, as that is THE only reason she and Paul 'took me on'…

A card came from Grandma Steele and a note from Ed wishing me good luck. There has been no word from my mother—or none that I have heard.

There is nothing I will miss from Avalon other than the ocean—oh, and of course dear Rip. I wonder how he will get on without me—I expect Jules will make him sleep out of doors— poor old thing. HE at least will miss me.

Later

We had a special dinner to wish me farewell with Sam and Adelaide Boyle who are staying in the cottage for the next few months. Jules made my favourite: chicken cacciatore and a baked Alaska and I was allowed a glass of wine which was quite horrible really but I pretended to enjoy it. Paul made a little speech saying that I was spreading my wings and that he and Jules expected great things and I couldn't have a better en- vironment than a school like Helicon—where I would be nur- tured and encouraged—and would have great fun! Sam Boyle laughed and said that he'd heard Paul say that boarding schools were Hell and why would this one be any different? But Jules cut him off with a cold look as only she can do and I saw Ade- laide kick him under the table—probably worrying that Jules would cut off his money if he offended them. They gave me a book on the Pre-Raphaelites.

It is rather terrifying—the idea of going to school. I do not know what Jules has been thinking all these years. She has kept me out of school and away from mixing with 'ordinary' chil- dren that she felt were not suitable—but now I have NO IDEA of how to behave in a school situation. Paul keeps saying that I am quite bright—but how does he know? What if, compared to other girls my age, I am quite stupid and ignorant? Jules says there will be other girls like me who've never been in school be- fore—some girls off properties like my cousins—and then oth- ers who have been raised with ARTISTIC PRINCIPLES as she likes to call them—and that the school will be quite aware of all the adjustments we will have to make—and that I at least know Marjory. But Marjory and I have never got on since she told me that her parents think that our household is full of Commies and Perverts ... I would love to see her say that to Jules's face!!!!

February 9th, Helicon

Day One

Well, this is to be my new life—here in this strange place—and there is too much to tell in a way ... Quite a few of the girls are new—they seem as lost and anxious as me. I am writing this lying on my bed, which is a sleepout on a veranda—like at Comebella, but there are 12 of us sleeping out here in our hard narrow little beds in what is called our 'dorm'. The older and the younger girls have inside dorms, and I'm not quite sure whether sleeping outside is meant to be a privilege or a punishment. The house mistress—the woman who is in charge of our 'house', Miss Lehmann, seems nice enough. They gave us a good morning tea with cream cakes and lamingtons and little crustless sandwiches while the parents were still here—'I'll bet this is all for show,' one girl whispered. And it was. After the parents left, we assembled for a luncheon consisting of dreadful hard brown bread, cheese and pickles—a Plowman's Lunch they called it. But the bread was stale, the butter was rancid and the cheese ... urg. The food is completely INEDIBLE and I cannot imagine even the hungriest plowman (whatever a plowman is?) eating it. AND even if it were edible there is hardly enough of it: at dinner we were all given one chop each and a tablespoon of cabbage that had been boiled for at least a month I'd say, with half a teaspoon of lumpy mashed potato. For some reason there was a little bit of food left on the serving platter, but I was told that no one was to touch it even though we were half starved. I suppose we will all end up very thin. We are not allowed to drink tea or cocoa—they are bad for our blood evidently; and are to drink at least 2 pints of water a day, and are to limit our milk—which is bad for something or other—we have an allowance of one cup of milk each day, which we can use on our porridge or drink. We are to have cold baths 3 times a week even in winter as these are good for our constitution AND our character, evidently. Sounds like <u>torture</u> to me!

The other girls seem decent enough so far. Marjory, THANK GOD, is in a dorm in another house. The girl who has the bed next to mine seems nice enough. Her name is Eleanor Leach, but she likes to be called Nell, and she has come from a property near Armidale and it is her first school too. She comes from a big family and is the eldest and the first to be 'sent away' as she calls it. She is very tall with bright red hair and is quite athletic looking. She seems even more lost and alone than me. She and her mother clung to one another and sobbed and sobbed when they were saying goodbye; her little sisters all cried, and even her father brushed away a few tears. My farewell, of course, was much cooler. Jules gave me the usual quick peck on the cheek and Paul squeezed my shoulder and gave me £10 and said to write if I needed anything. I am to go home for Easter so that is only 8 weeks or so away.

February 10th

There was a special assembly to welcome us new girls. The school founder was there—a really old lady called Miss Allegra Baird—she's tiny and frail and looks at least 100. She was dressed in draping old-fashioned fabrics—in different shades of purple—and has the oddest deep booming voice. I think she is probably crazy—mad as a cut snake, as Grandma Steele would say.

She told us about the school and about herself. She was an opera singer and an artist's model—Norman Lindsay painted a very famous portrait of her—and then with money she inherited from an aunt, she set up a music school which taught Eurythmics. Then when she inherited more money from her mother (she seems to have had lots of luck when it came to inheritances—Nell & I have decided that this is highly suspicious) she decided to set up Helicon, which is named after Mt Helicon in Greece—the place where the sacred springs of the muses come from. Our school motto is 'In youth doth run the sacred springs of inspiration.' Here is the school song—which we have to memorise. It is sung to the dreariest tune imaginable which is of course a song written for only the screechiest of sopranos so I will just have to mime the words—though I hardly mind this as they are rather daffy—probably because they were written thousands of years ago by someone whose name I have completely forgotten.

> *I begin my song with the Heliconian Muses;*
> *they have made Helicon, the great god-haunted mountain,*
> *their domain; their soft feet move in the dance that rings*
> *the violet-dark spring and the altar of mighty Zeus.*
> *They bathe their lithe bodies in the water of Permessos*
> *or of Hippocrene or of god-haunted Olmeios.*
> *On Helicon's peak they join hands in lovely dances*
> *and their pounding feet awaken desire.*

We new girls were invited to a special morning tea where Miss Baird drifted about with an overfilled cup which she seemed to constantly spill her hand was so shaky. When I told her who I was—she pursed her lips and frowned: 'Oh ... the artists' child,' she said. 'Not that these modern artists are artists in any True Sense ... Well, I hope you enjoy your time here, dear—and perhaps we can instil a love of the enduring and Universal Principles of Art, eh, make up for all the modern nonsense you've no doubt been exposed to ...' She dripped a little bit of tea on me and wafted away to find her next victim. Oh no! Not <u>more</u> Higher Things!!! I thought I had escaped ...

The school houses are of course named after the muses. Clio is history, Calliope is poetry, Melpomene the tragedies, Thalia the comedies and Polyhymnia dance and music. Ours is Clio, short and sweet!

The veranda is actually a decent place to sleep at this time of year—but we are only given one blanket each and it is freezing they say in winter. But no doubt freezing is good for our characters ...

We met all our teachers today—we have all the usual subjects: English, maths, science, history, Latin and geography and an art class which is in a terrifically huge studio with a pottery wheel and a kiln—and the teacher seems quite enthusiastic. There is also a library of art books almost as big as at home—but with very different books. Here there are only books and prints of old masters—Rembrandt, Leonardo, and some of the Impressionists, but there's barely any evidence of the art of the past 30 years or so which the art teacher—Miss Orville—seems to think is rather a pity and she is trying to persuade Mrs Baird to make some purchases. She will bring in some of her own books she says for us to look at ... When I gave my name she did not say ANYTHING about my parents which was a relief. As well as the ordinary lessons, twice a week we must take this Eurythmics class which we still do not know much about. When it's mentioned all the older girls get a peculiar expression on their faces—almost a smirk—and look at one another and say, 'just wait!'

February 18th

It is true, as Paul said, that I am quite bright—or at any rate it seems I am not a terrible dunce. I seem to know as much as all the other girls about all sorts of things—except for mathematics where I am a little bit behind. But Nell is a bit of maths whiz—she is a whiz at almost everything, I think—and she has promised to help me when I need it. Our English teacher is tremendous—she is a dull looking person, but she has all us girls enthralled and can explain like no one ever has to me why for instance we should care about poetry, or why it is that we love novels. Miss Orville the art teacher is very strict, and orderly, and not at all 'artistic' and so far in most of the art classes we are just going over things I have known FOREVER, but the art workshop itself is magical and we are encouraged to use it after school and as often as we want on the weekends. There is a girl in our house—she is a year older than me—Lois Dawson is her name and she is from some outback town near Boolah—and she knows Richard, who she said is a bit of a 'honey'—and she does the breeziest little portrait sketches in half a tick. It is quite a talent and she charges the girls 1/ each picture which they send home to their parents, or boyfriends. The girls have seen my drawings of Rip which I have pinned up beside my bed, and I have promised to draw their pets—puppies and kittens and oh God! even horses—if they can give me a photograph.

Jules sent on a letter that came today from Annie who sent me £1 and said she hopes I will do well and try my hardest at school as Jules and Paul do so much for me and that I should appreciate it and work as hard as I can to repay them for their kindness and goodness and generosity though she knows it is hard for a child to appreciate anything an adult does for them—God knows she never did herself—but now that she is a mother she understands it a little bit better. She says she is sorry I did not enjoy my stay with her and that what I did was very upsetting for all concerned but that it is water under the bridge and that Jules meant well but that it was an experiment best not repeated as too much time has passed and it is impossible to go back. That perhaps when I am older I will have some understanding of her situation. She thinks I should try to develop some sort of friendship with my siblings, as that is something she herself has never had and thinks that it would be a good thing all round and perhaps we could arrange to spend some time together. Perhaps Nesta & Eve—Troy is too young of course—could come to Avalon for a week or two in the holidays ... She is angling to get rid of them, no doubt, so she can spend more time alone with Clive ... I have torn up her letter into a dozen pieces—why would I keep such a thing? I REALLY cannot bear her and would like to post her money right back. How DARE she lecture me. As to understanding her when I am older ... I'd rather NOT.

February 19th

I have plucked up courage and sent a letter to Richard Howatt at Cranburn. There is not much to tell him—our life here is rather dull—so I did some cartoons at the bottom of the letter—two little comic characters in a strip that I am calling 'Nell and Zel in Hell'—and this might keep him entertained. A little like Scheherazade and the 1001 nights, Nell pointed out ... The first strip was of course about the terrible food and the lengths we will go to to fill our poor empty tummies which is a subject that occupies much of our time here.

February 23rd

We had our first Eurythmics class today. It is unbelievably ridiculous—I cannot believe they take it so seriously!! Some of the girls here have actually been sent expressly so that they can 'study' Eurythmics, poor things! Someone said that it was fashionable 20 years or so ago—when some of their mothers were young. I can't imagine why.

The other girls are mostly from rather odd families, as you'd expect—but there are some from very ordinary families too. One girl, Sheila Mason, lives in Killara and her father is an engineer. She is not certain why they chose this school, but thinks it may have something to do with the cost—which is substantially less than others around Sydney—and the fact that they don't care too much about academic achievement. It was either this or a school that concentrated on 'domestic arts', Sheila said, and as she is definitely NOT the type to be happy cooking and cleaning and sewing, they sent her here. There is no other sport here—Eurythmics class provides all our physical exercise—which suits me well enough, I suppose, though we can go on hiking trips on the weekends with the science teacher Miss Fletcher. She is a bossy girl-scoutish woman with very thick glasses and bad skin and a hideously repulsive habit of hawking and swallowing—which of all bad habits is the one I really cannot stand. So I doubt that I will choose to spend a weekend with her EVER, even if I wanted to hike, as I would be half the time retching.

Now, back to Eurythmics. It was invented by Monsieur Something-or-other from Switzerland and the idea behind it is that all music comes from the sounds around us: the birds, the wind, the rain, and even from our bodies—the rhythm of our heart, our blood, our breath—which makes sense and is really quite a beautiful idea. But what we actually do is just silly and in addition extremely embarrassing. The class is taken by Miss Parbury-Bucket-Smythe (or Buckethead as we fondly call her) and she is a truly a daffy old duck. (Not one of the teachers here is married and it is no wonder: they are all, as Grandma Steele would put it, as ugly as a hatful of dried frogs!) We must wear our 'muse' costumes—the calico toga and girdle—and first we sit in a circle under the special Eurythmical oak tree for a time—2 minutes or so, which we must spend 'listening with all our hearts'—and then we are forced to stand up and DANCE what we have heard—one at a time. After the stupid dance we must HUM the sounds—which Buckethead then writes out in musical notation on her special little board. <u>Then</u> each girl has to try and guess what each sound represents, and at the end the dancer must explain. Oh it is just ridiculous—especially as there are not so many sounds under the oak tree—birdsong, wind, leaves rustling. We are forced to make things up. Today I danced the 'pitter-patter' of a ladybird's feet—so silly—but Buckethead was most impressed!!!

March 10th

A letter from Jules. She says they are missing me terribly—especially poor old Rip who is moping dreadfully—he spends half the day asleep on my bed, and cannot be tempted even with his favourite food. Jules and Paul are planning a 6 month trip to Europe—she has been very 'under the weather' and her doctor says that a holiday away might perk her up a little. They are to go next month, and will be away for my Easter school holidays and then the next term break as well, but should be back for the Christmas break. They have arranged for Jenny Barstock to stay for the first break. I can, if I have made a suitable friend, spend the next holidays with them if I can arrange it. It is just remarkable how much they miss me—that they must go to Paris without me. I will just go home, I suppose. I would rather see Rip than anyone else in the world, anyway. And Jenny at least does not nag me from morning to night.

March 12th

A letter from Richard Howatt ... He hasn't got much to say—and is not, I'm afraid, a very interesting letter writer. The food at Cranburn sounds just as bad as ours—and the cold showers are worse—every day and then a run around the oval. URG! I wonder why they think all this cold water is GOOD for us. I see no reason. I'm not sure if I'll write back as he didn't even mention my little cartoon—if I had not actually spoken to him I would think him a bit of a dull stick from his letters. It has made me think, though. Perhaps I could go and stay out at Comebella for the winter holidays. I'll write straight away to see if it can be arranged.

March 20th

A letter back from Paul today. I can't go to Comebella, he says, perhaps another time, as they have already arranged for Jenny Barstock to stay and it would be difficult to co-ordinate times, etc. I'll bet Jules said no.

March 29th—Easter Sunday

Dull. Dull. Dull. Eating sleeping reading eating. Nothing to do & no one to see. Jenny is kind enough, but she is busy preparing classes for her new pupil & spends the rest of the day writing to her boyfriend and then is on the phone to him all night. The only good thing is the surf—& Rip of course. Couldn't imagine wishing myself back at school, but it is better than this—nothingness.

April 29th

One of the senior girls—a prefect—came up to me today and asked if I would do a long 'Nell and Zel' strip for a new school magazine they're planning to do once a month. Miss Reed, the Latin teacher, overheard us talking—and made a face—'Cartoons are not Art, Zelda,' she said in a strangled sort of voice, 'and I would think a girl of your pedigree would know that! You should aim higher, my dear.'

My pedigree!! 'It is as if I am some kind of racehorse,' I said to Nell later; her reply: 'Neigh! Neigh!'

RUTH

When I arrive home that evening, later than I'd expected and bone-weary, Chris and Lewis are sitting on the lounge, both engrossed in some hideously violent Xbox game, and looking so much alike, so obviously father and son—round cheeks flushed, eyes bright, hair sticking up madly—that for a moment I think that I'm seeing double. And they're both eager to get back to the game—their greetings are equally offhand, as if mildly irritated by the interruption. I'm so conspicuously excluded from their blokey companionship, my presence so utterly inconsequential to their happiness, that I feel my heart contract. But then comes the inevitable indignation: *How dare they?* This is my home too, after all.

For years I've worked hard to defy the stereotype, to not come over as the grumpy stepmother, but as Lewis moves into adolescence, it's becoming increasingly difficult to maintain this ever-smiling, all-benevolent, all-considerate persona. The wicked stepmother of fairytale and myth is becoming a far more sympathetic figure—I think of Hansel and Gretel—and for a moment, a long pleasurable moment, I imagine leading Lewis far far away, without maps, or stones, or any other means of return. My fantasy isn't a murderous one: I have no doubt that this particular stepson would survive his abandonment. Knowing Lewis and his never-diminishing curiosity and enthusiasm, his endearing engagement, his charm, I'm sure that with very little effort he would find himself a cosy gingerbread house, and a sympathetic, accommodating witch who would be happy to feed him sweets, embrace him, hold him to her hard childless bosom. But I've discovered, five years into the relationship, that no matter how hard I try, this accommodating witch is just not me.

Despite all my best efforts to maintain my composure, of late Lewis has become a source of minor aggravation: someone to be cleaned up after, provided with meals, money, transport—and someone to whose whims I am expected to defer. Like his father, Lewis is always meticulously polite, always earnestly appreciative, but there's something missing. I know that however sincere his occasional outpourings of gratitude are, on some level, I'm—if not quite invisible—then nothing special to him. No more special, no more necessary, than any chance acquaintance.

The issue of children had been raised early on in my relationship with Chris. It was Chris's weekend access visit and we'd taken Lewis to the Powerhouse Museum; we were sitting in a nearby park eating ice creams. Lewis was only a little fellow then, but already so much himself—bright, curious, charming—and so much a miniature version of his father that I felt immediately comfortable with him. I felt certain that he wasn't going to be a nuisance, his company wasn't going to put any real dampener on our burgeoning relationship. I'd heard all the horror stories of step-parenting but somehow I was going to prove the exception. Or so I thought.

'I don't want any more, you know.' This from Chris, looking up briefly from a makeshift game of pickup-sticks he and Lewis were playing with twigs they'd collected earlier. For one mad moment I thought perhaps he was talking about ice cream, but then he continued, head down again, his eyes back on the game, back on Lewis, 'I can't anyway. I had the chop after Lew was born.'

I swallowed. What did he want me to say? I could feel an ultimatum being issued; the sort of ultimatum that generally signalled the end of a relationship.

'It can always be reversed, you know. There are procedures ...' I made the comment as casually as I could manage.

'No.' He still didn't look up. 'I've always thought it would be tempting fate ... after all the trauma of his birth. I just couldn't face it again, you know. The terror that he wouldn't make it, the waiting ... And there was Janna, too—they made such a muck of it that she can't have any more. So it seems—well, it seems fair—that I don't have any more either.'

'Well, yes,' I offered cautiously, 'I suppose there wasn't really any point.'

'But now, of course, it's about more than Janna.' He looked up at me, eyebrows raised, chin jutting slightly as if preparing to defend himself. 'Now having another would be unjust to Lew, somehow. Blood siblings are one thing, aren't they—and really they're quite bad enough—but all this half and step bullshit ... Well, I reckon it could just fuck him up. I've made a no-sibling pact with him. Haven't I, Lew?' He gave the little fellow a friend-ly shove, and Lew looked up briefly from his pile of sticks, and gave a gap-toothed grin. His father smiled tenderly, brushed his cheek with a gentle finger, 'And I need you to know this, Ruth. Before we go any further. I won't be displacing him. Not for anyone.' He looked hard at me again, as if my reply meant everything. Relieved, I smiled widely, wildly, no longer fearful that I'd say the wrong thing. Chris couldn't have said anything more likely to appeal. His ultimatum fitted in with my own plans beautifully.

I took his hand and held it to my cheek, took a deep breath. 'It's okay Chris, I've never wanted kids. I'm happy that you have Lew, but I've never wanted any of my own. And I never will.'

We moved in together a week later.

This evening I take a deep breath, offer them a preoccupied wave, then stomp out into the kitchen. The room is a mess. They've had takeaway Indian and left the residue scattered ev-erywhere: the empty containers, dirty plates, smeared glasses, cutlery, soiled paper towels. I resist an impulse to sweep it all onto the floor. I had stupidly imagined a very different scenario: dinner made, the table set for two, a glass of wine proffered, Lewis asleep or—even better—not here. And I dislike myself for the thought. After all, his visits are generally only on the weekends, and it *was* the condition on which our relationship hung—our contract, so to speak. Chris had only agreed to move in on the proviso that every second weekend would be given, exclusively, to Lewis. There could be no jealousy, no argument, no expectation that our relationship should impinge on the father-son dynamic, or that our adult needs—or, more specifically, my needs—should take precedence even momentarily. He'd made the boundaries perfectly clear from the outset—and being in love, I'd agreed. Feelings, of course, can't always be negotiated around, or agreed upon. And after five years of being consigned to the periphery of my own life every second weekend, I was becoming increasingly pissed off.

I want, badly, to talk to Chris about the call from Douglas Grant. Really, I'd given him very little about my family's history—oh, I'd told him the bare bones when we'd first met, told him about my mother's death, a little about her life; and a few years into our relationship he'd read Grant's book on Annie. Despite my probing, his opinions and comments on these had been as equivocal, as circumspect, as his opinions always were: he had found them interesting enough—though the writing was perhaps a little florid, slightly pretentious. And though he admired my mother's work—how could he not? Like every other Australian child of his generation, he'd grown up with a copy of her *Tales Without Words* on the bookshelves—he was not so sure that my grandmother Annie's art was to his taste, it was too abstract, too grotesque, some of the portraits were the stuff of nightmares. Typically he had had very little to say about the actual content of the book—only that my grandmother seemed a fascinating woman, clever and cruel and beautiful. But the biography had, he felt, been a little too fulsome if one were to consider her rather limited output.

I need to talk to someone tonight—and it's obvious that Chris isn't going to be that person. I decide to ignore the state of the kitchen, and instead pop open a bottle of champagne, pour myself a glass, and try to work out the time difference between here and New York. I wonder if five in the morning is really too early to phone Andy. It probably is—and I know that I'm risking an irritable 'ring me later'—but I call anyway. He doesn't pick up, heavily asleep or perhaps not there, and I listen wistfully to his cryptic greeting. *Hey. Andy & Barry aren't talking right now*, spoken in his oddly breathless (and carefully cultivated) mid-Atlantic accent. I leave a message on the answering machine: 'Andy,' I say, 'it's just me. Can you ring? It's about Mum. It's urgent.' When I hang up I wonder about the oddness of my word choice; the way it echoes Douglas Grant's. *Urgent.* Nothing can be urgent about Mum—how can it when Mum's been dead for more than thirty years?

I say goodnight to the boys—who give identical charming smiles without lifting their eyes from the screen—and refill my glass in the kitchen en route to the bedroom. When Chris crawls in beside me, some time after midnight, I'm under the covers, feigning sleep. It's three in the morning, and I've just begun to drift off, when Andy returns my call. I take the phone out into the dark loungeroom and keeping my voice as low as I can so I don't disturb the now soundly sleeping Xbox warriors, I give Andy the gist of my conversation with Grant.

'You said it was urgent, Ruth,' Andy sounds bemused. 'Why didn't you just tell him to piss off? Sounds like the usual bullshit to me. There aren't any diaries.'

'Do you know who Grant is, Andy?'

'Of course I know,' he gives a pained sigh, and I can almost hear the bored-younger-brother roll of the eyes. 'He's the one who wrote that bio of Annie.'

'But that's not his only connection. You've read the bios of Mum, haven't you?'

'Yeah,' wary now, 'but, not, you know, not for years ...'

'Andy. Grant was Mum's lover. Before Dad.'

He takes a moment to digest this. Then: 'So? So what? That doesn't mean shit.'

'Well, it does. I mean, he didn't say as much, but he must

know that she kept a diary. Diaries. He must have seen them. Why else would he ring?'

Andy's not convinced. 'Oh, Come on, Ruth. She would have been so young. Eighteen or nineteen. Doesn't everyone write in a diary when they're young? And doesn't everyone dispose of the evidence once they grow up? She probably burnt them, or threw them in the—'

I interrupt. 'The thing is, Andy,' my words come slowly, 'since he rang I've remembered something. She used to sit at the table, after we'd gone to bed, writing in what looked like a school exercise book ... I'd honestly forgotten until now, and I'd always thought they were just work notes, anyway.'

'Well, they probably were.' But he sounds uncertain suddenly, as if he doesn't really believe what he's saying.

'But what if they weren't? What if they were diaries? What if they actually exist? I'll have to go back, Andy; I'll have to find them.'

He doesn't disagree.

The idea of heading back out to Boolah right now isn't at all appealing. I'd already flown there and back for the funeral, and as there's no direct air service from Sydney, it would mean two flights and considerable expense at short notice. The alternative, driving, is hardly an alternative at all. The journey takes me almost twelve hours and the last seven or so are dreadful—a completely straight stretch of road cut into a flat featureless landscape that seems to go on forever. At least it's bitumen these days—when we were kids half the road was still dirt and on our infrequent trips to Sydney, we'd bump and grind along the rutted road, one or other of us vomiting, Dad managing somehow to complete the trip a good two hours faster than I can now. Obviously, even respectable country doctors drove recklessly fast, sans seatbelts, sans airbags, back in the seventies. Back when the world was less dangerous.

I have to go back eventually—there's no escaping that. The job of sorting and disposing of all my father's goods and chattels—all the evidence, all the remains of his life—has to be faced. But I thought I'd managed to postpone the dreaded task for a month or two, the real estate agent who's taken on the sale of the house having convinced me that it would be well worth our while to have the house renovated before selling.

Really I'd be happy never to have to return to Boolah. That part of my life—of our lives—is over. Our stepmother, Judy, died almost ten years ago, and now with Dad gone there are no ties, no reasons to return, not even for occasional holidays. There are a couple of Steele cousins in town and of course Comebella is still there—run as a tourist camel-park of all things (a wonderful irony, as my great-grandfather was one of the few non-Afghan camel drivers out west) by one of Mum's cousins and her children—but all Dad's family left years ago. The town holds nothing, only what seem like long-ago memories—almost another life—and I feel very little compunction about severing all the remaining connections neatly and swiftly.

But now there is no escaping the fact that I need to go back again. And I need to go soon—to find out whether there is any substance to what Douglas Grant has told me.

My mother died when I was only eight, more than thirty years ago, and my memories of her are vague, fragmented, and, like so many childhood memories, based more on anecdote and reconstruction than any true recollection. Lately I've found myself gazing at women in their sixties with a raw sort of longing, especially when they're accompanied by a woman who might be a daughter, and have found myself wondering more and more about my own mother. I wonder who she would have become, what direction her life would have taken, what she would have looked like, what work she could have produced, where her imagination, her talent, would have taken her had she lived. But more than that, I wonder about what our relationship would have been—whether we would have been friends, loving companions, or estranged, distant, indifferent.

I even sketched her once as I would like to imagine her: my

mother grown old, lined, her eyes sad, but somehow wise, her customary melancholy leavened by humour, contentment— and some sort of resigned pleasure in the passing of time, some philosophical acceptance that even though life never quite works out the way you think it will, in the end it's still okay: that making the most of things doesn't always mean giving up. But the sketch was a failure, of course, every line false, and was quickly abandoned, crumpled and tossed in the bin. It was always an impossibility, my mother living into old age. And to picture it otherwise was far beyond my limited skills with a pencil or paintbrush, and, to be honest, quite beyond even my imaginings.

If these diaries really exist I need to find them urgently—not for the sake of scholarship—but for me.

I sleep in that first morning back at Boolah. I'd arrived late the previous evening, and though already exhausted from the long drive, had stayed up until the early hours, searching through Dad's papers. But I found no diaries; no evidence of their existence. I downed three whiskies in quick succession—this on an empty stomach—and slept heavily. By the time I get up, the builder, Walter Gatton, has already let himself in and started work. He's high up a ladder, sanding energetically, when I shuffle into the kitchen. He climbs down effortlessly—a tall, lean-faced, shaven-headed man in his early forties, vaguely familiar—and greets me with an outstretched hand.

'G'day mate. Hope I didn't wake you. Thought I'd leave the power tools till you emerged.'

We shake hands, and I have to consciously tighten my clasp, my fingers still half asleep, around his firm long-fingered grip. 'No, it's fine, I needed to get up anyway. I've got an appointment in—oh, shit—in twenty minutes, actually.' It is already past ten and I've arranged a meeting with Dad's solicitor at half past.

'Maybe I shoulda started with the power tools after all.' He smiles, his long solemn face suddenly full of humour, and all at once I recognise him. My startled realisation must show on my suddenly hot face, and his grin gets even wider. But he doesn't comment, just releases my hand and pushes me gently in the direction of the bathroom. 'How about I make you a coffee while you get ready. Wouldn't want you to be late, Roo.'

Walter Gatton. Like every other bloke who attended Boolah High, and the occasional girl, he'd gone by a nickname. For the boys these were generally a shortened version of their surname, frequently with a suffixed O: Shane Jackson was Jacko; Philip Patterson was Patto; Michael Henderson was Hendo; Jason Burden was Birdo, and so on. Sometimes a first name was used: David O'Reilly for instance, was Davo; and William McGuinness, Billyo. Occasionally a nickname would move away from the name to describe a physical feature: there were a couple of Blues and Reds, as well as a boy who was somewhat shamefully called Ears. Not so many of the girls had nicknames, though: in fact I can only recall two in my year. As the builder had just reminded me, I'd been nicknamed Roo, for obvious reasons; and another girl in my class, Julie Hubbard had ended up as 'Mother' because of the nursery rhyme. Most of the names were predictable, and certainly explicable. But occasionally the names' origins were entirely obscure. With the surname Gatton, the builder really should have been Gatto—but for some reason entirely unknown to me he'd always gone by the name Salty. Salty Gatton. I'd probably been dimly aware of his actual name, but Salty was the only name I'd ever heard used—even by the school principal.

He'd been a few years ahead of me at school and was something of a Boolah High legend: he'd captained the school football team, as well as the cricket, had made the state carnivals for swimming and athletics, and was made school captain in his final year. Salty had been pretty bright, too, as I recall. His father had died in his early teens, and his mother, left alone to support their three young children, had eked out a living as a cleaner and sometime-cook at the local bowling club, but there'd been some hope of Salty getting decent marks and receiving some sort of university scholarship—there'd been talk too of his trialling with a first grade football team. But at the end of year twelve all his plans had come crashing down very publicly when his young girlfriend—a girl in my year, Sheryl Biggers (Bigarse to the nastier members of the class) had announced that she was pregnant. He'd done the right thing of course, being a very noble sort of lad, stuck by the girl—but at considerable cost to his own future. There'd been no brilliant exam mark for Salty, and no prospect of university or professional football. Instead, he'd taken up an apprenticeship with a local kitchen firm, married Bigarse, and, as far as I knew, had proceeded to live out his life in the isolated poverty-ridden obscurity that was the fate of so many Boolah kids. At the time it had seemed a fate worse than death.

My first and last real conversation with Salty is still vivid more than twenty years later—and it wasn't a pleasant conversation, hence my burning cheeks. Tidings of Salty's impending fatherhood had just reached the flapping mouths and ears of the school population. A friend and I had been bitching rather loudly about Sheryl and the way she'd ruined Salty's life—naturally, we were all on 'his side'—and I have a memory of the words *stupid* and *slut*; *pill* and *abortion* being bandied about between the two of us as we stood surreptitiously smoking behind the weathersheds, when an incandescently furious Salty rounded the corner. I can't remember what it was precisely that he said to us, but I know I was utterly mortified—and completely ashamed. I'd avoided him zealously after that, though our paths had never really crossed once he'd left school, anyway. I do recall Dad voicing his great admiration for Salty's honourable action. He thought it was tragic that he'd lost his chance at the city and an education, and a career, but then pointed out—and it was something that had some impact on me at the time—that there were other more important educations; that Salty might regret that he'd missed out, but that he'd never regret sticking by his child.

Now, having showered, I survey him over the steaming coffee—and acknowledge that I've remembered him: 'You're *Salty* Gatton.'

'That's the one.' His smile is slightly rueful.

'It's not,' I gush, for some reason embarrassed all over again, 'that I didn't recognise you, or that I'd forgotten your name. It's just—I'm not actually sure that I even knew your real name was Walter.'

'No worries, mate. I think my mum's probably forgotten that she called me Walter by now.'

'But I'm sure the real estate agent called you Walter.'

Now it's his turn to look uncomfortable. 'Well, that's what I put on my business card—I was living up north for a while and thought it might be better to use my proper name ... more professional. And that real estate bloke's not a local—he wouldn't know me from Adam.'

'So, you're back here permanently, then?'

'Oh yeah. Had to come back to help out my mum. She's had to go into a home. Alzheimer's. Anyway, can't seem to escape the place. Same as you, I s'pose.'

My escape has been rather more successful—I haven't lived here for more than twenty years and am only visiting now, but I don't like to point that out.

'So, you're not with—it was Sheryl, wasn't it?—anymore.'

'Nah. We had two kids—daughters—and then she pissed off down to Sydney, left them when the youngest was only six months. Came back four years later and took 'em back. That's when I headed north. Only stayed a few years. Couldn't keep away.' His voice is bland, as if he's used to satisfying the curiosity of those who, like me, have not bothered to keep up with the town gossip.

He picks up both the cups and takes them over to the sink. Glances at his watch and then back at me. 'I don't want to hassle you, Roo, but you've got about two minutes ...'

I called Dad's solicitor, Roland Ward, from my mobile en route to Boolah the day before, and made the appointment with his secretary.

I last saw Roly, an old family friend, when Andy and I called in to discuss Dad's estate the day after the funeral. It was all very straightforward. He'd read the Will—everything was to be divided evenly between the two of us—and then he'd brought out various share certificates, details of savings, and superannuation assets that would be ours once the estate had been settled. There'd been nothing at all unexpected, and at Roly's suggestion we'd left everything in his capable hands. He would organise division of the shares and so forth once probate had been granted. All Andy and I had to do was arrange for the house to be cleared out and sold, which hadn't seemed a terribly arduous task—tiresome and sad, to be sure—and something I really wasn't looking forward to. But, we'd all agreed, there was no hurry, no urgency, I could take my time.

Now, after giving him a quick hug, declining an offer of coffee and discussing the state of the roads, the ongoing drought and the Sydney housing crisis, I ask him in a roundabout way—trying to avoid any direct reference to my mother's diaries—whether my father left anything else. If there is something he hasn't told us about.

'Anything else, Ruthie? I don't know what you could mean.' Roly sounds bemused. 'We've been through the Will, and you've been given the rundown on the estate. There are no secret hoards of cash if that's what you're after.' An afterthought: 'Though what he left was substantial enough, I'd have thought.'

'There aren't any other documents?'

'Nothing that you haven't already seen.'

'No, er ... keys or anything?' I'm grasping at straws here.

'Keys? Oh, you mean to a safety deposit box or something.' His laugh is unexpectedly merry. 'Ruthie. Roo. What are you thinking, girl? Your old man was the most open bloke on earth—what do you think he'd be hiding?'

'I'm not sure. Maybe ... letters? Journals?'

He frowns.

'If you're looking for letters, there's nothing, really. Nothing's been given to me to keep. You'd be better off going through the house. Have you looked in his desk? Your father wasn't exactly a hoarder, though. We both know that. If you're looking for his personal correspondence, most likely he hasn't kept any of it. And I doubt he'd keep a journal—he never struck me as the ... writerly type, to be honest. He was never one to look back, was he?'

I explain that I had a good look through the house and the surgery last night. There was very little in the way of files—the only papers in the surgery were the various medical journals he'd subscribed to, and his current patients' files. And not so many of these either since he scaled back the practice.

Roly looks thoughtful. 'How about his old notes? You have to keep medical records for a number of years, don't you? Maybe he's stored his personal files wherever he stores his old patient records.'

This sounds like a possibility. I say as much and thank him, stand, ready to go. I give him another quick hug and Roly takes my hand between his two, then, distracted, stares absently off into space, my hand still held captive.

His face clears, and he lets me go, giving me a reassuring pat on the shoulder. 'I'm not sure what you're after—and for some reason you don't want to tell me.' He waves away my embarrassed excuse. 'No, no, it's okay, it's none of my business anyway—but I've an idea who might know.'

'Who?' I can't think of anyone else Dad would confide in. He had plenty of friends, but Roly was his best mate, his closest confidant.

'Linda,' he says with airy confidence. 'Linda Fraser.'

Linda. Of course. I don't know why I didn't think of her myself.

During the seventies, the first federally funded Aboriginal housing co-operative—the Thulli Co-op—was established in Boolah. The initial phase of the co-op's programme entailed a complete makeover of the old reserve, which was then home to most of the town's Aboriginal population. All the substandard buildings—little more than shacks, some of them—that lined the river-bank were to be demolished and replaced with three-bedroom brick veneer homes. My father and several other town worthies known to have progressive views were contracted by the Whitlam government to help set up the administration, and oversee the construction. Linda's father, Charlie Fraser, a much-respected member of the Ngemba community, had been employed both as a builder and to co-ordinate the mostly Aboriginal labour force.

That summer, he and Dad spent every second afternoon locked away in the surgery, poring over site plans and discussing drainage systems. Charlie often brought his two children, Linda and Mick, along with him. Linda and Andy were the same age, and the two would play together happily, while I would be left to baby-sit the wild toddler, Mickie. I didn't take too much notice of Linda after that—in the way of older children, she just wasn't on my radar, though I'd hear about her every now and then from Dad or Andy.

Strangely enough, though, we met up again in Sydney years later, when I was doing my residency at St Vincent's and Linda was in her first year of nursing. We spent a year together in Casualty, and beyond the initial surprise and pleasure at having met a fellow Boolan, we became good friends, and even flatted together for a few months while Linda was between boyfriends. One of these boyfriends—a spectacularly good-looking guitarist—knocked her up and then disappeared, leaving her literally holding the baby—a beautiful little girl, my goddaughter, Nadia. Linda went back to Boolah then, and nursed casually for a few more years before taking on the position of practice nurse with my Dad—who tailored her work hours around school, so eager was he to have her there.

Linda's house is in one of the new housing estates: large blocks, new brick homes, all properly oriented, with fully land-scaped gardens. I ring the doorbell and within seconds Nadia, who is no longer a baby but a lively sprite of a child, quick and smart and unrelentingly chatty, answers the door. She gives a great whoop of delight on seeing me: '*Muuuum,*' she yells, 'it's Aunty Roo!' and then launches herself straight at me, wrapping her skinny arms around my middle, almost knocking me off my feet in her enthusiasm.

Her mother is no less enthusiastic. 'Roo. What are you doing here, girl?' She bats her daughter away playfully—'Shoo you, let me have a go'—and gives me a great bear hug. 'You never said you were coming back. There's nothing wrong, is there?' I lean into her warm solidity, rest my head on her shoulder momentarily, grateful for the uncomplicated physical affection of an old friend. 'No,' I start, 'There's nothing …' but all at once I'm overcome by a confused misery. I feel my eyes sting, the breath catches in my throat. Linda pulls back and looks at me hard.

'There is something. Come on and I'll make you a cuppa.'

I follow her up the hall, protesting weakly. Nadia jumps up and down by my side, her non-stop commentary interspersed with rapid fire questions: The new Harry Potter is fantastic; what have I brought her; did I know that her Aunty Jenny was going out with that horrible new year three teacher, the one with the bristly moustache; had I seen their new car? Would I like to look at her merit certificate? She has just got her report and she's come top of the class in storytelling.

'Well, Miss Hester's right about the storytelling,' her mother comments wryly, filling the kettle. 'Now would you rack off for a bit, Nades. We've got some grown-up talking to do.'

Even before Nadia's stomped from the room—only partially appeased by promises of a sleepover and McDonald's—Linda has conjured up a large buff envelope, addressed in my father's instantly recognisable scrawl. She hands it over. 'Your Dad gave me this when he knew ...' she gestures, grimacing, 'when he knew he was on his way out. He asked me to post it to you a month after the funeral.' I open my mouth, but my voice seems to have disappeared.

'I know.' She grimaces again. 'I told him that if it was something important—and I can see that it must be—that he should let you know before. In person. While he still could. But,' she shrugs, 'you know what a stubborn old bastard he can ... he could be. He insisted. He said he didn't want to tell you—and he didn't want you to have to deal with *this* until you'd had some time to get over it.'

'To get over it? Over what?'

'Over his death.'

I take a breath.

'I know, I know, Roo. I told him that too—that you don't miraculously get over your father's death once a month's expired. I explained, really I did, that you would never get over it—that you'd just get used to it. But he wouldn't listen. So, girl, what else could I do?'

'But, Lin, it hasn't even been two weeks.'

'Well, I figure that you've found out something. Something to do with whatever's in that envelope. Can't be any other reason that you're back out here so soon—not like you'd come up for the shearing. Shit. I hope he doesn't come back and haunt me or anything—I mean what's a week or two between old friends, eh?'

I smooth the envelope with my hands, desperate to open it, but afraid, too.

'D'you have any idea ...?'

'Not a one. For some reason he didn't want to give it to Roly, and I respected that—it'd have cost him another hundred quid for the favour—and that's mate's rates. And Roly'd have asked questions, wouldn't he? Soul of discretion, me ...'

I stay for another hour, drink my coffee slowly, try and answer all Nadia's questions satisfactorily, exclaim over her latest paintings, admire the merit certificate, claim my copy of her latest school photograph—all the while, the envelope is shoved casually into my handbag, unopened, waiting. It isn't until Linda looks pointedly at her watch and tells me in her blunt way that she's got better things to do than sit about gasbagging with me all day that I make a move. I remember to ask just as I'm leaving: 'Lin—if Dad had anything—any papers or anything, that he wanted to store—where would he keep them?'

She doesn't even have to think: 'He stores all the old patient files up in the roof-space. Every six months or so he'd get what he used to call the tidy bug and out would come the ladder, and then he'd ask me if I'd lost any weight yet!' She smooths her hands down her plump hips, laughing. 'Did I think I'd be able to squeeze through the manhole—cause he was getting too old and arthritic for that sort of caper. I used to tell him that he'd never get no skinny little miss to do that sort of work anyway, and he was lucky to have a big strong girl like me who could at least lift the bloody stuff.' She shakes her head. 'He was a *gwani* bastard, your old man.'

'He was a bit,' I smile at Linda's use of the term *gwani*—mad, loco, crazy—an old Boolah word I hadn't heard used for years.

'And what, I have to climb a ladder and actually crawl up in there?' I shudder at the thought. 'But won't I fall through the ceiling?'

'Jeez, Louise—what a bloody princess. Why don't you get that sexy feller to take a look?'

'Eh?'

'You've got Salty Gatton working over at your dad's place, haven't you? The carpenter. Always thought he was a bit of a hunk.'

'A hunk?'

'Oh, Jesus. Honestly, Roo—sometimes you're as *gwani* as your dad.' She gives me a squeeze, then pushes me gently out the door.

'And we'll be taking you up on that sleepover. Don't think you'll be getting out of that promise too easy.'

ZELDA

January 5th, 1962

It's clear that I am not one of the world's most diligent diary-keepers. It has been a good three years since I last wrote, so I won't make any promises of fidelity and observance that I just won't keep. I don't suppose I shall write in you faithfully now, either, dear diary, but perhaps just every now and then—when there's something that's worth recording, worth remembering. Though I suppose such a restriction might mean that I'll NEVER have reason to write. It's very odd looking back at my old diary, which I'd really quite forgotten about until now. It had fallen down the back of my desk drawer and only dislodged when I was clearing my bedroom out. They were such funny days, those first days at Hel. I'd forgotten how VERY strange it seemed at first—& how difficult. Now in some ways dear old Hel feels far more like home than home—& yet it's not a home I can ever return to ... unless I go back as a teacher, like poor Melissa Isles, which would be a fate worse than—well almost any other I can imagine, really.

Actually—I can't really call any place home at present. Paul and Jules are having the studio cottage renovated and are going to move in there: they've had enough, they say, of indigent artists and their endless requirements. Paul's father has died and left him a squillion pounds and they plan to have the house 'rejuvenated'—they have architects and designers and National Trust people swarming all over the place and it's to be taken back to its original state—and then eventually they're going to use it as a gallery that's to be called HOLLAND HOUSE GALLERY. Urg! I can't imagine it will actually be a <u>public</u> gallery—Jules really couldn't bear all 'those people'—she'd have to don a face mask and gloves. And anyway I'm quite certain a public gallery wouldn't really be the done thing here—in fact there's probably some statute prohibiting it—so I guess it'll be for private viewings only. There's no doubt that it's about time they did something with all the paintings. Three more were damaged last year—one of Jules's stupid spaniels piddled on a couple of Ray Tebbut landscapes during a thunderstorm—but they will just leave them lying around ...

Back to the cottage. Though the extensions are to be extensive, basically it will be a new house inside the old shell. (I don't know why they don't knock the thing down and start again, it's not like it's an architectural wonder, like the house, but Jules insists that the cottage has historic value, being both 'womb and cradle'—urg—of so much significant art work.) In any case, Jules has made it very clear that there will be NO ROOM for me. 'There will be a <u>spare</u> room, darling—and you'll be more than welcome to it whenever you visit.' I gave her a bit of a turn—looked terribly distressed momentarily, said: 'Oh, but where am I to live?' in a plaintive little voice. She really did go pale. Brightened up considerably when I laughed and admitted I had no intention or desire to live all the way out here. The upshot is that I'll move into one of Paul's rental properties—which'll be fine whatever I decide to do with myself.

It's too exciting—the prospect of all this freedom. But what to do with it? Paul is hinting in his gentle way that I should perhaps forget art for now. After all, he says, art is something I can always do. I could go to art classes at night, he says, or perhaps it should be just something I do for pleasure ... And I've got such good results, he says, what a pity to waste them. Have I thought of doing law? And medicine would be quite a good career for a bright girl. Or even if I just do my B.A. and then go into journalism perhaps ... Things are really opening up for women now—so many opportunities. This is an attitude that enrages Jules, who thinks that I MUST MUST MUST study art.

'After all the effort we've put into her training, Paul!' she wails. 'What a tragedy to let it go to waste.' Paul says nothing directly to her; looks pained. After all the work <u>they've</u> put in! Most of the time she's berating me for my lowbrow taste—for my silly adolescent passion for fairytales and comics, for my lack of interest in the works <u>she</u> considers worthy.

Later

A letter came from Annie today—the first in almost two years. It is quite shocking—in fact I was so angry that I tore it in several pieces & threw it away. But I've fished it out of the bin and have taped it back up—as EVIDENCE. It is almost impossible to believe that this woman is actually my <u>mother</u>.

> *My dear Zelda,*
>
> *I know we haven't seen eye to eye on anything much over the years and that to be honest I have not made any real effort to see you, our meetings being always so painful—for me of course, but also, and especially, I feel, for you. Paul has told me that after that disastrous last visit—three years ago now—you were terribly upset. Anyway, I know you do not want to hear from me my reasons for your adoption, as these you already know, nor is it appropriate for me to discuss my guilt and unhappiness over events—though don't ever think, Zel, that it is only you who suffers. And there is your father, too, to think of.*
>
> *I am glad that you have at last made some effort to get to know your sisters and brother, and I know they appreciate your little letters and cards—and Nesta says she enjoyed the afternoon she spent in town with you before Christmas, though you might have chosen the movie a little more carefully as I am not sure that 'Godzilla' really was the best choice for a nervous child like Nesta. Even if*

you are not close and do not <u>really</u> think of them as siblings there is something in blood relationships that we cannot— and perhaps should not—avoid completely. (Though I'm afraid that I don't have a rosy view of family life myself: my own sister and brother are not close to me at all, in fact we heartily dislike one another and the dislike in me runs VERY deep and VERY bitter.) But you must know that what I did, I did for your own good as well as my own. It was obvious that there would be no true marriage between your father and me once I had met Clive—only one of unhappiness and regret and increasing frustration and bitterness—and once I had made that decision to be with Clive and knowing that with his illness and our shared passion for art we were unlikely to be living any sort of an easy life—and we have NOT as you know ever had the sort of privileges and comfort that you have grown used to—the decision to leave you was virtually made for me. Despite the pain I experienced in relinquishing you, I have no doubt that there would have been even greater pain in store for us all had I not. The decision for you to be adopted by Paul and Jules was a joint one made by your father and I—your father for all the same reasons—both of us wanting your upbringing to be safe and secure, something we could not offer with what seemed then to be our very uncertain futures. And Jules loved you, she did, Zel. From the moment you were born I could see how much she coveted you. You have probably seen (they were at the 'Antipodes' exhibition last year) my 1945 Madonna and child pictures—they were modelled on you, you and Jules, Zel. It was as if she was MADE to be a mother, as if you belonged to her. Her every look, every gesture was all gentle bountiful maternity—unlike me, who seemed at that stage of my life made for anything BUT motherhood. I was incapable of giving anything to a baby who is all need need need. I did not have what <u>I</u> needed, so how could I give to an in-

fant? And Jules's desperation, her despair and grief over her barrenness—it is hard to express just how much I pitied her. We were so close at the time, like sisters almost, and her sadness inevitably became my sadness.

There are other things, too, that occurred later and that I could not necessarily have anticipated, Zel, which I imagine you will have been told about or guessed by now. I am talking about Jules and Ed's affair, which went on for several years after your adoption. I think that Jules had probably been in love with your father for a long time, though I had not been aware of it. And once I left him, your father reciprocated—he certainly did not make the advances, but has always been a weak man and would not be able to withstand any woman's flattery (though, unlike me, during our marriage he was always loyal).

So it worked out extremely well for us all for the first few years—the break was not too severe or sudden—you had your father in the cottage as well as your adoptive parents. You had a secure, comfortable, affectionate home, and a mother's love that was much stronger and more real than any I could provide. And Paul has been a wonderful father—you could not be in better, more thoughtful and considerate paternal hands. He has always had your best interests at heart—the only matter in which he did not have his way was the decision to send you away to school—but this occurred at a difficult period in Jules's life. It is a critical period in many women's lives, Zel, one you cannot imagine as you stand at the brink of adulthood—all the energy, the enthusiasm, the joy of being alive can so suddenly dissipate, to be replaced by—well, something else, something dark and terrible—awareness of your own mortality, the inevitability of decay and dissolution, and all around you the evidence of new life, of youth. Still, from all accounts, school has worked out well enough, and you have after all the good marks to your credit and the means as well as the capacity to further your education at the University.

Which brings me to the crux of this letter—you will forgive my rambling, Zel, for it seemed there were a few wrinkles that needed ironing out before I could presume to go any further. As you probably know, I had lunch with Paul in town last week (Clive had to come for a visit to the specialist—but that is hardly news that will interest you so I will not dwell on this) and he spoke to me of his concern for your future. He says that you still seem determined to go on to art school despite your excellent results and his willingness to pay for whatever degree you should choose, even, he says, if you wanted to make a career of being a scholar and go on to do your doctorate—which is a pos-sibility that is way beyond any expectation I ever had for myself when I was your age. This may be painful, Zel, and I really hate to be the one to say it, but really it is always better to be straightforward in these matters—but Paul is VERY concerned that your strength does not lie in the ar-tistic realm—regardless of what Jules may say to the con-trary, whatever hopes she holds out for you in this area. It is not always a matter of talent, but of perseverance—I do not think in fact that I have a great talent in the way that your father has, but I do have the compulsion—and it is this LACK of compulsion in you that so worries Paul. He knows you have a great interest in drawing and is a great admirer of your dinky little comics—and he tells me you have produced one or two charming woodcut prints—but he does not think, and I have to agree, that these are an indication of that overriding, overwhelming passion for art that is the first requirement of the artist. You can do without drawing and can progress as I have managed to do—much to your disdain, I realise—without a technical knowledge of all sorts of things, but you cannot do with-out PASSION. And while your cartooning shows talent, what Paul fears is that it will be exploited in a commercial sense, that you will end up frustrated, disappointed and bitter, perhaps never progressing beyond drawing and colouring in advertisements for women's magazines. He has said too that your interests are quite idiosyncratic, that you don't appear to be at all interested in the sort of art that SHOULD interest you as someone who has been exposed to the highest forms of art since they were an infant. It is as if the young Mozart, despite all his intensive training, his access to the finest traditions of European music, had decided that he preferred Austrian peasant tunes.

If you do determine on a life of art you should prepare yourself for a great deal of suffering—and not only yourself—but those who love you as well. I am not sure that for most people, and women in particular (though men seem to have NO TROUBLE, it does not seem to necessitate such a compromise for them) that their art is worth it, and think perhaps they would have had better, more satisfying, less disappointing lives had they stuck to something else: teaching, nursing, writing for a newspaper—anything. It is a road strewn with fatalities: drunkenness, ill-health, broken hearts, broken marriages, broken spirits. I speak from experience as you well know. And in the end—perhaps it hadn't been worth it. What is a body of work—is it really worth more than children, friendships, family etc? I cannot say—only that once I discovered art there was NOTHING ELSE I could have done. This is how you must feel—utterly uncompromising. The work must supersede everything—and every one—else in your life. Only you will know whether that is what is in you ...

There are many people who have a great deal of talent—more, no doubt, than me, and it is no judgement against them that they have made that decision to put art (or music, or poetry ...) at the periphery of their lives rather than at the centre for what are usually very SOUND reasons. They do good work, contribute to society in various essential ways, and perhaps the weekend landscapist, or portraitist, gets MORE real, uncomplicated pleasure from their work than the professional who makes their work their sole endeavour. I am not sure that the uncertainty, the emotional trauma, the sheer hardship of working and waiting, waiting, waiting for recognition is worth all the pain. There is no doubt that a finished work can sometimes give an intense feeling of satisfaction, and that there is no better feeling than during those moments where the 'muse' is in evidence—it's almost a euphoria—but these moments are rare. For the most part there is frustration and uncertainty, both from the requirements of 'the world' and from the artists' own feeling of lack, of inadequacy.

There is no doubt that you have other talents that could be nurtured, which is very different to my case—there was nothing else I was ever particularly good at, and indeed it was not until I had left your father, and you, when I was with Clive, and our circumstances became extremely difficult, that my calling really became clear. Until that moment I was really no more than a dilettante—Ed's wife, Ed's model, Ed's muse I suppose. You are more like your father than me in that you are VERY CLEVER—but far more fortunate than him with all your monetary and social privileges.

The world is truly your oyster, Zelda, and I hope that you will think carefully and weigh up all the possibilities that are open to you before you make any binding decision about your future.

I hope that my frankness has not offended you, but as you know I have always held honesty to be the best course, sometimes to my own disadvantage.

With my sincere best wishes for your future,
Annie.

There is no reply to be made to this. I do not think I will reply. Ever.

Later

What a way to make such a revelation. She must have known that I did NOT know about my father and Jules. My God, how ridiculously naive I am.

All that time Jules spent with my father—how could I have been so stupid not to understand why Jules was so often with him when I was little, accompanying him on his trips, to exhibitions. And then to be so terribly excluded—I had never known why we did not then see him for so many years. And how could Paul have stood for it? He has been cuckolded in the most humiliating way. And now, how can it be that he is still so hopelessly besotted with her? It is dreadful the way Paul is always watching her, considering her—as if she were some sort of an invalid, when she is anything but. How do women like Jules get away with it? She has everything: money and a man who will do anything for her, whose first thought is ALWAYS her. You should go to bed, darling, you look all in. Do you really think you should be doing that, my jewel? As if she might be mortally wounded peeling potatoes. It makes me sick! And all these years she has been—and it seems that everyone knows it—completely unfaithful. How could Paul bear it? And I've never ever felt that he hated Ed. Surely he has every right? Surely he can't have felt it right to sacrifice his manhood, his pride, for the sake of art? This would take the soul of a saint. And then to have to bring me up—and yet he's always been so kind to me—there's never been any sign at all ... And Jules, it is staggering—her ingratitude—to have a man, to have anyone! love you so much ... she does not know what it is she has.

As to the <u>crux</u> of her letter, Annie should not have wasted her breath: I had already decided on Arts. Still, honesty has, as she points out, its uses. Wonderful to know that they all have such faith in me. And my talent.

January 6th

Spent all day at the beach. I think they know I am avoiding them—both Jules and Paul are being very courteous and gentle. They must have had some idea of what was in the letter, though I'm sure they have no idea of the revelation about Jules and Ed. I wonder if I should tell Jules that I know—but how would I even begin such a conversation? Jules dear, is it true that you had an affair with my father? How absurd!

Anyway, the day began pleasantly enough, then rapidly went downhill. Marjory was down at the beach with a big gang: some of the local girls, as well as her brother and a few of his Cranburn mates, so I sat with them some of the time. Marjory's brother, Alan, is not quite as awful as her, and he's rather good-looking in a blond, beach-boy sort of way. He was impressed with my bodysurfing skills, but spoilt things rather when he pointed out that I was the only girl there who got my hair wet. It was, I think, meant to be a compliment, but Marjory and her friends looked at one another, then Marjory gave me the benefit of her devastatingly nasty smile: 'Zelda never did give two hoots about what she looks like.' Well, I managed a retort, at least: 'I come to the beach to surf, not to sit around like some corny Christmas decoration.' I wandered casually back down to the water (really to cool my flaming cheeks), and I could hear them all laughing. Girls are SUCH cats. If only I could have thought of something a little more cutting.

Told them over dinner of my decision. Paul's relief was obvious, though poor Jules looked a little deflated by my compliance. Perhaps she'd secretly hoped that I'd insist: rally, argue, prove my mettle, show some determination; become the person she'd hoped for, planned for, carefully nurtured. Instead I am just me, Zelda: plain, pale, plump, with my plebby taste for the surf, for comic books and true romance novels. With none of my mother's grace, wit, beauty or passion; none of my father's charm—and none of their painting talent—all I can claim is a 'certain knack for depicting the whimsical' as the art teacher at Hel so patronisingly put it. And now it seems that Jules has suddenly noticed my lack of polish (how this has managed to escape her attention for so long I can't imagine): she is threatening to send me off to a Swiss finishing school in the university holidays. We argued about it at the dinner table and in the end I stormed off in a huff.

But instead of going to my room, I stood outside the door, listening. Paul had said very little in my defence while I was there—he rarely argues with Jules when I'm around, but once I'd left he made it clear that he disagreed.

'Good God, Jules! A finishing school! You can't be serious! Whatever for?'

'Oh God, Paul. She's just hopeless. Really, I'm at my wits' end,' hissed Jules.

'Wits' end? Oh, come on, Jules. About what?'

'Well, there's her weight, for one thing. She's far too plump and I'm sure these places can do something about that. Did you see how many potatoes she ate during dinner? Ridiculous! And she needs to learn to hold herself properly. That slouch! And then to dress with a sense ... to develop some sense of style. She's just so *drab*, somehow! To look the world in the eye—sometimes she's so awkward, so graceless. And quiet, she has so little conversation. It's hard to imagine how it happened, living here with us, and with such parents ... Annie's so beautiful, and so full of life ... Zelda doesn't seem to have inherited anything of her.'

'But those places train girls to be—well, to be wives, darling. And a certain type of wife. A society hostess. She doesn't need that rubbish.'

'No? Well, what on earth do you think she's going to do if she doesn't get married? And who'll have her as she is? She's got no feminine graces, no sense of being a woman, Paul. And I know you think she's bright ... but she's not going to be any sort of a scholar—she's got no energy, no passion. Both her parents ... well you'd think she'd have some sort of drive. She's such a—I don't know—such an aimless, lumpy sort of a girl. And so fleshy. Like a big pale pupa …'

'But these are things we've always said don't matter. She's very bright, and she's a good kind girl. She'll make her way like everyone else … the way we all had to. She's just a child, Jules—she's not even eighteen. You expect too much—far too much. This stuff, these externals, surely they don't matter?'

'Oh yes. I think for a girl like Zel—especially a girl like Zel—these things will matter a great deal. Unless we settle a great deal of money on her, Paul, and I'm not sure that that would be such a good idea, but unless we do, really, she has so little to offer.'

I stood there cringing, trying not to cry, wishing with all my heart that I had the courage to confront her. Instead I slunk back to my room before they caught me there—a big pupa—hanging at the doorway slowly digesting her poison.

It is true, I am not at all beautiful, certainly not in the way that Annie was, and still is I suppose—I can see nothing of her in me at all and only a little of my father. But why is it always a comparison anyway? And surely, surely, I am not THAT bad?

Later

It's odd, in some way Jules's cruel description of me IS how I feel—like I'm a big fat pupa waiting waiting—but I don't know what for. I wonder whether a real pupa KNOWS that when the cocoon breaks open it'll emerge with glorious wings, tentative and sticky and grounded at first, but then with everything it needs to take flight. How could it ever have imagined such a metamorphosis? Perhaps this period of gloomy uncertainty is necessary before I emerge into the light, anyway. A regrouping, a rethinking while I grow. And then soon, soon, I'll burst out of my skin.

It is utterly impossible to know what it is that I actually want to do, what I want. One moment I feel as if I am capable of great things—as if the idea of the world itself could spring from my own head—and I am giddy with my own power: it is all there before me. And then the next moment the reality—the terrible limitations—crowd in. It is, after all, <u>only me</u>. Only Zelda in her grimy pink dressing-gown, spooning some prohibited substance into her mouth, happy to stay in bed the entire day with a book whenever she gets the chance, with every grand idea, every brilliant thought, too much trouble, too difficult to put into any action. It is, after all, <u>only me</u>: plain, inadequate, bone lazy. The thought of anything to do with any sort of art beyond my own little sketches seems quite absurd, impossible, requiring an effort that I can't possibly make, attention I'm incapable of giving. It is what they have always wanted though, what they have all but given up hoping for: great things from me—and yet I know and they know that it is an impossibility. I am NOT Annie Swift or Edward Steele, but just myself. It fills me with terror: the idea that I have to perform, to show Jules, Paul, Ed, Annie—EVERYONE—that it hasn't been a completely wasted effort ... Does everyone feel this—this pressure to be SPECIAL, to somehow give back what they have been given? I'm sure Nell doesn't. Her parents love the Nell that is, they don't constantly desire someone bigger, better, more clever, more beautiful. Lord, what would they think if I told them that half the time all I want is what every girl I know dreams of: a man, babies, a house, a garden ... that I don't yearn for Higher Things at all.

Deep down I feel as if I am a bitter disappointment to everyone: Jules and Paul; Ed and Annie; even my Steele grandparents if they even bother to think of me at all, since I have never been back since that visit, and have hardly ever written.

And what would be worse, I wonder: their disappointment in me, or my own? At any rate there is no doubt that at some stage I am bound to disappoint someone.

January 14th

I have never really thought much about the fact that I was named after someone—after Zelda Fitzgerald, the writer's wife. Jules told me that Ed had wanted to call me Caroline after Grandma Steele, but Annie had said no, she wanted Zelda, as, Jules says, she identified so strongly with her. Yesterday I came across a copy of Zelda Fitzgerald's book *Save Me the Waltz* in Paul's study—I had not known that she was a writer too, I said to Jules. Oh, yes, yes, she was—a much lesser writer than her husband of course, Jules told me, she only wrote to spite him, to compete, she was never a real artist. No wonder my mother identified with her, I thought, then sat down to read it, intrigued. I read all day. What a person to name a daughter after! Was this what she wanted ME to be, I wonder—wild, tragic, talented, unfulfilled, bitter, restless, dissatisfied—or how she saw herself?

January 18th

Jane Steele phoned this morning. Grandpa has had a stroke and is dying. He is in hospital in Boolah and has expressly asked to see me, she says. Jules has arranged for me to fly to Dubbo tomorrow—Albert is to pick me up there—and back next week. Ed and Ynez are flying over from London. Jules has said that it's not necessary that I go—it seems to me that she would rather I didn't—in fact she says that it is ridiculous, I barely knew Grandpa Steele. I'd only spent any time with him that once and that all this 'blood' business that the Steeles go on with is just sentimental rubbish! I cannot say that I am anything but dreading the meeting—but it would be a victory for Jules if I don't go. For some reason she cannot bear the idea that I am connected to that world—and it galls her that I don't despise it as she does. Jules hates the fact that both Ed and I have come from such ordinariness—such flat, poverty-ridden lives. Though I suppose, in her mind, Ed has at least transcended it. It is so odd that she does not, will not, see that there's as much richness in others' lives as in her own. But then there is so much that Jules misses. Perhaps it is having so much money—she can be detached from real people, in a way. I remember once when we were heading up the coast for a holiday, Jules would hold a cologne-drenched handkerchief up to her nose whenever we drove through the countryside. She couldn't bear the stench—it was the cattle, she said, the dust. Sometimes I think she would like the equivalent of that perfume in all social situations—to hide the reek of other humans.

January 20th

Grandpa died before I arrived, so Albert took me straight back to Bella. I have to say that I was more relieved than upset. I was terrified all the way out there: I have never seen anyone on their 'death bed' before—what is one to say or do? Everything would be awkward, and everything would be wrong. Poor Grandma Steele. She is brave but it is obviously difficult for her—she is going to move into town into the house that she and Grandpa had just had built, but now it will just be Grandma, alone.

Everything here is different to the way I remembered it. Comebella itself seems hotter, drier, flatter, redder, more barren, than in my memory. But more prosperous too—there are new fences everywhere, the old sheds have been replaced, new cars and utes. Grandma & Grandpa's house seems so tiny, and so primitive it's almost impossible to imagine bringing up a family in it—and it looks like it is collapsing into the earth. Albert and Jane's house has expanded. It has had a brick front put on and three new rooms out the back as well as a veranda. The twins are taller and prettier, but despite boarding school are just as horsey as ever, and little Diana is set to follow in their elastic-sided bootsteps! Everyone—especially Jane—is being very kind, but I feel much more of a stranger—a visitor, not family—than I did last time. They are all grieving, telling stories, sharing their memories of Grandpa, and I have nothing to offer. I hardly knew him. I hardly know any of them. I feel like an intruder.

January 22nd

The funeral—the first I have ever been to, but not the last, I'm sure—was very very strange. People behave so oddly, so unexpectedly. Ed, who had arrived by train only this morning, was shockingly upset—the most distressed of anyone, really. After the church service he had to carry the coffin from the hearse to the graveside, along with Albert and some second cousins I've never met, but they had to set it down—they almost dropped it—because poor Ed just couldn't manage, his shoulders were shaking so much. Then he stood at the graveside and howled and howled—the most terrible, frightening sound, it was just awful. Ynez tried to comfort him, but he pushed her away. Only Albert was able to calm him.

It was quite surreal—the red red redness of the earth there, swallowing up the coffin, the withered-up old priest in his great black robes, & my father howling away like a crazy wounded animal. It was impossible to connect Grandpa with the coffin—I couldn't quite believe that all that was left of him was in there. His earthly remains. It hardly seems possible ... Grandma did not cry. She stood very upright with the twins on either side. Jane said I should stay close by, and that it would please Grandma to have me near—as Grandpa was so fond of all his granddaughters. I felt a complete fraud. Pen and Pam and even little Di were obviously really upset, and there I was, like a shag on a rock. I would have been pleased to have been able to shed even a crocodile tear. Anyway, Grandma did not seem annoyed by my presence, but she seemed very distant—as if her mind was elsewhere ... which of course it was.

I spoke to Richard Howatt later at the wake (which was at Tattersalls) and he has grown up to be pretty cute—not handsome exactly, but with a big smile and an open friendly sort of face and an easy way of talking. I told him I still felt guilty for being such a bad correspondent all those years ago, but that I was SO offended that he did not make any comment about the little cartoons I'd drawn him & which I'd thought were so very amusing, that I'd decided he just wasn't worth another letter. And he laughed and said that he can remember thinking I was a pretty funny kid—and that from what he recalled my school had sounded even worse than his!

He is at Sydney Uni—in his third year of medicine—and we exchanged numbers and promised to get together sometime soon. He has just moved out of college and is boarding in Chippendale.

The wake itself was very subdued, although there seemed to be hundreds of people there—half the town turned up—and most of them were related in some way or other. Ed got very drunk and maudlin and Ynez took him off to bed, which was a pity because he had started to sing—he was in the middle of 'Danny Boy', which was Grandpa's favourite, evidently, when she dragged him away. His voice is pretty good—deep and sad—and I noticed a few people wiping their eyes.

When I said goodnight, Grandma patted me on the shoulder and thanked me for coming. I felt rather hurt—she did not need to thank me—he <u>was</u> my grandfather after all.

RUTH

My darling Ruth.

By the time you receive this letter I will be dead. It is painful to think, writing now, that I really will be gone, that I won't be around to advise you, to guide you, on what I know will prove a difficult journey—perhaps the most difficult journey you will ever undertake.

I have entrusted this letter to Linda, and have asked her to let four weeks elapse from the time of my death, before sending it on to you, in the hope that this will give you time to recover a little, to have made a start on the arduous process of sorting and sifting and resettling—both physically and emotionally—that's required after the death of a parent. I have always thought that you and I have been blessed, Roo, that despite our shared sadness we've managed to forge an incredibly strong and loving bond—and I hope that the memory of this will help sustain you in the difficult period ahead.

Up in the crawl-space—the access door is just outside the big bathroom—you'll find a parcel, wrapped in brown paper, and addressed to you. (It's possible, if I haven't managed to clear it out before then, that you'll also find forty years' worth of patients' notes, which I'm afraid you will have to deal with. Most can be burnt, but some will have to be put into storage elsewhere. Perhaps you can speak to one of the other doctors in town about this—Ray Belling might be of help here.)

This parcel contains one hardback 'diary' along with eleven school exercise books—the journals that your mother kept from her fourteenth birthday right up until the night of her death.

I have asked that you be the first to go through these journals not only because you are the eldest child (and I realise that like so many responsibilities heaped on the first-born, it may seem an unfair burden), but because there is material in these papers that is relevant to you alone.

While I was aware of the diaries' existence—they were never a secret, and your mother wrote in them frequently enough during our short time together—I have only had access to them for the past ten years. After your mother died, I was in a terrible state for some time— blasted by both grief and guilt—and could not bring myself to clear up your mother's belongings. It was just too hard, too traumatic. In the end, Ed Steele and Paul came up for a week and cleared the house and sorted out all your mother's effects. I had given them permission to take away the works as they saw fit—your mother had made no provisions of course, there was no will, but I thought it in your best interests to make Jules and Paul her literary and artistic executors. And so they packed away everything that your mother had written or drawn and had the lot transported back down to Sydney. Most of the prints and illustrations—other than those that were given to you and Andy—have been sold or published, but the journals and the manuscript seem to have been 'lost' somehow—either in storage, accidentally, or perhaps, though I don't like to think it—deliberately.

It wasn't until after Jules's death, and a few months before his own, that Paul saw fit to send them on to me, in trust for you and Andy, thinking that we might want to see them published, or perhaps sent to the National Library; or even sold to the highest bidder, as one does these days, but it is up to you now whether you wish to make them public or not. I suppose my instinct would be for you to keep these to yourselves—neither of you suffers from any real shortage of funds (though your brother does like to fancy himself poor), and there is still the sale of my estate to come—but this is a decision I must leave to you, Ruth. Almost all of the main players in this story are dead now—there are very few who can be hurt by the revelations contained within.

The diaries contain very little information that's new to me, but in reading them I was able to see again the young woman I fell in love with all those years ago and who, if truth be told, I still love. And I was able to experience some slight alleviation of the guilt that I have carried for many years. I only wish poor Judy were still here, as she too felt the weight of your mother's death terribly.

You will, perhaps, be upset that I did not pass the diaries on to you and Andy immediately their existence was made known to me, but I hope that after you read them you will understand—and forgive— my silence.

Now I will say nothing further—this is your mother's story and I will let her be the one to tell it to you.

With all my love,

Dad.

ZELDA

February 10th, 1962

Here I am in my own little house! For it IS actually, really and truly, ALL mine. I have the deeds (or at least my solicitor does) to prove it.

I had thought, when Jules told me that they would be transferring the house to me—as a part of my 'inheritance'—that this would mean I could live here alone, or at least find a friend to share with me. But as always, Jules has already arranged things to her liking. She has told Marjory Fanning's parents that she would be welcome to share, and she'll be moving in early next week. I kicked up a bit of a stink at this, said that I would rather share the house with anybody else—surely there is some poor homeless creature out there somewhere?—than with Marjory, but Jules very icily explained that while they were willing to pay me an allowance for food and transport and to help out with clothes and so on, they felt that a small contribution from a tenant would be helpful—and would help cover some of the expenses of the house itself—electricity, rates and so on. And that Marjory, naturally, would be a most respectable and reliable flatmate. So unless I wanted to go out working rather than studying, and pay my own way, Marjory's tenancy was a condition of my living here. As always, there are strings attached to their gift. Why does it sometimes seem that Jules HATES me? Everything I do seems to annoy her. Paul is kind as always, but distant, distracted, and always always considers Jules first. He did say to me last week—and perhaps he was trying to tell me something—that moving out of the house is proving more difficult for Jules than she imagined: the place holds so many memories, so many hopes and dreams, that in a sense it is admitting old age, defeat, the end of something, to move out ...

Still ... I have a week's grace—and I'll make the most of it. For one week more it will remain unshared: my own private place, my sanctuary. Such a quaint little place it is too—from the exterior it's in every way exactly the same as its neighbours (it's one of six terraces that Paul bought during the war), other than the door, which is painted a dark green, and the lovely brass lion-head knocker.

It's only six rooms inside—a loungeroom at the front, a little kitchen at the back, a bathroom off that (& it is literally only a bathroom—there is no shower, and the toilet is outside). Upstairs there are three rooms, two that open out onto the little front veranda, and one funny little odd-shaped north-facing room at the back that I thought I might use as a studio.

I am full of ideas for its improvement—but so far all I've been able to do is to clean it up a little and splash a bit of white paint about. It has been rented out for years and years—since before Paul first bought the row—and is really pretty dingy. We've furnished it with odds and ends from Avalon—all my bedroom furniture, the old club lounge and the little oak dropleaf dining table from the cottage, six mismatched bentwood chairs that I found stacked in the garden shed, a little cedar coffee table that Jules said Ed knocked together years ago ... Plates and cups are all throw-outs I found stored in the pottery-shed, all unsigned, all imperfect—but quite perfect enough for me ...

February 12th

I walked through the Cross today—what a place! I feel so excited to be here—right in the centre of the city—it could be the centre of the world. It seems such a long way from Avalon, and a lifetime away from Helicon. (In fact I wonder sometimes whether the whole of my high school years were just some bizarre dream. What a strange out-of-time place it was—is—and what a strange way to prepare young girls for the real world.)

But here—here you can feel everything, all the life that I have been burning to feel: it's as if it's pulsing in the air—youth, beauty, passion—and then the other side of the coin, the depravity and dirt and licentiousness for which this place is known. All the sights and sounds are so strange and wonderful—and even the smells: from the delis, restaurants, pubs and all-night strip clubs, and the rotting garbage that never seems to be carted away, and God knows what else. Anyway, to me it is all exotic. It's almost as if I have been transported to a foreign country, as romantic as Paris, Venice, Rome ... It seems that there are no ordinary people—everything, everyone, is louder, larger than life—lovers quarrelling, people begging, down-and-outs sleeping it off in the park. Housewives, students, sailors, beatniks, whores—all going about their business. I am afraid in so many ways, and yet exhilarated too, knowing that I am amongst all of these people, a part of this great living breathing metropolis. And yet somehow I am feeling simultaneously lonely, left out, invisible—I want to be a part of it all ... I want so badly to <u>be</u> that beautiful dark-eyed girl, sitting outside the cafe, arguing passionately with her young man, a cigarette in her hand, gesticulating wildly, so gracefully gloriously angry. I wonder what it is they're fighting about? And her young man—looking so cool, almost bored. How could such a beauty be boring? Are they arguing about poetry or politics, are they having a lovers' quarrel? Does he want nothing more to do with her? Perhaps she's pregnant ... I suppose they could be fighting about him not wiping his dirty feet on the doormat, tracking mud inside their flat, or something equally banal, but that's not possible, surely?

February 17th

Oh God. Marjory has arrived today and she is exactly as I thought—<u>completely</u> unbearable! (Did I stupidly think that perhaps—being out in the big wide world—she might have improved???) First, though and most important to record for posterity: Marjory has, for some reason, decided to change her name to Margot. Which means I shall henceforth call her Marg to her face and Maggot behind her back. Margot!!!!! I wonder what her mother thinks of this? I just wish Nell were here to tell—how she would laugh. After giving me this side-splitting piece of information and before we'd made it up the staircase with her luggage, she thrust her hand in my face. Look at that! she shrilled, waving the hand about so wildly I thought she was having some sort of fit. But no—she was showing off the great chunk of rock on her finger. A three-pound diamond on a two-hundred carat band!!! Yes, she's engaged—oh, Joy!—to David George. A Cranburn Boy!! An accountant at Phillips Henshaw Rex. I tried to say the right thing, I really did, but I could tell that my response was somewhat disappointing—no doubt I did not quite manage the tone of seething envy she'd anticipated ...

When we eventually lugged all her baggage up the stairs, Maggot, typically, found a great deal to complain about. The walls of her room were far too dark, she could hear the noises from the street, from the dripping tap in the bathroom below, from the wireless in the terrace next door ... and then there were the smells: next door's cabbage, car exhaust, old carpet, new paint ... So—I gave her what she wanted—the sunny room at the back which I had thought I might use as a 'studio' ... (But WHY would you need a studio, Zel—it's not like you paint, is it? You only ever do those little sketches ...) And then, of course, once she had that fixed, she said that seeing as it was a smaller room, shouldn't she pay less? It really is only smaller by a couple of inches ... These are the perils of being a landlord, I suppose. I hope her Dave takes her off my hands sooner rather than later.

February 20th

Margot—Maggot—is a cow. This evening I was sitting peacefully in the loungeroom with a cup of tea, settling into a lovely nice quiet night of reading and sketching ... when in flounces Maggot with all her nail-care accoutrements. She was quiet for all of about two minutes, and then obviously couldn't bear it, and off she went. Onto her favourite topic: the scandalous goings on at the Hollands ... Did you ever think that your father was having an affair with Jules? Everybody wondered, you know. He lived there for all that time ... and then what about that American artist? Max something or other—Cohen was it? A Jew anyway, who lived with you a few years back? My mother swears that our cleaner—she worked at your place too; was it Mavis then? or maybe Imelda?—anyway evidently our cleaner saw Jules coming out of his bedroom, with NOTHING ON!

I deflect deflect deflect ever so politely—when what I really want to ask her, what I would love to have the courage to ask her, is whether it's true what they all say about her—that she had nothing better to do than listen to her mother's third-hand gossip ...? It was actually a relief when she gave up on this line of questioning (getting no satisfaction whatsoever from me) and started with her inane gossip about her job at the florist's, and then her interminable tedious bragging about dull old Dave. (A Cranburn Boy! An accountant!) Oh, the money he earns, the people he knows! The car he's going to buy! The house they're considering! The places he'll take her! ... At nine-thirty I yawned mid-Maggot-sentence and went to bed without saying a word. If only one didn't *need* electricity ...

Later

I wonder, though, I really do—did Jules really have an affair with Max Klein? Good lord! He's only a few years older than me ... URG! The mind boggles.

February 2nd

It strikes me—every day, every moment—how it is all ahead of me: the whole of life. It is such a dizzying idea. Dizzying too to

contemplate what it is that I want from this life. What is it that I
DO want? There are the big things, the universal things: I want
freedom, I know that—freedom from other people's ideas about
me; I want knowledge, understanding, wisdom of course—to
know what the world is and where I am in that world—where I
fit in. I want—oh, I want, I think, my life to matter in some way,
to count, to do something good. I want to be wise, and to find
a way of expressing myself that is my own—that is not some
faint echo of my parents, not what Jules thinks I should do, nor
what's fashionable or proper. To be good at something—to be
expert, admired, consulted ...

But I know that what I want more than anything—and it
is so clichéd, so dated, I suppose—is to be loved. To find THE
ONE. To have someone—a <u>man</u> of course, why beat about the
bush—want <u>me</u> more than they want anyone else in the world.
To look at me and to see no one else. To not be looking through
me or behind me or beyond me searching for someone else.

Is this what everyone wants? I wonder if this is what Margot wants—& what she is getting—from her Dave? It's hard to
imagine—it seems to me that what she wants is a white dress, a
Mercedes and a 'naice' house in Killara. But how unkind. What
would I really know about Margot?

February 26th

Enrolment day today. How very confused and confusing the
whole thing is—but somehow it didn't seem as if anyone was
quite as confused as me. Three times people came up to ask
if I was alright. I did feel quite bewildered—but had forgotten
to have breakfast and was too busy for lunch so that probably
contributed. I have enrolled in English, French, History and
Philosophy for first year—at least I think I have. The grounds
are wonderful—quite inspiring—and you could imagine that
you were really at Oxford or Cambridge, and not just Sydney.

I had thought that there would be a few familiar faces from

school, but didn't see anyone other than Laura Bevis. I waved and called out but she did not deign to know me and hurried to the other side of the quad with her college friends. She is at Women's. I wonder whether I should have taken Jules's advice and moved into a college—but I really don't think I could bear one more moment of institutional living. Far better to be on my own (well, alone with Maggot)—than to be with people I don't want to be with, forced into joining in when I don't want to, doing things I really don't want to do, eating instant mashed potato and shop-bought coleslaw three times a week ... And it is such a lovely feeling—to put my own little key into the lock of my very own front door. And then to make a cup of tea and sit wherever I want for as long as I want. I can read or even draw at the table if I get the urge: it is my table after all and there is no one to tell me I should not. I think I might, although Jules has said not to (or is it <u>because</u> Jules has said not to?) get a puppy. I still miss poor old Rip, and I suppose in a way it would be a betrayal, but it has been more than a year and there is a yard here—though small—and anyway having to walk a dog would be something I HAVE to do ... feeding it, walking it, keeping it clean, otherwise I can see myself just wasting time doing absolutely nothing.

Forgot to mention that Richard Howatt called. He wanted to know if I'd like to see a film (to be decided) with him on Friday. I said yes—why not? Who knows: he could be The One.

February 28th

Paul rang to tell me that Grandpa Steele has left me £1000 in his will!!! Paul says I should bank the money, but really I fancy spending just a bit: some paints, a new record-player, a couple of records, and I think perhaps—<u>quelle horreur</u>!!—I will buy myself a television!

March 2nd

Well, you can relax, diary dear: Richard Howatt is most definitely not THE ONE.

The afternoon was pleasant enough. Such terrible weather, we got completely soaked—we had his car, but had to park miles away from the theatre—but it was fun, running through the rain and not caring at all that we were dripping wet. Richard was very chivalrous—offered me his coat ... We had coffee after the film (which was <u>so</u> terrible it was hilarious). Richard's very easy to talk to—intelligent, quick-witted, funny. And interested in <u>me</u> for some unfathomable reason. He's a really nice boy—man, I suppose I should call him—and really everything a girl could want: intelligent, thoughtful, kind, good-looking enough, sincere—and he actually has his own car—which is completely desirable! And he'll be a doctor in a few years, which is something every girl wishes for—or so Maggot informs me.

We talked away a couple of hours effortlessly and enjoyably, but something, well, something didn't click between us. Still, he's asked me to a party tomorrow night and I've said yes. Is this leading him on, I wonder, when I already know I don't want anything more than friendship? Perhaps I should have told him no, I'll be too busy washing my hair? What would Maggot do, I wonder. (Hmm. She'd have already jumped over the broomstick with him by now, I imagine—a Cranburn Boy! A Doctor!) Should I perhaps ask for her advice on this delicate question of dating a boy you have no intention of marrying? No, I fear I would shock her with my sadly romantic ideals.

Later

It turns out that Dave the Dull was a schoolmate of Richard's at Cranburn and that Dave and Maggot will be going to the party too. Hooray.

Of course, Maggot was able to fill me in on all the gossip

about Richard—or Rich as she insists on calling him, having met him at least once, and spoken to him for a full twenty seconds. Evidently he was engaged to a girl from a big station out near Boolah (an Abbotsford girl—which of course impresses Maggot no end)—but she dumped him just weeks before the wedding & broke his heart ... They were childhood sweethearts, Maggot thinks, and there were ties between the two families—the two mothers were best friends or something—but the girl fell in love with some other, richer fellow. It may even have been that handsome so-and-so—the son of an American newspaper magnate who was sent out here to run something or other—don't I remember the photos in the social pages last year!? At the very least he's worth a billion. (A Harvard boy! A magnate!) Hmmm. Richard was heartbroken. Do I take this with a grain of salt or swallow it whole, I wonder? At any rate Maggot thinks he is a very good catch—and that I would be foolish, nay, delinquent, to NOT try and land him ... I could see her thinking, though she didn't say it: what on earth would HE want with a girl like you?

I think I may need a new dress for this party: Maggot says so, anyway. She's insisting that we spend a morning shopping together—and she'll help me find something decent. You just can't wear one of your dreary old grey skirts—and those awful cardigans, Zelda. It's at the yacht club! According to Maggot, I'm something of a joke in the fashion stakes. 'I'm sure we'll find SOMETHING,' she says, head tilted, lips pursed, eyes wide and doubtful ... 'It amazes me how rich girls always manage to look good—even when they haven't got much to start with—Oh, I don't mean you, of course, Zel. You've got some really lovely features. Your eyes are such a pretty blue ...'

March 3rd

A strangely fun morning with Maggot. She's actually quite useful—knows where to go—and to be honest, she really <u>did</u> know just the sort of thing that suits me. We walked and walked and walked all through the city and must have tried on three billion outfits, but eventually ... it's amazing: she's effected quite a Cinderella-ish transformation, though I don't look at all like Cinderella—no frilly ball-gown or glass slippers for Zelda. Instead, Maggot suggested that a more 'arty', beatnik look might suit me better than the usual formal party dress. So, I've been squeezed into a pair of breathtakingly tight black capri pants (you know, Zel, she mused, your legs aren't at all bad ...!), donned a daringly low-cut red and white striped sailor-shirt, and have a pair of the daintiest little flat black suede slippers adorning my feet. My hair is as smooth and sleek as some film star's and she organised a beautician who darkened my eyebrows, kohled my eyes and glued six-inch lashes to my eyelids. I don't look at all myself—for some reason the clothes and the haircut make me look six pounds lighter—and a few inches taller, too. I feel quite a different person: as if—well, as if I've suddenly become the sort of girl to whom almost <u>anything</u> could happen. In return for her services I shouted Maggot lunch. Of course she ordered the most expensive items on the menu—and had three sherries ... Now she's sleeping it off before the party.

I am not going to try and LAND anybody at this party—and of course I'll be there with Richard anyway—but just put a toe in & see what the temperature is. And—more importantly—see who I am—& who I can be. Perhaps the transformation is more than skin deep. Perhaps I can be somebody quite different to the Zelda Steele I have been thus far & am expected to be. Perhaps I will surprise everyone—especially ME.

Later

Richard's eyes lit up and he made a soft wolf-whistle when I answered the door—which was completely and utterly gratifying. Maggot had to spoil it by opening her big mouth: 'Doesn't she look like a different girl? You'd never have guessed that Zelda could scrub up so well, would you, Rich?'

Richard didn't bother to reply—which showed her to be the bitchy fool that she is—just looked at his watch and suggested we should all get going.

For some reason the Maggot—possibly irritable after her late-afternoon nap—grabbed me as we went to get into the parked car and said 'Oh, you boys can sit in the front—Zel & I'll cuddle up in the back,' but 'Rich' was having none of that either, and quickly made it quite clear that I was in the front with him, not Dave.

Maggot glared—she does hate to be resisted or denied—but Richard handled her so deftly, and with such dazzlingly brilliant courtesy that there was nothing she could do or say—and she and Dave clambered into the back.

The dinner was a much posher affair than I'd expected. The yacht club is rather swanky (I had for some reason imagined it would be a ramshackle old boathouse) and all of the girls were in frocks and heels—so of course my 'arty' clothes were rather out of place (which Margot must have known—so did she set me up?)—but somehow it didn't seem to matter ... perhaps the fact that I was with Richard—who was flatteringly attentive—stopped it from mattering in the way that it usually would and I really managed to enjoy myself. I didn't drink enough to make myself stupid—just enough to get pleasantly fuzzy and able to talk easily to people both known and unknown! A few familiar faces from school—Diana Brearley and Selma Warrington—who actually went out of their way to speak to me, which I thought very odd as they had barely spoken to me in three years at Hel, but both batted their eyes desperately in Richard's direction, and begged to be introduced, so that was cleared up.

The band—a jazz trio called 'The Skiffs'—was wonderful—and Richard is an excellent dancer, much better than me, but somehow able to make me feel as if I <u>can</u> dance.

We sat at a table with some of Richard's med student friends—Dave & Maggot were at a table with their own gang (accountants? Cranburners all, no doubt) which was a relief.

Richard's friends were all very pleasant—the boys nice looking, earnest, clean-cut. Most had brought their girlfriends, who all seemed to know one other, though they were friendly enough. There were two female med students too—one very beautiful, and glamorous—Jenny, I think her name was—who smiled vaguely when we were introduced, and directed not a word to me all evening, though we were seated together at dinner—she obviously had bigger fish to fry; the other was plain and intense and had her cleverness writ all over her. For some reason she was the more intimidating of the two. At any rate she had, for some reason, made up her mind to disapprove of me. 'Oh, you're studying art are you?' She asked, lips pursed expectantly.

'No not art. Arts,' I replied.

'Oh. Arts.' Her lips twitched, her piggy little eyes blink-blinked, and that was the end of our conversation. I suppose she is the sort of girl who thinks that Arts is a lot of nonsense—only ever the choice of working-class kids on teaching scholarships or rich dilettantes who are filling in time before marriage ... Oh.

Anyway, the food was rather good and I had a really lovely time—came home feeling as if I'd been—if not a complete social success—at least a moderate one, or at any rate not a complete and utter failure. Will have to write to Nell—who'll be most impressed with my effort ...

I know what it is that you're wondering, diary dear—and have been thinking about it myself. Yes—there was a kiss on delivery home (and we were alone, thank the heavens—Dull and Maggot having disappeared somewhere earlier in the evening)—it was a gentle, tentative, exploratory sort of a kiss—and there is definitely some interest from the boy. But from the girl—I don't know—and I guess not knowing is actually rather significant. I'm certain that whatever it is that I feel for Richard is too low-key, too subdued. I like him a great deal—how could I not? He is quite lovely: kind considerate gentle and makes me feel GOOD about myself—as if I'm quite worthwhile, just as I am—in a way that I've never really experienced before. He takes my opinions,

for instance, quite seriously, even when they are only half-opin-
ions, barely thought out and expressed in panic. He soothes me
somehow, and makes everything calm, secure: I can feel myself
expanding. But but but. That's not what love is, surely?

I know I don't feel for Richard what it is I know I am capable
of feeling: something immense, all-consuming, overwhelming.
Surely there's more than this simple pleasure and contentment:
what I want is to feel myself turn to a jelly, to a liquid, to melt,
to be overcome. I want heat and passion and even anger. For
my heart to beat so loudly in my ears that it drowns out every
other sound.

March 22nd

A little bit of excitement. I sent four new comic strips which I've
called 'Zel in the Under (grad) World', to *Honi Soit*—and they've
been (wonder of wonders!) accepted. AND the editor actually
asked me for four more and then perhaps will make it a regular
feature if they prove popular.

I told Maggot, who was rather less than impressed. 'Oh, don't
tell me you're still doing those little pictures are you, Zel? I'd
have thought you'd have grown out of them by now,' were her
actual words. Thankfully Richard, who had called over to lend
me a book, was a little more excited, especially as he'd been
the first recipient of one of the original Zel comics. Wondered
whether he should find that letter and have it framed. 'It might
be worth something one day,' he said to a sceptical Maggot.
Well you never know, maybe it will. He stayed for dinner in the
end; and the three of us played Scrabble. R won which wasn't
much of a surprise. I came last—my score quite shamefully
low—even Maggot is far better than me. This is because, as she
so helpfully pointed out, I'm not competitive enough. R says it's
because my brain isn't mathematically oriented—it's a game of
strategy, he tells me, and not vocabulary. I must think in terms
of word scores rather than length next time.

April 4th

IN WHICH OUR HEROINE PONDERS ABSENT FRIENDS, THE POSSI-
BILITIES AFFORDED BY OVERSEAS TRAVEL ... AND LIFE. AGAIN.

A letter from Nell. She's having rather a lovely time in London, has moved out of her Gran's and is sharing her flat with
another girl, a nurse from New Zealand. She says I should come
over, too. She's working at a women's magazine—a newish
weekly magazine called *The Woman*—and is mostly concerned
with the usual stuff—makeup, men, food, clothes ... Nell says
her actual job is deadly dull: just typing and making endless
cups of tea, and the pay is terrible, hardly enough to live on;
but the staff are all fun and friendly which makes it bearable.
She reckons that she'll be able to apply for work editing or even
writing soon, as a number of the girls have got their jobs that
way—having first started out in the typing pool. The magazine
publishes short stories in every issue and she has shown several of hers to the editor, who is very encouraging and says that
she shows promise and should keep trying. She has a wonderful social life too—there is hardly a night where she does not
have someone or other to go out with. She says I would love it
there—and that I should get a ticket without delay. She has met
quite a few Australian art students ...

It <u>is</u> tempting—perhaps when this first year is over. I could
always stay with Ed and Ynez, if it came to that. I wonder if my
allowance will stretch that far?

April 12th

IN WHICH OUR HEROINE DOES NOTHING MUCH.

A mooch-about sort of day. It's almost dinner time, and I'm still
in bed, and there's nobody, NOBODY to say I should do otherwise. What freedom. Read a book—and NOT one I'm supposed
to be reading. Ate piles of toasted cheese sandwiches. Watched
TV. Listened to records. Made some halfhearted sketches.

Ignored Maggot's banging and whining about the state of the kitchen: if you don't like it why don't you clean it? I thought, but did not say. I have a feeling that Dave stayed over—though M must have hustled him out in the early hours. Hmm—perhaps he's not so Dull—shall have to call him Dirty Dave from now on. Oh well—just the fellow for a Maggot I s'pose.

Feel even more certain that R is not the one—but what to do in the interim? I guess I'm being very unfair—I wonder if this counts as leading him on? But he's such good company. Oh dear. Oh dear. I wish there was someone to ask. I could write to Nell, but then what could she say? And really, she's had no more experience than me.

Wonder what it is exactly that M and D feel for one another. Shall I ask M? Would it even be possible to have such a conversation with her?

April 15th

IN WHICH OUR HEROINE LEARNS NEVER TO TRUST IN SURFACES. EVEN—ESPECIALLY?—SQUEAKY CLEAN ONES.

Finally gave in to M's nagging & spent the day putting the house in order—under her direction, of course. It must be admitted that she's far more efficient and knowledgeable about domestic matters than me. We scrubbed, dusted, swept, mopped the day away ... activity which, if undertaken infrequently, can induce a strange kind of physical satisfaction, almost pleasure. (Or is that just the effect of the fumes?)

A day spent with M. is not without its irritations: at the very first opportunity she brought up the subject of 'Rich' as she will keep calling him. Urg. We were in the bathroom—M doing the bathtub, while I had been given toilet duty. I concentrated very hard on plunging the brush as deep into the bowl as I could & tried to stay cool and not divulge too much—just said that he was a very nice fellow and a good friend.

'Well,' said Mag, her head well down in the bathtub,

scrubbing vigorously at some terrible, quite possibly toxic scum flourishing there, 'it's as clear as the nose on your face that Dick really fancies you—in a big way. I'd say he thinks YOU'RE something more than just a nice fellow.'

She scrubbed even harder, muttering, almost to herself: 'You ought to appreciate it, too—it's not as if it lasts long. Once they've got what they want you may as well be … you might as well be this bathtub.'

This last sounded so unlike M. that I almost dropped the toilet brush. 'Is everything okay, Margot? Are you all right?'

'Yes, it's fine. I'm fine.' She sprinkled the Ajax liberally, carefully avoiding my eyes, scrubbing crazily now, over and over in the one spot.

Suddenly she threw her brush hard into the tub and sat back on her heels, wiping her nose on her sleeve. Her eyes were red and not from the fumes or the exertion. She regarded me silently for a moment. Then: 'He's being odd, Zel. Cold. Distant. And yesterday afternoon—you remember I met up with Alice Forsyth for lunch? Well Alice mentioned that she'd seen him out last week at some uni bash, and he had this girl with him.'

'Oh.' I try to be reassuring. 'Maybe it was a spontaneous thing?'

'No. It was last Wednesday night. Remember—we were supposed to be going out to dinner with my parents to discuss plans for the engagement party? And Dave called at the last minute to say he'd had to work late. That he couldn't make it …'

'Well, maybe there's an explanation, maybe he just—'

'Oh,' Margot was sobbing now, 'but that's not the worst thing.' She sat down hard on the cold tiles, legs splayed. 'Oh God, Zel,' she squeezed the Ajax tin convulsively, took a deep breath. 'I'm pregnant.'

I suspect my jaw dropped, but M. was beyond noticing or caring. 'Now we've got no choice,' she wailed. 'Now he'll have to marry me and he's already gone off me. That's my life … My life is OVER.'

'Can't you ...?' Shocked, I fumbled for something helpful, something sensible to say. 'Isn't there something you can do? I mean—aren't there ways you can get rid of it?'

'You mean an abortion. Of course. But Zel, the thing is, I don't want an abortion. I won't have an abortion. I want this baby. And I want Dave.'

Poor old Maggot: she really DOES love him, I suppose. What on earth is she going to do?

April 30th

A DAY IN WHICH OUR HEROINE ADMITS HER LAZINESS—AND ONCE AGAIN PONDERS THE RIDDLE OF HER DESIRES.

Really must start studying. I have three essays due next week and I haven't even read the questions yet. But it is all so dull. History—urg. Philosophy—double urg. French is just too difficult—too much work. And even English—bah! I just don't care—every time I take up a book I am supposed to be reading, I feel a terrible urge to toss it out the window or throw it against a wall. I cannot take an interest in any of it—even when I make the effort: I read a paragraph and somehow an hour has passed, and I have taken nothing in. Twice I have fallen asleep in lectures. I have filled an entire notebook with doodles and sketches and have barely a page of notes. Yesterday I missed three tutorials and instead spent the day in bed rereading a Georgette Heyer that I've read probably ten times before. I am wasting time. Wasting my life. I wish, I wish ... what do I wish?

WHAT on earth do I want?

May 3rd

A DAY IN WHICH AN OFFER IS MADE—AND CONSIDERED. SHOULD SHE OR SHOULDN'T SHE TAKE IT UP??? THAT IS THE QUESTION.

Jules rang today all excited over an offer of work—for me. Georgia Blandish needs someone to work in her gallery and for some reason thought of me. It is only secretarial and front desk work—and I would have to go to typing and shorthand classes. Jules sounded SO pleased. This is JUST the thing, Zel. The perfect opportunity for you to get your foot into the art world. And to extend your interests a little.

But I AM extending my interests—at university! She is so dismissive.

'Of course it's not a question of the money, Zel,' she assures me, when I ask whether putting me through uni is just too much of a strain, 'but of experience. This is exactly the sort of work that would suit you, darling. You already KNOW this stuff. Georgia thinks that you'd be just PERFECT for the job. Why not forget all this university business for the time being? Why, you can discover all that nonsense for yourself. You just have to read the right books, Zel. Why, I left school at fifteen ...' she says airily.

In the end I told her I'd think about it. There's no great hurry as Georgia will be away for a week or so. I suppose I could drop Philosophy and French and just do English at night ... it's tempting, I have to say—and no doubt the temptation will increase as I get further and further behind ...

Later

Paul rang. He thinks I should consider this offer very carefully, not rush, not burn any bridges. The same old lecture: perhaps the world of art is not for me—I shouldn't feel pressured into it just because this is what Jules would like me to do. Perhaps there are whole other worlds that I haven't thought of yet—worlds where I might find my niche. What about journalism—you have good language skills, he said, helpful as always, what if I give a fellow I know at the *Herald* a ring—or have you thought of the ABC?

Paul's attitude is *so* bewildering. What is he saying? That I have no real talent for art and so should keep well away to avoid disappointment? Or does he genuinely think that I have other talents????

Who to ask? What to do?

May 4th

Poor Maggot—she had to stay home from work again today. Morning sickness has struck—only it seems to be all-day sickness rather than just mornings. She's very green about the gills—and can't go anywhere without a bucket. I suggested again that she tell Dave, but she says not yet—he hasn't been in contact for over a week now and she wants to wait and see, she says.

She had better hurry up and do something—come to some decision—or it will be too late. The baby won't wait for Dave.

May 5th

IN WHICH SECRETS (OTHER PEOPLE'S) ARE DIVULGED.

Dinner with Richard. Told him about gallery job offer & he said why not—if I really am interested in art then surely it's an opportunity too good to be wasted.

I'm interested in everything, I protested. He laughed. 'Considering you've said that you've barely opened any of your textbooks since uni started—and you've got exams coming up in a week or two, it doesn't seem to me that you're all that interested in studying.' I had to concede that he had a point.

Very indiscreet of me—but really I couldn't help it—I told Richard about poor old Maggot. Of course he wasn't a bit shocked—but felt very strongly that Dave should be told immediately, that it was only fair. He's quite certain that Dirty Dave would do the right thing—do the gentlemanly thing—the only thing to do. I told R that M didn't want Dave to be forced into marrying her, but wanted him to WANT to marry her. Poor R looked utterly confused. Gave me the number of a doctor that he knows who would be able to help Maggot—but said that she would have to make the decision very soon or it would become far too dangerous.

I asked him what he would do if it was him—and what if he'd fallen out of love with the girl. He said it's not a question of love, but of duty and responsibility.

'But that would be it, Richard. For life. Like a prison sentence.'

'It's risk you take anyway, Zel, don't you think? In every marriage.'

'A risk? What do you mean—a risk?'

'Well, whether the love will last. I mean, there's no guarantee, is there, that what you feel initially will last forever? Though every couple thinks it will when they start out. My parents, for instance. I'm sure they loved each other once, but now ...'

I am fond of Richard but it is this sort of attitude that shows the great gulf between us—& why I could never love him. He is far too <u>practical</u>—I cannot imagine him EVER in the throes of a grand passion. And to be honest, I really don't think that he is in love with me either. He is friendly enough & I know he likes me: but he is cool, detached. I could be his little sister.

Later

I gave M the phone number. She tore the paper in two and said that she would never ever consider it—not for a moment—she would rather have the baby without Dave, than do that.

And then what? I asked—trying not to sound unkind, but just curious.

She could always, she insisted, have it adopted out—at least then there would be something to show for it all.

'Not something,' I couldn't help saying. 'It won't be something, Margot, but someone.'

May 9th

Dave has called ten times, but she will not speak to him. I have had to tell him that she can't take the call—she's indisposed or washing her hair or working late or at the library (!!). Very soon I will run out of excuses. Poor fellow—I wonder what he's thinking.

I think she has gone a little mad—& am not sure what to do. I wonder if Richard can help.

May 11th

WHEREIN A DECISION IS MADE, ALMOST BY ACCIDENT.

Plucked up the courage and rang Georgia Blandish to discuss the job. Actually there was no real discussion about WHETHER I was going to work at her gallery—more an assumption that in fact I was. So I suppose I am ... The gallery hours are 10–3, Tuesday to Saturday, then every second Sunday, but I have to be there at 8 o'clock—there's plenty to do, she said: cleaning, accounts, deliveries, mail, all that sort of thing. I'm to wear something decent and respectable. Nothing too studenty, she said and I have to appear knowledgeable about art without seeming too clever or scholarly—as that only puts people off buying. She didn't actually mention money, and of course I was too polite, too intimidated to ask. She seemed very brisk and quite impersonal and businesslike and then surprised me by saying that she remembered me as a child—that I was a dear little thing. She came to Holland House for Christmas once, she said, I must have been four or five, and I ran into the house, naked, covered from head to toe in mud—I had thought it a very good trick—I was pretending to be some monster from a fairytale—but had got into terrible trouble from Jules, and was taken outside and hosed off. 'You seemed such a lonely, lost sort of child, all alone out there, with no one to play with, and all those adults, so intent on their own lives,' she said, then coughed and quickly changed the subject. Strangely, though I can hardly remember anything about my childhood I do remember that incident quite well. Jules had read me the bunyip story from the *Brown Fairy Book* the night before, and I'd been thinking hard about what a bunyip might actually look like—I had done pages and pages of unsatisfactory little drawings in my scrapbook, but my muddy brown body had seemed JUST the thing, and I'd thought Jules would be very impressed when I came roaring in with my bucket threatening to drown everyone if they didn't return my baby. I can remember being so shocked by the coldness of that water, but even more shocked by Jules's fury. I wonder if that was when things first started to go bad with Ed? I don't recall him being there—but then I don't remember Georgia Blandish either.

I rang and gave Jules the news. She was over the moon, of course: You've made the right decision, darling, you're heading in the right direction now, gush gush gush. She is coming in to town tomorrow morning to 'fit me out' as she calls it. 'I'm sure we can smarten you up, darling, if we make the effort. Make you look the part.'

I do so love the 'we'.

May 14th

Have withdrawn from uni. The fellow I spoke to at the *Honi Soit* office said he didn't think that me not actually attending would make any difference to them publishing my cartoons. Can't say there was much regret—oh, I'll miss the library & my occasional lunches with Richard, though I'm sure we'll keep in touch. Was pleased to toss away all my notes. Don't suppose anyone in any of my classes will even notice—I've barely said a word all term.

May 16th

Maggot's mother called this morning and insisted on speaking to her, though at Maggot's panicked insistence, I tried to convince her that Maggot was out. But she would NOT be put off and eventually she started shouting down the phone at ME, and actually threatened to send the police if I didn't put Maggot on AT ONCE. So M gave in & spoke to her & Mrs F got it out of her somehow & then both her parents drove over immediately and took her home. When she got here, Mrs F glared at me and warned that if I opened my mouth to ANYONE there would be hell to pay. Oddly though she was very kind to poor Maggot. When she first walked in she was yelling and angry: 'Marjory Elizabeth Fanning, how could you?' But then when she actually saw poor Maggot properly—how very thin and pale and dishevelled she is—she stopped all at once and hugged her. 'Oh my poor darling, my poor, poor little girl,' she said. 'Whatever are we going to do?' Margot was very teary, but she's relieved, too: it's out of her hands, now. If Dave calls—though just this last week he seems to have given up—I'm to tell him to phone her parents. I wonder if they'll tell him?

Anyway, I'm all alone here now. Think I might even miss the Maggot. How odd.

May 19th

Jules arrived early this morning in her usual whirlwind. First she insisted on knowing why Margot was back home—she'd noticed her at the greengrocer's yesterday. For someone who appears so vague it's amazing how so little seems to escape her. Anyway, I said she had been sick with a bad flu and that her mother wanted her home to keep an eye on her—which didn't quite satisfy nosy-parker Jules, but what could she say? Next she wandered about the place, poking her nose into this and that, carping about the cleaning, sneering at the television, smirking at the bits and pieces of furniture I've bought. 'Oh darling, what on earth possessed you to get THIS awful old thing; I just DON'T understand what you see in all this dreary old Victorian furniture, it's so dark, so heavy, everything's so cluttered ...' etc etc ad nauseam. She patently ignored the three or four sketches of my own that I've had framed & hung about the place and flicked through my sketchbook with the most bored, disdainful expression on her face ... 'I can give you a couple of good things if you like, Zel, to cheer the place up. How about a couple of Annie's little charcoals, and why don't we bring over some of those Japanese prints ...?' So then I couldn't resist, I had to tell her: 'It's so exciting, Jules,' I gushed. 'You remember my little "Nell and Zel" cartoon strip from Helicon? I've had a few published in *Honi Soit*, it's the uni newspaper, & they really like them, in fact they said they might want to make it a regular feature ...' my voice petered out by the end: Jules's stoniness, her total lack of interest, was so apparent. And she made no comment, went on as if I'd said nothing: 'Well, we'd best get going, darling, we've a lot to get done this morning.'

You would think that by now I'd know better, that I wouldn't bother—nothing I do without her approval can ever impress her.

Strangely the rest of the morning went smoothly enough—I let her have her way with me & have been bought some wonderful new clothes, so I can hardly complain. I wore the outfit that Maggot helped me choose and Jules was quite surprised. 'It's not the sort of thing I'd have chosen myself, but—well, it does suit you, somehow,' she said. And she was amazed at the difference the shorter haircut makes. 'You've quite a pixie-ish face,' she commented. 'I'd always thought it was long and heavy like your father's but it looks a little more delicate with that cut—it takes some of the emphasis off your jaw, somehow.' Her compliments always contain a nasty little edge—rather like those cakes that are smuggled into prisons with a hacksaw inside, only without the good intention, in her case! So anyway, I managed to persuade her that we should stick to the more modish new boutiques that Maggot took me to, instead of being forced to dress exactly according to Jules's ideas of what a Bright Young Thing should be wearing (ie a Bright Young Thing circa 1929). She actually seemed to enjoy herself—the clothes weren't as expensive as she'd imagined, and she said as we sat down to lunch that she'd forgotten just how many clothes a 'young lady' needed. She'd been wearing what she calls her 'gardening gear'—her old shirts and pullovers and men's trousers—for so many years now that she'd practically forgotten that she'd once been an age where clothes—and looks—had been so important. She didn't mean this nastily, I don't think ... Though it's rather odd that she would say that she doesn't consider looks to be important when she's certainly not indifferent to her own. I can remember her howling once over a sketch that Annie had sent her—it was a candid charcoal portrait that she'd done quickly when Jules was visiting one summer. 'Oh my God, oh my God, I'm so OOOOLD!' she cried, and then Paul had to spend the rest of the day reassuring her that the picture did not look one little bit like her ... that it was a very bad picture indeed. Though as I recall it was a fairly reasonable likeness—for Annie, anyway ...

So my work outfits—of the utmost importance, according to Jules—have been purchased. And I now have the beginnings of a decent wardrobe—and I have to say I feel quite stupidly pleased with all my purchases. I have three new skirts. One grey, one black wool, one a sort of greeny-blue plaid. For my first day I will wear the grey, which is very sweet skirt: at first glance it is nothing out of the ordinary, but it is cut on the bias, so has a rather cute sort of a swing to it; patent red pumps; and a rather stylish black cowl-neck jumper. As well I have two new shifts for winter—one covered in red and black geometric shapes, the other a tunic in the most beautiful sky-blue wool. Also two 3/4 length sleeve silk shirts, and two cashmere cardigans. Nothing was terribly expensive, but it was all, as J. puts it, 'rather chic'. Then to DJs for underwear: three pairs of stockings, six pairs of cotton undies and two new bras. 'Good Heavens,' said Jules when we were in the change room, 'You can't possibly keep squeezing that lovely bosom into those old things.' Good Heavens! A compliment from Jules. This is certainly worth recording for posterity.

We visited the secretarial school that I'm to attend one afternoon and one evening a week to learn typing shorthand and double-entry bookkeeping. It looks deadly dull, but I suppose whatever skills I learn there will come in handy. The college is just downstairs from the Ashwood School of Art and J was tickled pink when I suggested that we have a look at the class list as I had been thinking that it would be fun to do some sort of art class. The only one that I could go to is on a Thursday night—it's a print-making class, and I would really have preferred life-drawing, but I put my name down for it anyway. Jules was so pleased—she pulled out her chequebook without being asked, and would, I think, have been happy to pay double. The class is run by someone called Douglas Grant, who Jules had not heard of, but the woman at the desk said he was a very fine teacher. He trained at the tech—where Annie now gives the occasional drawing class—and does some teaching there, too. He has been in the UK for a few years—and has been making a name for himself writing reviews in the London papers. He is only back in Australia for a short time—he's been commissioned to write a book on modern Antipodean art, and is here doing research. 'He's very popular with the young ladies, our Mr Grant,' the lady at the desk tittered, 'and the old ones too.' 'Poor man. Some non-entity no doubt,' said Jules when we left, 'but so often the best teachers are.'

Lunch was actually good fun—Jules had a few glasses of sherry and relaxed a little—for a while at least. Told some funny stories of her own misspent youth. She worked as a secretary to a rather grand newspaper editor for a few months, but was so terrible and unreliable—such a flibbertigibbet—that she was sacked. And this was despite the fact that her <u>uncle</u> OWNED the newspaper! Then she travelled on the continent with a cousin for six months, and it was during that trip that she had her greatest good fortune—she discovered ART. When she came home she took classes at Justin Ashwood's school for a year, where she learned very rapidly that she had no artistic ability whatsoever. But what she did develop was an insatiable PASSION for art along with what she quite immodestly referred to as her 'uniquely discerning eye for others' talent', which meant that at long last she was able to find that place for herself that meant something. That made her feel as if she was worthwhile, as if she was doing something important. And then she had been incredibly lucky to meet Paul, who shared so much of that passion. She said that even if she and Paul sometimes felt rather dispirited, sometimes even bitter when they considered all the time, the money, the energy, the WORK they'd put in to advance the careers of so many Australian artists they'd mentored—even if after all this their contributions seemed to have been more or less forgotten by so many of those they have supported—she could at least always know that the resurgence in Australian art was in part attributable to their efforts. And that could only be a good thing—a wonderful thing—and whatever pain she had suffered as a result was truly immaterial measured against that. She sincerely believes that one day their contribution will be honoured.

I suspect that all this was directed to my current state of aimlessness. 'There's something out there waiting for you,' she said. 'You might not know what it is right now, but this job at Georgia's might be a door that's just waiting for you to walk through.' She said that she knew that Paul and Annie had both tried to discourage me from a life of art—and perhaps they were right—perhaps it would be more sensible for me to set my sights elsewhere—but but but ... 'Consider who your parents are, Zel,' she said, 'and then if you factor in your upbringing!! Oh, darling—we just don't know what's latent in you: what gifts, what power!'

It's so odd—this tug of war between Jules and Paul about my direction—Paul trying to steer me away from art, Jules determinedly pushing me towards it. (And then Annie in the middle, pushing me as far away from HER as possible.) It's so hard to know what to make of it—and impossible to know which way it is that I actually want to go ...

Jules put me in a taxi outside the restaurant—said to make sure to set my hair on Sunday night and not to stay up late reading ... and she would give me a call about the opening of my father's new Australian exhibition. She had a letter from him last week to say that he would be flying home for the opening, and would like the three of us to attend if possible. 'It's been three years you know, Zel,' she confided, her cheeks pink, her voice all bubbly with excitement, 'since I last saw him.' It seems crazy—after all this time, and everything he put her through, that she would still care in any way about Ed. She would do better to return some of the affection that Paul lavishes on her—he is twice the man my father is.

June 20th

IN WHICH OUR HEROINE REALISES HER WORTH AS 'BAIT'.

The work in the gallery is not so bad, though Georgia Blandish is the most dreadfully snobby woman. Luckily her snobbery somehow encompasses me, or it would be impossible to work with her. Some days I really thank God for my pedigree! (Neigh! Neigh!) I am mainly in the office, typing out letters (quite a slow process at this stage—but I will get faster) and invoices. When the gallery 'hostess', Rowanna, a VERY thin, beautiful stylish girl—she's an artist, of course!—goes to lunch, I work on the front desk. I am only allowed to talk to those patrons who are unlikely to buy—students, middle-aged suburban matrons etc etc. I'm meant to subtly discourage these tyre-kicking types from hanging about for too long (ie tell those who look too poor to buy just how VEDDY VEDDY exclusive our pictures are) or to inform Georgia immediately—by means of a cleverly-concealed bell—when any obviously well-heeled potential art buyers enter the door. She's taking no chances on my sales ability yet. At the moment whenever any suitably wealthy types walk in (which happens more frequently than I'd imagined) I follow Georgia about like a shadow—taking in what she is saying about the art itself—so that eventually, when I learn the spiel to her satisfaction, I'll be trusted to talk to them myself. Most of it's a lot of rot if you ask me—some of the terrible stuff they are selling, and for such prices! She has three horridly busy still-lifes of Marian Ellison's which have been given the most outrageous price tag—three times my annual wage! I have seen Marian at work and if she can be regarded as an artist then I really AM an absolute genius! Good luck, I suppose, to them for being able to get the public to swallow such nonsense. There are a couple of my mother's seascapes—with a fair price on them too, four of Ed's early 'West' paintings and, as well, three of his little 'shoebox oils' for another ridiculous sum. It makes me laugh to think that these were a party trick, done in only two or three minutes when he was a student, according to Jules!

Despite my complete awkwardness, I must say that Georgia actually seems to find my presence very useful occasionally—as bait! This afternoon she introduced me to a couple visiting from Queensland who were interested in one of Ed's landscapes, and was, naturally, far more friendly than she usually is: '… a very great artist, perhaps Australia's finest, and just imagine, this lovely girl who I'm honoured to have as my assistant, is the great man's daughter …' Urg. Such rubbish—but it certainly hooked them.

'And do you paint too, dear?' The woman, a rather buxom bottle-blonde, was much younger than her husband, and wearing fur though it is only just autumn. Her accent was rather like Grandma Steele's.

I was honest and admitted that, no, I didn't really paint, but that I was currently doing a cartoon strip for a university magazine … at which point Georgia interrupted.

'She's got such a lot of time to develop artistically, though—and with her remarkable lineage I've no doubt we'll be seeing her serious work on these walls in the not-too-distant future.'

I drifted back to the desk then and left them to Georgia's ministrations. In the end they purchased one of Annie's as well as a rather dark, dreary landscape of Ed's—not one of his best, though of course I didn't point this out.

The man looked at me very kindly as I was writing out their sales receipt and arranging for the delivery—Georgia having disappeared into her office once the deal was done—& said that he thought that sometimes the child of very talented parents needs to look in quite another direction ... that expectations could be paralysing—and that he knew a little about this being the son of a very eminent man, a Queen's Counsel. As a lad he'd been under some considerable pressure to conform, to follow in his father's footsteps, but he'd decided early on that the law just wasn't for him. Which was fortunate, he'd said, as he'd made a great success and a great deal of money eventually, in his chosen field—manufacturing and selling pharmaceuticals.

I was surprised by him telling me all this & all I could think to say was that I was beginning to enjoy this other side—the business side—too.

He left to whistle down a cab, and after he'd gone his wife leant back in her chair and gave me a funny look: 'Joe's right, you know, love,' she said softly. 'You'd do well to stay on this side of the business. I was an artist's model for a few years during the war (not that I've ever told him) and I know how fellas like your father live and how their women are treated. They get the rough end of the stick, believe you me. And you don't want any of that, believe me. You stick to the gallery, love, and find yourself a nice businessman like my Joe.'

She gave me a wink, heaved herself up and out of the seat, rearranged her furs, and tottered out the door.

Later, Georgia suggested that it would be best if I didn't mention what she called my 'foray into the slum of commercial art'—meaning my cartoons, I guess—as it didn't really 'set the right tone'.

'You're going to art classes aren't you?' she asked. 'I'm sure Jules mentioned something ...'

'I start next month at the Ashwood School ...'

'Well, see if you can't discover some latent talent in a more suitable medium, dear—something that we <u>can</u> mention.' Her beady eyes lit up suddenly, 'And if they're any good, I'll be more than happy to sell them for you. At a discount.' She paused, and then, fiddling with a vase on the desktop, and carefully avoiding my eye, added: 'And your hair—you really should do something about the colour, Zelda dear. It's too ... it's really far too pale—too fair to seem natural. You know, a really good colourist could work wonders—make it look a little less ... albino, if you know what I mean. And they can do your eyebrows, too. I'll give you the number of my man. He's expensive—probably a week's wages for you—but he's worth it!' She looked up then and, smiling sweetly, gave me the once-over with those nasty little eyes: 'And perhaps you could try a little kohl, Zelda; maybe even frosted eyeshadow. It really does helps with that rabbitty look, I find.'

June 29th

A letter from Margot today. Amazingly it's all no-go with Dull Dave: 'It was obvious that Dave's feet were very cold. He said that he would marry me if there was no other way out of it and I have refused to take him on those terms. My mother and father have been very good about everything—though I know my mother thinks I am being stubborn not to take up his offer. Dad, on the other hand, seems to understand perfectly. I have told Dave that it has all been arranged and he is free to go—and I've heard that he has a berth booked and will leave for England next month. He is off to stay with his grandparents there. I am not sure what has happened with the girl he was seeing—he appears to be going alone—so perhaps it is all over between them.'

So lovely and easy to be a man and escape the consequences; to behave & even to <u>feel</u>, perhaps, as if nothing of any import has happened. But then I suppose nothing has—to him. He has merely fallen out of love. Margot is to be sent next week to some home in the country especially for unmarried mothers, where she will stay until she has had the baby. She says they spend the months before the pregnancy in exciting domestic pursuits—knitting a kind of layette for the baby (too bad that it's due in the middle of summer!) and cooking and gardening. When the baby is born it will be adopted out immediately.

She writes so bravely, so bleakly: 'I'm okay—but I do not think that anything in life will ever seem the same again. Love is—love can be a very black and empty place.'

July 6th

Richard took me out for dinner after work today. Introduced him to Rowanna before we went. He was very obviously taken with her as everyone—every MAN, I should say—always is. Like most young fellows he became completely tongue-tied in her goddess-like presence. The older ones talk far too much, become embarrassingly bluff and hearty. 'Goodness, Zelda,' she said when I went into the office to get my bag, 'such a clean-cut young man—he's not exactly your typical art student, he's far too wholesome-looking.'

'Actually, he's studying medicine.'

'Ah—well that explains it—he's too tanned, too healthy-looking for an artist.' She lit a cigarette. 'Can't imagine he'd be too impressed by your lot.'

'My lot?'

'Oh, you know: the whole set-up: the Hollands, your mother, your father ... You're not exactly the respectable suburban type ... or haven't you told him yet?'

'There's nothing to tell, Rowanna. Anyway, it's not really—it's got nothing to do with me. And that's all years ago now. They're all middle-aged. Old. And boring as hell.'

'No. I suppose you're really not a chip off any of the old blocks are you, Zel darling?'

I shrugged. 'To be honest, Row, I try hard not to be.'

She blew a smoke ring in my direction. 'Well, he's lovely, dear. Like a new-born lamb. *Verrrrry* sweet. Is he from the country?'

'He is, actually. He's from Boolah.'

'Oh, Boolah—that's where your dad springs from, isn't it? I'm from the country too, dear—though I've managed to disguise it ...'

I tried to change the subject. 'Where in the country?'

'Oh, down south. Nowhere you'd know.' She waved away my polite interest. 'A word of advice, though, Zelda dear: be careful. He's probably a lot keener on you than you realise. You don't really want to break any hearts, do you?'

'*Row*.' Exasperated now. 'We're just friends. Really.'

'Oh, I think not. Anyway—just be careful. You might think it's just a notch on one's belt—and sometimes it is—but other times ... well, other times you'll end up doing things you don't really want to do just to avoid hurting someone. Oh, not me—but I've had to learn the hard way. You have to be sure that you're both playing the same game ... that the stakes are equal, so to speak.'

'It's not a game, Row.' I said it again: 'We're just friends.'

'Uh huh.' Suddenly bored, she dismissed me with a wave of her perfectly manicured hand. 'Well, on your bike, Zel. I can't stand around all day gabbing.'

Dinner was pleasant, as it always is with R. But I was glad to get home, nonetheless. What if Row is right? M said the same thing. But he's just the same Richard as always. Light, teasing, easy-going. There's nothing deeper. Nothing more serious. Surely I'd notice; surely I'd know.

RUTH

The first one turns up late that afternoon. I'm sitting alone in the dustsheet-shrouded surgery, stunned by the contents of Dad's letter and staring blindly at the little pile of books that I had easily located in the roofspace, when Salty knocks and peers into the room. 'Sorry to disturb you,' he says in an apologetic whisper, 'but there's a lady here wants to see you?'

'A lady?'

'It's—er—it's old Mrs Gaffney.'

'Old Mrs Gaffney? Oh, God. What does she want?' Then: 'How does she even know I'm here?' Old Mrs Gaffney—her sixty-odd-year-old daughter-in-law was still known as young Mrs Gaffney—had been one of my father's most loyal and regular patients. She's a close neighbour—with only a laneway between the two houses and access from the rear. It's a rare complaint indeed that Mrs Gaffney hasn't suffered from over the years, and I remember Dad once showing me her patient history, which was his most substantial file by far, taking up a good four inches of his filing drawer. It has to be some sort of miracle—and a great source of anxiety to her—that at eighty-eight she is still vigorously alive. I imagine she's here to proffer her sympathy again, or to bring me a container of her pea and ham soup to help me through my troubles.

'Well, actually,' now Salty looks embarrassed, 'actually she reckons she's got a bit of a pain in her chest. She's worried that it might be a heart attack, and thought it'd be quicker to see you than to call the ambulance.'

'What? Oh shit.' Old Mrs Gaffney's heart attacks were famously non-existent—she'd been disappointed by her chest pains for a good twenty-five years now. Practically every one had been diagnosed as reflux or heartburn, though I recall that there was one exciting instance when, on complaining of referred pain in her arm, the cause was found to be bona fide muscle strain.

'So—er—what do you want me to do, Roo?'

'It won't be a heart attack, Salty. I can virtually guarantee that.'

'Well, she's in a pretty bad way, pale and shaky. Maybe I should just call the ambos, just in case.'

'That's probably from the exertion. No, don't worry. Just send her in.'

I look around the surgery. It's coated in a layer of grimy dust, but it's more familiar to me than my surgery in Manly. I find what I need easily. My father's stethoscope, his old fashioned hand-pumped sphygmomanometer, tongue-depressors, disposable plastic gloves. There's a row of white coats, scrupulously bleached and carefully ironed, hanging in a cupboard. My heart twists a little, but I take a deep breath and put one on. It's worn, a little frayed, and smells of antiseptic wash, the smell of my father. I pull the dustsheets off the examination table, the desk, the chairs.

I go out into the office and find her file, just as Mrs Gaffney hobbles in, a wide-eyed Salty supporting her. She's clutching her chest, moaning.

'I think it might be the real thing this time, Ruth love. Oh, I'm sorry to be such a trouble. If only your poor father were here.'

I smile and lead her over to the chair.

'Sit down here and let me have a look at you, Mrs Gaffney,' I say. Salty smiles uncertainly and removes himself. 'Now, let's have a listen, shall we?'

The next morning, despite my pleas to Mrs Gaffney for discretion, my defence that I really shouldn't be practising, that I am here on family business, that the surgery is closed, closed, closed, word has somehow spread. Salty has to field numerous phone calls from my father's former patients, all desperate to make an appointment with young Dr Howatt, who they've heard has reopened the surgery. I determinedly turn away another three of my Dad's ex-patients who've actually made the physical journey—all elderly, and all with ploys at the ready to engage my sympathy. 'Oh, I just thought, as I was your kindergarten teacher, Ruth, that you wouldn't mind ... just this once'; 'I've had this terrible cough for a good fortnight now. And I can't really be expected, at my age, to sit up at emergency for hours and hours, can I, Doctor?' But there are more visits in the afternoon, and eventually I give in; give up. I prescribe antibiotics for Mrs Hobson's infected throat; corticosteroid cream for George Mallinson's itchy knee, and write out yet another prescription for double-strength Mylanta for Gordon Ebsworth. I swipe their Medicare cards through my luddite father's ancient click-clack machine at their insistence. We are both Dr R Howatt, and this will have to do for the interim—if I ever bother to claim the payments, of course. Anyway, that part of the treatment—the financial transaction—seems to be as essential to the patient's well-being as any of the advice and prescriptions I provide. Though I try to wave away their payments, they all insist that it wouldn't be right, and that anyway, it is the government's duty to keep them well. They have a point, I suppose. Anyway, I tell Salty, as I lock the surgery, it's only a one-off, there won't be a repeat. There might be a rural medical crisis, but Ruth Howatt isn't going to be any part of the solution.

The next day there are a dozen calls before 10 am. I unplug the phone, but by midday eight of my father's ex-patients have knocked tentatively at the front door, wondering whether they've heard right, whether they really can make an appointment. By mid-afternoon, I give in. I make a few calls—to the local hospital, to several of the other doctors in town, and finally to Linda, who laughs loudly at what she terms my soft-headedness, but agrees to help out. I take a thick black texta and alter Dad's surgery hours—*Surgery open 8.30 am to 10.30 am*. It seems that whether or not I want to be, I am in business.

ZELDA

July 27th, 1962

So Diary dear, it's happened at last. Finally, finally I have met HIM. The ONE. I had my first class at Ashwood's last night. To begin with it seemed most unpromising, & I almost left before the class started—the room was full of middle-aged spinsters in grey flannel skirts with black berets jauntily angled over their mousy curls, and a few bearded fellows with brylcreemed hair and cable-knit cardigans. It all seemed hopelessly amateurish and not at all the class I had hoped it would be. (What had I imagined, I wonder—classical sculptures draped in white, young men in striped shirts ...?) Anyway, then HE walked in— our tutor—Douglas Grant.

How to describe him? Is he tall dark handsome? But of course! Aren't they all the characteristics that we wanted, that we insisted on, in our lists describing our perfect men—our knights in shining armour—all those years ago, Nell & me? Well, he's not exactly TD&H. He's dark—in a powerful craggy Celtic way— brown curly hair, pale skin, coal black eyes. His nose is hooked in a Jewish manner, though Grant does not sound at all a Hebrew name, and his lips are—oh, dear, his lips are quite quite beautiful—they're thin, and they're a little sad, & slightly feminine I suppose, but oh so kissable! And he has a little mole right at the corner of his mouth—a beauty spot, I suppose you would call it if he were a woman. He is not so tall—perhaps he's a little shorter than me—but he is powerfully built so you don't notice his lack of height, with wide shoulders and a shortish neck and the most deliciously sinewy forearms. His voice is something special too—he told us he has lived in Dublin for a few years & his voice has lost all the tedious flatness of an Australian accent and the slight burr somehow injects humour and warmth into everything he says. He is very serious though and smiles only rarely … Yes, diary dear—I did spend most of the lesson looking at him (as I think did half the women in the class—even, especially, the old ladies) and even managed a few surreptitious sketches …

Needless to say my efforts sketching the objects he'd actually arranged for us to draw—an egg, a feather, a felt hat—were far from interesting and initially he dismissed my pictures—and me—with a yawn. He was all charm to the old ladies, however, taking their efforts so seriously and responding to their appalling flirtation with kindliness. Though I suppose it was in his best interests not to shoot them down in flames as four of these old ducks—not one of them under forty!—had brought in food for him. One had made a pavlova, of all things, another her special ten-egg sponge, one had even made an Irish stew with dumplings … These meals, he said charmingly, were works of art as much as anything that could be produced on a canvas.

I had to leave briefly to go to the loo and when I came back he was flipping through my sketch book, frowning. I was ready to be humiliated again, could have run from the room & never returned, knowing that he could not have missed the little sketches—of course some of them only caricatures—of him. But he did not mention them—and turned the page he was regarding towards me.

'Is this your sketch, Miss … er …?' He had chanced upon some fantastical scene—which was actually an image from a half-remembered dream—and really not much more than a doodle: princesses, witches, apples, thorns and, of course, a knight, all tangled together, swollen limbs and everything overblown, with grotesquely exaggerated expressions and features. I'd coloured it in, testing out a new set of pencils, but it was really nothing more than the shameful doodlings of an overwrought adolescent, if truth be known—the sort of thing that ordinarily I would never have considered worth working on, would have torn out and tossed away.

'Miss Steele, Zelda,' I stammered, my voice catching as it always does when I'm nervous. 'And yes, it's mine,' I made to snatch the book out of his hand, but he moved it quickly out of my reach.

'Zelda? Your name's Zelda ...' He looked me up and down—subtly, but still, I noticed—and I wished immediately that I had worn something more flattering than that blue dress that makes me look so thick around the middle.

'I've never met a Zelda, before ... what an intriguing name.'

I stood open-mouthed, not sure what I should say, my face burning, my heart pounding.

'Well, it's—it's just what my mother called me,' I offered lamely. 'It's not terribly common—there's Zelda Fitzgerald, she was married to F. Scott ...' He'd stopped listening, and was regarding the sketch book again, frowning.

'This is really good, y'know,' he said suddenly. 'Really bloody interesting stuff—you've got something here ... It's primitive and raw—and yet it's incredibly sophisticated ... I don't suppose you've ever seen any Spencer—no, you wouldn't have. Not here.' He closed the book with a sigh and passed it back to me.

I clutched it to my chest, feeling ridiculously disappointed, and watched him move towards the next eager student.

But then he stepped back; moved close. 'Listen,' he whispered. 'Why don't you come and have a beer with me when this interminable class is over. You don't have to be anywhere, do you?'

'Oh no,' I whispered back. 'Nowhere. I don't have to be anywhere.'

'Well, bring your sketchbook, Miss Steele, and we can continue this lesson later. Elsewhere.'

We went to the Blue Mood, just up the road, where they had a jazz quartet playing. There was quite a crowd for a weeknight, but we still managed to find a little table in a dark corner. He bought me a sherry and himself a black beer and sprawled back in his chair and lit a cigarette and then without saying a word put out his hand for my sketchbook, which I released with an apology and a fumbling explanation—'This is just my everyday things sketchbook—just doodles really—there's nothing serious in here. Nothing worth looking at. Really.' He took it from me without comment and then went through it page by page, his face completely expressionless other than an occasional narrowing of his eyes, while I sat in terrified agony. I gulped down my sherry in one go, and sat waiting, my heart pounding so hard that I thought it might burst through my chest. Just as the wait was becoming almost unbearable, just when I thought I might die from the anticipation, the heat, the noise—he closed the book gently. Then he sat for a moment, considering me through the haze of smoke, his face completely inscrutable. Finally finally—his verdict: 'They're good,' he said. 'Actually, I think they might be quite remarkable.' He gave a lightning-flash smile, a slight inclination of the head.

I could barely manage to squeak out some lame expression of surprise and doubt ...

'I'm not known for giving out praise easily, Zelda. I tend to—er—conserve my compliments. So if I say you've got something—well, you have to believe me. This piece for instance.'

He opened the book to a sketch I'd made of Maggot scrubbing the bath, a very spare sketch I'd done from memory weeks ago—though again I'd more recently coloured odd bits of it, testing out some new inks and brushes this time.

'I can't work out what it is that makes this so remarkable: is it the model's body, the proportions, the way you've indicated the interior of the bath, the harsh angles of her limbs, the slightly askew perspective? And somehow you've made it real: the physicality of the scrubbing, all the effort, and there's so much pain in her expression, a feeling of submission to the work. And to life, I suppose. God, it's all there. So many things you've managed to show in just a few lines. And then the touches of colour—like hints of emotion. Some of us spend a lifetime attempting this sort of thing—and failing miserably.'

He lit another cigarette, sipped his beer, and eased back in his chair, contemplating me, waiting for my response, but I sat there in front of him, stiff and upright, my purse clutched tightly, my face aflame, struck dumb, a paralysed fool ... When I eventually managed to speak, it was a croak: 'I wonder if I could have another sherry?' He looked surprised for a moment—as if this was the last thing he'd expected me to say—but then he laughed and laughed as if it was the funniest thing he had ever heard, and then all of a sudden I was laughing too and I did not really need that next sherry or the next ... and the conversation flowed easily between us and we talked and talked and talked ... about what? About a million different things—infinitely memorable, utterly forgettable. Suddenly I was inside that magical bubble that I have only ever glimpsed from the outside. It was me, Zelda, with a man—and not just a man but a man who is everything I have ever imagined was desirable—handsome, clever, witty—and we were discussing things of import, momentous things: art, literature, the war, the bomb, ourselves, Australia, Britain, our families, our regrets, our sadnesses, our hopes, our dreams. It was just as I had always wished it, always dreamed it would be. For once this was not banal small-talk, but real conversation: passionate, significant, and suddenly I <u>was</u> this other person—forceful, opinionated, amusing, intelligent—and not the shy and retiring, the almost invisible Zelda Steele that I have felt myself becoming, but instead someone sharper, smarter. And he—this man—this most desirable of men—he was actually listening to me, listening seriously to what it was I had to say. This new me: so utterly unlike myself—and yet at the same time never so much myself. It was as if there were only the two of us—and time moved so slowly and so sweetly and yet in less than a moment it was over and we were outside, shaking hands, preparing to part—and then: 'What the hell,' he whispered—or did he shout? 'Do you ride?' he asked. And there I am, perched behind him on his motorbike, squeezed up hard against him, my arms encircling his waist, and we are rushing through the night, speeding through the tilting flashing city and somehow I am not afraid but exultant and soon too soon we are outside my little terrace, home, and I am floating to the top of the stairs, I am opening the door and he is standing politely at the bottom of the steps waiting for me to turn the handle, to say goodnight, but I do not want this night to end—surely it can last forever? And suddenly I know what I want and how to get it, and here, now, I realise that it is so easy. I say, 'Come inside, Douglas.' I say, 'Come in.' But he stands at the bottom and shakes his head. 'No, sweet girl. Go inside. You need to go to bed. Work tomorrow.' He blows a kiss and 'Go inside' he says again, and then he is back on his bike & has sped off into the night and has gone—almost as if I imagined him, as if he materialised—a knight in shining armour—directly from my imagination.

And I am writing this while it is still fresh in my mind, still slightly drunk, but filled with the wonder of it—needing to see it written to know that it is really real, that it has truly happened. To me.

July 28th

There is too much to say & nowhere to begin. I am in love & it is everything I had imagined—but it is more even than that. It is as if the world is a different place today. And I a different person: infinitely bigger brighter all my edges clear and defi-nite. But I look into the mirror and am surprised when it is only me—there is not even one aspect of me that has changed phys-ically. How can it be ...?! I feel like a butterfly newly hatched from its cocoon, and after the first trembling fearful fluttering comes the realisation of what it means—to fly—to be up above the ground. And oh, the earth looks so very different from up here. Everything somehow smaller—but so much vaster too—and look: surely now I can see beyond the horizon ...?

July 31st

Work was interminable. Everyone—Georgia, Rowanna, the clients—unbearably closed and earthbound, and concerned ONLY with the shallow and the trivial. Even the pictures seemed insipid somehow: every one of them showed life at its most banal, the most tedious aspects of existence—without any sense of wonder.

D is coming tonight—he said that he had an article to finish and wire & then he'd call ... I was supposed to be going out to the theatre with Richard, but have cancelled. I lied—told him that I was ill & he was of course concerned—did I want anything, need anything, was there anything I'd like him to do? Which made me feel horribly guilty—but not guilty enough to tell him the truth. We'd planned to go down and visit Jules and Paul on the weekend, but coward that I am I did not have the heart to cancel this.

Later

Midnight—and he has not called.

August 1st

He did not call. And did not call again today, though he knows where to find me. I tried phoning him at the studio, but no one answered; and so I walked over in my lunch break, but the woman in the office did not know where Douglas was or how he could be contacted—'He only comes in for his night classes, dear,' she said. 'Other than that he's a free agent.' I told her that we were to have met the other night and he did not arrive and that I was worried, something might have happened—an accident; an illness? Perhaps I could leave him a message? She gave rather a nasty smile and said I was welcome to leave my number, but she could not guarantee that he'd ever get back to me as there was always quite a long list of 'messages' for Mr Grant.

Richard wandered into the gallery in the afternoon—just at closing time, so there was no choice but to leave with him when he offered to drive me home. He knew immediately that there was something wrong—I made the mistake of telling him I was still under the weather—so he insisted that I see a doctor. 'You look terrible, Zel,' he said. 'Really tired, and you're quite pale, maybe it's some low-grade infection ...' I had to promise to make an appointment next week. I hate lying but how can I tell him what is really wrong? And how can I feel this bad when a few days ago I felt as if I could conquer the world? Perhaps I imagined it all.

August 3rd

IN WHICH VIRTUE IS REWARDED; AND THEN LOST.

My second Print class last night—and there HE was. I hadn't conjured him up after all.

He gave me a quick cool look, but no special word or greeting—though I had arrived early and it would have been easy enough for him to snatch a moment before the rest of the class came in. I could feel my face burning shamefully, and thought I might burst into tears then and there. I shuffled to a desk at the back of the class, alone, so nobody would notice. And sat there in a daze, barely taking anything in—wondering what on earth had happened, thinking that I must have imagined it all—or worse, that I had given it a weight, a meaning, an importance that Douglas doesn't share. Of course, I was just so naive, so inexperienced—this falling head-over-heels so instantly—after one evening out—one single conversation. Oh, it is such foolish childish schoolgirl behaviour, or so I berated myself, barely hearing anything that was going on—taking no notice of his instructions, his descriptions—mechanically picking up the instruments we'd been provided, making lines on the paper in front of me, tracing, and then making the cuts and gouges as directed.

He moved through the class gradually, commenting on this, correcting that—giving all the old girls a thrill no doubt as he moved close to examine their work, sometimes guiding their trembling hands with his, so certain in their mastery of each trajectory—and he finally approached the workbench at the back, and moved behind me to check on my progress. I sat rigid, did not turn to look at him, but I could feel him with every part of me. It took every ounce of strength not to turn towards him, but to keep cutting cutting cutting while he stood behind me watching. 'You've got something,' he said, quietly, 'there's no doubt about it. And you're not even trying, are you?' He stood for a moment, as if waiting for an answer, but I could not speak, didn't dare even raise my head, and eventually he made his way to the next student.

Of course, I stayed behind, I could not help myself. I packed my work away as slowly as I could, and waited while he chatted patiently to all the old ladies, explained over and over how the class was to be run, that he would be concentrating on woodcuts and that yes, he would bring in some of his own work; and that there would be another teacher, an exceptional woman, who would visit to discuss etching techniques. And that yes, he was of course, familiar with the work of Margaret Preston and that she was certainly a wonderful artist, but that he had no time for flowers and still lifes himself, that figurative work was his particular area of interest and expertise ... and then finally finally they had all twittered away and it was just the two of us and I stood before him, practically quivering with anticipation, not trusting myself to speak—the humiliation, the aching disappointment of the last few days somehow dissolving, as if forgotten, in his presence.

'Well hello again, Miss Steele.'

It's the barest, emptiest salutation, his eyes are cool, giving away nothing, his voice is brisk and distant. I feel myself shrinking, freezing again. And then he smiles—deliberately, knowingly, a smile that's long and slow and infinitely warm—and I expand, unfurl like a flower in spring sunshine, welcoming his heat, his grace, his benediction.

And then, just as abruptly, the chill returns. He turns his back, sorts through papers, packs away cutters, blocks.

'So, do you want to come out again tonight?' He's offhand, casual, says it without taking the trouble to look at me. 'I'm meeting some of my students from the tech. I thought it might be useful for you to meet,' he hesitates, 'to meet some real art students—see what it is they're doing—what's happening. This crowd here—well, you're hardly going to get a sense of the art world mingling with this lot, are you?'

'No. I mean, yes. That would be nice ...' I've hardly taken in what he's saying, but the spirit of the invitation is crystal clear. It's that of a teacher, a mentor—not that of a potential lover. I'm confused. My heart has slowed a little, my breath comes deeper. And for a moment I hover between the old world and the new, not sure which world it is that I should be in: it is as if I have rushed headlong to the top of a mountain, ready to fly, only to find myself halted, pulled up short at the edge of the precipice, not sure whether to fling myself over—there will be no way back, after all—or to move, ever so cautiously, back from the edge.

And then, as I stand there, wavering, irresolute, he turns and takes my wrist, kisses it casually, almost indifferently—then goes back to whatever it is he is doing, humming softly under his breath. Now there is no possibility of any reversal, any tiptoeing back from the brink, and I am over the edge.

We go to the Blue Mood again, where his students are waiting: there are half a dozen or so—four or five boys, two girls—rowdy, exuberant, drunk on cheap red wine and full of themselves and their ideas, and outdoing themselves to impress Douglas. We are all pretty much the same age—and yet I feel a hundred years removed. Once the introductions are over, I am pretty much ignored—the two girls, who are both vying desperately for Douglas's attention, especially go out of their way to disregard any comments I might make. But though he is attentive enough to them, he makes it very clear that we are together—keeps one arm slung along the back of my chair, stays close—and I can see the girls look at me quizzically. They prattle on and on about art school gossip: whether this or that artist is really any good or a pseud; which model is sleeping with which student, or which teacher; which classes are least inspiring, none of which requires any contribution from me— not that this bothers me in the slightest. I am in such a contented daze, sipping my sherry, leaning up against Douglas in the warm noisy room, that it takes me a moment to absorb a remark that one of the students has made about a recent guest lecturer at the tech, Annie Swift, who was 'easy on the eye, and a bit of a goer if you get what I mean'. One of the girls, a tall dark kohleyed girl with a plunging neckline, laughs scornfully: 'Easy on the eye? Oh, God Robbie. That lightweight. She has to be old enough to be your mother,' and when I interject, as I must, and tell them that actually she *is* my mother, the laughter stops, and the table is silent and they are all—Douglas included—looking at me as if I have dropped in from another planet. Someone sniggers. Then one of the young men—quiet, serious, perhaps less drunk than the others—asks nervously: 'You're joking, aren't you?' and when I say no, he blinks rapidly, once or twice, and shakes his head as if to clear it.

Douglas has hold of my wrist, is looking at me disbelievingly. 'You're really Annie Swift's daughter?'

I nod, give an embarrassed smile.

'So, Ed Steele is your father?'

'Ed Steele. The Wild Colonial Boy. Jesus.' The sober boy whistles, and blinks again. 'I guess you're probably some kind of artistic prodigy then,' he says. 'I mean, they're both—well, your mother's pretty good too, isn't she? Wow. Talk about winning the parental lottery ...'—and then: 'So, why aren't you at the tech—I mean—what are you doing at the little old ladies' classes—no offence Doug—but they're not exactly, well, not exactly where you'd expect to find someone with your—your ...?'

'Pedigree? Exactly my thoughts,' murmurs the dark girl. 'What's the daughter of the Wild Colonial Boy doing at a third-rate night class? Maybe Miss Steele isn't such a genius—I mean, parents don't count for everything, do they? My father's a shoe salesman—but so what? I certainly haven't inherited his interest in leather uppers and synthetic soles. Plenty of talented parents produce duds—and there are plenty of duds out there who have immensely talented children. And nobody, nobody in their right mind, would ever say that Miss Steele takes after her mother physically, would they? So why would they expect that she take after her in any other way?' She smiles sweetly, beams around the table, eyes wide and guileless as if this might take the sting out of her words.

I open and close my mouth, not sure what reply to make, but Douglas is there before me, his voice low, gritty with anger, 'Kelly, darling, pedigree or not—there's more talent evident in Zelda's doodles than in any of your pretentious canvases.'

And then he's stubbed out his cigarette, pulled me to my feet and we're back outside in the cool air. 'Christ,' he says. 'I had no idea that Kelly could be—well, such a bitch. I think—well—I think perhaps she thought that she, that I ... she's done a bit of modelling for me. But Jesus, Zelda. Why didn't you tell me? About your parents.'

'I don't know.' It's true. I don't know. But I tell him now, here, standing on the footpath outside the nightclub, and once I start I can't stop: I don't actually live with them, I tell him, I was adopted, they gave me away when I was only a baby, to their friends, their patrons. Neither of them really has anything to do with me—and I don't really regard them as my parents. And as far as they're concerned, that girl Kelly is right. There's no evidence, nothing to say that I've inherited any talent whatsoever, in fact, thus far, I've been nothing but a disappointment, a dud, and regardless of what he, Douglas, can see in my work, my mother and my adopted father had done their best to dissuade me from any artistic pursuit ...

'Shhh. It's okay' He gives me a little shake. 'For God's sake; shut up, Zelda. Bloody hell. What a disaster. Look, I'll take you home.'

And then we are off again, on that wild ride through the night and I am thinking of nothing else, nothing beyond this moment, the now, leaning hard against him, holding tight, and then we are home, and this time we kiss—slowly slowly slowly—and when it ends, as it shouldn't but as it must, as everything does, he holds my face close to his for a moment—a pause, a heartbeat, a breath—and then pushes me gently away, 'Go on, Zelda,' he says, 'it's late.'

I walk slowly up to the door, then turn, and he is still standing there, as if waiting. I beckon—it is no more than the slightest tilt of my head—and this time he bounds up the steps two at a time, and: 'I hope you have some etchings to show me,' he whispers, as I unlock the door.

For a moment I don't understand, but it's the old joke, and I laugh and take his hand and pull him through the doorway after me, and what happens after that I do not care to write about. And really there is no need, as it is not something I am likely ever to forget.

August 23rd

He arrives late, after midnight & leaves early, before light. I am tired, but I am always up waiting—it is as if my day, my life, doesn't begin until he arrives. Oh, I go through the motions: on the surface nothing's changed. I get up in the morning, bathe dress eat my breakfast, call a cheery good morning to the flower lady on the corner as I walk to work; I talk and smile, I eat, keep busy. But I am not really there—I'm drifting, dreaming, waiting waiting waiting. All day I can think of nothing but him. The world has shrunk to this—to the two of us—nothing else exists. Nothing else matters.

RUTH

The days fall into a pattern of sorts. I spend a couple of hours of the morning in the surgery, and then help Salty with the house until lunch. Painting, cleaning, sanding, depending on what needs doing; or else running over to the hardware store with a list of necessary items: brushes, turps, paint, rollers, plastic piping. I place orders for lengths of timber, sheets of masonite; choose tiles, sinks, taps, toilets, basins. I'd always found the idea of home renovations tiresome in the extreme—had never taken much interest in friends' tales of the trials and tribulations of their renovations and extensions, had always been smugly pleased with our small, neat apartment. I had focused most of my energy on work, on Chris, and to some extent—inasmuch as he required my energy or attention—on Lewis, and had never found any particular pleasure in homemaking. The house was a place where I lived. It fulfilled some very basic but essential human needs, provided shelter—a place to eat and sleep, to feel comfortable and secure. But I had no sense of it providing the creative, expressive space enthused about endlessly by so many of my peers. So I am rather surprised at how perfectly this sort of work suits me right now, amazed at how much I enjoy thinking about all the endless small details that need thinking about; bemused by my own satisfaction when the blue paint I'd chosen after much tedious consideration and consultation really does make the loungeroom look not only brighter, but considerably larger. There is something so unexpectedly satisfying in this work, and I barely notice the time passing.

We take our lunch break on the side veranda, the old sleepout. Salty insists on a decent break from the work—a solid hour—so there's time for one cup of tea with our sandwiches and another after. Salty makes a pot for us both, and he brews it until it's bitter with tannin. He takes his black and sugarless, and winces at my pale milky drink. 'Dunno why you bother with the tea, you may as well just have a cup of warm milk.'

Usually we spend the hour in companionable silence—Salty reading the newspaper, or some fat paperback novel, while I sit daydreaming or doing the crossword. Occasionally we chat desultorily about this and that—the weather, the town, what bit of the house we'll be doing next, what does Salty think I should do with the garden. Every now and then little bits and pieces of our real lives drift into the conversation: Chris, Lewis, Andy, my practice; news of Salty's ex, Sheryl, his teenage daughter's underage drinking escapade, his trip up the Murray last year, his elderly mother's Alzheimer's, her recent admission to a nursing home. I remember his mother pretty well, I tell him, probably better than I can remember him; and I can remember her famous pavlovas—provided for every school function—even better.

He laughs. 'You know, Mum'd love to see you, if you get the chance.' He gives a snort. 'I mean she *would* have loved to see you—though I don't suppose she'd have a clue, now. She loved your father, you know. He was really good to her when Dad was sick—visited every day, came in the middle of the night when we needed him, and never charged a penny. And she always reckoned you were a nice sort of a girl.' Salty rolls a cigarette and lights it, ignoring my obvious disapproval. 'She was always worrying over you and your brother. Those poor little motherless Howatt children.' He gives a resigned sigh. 'Well, we're all poor motherless mites now, I guess.'

'I wouldn't have thought she'd have even really noticed me, I mean, I was so much younger than you.' I'm surprised at how pleased I feel.

'Eh?' he glares at me, 'I'm not that much older than you, mate. You must be past forty.'

'And you must be well past.' I hit him lightly on the head with my newspaper. 'Didn't your mother ever tell you that it's rude to ask a lady her age?'

'Where's the lady?'

I groan.

'Actually, I remember thinking you were a pretty good sort when we were at school—or at any rate thinking you'd be a bit of a goer once you grew up.'

'A goer—me? Really?' I blush.

'Oh, you weren't bad. A little bit stuck up, I guess, but then you were a doctor's daughter.'

'And now I'm a doctor. And the doctor says you should put that disgusting thing out.'

'Actually, you haven't changed that much.' He regards me thoughtfully.

'No?'

'Well, you're not quite so stuck up, I s'pose; but you're still a good sort.'

I leave my reading until the late afternoon, and only then, when I'm quite exhausted, settle down in the loungeroom with a cup of coffee and the diaries. It might seem unnatural, not to gobble them up all at once, to read them avidly, in one long unbroken stretch, but somehow, I can only bear to read them—these messages from the dead—in short bursts. I go through them for only an hour or two at a time, slowly and methodically—more as if I were assembling case notes than reading my mother's life story. I read them sparingly and carefully and only in the daylight hours. Andy—who has rung several times to see how far I've got, desperate to read them for himself—is annoyed by my lack of progress. 'Christ, Ruthie, what the hell are you doing? It's a woman's diaries—it's your *mother's* diaries. You don't have to make a bloody diagnosis you know.'

And really, I don't understand either. It is as if I am resisting something, as if my urge to know my mother isn't strong enough to dispel my unconscious fear of being sucked into some netherworld, abducted like Persephone—or that gazing back, I will be turned into a pillar of salt like Edith, Lot's wife. One thing I do understand, though, is my desire to keep the diaries for the daylight hours. This is a psychological strategy I'm already familiar with from my work. I learnt early on in my career that it is always far easier to distance myself from the suffering of my patients if my contact with them is restricted to daytime. Somehow, if my work ends early, if I am able to leave the hospital or the surgery before sunset, I'm better able to slough off their lives, to move beyond the pain and sadness, to keep the constant awareness of decay and death at bay. If my evenings are free I fill them up, keep myself busy—after a session at the gym, a few drinks, a good meal, an hour or so in front of the television, my thoughts are successfully diverted, and then I can sleep well, without dreaming. During my residency I'd come close to giving up medicine. With weeks and weeks of unavoidable nightshift, and frequently enough a dayshift that would continue late into the night, all the events of the day would somehow imprint themselves more deeply, and my dreams would be tainted, contaminated, as often as not becoming nightmares that were impossible to shake even the next day. They would surround me, like a miasma, a dense grey cloud—like a perpetual hangover that coloured the day in the night's dark and dolorous hues.

And I approach my own mother's writing, now, with a certain inbuilt resistance: how much of what she wrote is the truth—and how much fabulation and self-mythologising?

I have no desire, and to be honest, no real understanding of diary-keeping. In fact, these days I find even the process of writing things down strangely awkward, irksome. I was a good English student as a child, a fluent reader and speaker, and never had any problems putting my ideas together coherently in essays and reports, but I suspect that 'real' writing is another matter—and that whatever gene or environmental factor it was that compelled my mother to write, to keep a record of her life, has completely bypassed me.

Strangely enough, I did keep a diary during my adolescence. Only sporadically, it's true, but I've kept them and every now and then treat myself to a rereading. I use the word treat ironically; actually they're almost unbearable to read now, those painfully clumsy outpourings of a younger self who's simultaneously known and unknown, utterly familiar and yet wholly transformed and irretrievably lost. Whenever I've reread the various jottings—a few in fancy journals provided with a lock and key, but mostly in a series of thin feint-lined exercise books—I've had to resist the urge (and once or twice couldn't) to tear out certain pages that seemed too awful to contemplate. In adolescence the physical traits are not the only ones to undergo a period of intense growth and temporary exaggeration. Like a sort of literary version of the adolescent's too-long, too-thin legs, the sticking-out ears, the nose that's suddenly, startlingly, too big for a face, my old diaries provide an hormonally enhanced version of events and emotions, and all in the very worst, most purple-hued prose imaginable. Then there's the problem of reliability—it is rare that the truth is actually told, outright, straight. It seems that not even the youthful diarist's oath—*that here I swear to set down the absolute truth*—can overcome the urge to aggrandise one's own role in events: *When that bitch Armstrong told me to go to the back of the class I completely ignored her, and sat down next to Jane S and she was too scared to say anything, the stupid cow!*; or to master the desire to exculpate oneself from agency or wrongdoing: *Anna should know that there's no way I would have meant it like THAT*; and impossible to NOT romanticise: *And then when Felicity and I walked past him on the bus, he turned and looked right at me, I swear, and I felt my heart soar. I'm positive he likes me.* And there's so much that isn't written about, so much of what's significant is omitted, excised: where is the entry about my first, humiliatingly aborted, love-making attempt, for instance? The diary is so often at odds with my memory that I wonder occasionally if I'm reading about someone else's life, and not my own.

The essential transience of thoughts and experience, all so assiduously recorded in personal diaries, makes me wary, too. The shift in ideas and ideals—why set them down so indelibly when they're by their very nature so mutable? What is this desire to trap time, to consider, to recall, things that are better left unexamined, and in some cases even forgotten?

These days I avoid writing wherever possible. If an extensive report is required, my patients' notes, symptoms, history and my subsequent diagnoses and referrals, are all spoken into a dictaphone initially, and then typed out by the practice secretary. My notes are always brisk, aiming for precision and brevity rather than expansion. I keep my explanations to a minimum, and never say more than just what's necessary. I avoid embellishments, eschew flights of fancy, and in this I'm aware that I resemble, or perhaps emulate, my father. As a practitioner I'm methodical, but would never say that my treatment is unimaginative—obviously I'm frequently compelled to surmise—but I much prefer to have my diagnoses backed up by cold, hard, indisputable fact.

My grandmother, too, was usually loath to express herself in words, and the letters that my mother has pasted into her diary are an aberration and something of a surprise—perhaps representing some sort of guilty effort to connect with her lost daughter. They're evidence of thoughts that were better left unexpressed, unsaid; regrettable and perhaps regretted, and are, conceivably, why Annie avoided written communication later in her life. According to Jules, she became a devoted user of the telephone as she got older, or sent the occasional telegram— *train arrives central 6 pm platform 6*; *painting en route*; *cheque received, thanks*. That way she left no trace, no evidence.

And it's not just written lives that I'm wary of. After years of hearing people's stories about their health and their behaviour, it's hard to put much faith in what most people say about themselves. Time and time again a patient, presenting with immediately recognisable aches and pains, symptoms both physical and psychological, will insist *Oh no, doctor, I hardly ever drink, or only socially, occasionally, a glass or two at most, doctor!* when I can smell the grog, see it in the yellowing eyes, feel the tremors in the hands. Sometimes I wonder whether they believe what they're saying, and I'm beginning to think that perhaps they do; perhaps, in order to survive, we all have to believe in our own versions of our lives, of ourselves.

Linda makes certain that I'm true to my promise of a sleepover—she arrives on Saturday morning with an excited Nadia in tow, her little overnight bag bulging with all her essentials.

'I've got a hot date tonight, Roo,' Linda tells me, stopping to primp in front of her reflection in the hallway mirror.

'Oh, yeah? Who with?' I'm pleased for her. Linda's had some hard times and she's coped by being tough. She's not easy, not accommodating in any way—and it seems that men who can cope with a strong woman are thin on the ground.

'He's a copper, love. A new bloke in town. Jason. Jason Freeman. He's a bit of a honey, actually.' She hesitates. 'Don't laugh, but he's ten years younger. Still in his twenties. A baby, really.' Her smile is slightly bashful.

I do laugh, I can't help it. 'You're a bad woman. Does he know what he's letting himself in for? Don't you eat him up, Lin, he'll be permanently traumatised. Poor little fella.'

'Oh, don't you worry 'bout that, mate. He'll be the one doing all the eating if I have my way.' She gives me a suggestive wink, and runs her tongue over her lips. 'And I dunno what you're imagining: he's not one of these weedy, pissweak, pasty-faced young pigs—Jason's a great big bloke. Taller 'n heavier than me. Works out—done a bit of wrestling. He's got muscles on his muscles if you get my drift.'

Linda gives the impatiently hovering Nadia a list of instructions: 'Now, don't you give Roo no trouble, Nades—no asking for lollies and ice-cream every five minutes. And if Aunty Roo gives you cabbage and turnips for dinner you're to clean your plate without whining. And you make sure you go to the toilet before you go to bed. Don't want you peeing in Aunty Roo's nice clean sheets. I'll pick you up before lunch tomorrow.' She gives her daughter a good-bye hug, and I watch as she steams off down the path, humming tunelessly, aimlessly pulling the dead heads off a few of Judy's prize roses on her way. She meets Salty at the front gate, they chat for a moment, then as he heads on up the path towards me, Linda turns and gives me a thumbs up, before striding off down the footpath.

'It's Saturday, Salty,' I say by way of greeting. 'It's your day off.' But he's not dressed for work, I notice. He's wearing jeans and a pale cotton T-shirt instead of the trademark King Gee overalls. He's shaved the stubble that he's sported all week and I can smell the faint tang of aftershave.

'Yeah, I know that.' He stands beside me on the veranda, obviously ill at ease, his cheeks rather pink. 'I didn't come about work.'

'Did you leave something? Do you want to come in?'

'No, that's all right. Actually, I was just thinking that you might want to do something today, a picnic maybe, being here alone and everything.'

Just then there's a bellow from the loungeroom, 'Aunty Roo. Roo. How do you get the video to work?'

'Hold on, Nadia,' I yell back. 'I'll be there in a minute.'

'Oh. Sorry, I didn't realise you had company.' Salty's face has turned a darker shade of red. 'Maybe another time.'

'*Aunty Roo.*'

'Listen, what if I give you a call later, maybe.' He turns to go.

'Oh shit. Hold on Nadia. Listen, no.' I grab at his shirt. 'Come in, Salty. I think I might need you. I don't suppose you know how to connect the bloody video machine?'

'Dunno.' He gives a grin and follows me inside. 'But I'll give it a go, mate. Anything to oblige.'

Nadia wants to go out for McDonald's—after all, I did promise—but Salty has a better idea. 'Have you ever been yabbying, Nadia?'

'Course,' Nadia looks at him scornfully. 'I been yabbying thousands of times when I was little. I used to go out with me Uncle Mick all the time. Before he—' She pauses, looks down at her feet. Linda's younger brother died in a car accident late last year. He'd just finished a stint in prison, was off the junk, had a new girlfriend and things were looking up. I squeeze Nadia's shoulder and she takes a deep breath. Says solemnly, 'ack-shually—that'd be really fun, because, ack-shually, there hasn't been anyone to take me for a while.'

There's nothing in the cupboards to make up a picnic basket, so we call in at the local supermarket and buy a barbecue chicken, several unappetising tubs of anaemic pre-packaged salad, and bread rolls. I hesitate over a drink for my young charge, but Nadia heads straight for the Coke. 'Yeah, 'course Mum won't mind,' she says, indignantly, when I express my uncertainty over her choice. 'I'm allowed to have Coke every single day,' she insists, careful to avoid eye contact.

Salty drives us about ten minutes out of town to a stretch of the Darling that's not at all familiar. The river itself is wide and quite shallow here—perfect for yabbying, Nadia tells us. Despite the lack of depth, the water runs smoothly, and there's a familiar watermelony tang of river in the air. The bank is reasonably level, and the thin strip of green that runs along the river is shaded by gums and relatively cool. It's a gentle, peaceful, bucolic scene, deceptively so—the illusion's lost as soon as you lift your eyes to the parched, flat land, the straggly saltbush, the crazed red earth that stretches forever and ever beyond. The land that simultaneously intrigued and horrified my mother; that terrified and inspired my grandfather. The land that's so familiar to me—despite my long absence—that I can barely appreciate what it is I'm seeing. This sweep of the Darling is currently neither a muddy gutter nor the second Mississippi of Henry Lawson's famous quip, though it's clear that it's nowhere near capacity and is much muddier and slower than I remember it being during my childhood. Back then, speedboats would power up and down on weekends, pulling water-skiers in their wake, but Salty tells me that even though the surrounding area is still in drought now, the river itself is in slightly better condition after the floods up north, earlier in the year. That it's better than it has been for years.

I find a comfortable shady spot to spread out the blanket, while the other two head down to the water to set up the mesh traps. Nadia holds the bag of slightly tired mince that Salty has charged her with carrying, her arm stretched as far away from her body as possible, cheeks distended with her exaggerated-ly-held breath. I've managed to wriggle out of any involvement with the fishing, but thought it best not to mention to either of them that I'm no great fan of freshwater crays, and that all freshwater creatures taste to me of mud.

I open the wine that Salty has thoughtfully provided, pour myself a glass and stretch out on the blanket, planning to watch their antics, but by the time they've got all the traps baited and tied, I'm adrift, properly relaxed for the first time since arriving in Boolah. 'Now,' says Salty, easing his long body down beside me, and pouring himself a glass of chardonnay, 'we just sit and wait.' We watch Nadia for a while. She's right down at the river's edge, building a mud-castle with twigs and leaves, filling up a dirty old beer bottle every few minutes with the water that's essential to any such building enterprise. She's unaware of our scrutiny, completely absorbed in her game.

'She was a premmie, you know. Thirty weeks. We didn't think she'd make it. Wouldn't guess it, looking at her now. She's a precious little thing.'

'Precious? I'd say she was tough as an old bootstrap, *ack-shual-ly.*' Salty gives a rueful grin. 'I s'pose she got that arguing gene from her mum.'

'You didn't actually think it would be a straightforward exercise, setting up your yabby traps with the help of an eight-year-old girl, did you? I thought you were an expert—you've got two daughters, haven't you?'

'Well, yeah.' The humour has gone out of his voice. 'But I barely saw them at all at this age. I missed all that.' He pauses, adds lightly, 'I could fill a book with what I don't know about eight-year-old girls.' He considers me for a moment. 'It doesn't get any clearer as you get older, either.'

I laugh. 'Yeah—well it's no different for us. No easier. Believe me.'

Nadia scrambles up the bank, damp and muddy and *staaarving*. 'What's there to eat, Auntie Roo?' The three of us tuck into the makeshift picnic lunch. When Nadia complains that she's still hungry, despite having speedily demolished two huge rolls, Salty miraculously conjures up an intact packet of Tim Tams. Nadia gleefully demonstrates her gut-churning version of a Tim Tam slammer—sucking her Coke up through the biscuit. The very idea of it makes my teeth hurt and I can't resist *tut-tutting* over the sugar content. 'I think we'll need to scrub out her mouth with soap after that effort,' I comment to an equally revolted Salty. Nadia glares at us and chomps the crumbling remains, then reaches for another and has the ends bitten off and the biscuit dunked before I can even think about demurring. 'Hey, Mr Salty,' she pauses mid-suck and turns her gimletty eye on Salty, who's leaning against a tree, smoking, with his eyes half-closed, watching the performance with a benevolent smile. 'My mum reckons you're a bit of a spunk y'know.'

'Nadia. Shhhhh. You know you shouldn't repeat things.' For some reason I'm blushing, embarrassed not on Linda or even Salty's account, but my own.

'She does, does she?' Salty responds solemnly. 'A spunk, eh? Well, I dunno about that, mate.'

'No. I dunno either.' Nadia gives a bemused shrug. 'You're ack-shually a bit old to be a spunk, I reckon.' She looks him over critically. 'Maybe if you had more hair. And if you wore some cooler clothes. You, know, maybe tighter jeans or something.'

'Nadia,' I say warningly, but she ignores me and keeps her eye on Salty, who's trying hard not to laugh. 'Mum told me that you were at school with her, but that you were a bit older. But I reckon you look heaps older than Mum. She's hardly got ANY wrinkles.' She slurps up some Coke, gives a burp, squeals and puts her hand over her mouth.

Salty runs his hand over his jaw, grimaces. 'What can I say, mate. I've had a hard life.'

'Yeah. I reckon you're more Aunty Roo's age.'

'But, Nades,' I splutter, 'I'm hardly that much older than your mum.' Now Nadia sizes me up.

'Yeah, well Mum says you've had a hard life too. That must be it.' Her eyes flicker over me briefly then settle on Salty again. He's standing up straight now, as if preparing for the next sally.

'And I know why you're called Salty, too.'

He blinks, surprised. 'You do?'

'Well, that's something I don't know.' I'm relieved to be in safe territory. 'Why don't you tell us why, Nades?'

'Well.' She takes a deep breath before she begins: 'My mum's second cousin Willie Dermott was in your class at school and he reckons it was because you were such a sickly little fella who cried all the time and all the teachers used to feel sorry for you and say how sweet you were and all the other boys used to tease you about it until one day you stood up and yelled that you weren't bloody sweet and ackshually you were salty not sweet and that from then on you were Salty.'

As soon as she finishes her long narration, Nadia's reached for her third Tim Tam and again I'm too slow to do anything to stop her in time and she's sucking away for all she's worth.

I look up at Salty. 'Is that true?'

He looks mildly embarrassed. 'Yeah. Well, I guess it is. I haven't thought about that in a long while. Not sure that I ever used the word "ack-shually", but—I wasn't quite as advanced as Miss Nades here.'

'I always wondered, y'know. I'd heard a few other stories, but none of them really made sense.'

'Probably put about by me. Doesn't do a young fella much

good to get a reputation for being sweet.'

'Oh, but you are.' It's out before I have time to think.

'Eh?'

'And Mum said,' Nadia pipes up again unexpectedly, 'Mum reckons you're just the sort of bloke that Aunty Roo needs—instead of that fat, boring city feller.'

'Nadia Fraser,' I hiss, 'that's enough. I'm sure your mum wouldn't want you repeating this stuff.'

I stare down at my clenched fingers, my face burning. I can hear Salty chuckling, Nadia's biscuity slurping. The grass crunches as he moves back to the blanket, and there's a faint tinkle as he tops up first his glass, and then my own.

'Well you can thank your mum for the compliments, Nades. 'Bout time we checked those traps, don't you think, mate?'

'Mr Salty,' I hear Nades trill, as they scramble back down the bank. 'I hope we're not gonna have these yabbies for dinner.' When he murmurs in the affirmative her response is carefully enunciated. 'I ack-shu-ally really really really hate yabbies. They make me feel sick, y'know. In fact, sometimes just the smell of them can make me spew.' Then, quite offhand, as if it's a thought that's only just occurred to her, Nades adds: 'But if youse get me some McDonald's for dinner—you and Aunty Roo can have 'em all.'

ZELDA

September 17th, 1962

There was no escaping it—had to go out to Paul & Jules's on the weekend, with Richard, who I'd invited weeks ago. It was a lunch to celebrate their move into the renovated cottage—& the beginning of the preparations to convert Holland House into a gallery of contemporary art. First there was the drive to endure—it was interminable, with me resenting every moment that I had to spend away from Douglas (who, of course, would not have been there in any case—he had his own work to attend to), and worrying about what & how I would tell Richard, because I had made up my mind that tell him I must. Whatever it is that Richard feels about me it is only fair that I tell him about Douglas. Luckily for me Richard is such a serious driver, he doesn't encourage conversation, anyway.

Once we arrived it was far worse than I had imagined. I had thought it was to be an intimate luncheon, with just the four of us, casual (if anything Jules does can EVER be described as casual) and easy, and with the opportunity for a surf—which I have not done, it feels, for months! But NO. There were a dozen others present—including Annie and Clive, which I was completely unprepared for. Jules looked a little guilty when I asked her why she hadn't warned me beforehand that there'd be others—but only said that this would be much more fun and since when had I become such a party pooper anyway? And that the luncheon was partly a 'strategic' gathering as one of the guests—Roy Luthy— was a journalist who was doing a series of interviews that would be published to coincide with the opening of Holland House, and there were several business types as well who Paul is trying to impress. Jules said she was hoping to give them a sense of what art <u>should</u> mean to a culture, and was attempting to recapture a little of the 'essence' of the good old days for these people, when the place was full of art and artists and their conversation. It seemed quite sad, really, as if Jules was trying desperately to recapture her youth, but the only one of the old crowd to come was Annie—all the other artists were much younger, people I've only heard of vaguely. Some of them have their work at Georgia's, but I've never met them, and there was some government official—a representative of the Minister for Culture and a more unmitigated bore (and boor!) would be hard to imagine—and the others were potential investors, bankers and businessmen and their wives, and they all seemed rather bemused by Jules's enthusiasms.

Suddenly she seemed terribly old-fashioned, rather old hat, and not the influential doyenne of the avant-garde she imagines herself to be. The idea of 'patronage' seemed completely foreign to these people with their smart clothes and fast cars and artistic 'careers'. I could see that even the food—the home-grown vegies, new-laid eggs, fresh-baked bread—seemed quaint to these folk, and that the house, & the furniture—we ate in the courtyard of the old house—seemed dark and dank and run-down, like a relic from before the war. Hardly cutting edge. One of the wives—a very stylish brunette—whose husband was, I think, some sort businessman they were trying to interest in investing in the gallery, asked—her pretty cheeks quite pink and her eyes all alight with speculation—whether it was true that Holland House had once been some sort of free-love society ...? Annie, who seemed to get a great deal of malicious pleasure from the whole event, answered with a straight face that it was more than just free love, it was free *communal* love—and that it wasn't just a thing of the past—at which the businessman's wife became furiously red, even the tips of her little ears, and moved closer to her husband. There was not a great deal of conversation about art—and certainly not the sort of conversations that

I know Jules was hoping for—instead there was a great deal of talk about who's showing where, who said what about whom, and most importantly, in this brave new world, who's worth what. It *is* a new world and it's evident that it's not one that Jules is comfortable in. The poor thing seemed quite bewildered, and for her, a little dithery. Paul was his usual urbane, polite self—he managed to keep the conversation going when Jules faltered and once or twice was able to stop Annie from making some outrageous statement or other.

The cottage is almost unrecognisable & is certainly not a cottage anymore. It's so much grander than the old place, and strangely—though it is the one they are to live in—IT feels like a museum. Everything is so clean and light and new—and somehow horridly clinical. All the old furniture has been replaced and everything's plastic and chrome and glass and marble, all cold, hard and uncomfortable. Some of the wives were very taken by it though—I guess it is more to their taste, being freshly painted & full of the latest gadgets ...

Throughout the afternoon Richard was entirely at ease—he'd seemed a little nervous on the drive down, but once he had shaken hands with Paul, and found a way to make himself useful—he mixed the drinks, carved the meat—he was entirely comfortable. And everyone found him delightful, as they always do.

It was embarrassing. Jules, Paul, Annie, Clive and the other guests, I suppose, all assumed that Richard and I were there together, that we were a couple—and I think even poor Richard too in his tentative non-demanding way has begun to assume this—and I spent the day agonising over how on earth I was to tell him about Douglas.

Annie was cool and indifferent as usual. She asked a few questions about what I was doing and didn't really listen to the answers—except when I mentioned the night class I was taking & she raised her eyebrows and gave a scornful little laugh.

'Good God—don't tell me old Justin Ashwood's still running those classes! He must be getting long in the tooth!'

I told her that he just administered the school now, and hired other artists to teach, and I prepared to make my first public mention of Douglas, without any telltale blushing or stammering, but she'd lost interest by then, anyway, interrupting to say: 'Oh well, maybe—despite all our attempts to discourage you—maybe you will make an artist of yourself, Zelda.' She then started to interrogate poor Richard—who was he, again? What was he doing? And oh, that's right, he was the doctor's boy—the doctor from Boolah—wasn't his name Richard too? Oh, yes, she'd met his mum and dad, she remembered them from her one visit to Boolah—as a matter of fact she remembered them rather well. She put back her head and laughed, then clutched Richard's forearm: 'Actually, Richard, you won't believe this, but I had the most God-awful row with your mother.' She laughed again. 'Oh, dear—we met them at some party, it was just after the war, and it was some welcome-back do. Ed knew them both of course, Ed knew everybody in Boolah. Anyway, there was dancing, and Ed was the most dreadful dancer, but your father—now he was terrific. He must have asked me up to dance once too often, and I suspect your mother thought we were flirting. But we weren't—at least I wasn't. Believe it or not I was as pure as the driven snow, on that count. Your father must have been in his thirties then, and I was very young, only twenty or so, and it was quite ludicrous—I thought him quite quite ancient, not worth flirting with. Anyway, I can remember your mother looking daggers at us both, and hissing something about me being a cheap little tart when she caught us outside having a smoke together. And as I recall—never being one to let an opportunity for a dust-up go by—I really let fly. Oh dear.

'Poor old Ed was so humiliated, so embarrassed. I don't think he ever forgave me for that. And Mrs Steele, his mum—well, she didn't speak to me for the rest of the visit. And hasn't since,' she snorted. 'God—that dreadful place. Well, good on you for getting out, love.' She patted Richard on the cheek, then, and drifted back out with the others—having fulfilled her maternal duty for the next twelve months or so. Richard looked at me, as-tonishment writ large on his face—'So that's your mother?' and I just nodded. I was feeling quite nauseated by her performance & couldn't speak. I'm completely grown & yet she still has this effect on me—after any contact, I end up feeling—well, slightly mad, slightly sick ... all churned up, anyway. My *mother*!

We didn't stay for too much longer, after that. We were the first to leave—Richard by then as eager as I—and Jules only made the most cursory of appeals for us to stay longer—she seemed suddenly weary, old, small. I suspect that the luncheon was not what she had hoped for—on any level. I'm not sure what Paul thought of it all—what Paul actually thinks, as op-posed to what his Jewel WANTS, is one of the great mysteries of the world, even to him, I suspect.

In the end I told Richard on the drive back. We stopped at Collaroy, at my request, and had a quick swim, and then walked along the beachfront in the dark. It was probably not the best place to do such a thing—we still had quite a long drive home, but I felt that I would burst, if I couldn't get it off my chest once and for all. At first I tried dropping some not so subtle hints, hoping he would pick up on what I was saying & that I could manoeuvre the conversation from there—but he managed to deflect my every attempt—and in the end I was forced to blurt it straight out. 'I've met someone else, Richard.' I was shouting into the wind, facing the ocean, so I didn't have to look at him.

'I know,' he said quietly. 'I mean, I didn't know exactly—but I could tell that there was something; that something had changed.' We were both silent for a moment. Then: Who is he?'

'His name's Douglas. Douglas Grant. He's my art teacher.'

'He's an artist.' A statement, his voice rather plaintive.

'Oh Richard, can't we still be friends?' I winced over my lameness, the apologetic gush of my question, but as always, Richard was consideration itself.

'Be friends? Well of course, Zel. If that's what you want. That's all we've ever been, anyway, isn't it? Friends.'

I felt for his hand and squeezed it gratefully; he returned the pressure briefly, then walked on. 'You know how I feel about you, Zel,' his quiet words were almost lost in the boom and rush of the incoming tide. 'This doesn't change that. Nothing will.'

November 16th

I haven't written, I know—there is too much happening. I have found love—but also found what it is that excites me—what I want to do. And what I CAN do.

I have been, with Douglas's help and encouragement, his insistence, I should say, working hard on a series of woodblock prints. And somehow—what a discovery!—this is a process that suits me utterly. Somehow the clean lines of my drawings—in some ways not so unlike my dear little cartoon figures—are completely suited to the process. And the images work so well, feel so right. What is it, I wonder? The feeling of making something solid, the carving away of all that negative space? It is so physically satisfying—the smell, the feel and the way my mind just disappears into the work. No, I think it is more than satisfying—it feels like breathing; it is what I was meant to do. And the pictures, the prints. They're <u>something</u>. Astonishing, Douglas says. I think—for the first time ever—that I am doing something right. Something good. Something for me.

December 4th

Georgia Blandish has taken three prints—the first three I showed her, in fact—and has said that she thinks she will be able to sell as many as I can give her, and has agreed to reduce her commission by 5% because I am staff. She is even saying that if I keep on working like this she will give an exhibition. 'We'd get some people coming in just to see you—"the prodigy"—even if you weren't any good. But, my dear, these are—well, they're exquisite.' Douglas was there when she said this, standing back modestly, and I could not resist telling her that really he deserves half of the credit. And he does. For the past few months he has been coaching me furiously—dragging me along to galleries, libraries, exhibitions. We have spent hours, and hours, when we are not in bed—looking at different prints, from medieval block books to Japanese erotica or Shunga— which he says is his particular favourite.

I have still not seen any of his work—it is all in storage he tells me, and he is far too busy writing his book and teaching to collect it.

December 14th

Douglas says I should think about applying to the National in London, that I'm quite likely to get in. What I need right now, he says, is to consolidate my skills—and this really is the place to go. He thinks that they would overlook my lack of formal training—that my talent will speak for itself. I think he knows, too, that my 'pedigree' will mean something even over there—Ed being the flavour of the month, the 'wild colonial boy'. Douglas will probably be going back next year to take up a position at *The Times* so maybe it would be an idea to start making enquiries now. Imagine! Me and Douglas in London—*together*!!

December 15th

An argument with D this evening. I was musing on the fact that so few women have left their mark in the world of art, and wondered, just idly, whether it might be that even when women did manage to express themselves artistically—and often in other ways: sewing, potting, gardening, embroidery and so on—their work was not regarded as art, but craft. But D gave a scornful laugh and said that the fact that most women are at best only second rate has nothing to do with men's attitudes, and everything to do with the attitude of the women themselves. It's not, he reckons, that women have any less talent or ability, but the lives that most women aspire to—the conventional, secure, domestic lives—are of no use when it comes to artistic expression. He says that women need to bite the bullet, to sacrifice all their security, their comfort, their children even, for art. Women need to be prepared to lash themselves to the mast of a boat, like Turner, just to see what it's like. 'There's no point,' he said, 'in trying to live an ordinary life if you want your work to be extraordinary—there can be no transcendence, no kicking off of inhibitions and expectations, if one is to be forever subject to the whims and wants of others—however well loved. There can be no brilliance, no realisation of potential, if art isn't first. Always.'

Perhaps he's right—but I fear I must be hopelessly conventional, and definitely not sufficiently committed to the creation of art, lacking the right degree of passion, and genius, but somehow a life where art is all-consuming just doesn't appeal. In fact even the idea of such a freewheeling, unattached existence—where you care for no one, and no one cares, truly, for you—fills me with fear and dread.

December 18th

It is clear that Richard has nothing but disdain for Douglas and what he calls his phoney friends—and I expect that these days I'm included in this ... For some strange reason Douglas insists on inviting him out for drinks whenever they bump into one another—which is far more frequently than I'd like—and for some equally strange reason, Richard always accepts. But he then spends the night in obvious discomfort, he never says a word himself, just sits smoking and glaring, and only just refrains from sneering whenever anyone else actually speaks or has an opinion. Yesterday I confronted him—asked just why he felt himself to be so superior.

'Is it because they're artists—because they're interested in more than just beer, football and girls? I hadn't realised you were such a philistine, Richard!'

He rolled his eyes. 'It's got nothing to do with that. It's just—they're pseuds, Zel. They're not <u>real</u> artists—they're just playing at being artists.'

'Who are you to judge? You don't even know any of them. And anyway, who are these real artists you're comparing them to?'

'I dunno, compared to men like—well, like your father, for instance, and any number of other blokes who've really had to work hard, who came up from nowhere. I know these boys, Zel, I went to school with boys just like them. They're all incredibly privileged, from wealthy families, North Shore, Eastern Suburbs. They'll never get anywhere—they're not hungry enough, they don't have the drive, the dedication—honestly, they couldn't work hard in an iron lung. They'll all take the easy option—end up working in their daddies' law firms, or in banks, or advertising ... It's just rubbish—all this anti-bourgeois, anti-establishment posing. It's just that, posing. Whatever they say, whatever they do, this lot aren't taking any risks—they'll always land on their feet. I don't see any of them sacrificing anything, *or* making the world a better place ...'

'Oh, I see,' I made my voice as heavy with sarcasm as I could. 'Unlike you, Richard. Or perhaps that should be *Saint* Richard. Who'll single-handedly change the world for the better with one swoop of his almighty, er, stethoscope ...'

'Oh, come on Zel. They've obviously got brains, and they've certainly been given the opportunity to do something useful. But what are they doing—grandstanding, posturing, fighting straw men—while the kids from really difficult backgrounds—the kids who've got reason to see the system as corrupt and unfair—just bloody get on with it. You know, Zel, there's this bloke in my anatomy class—Tony Corbert—he's from a small outback town like Boolah, got to uni on a scholarship, and his parents mortgaged their house to get him through ... his dad drives a taxi, and his mum's a cleaner ...'

'But that's the sort of person they're trying to help, Richard, they're trying to make everyone see just how unfair it all is. I don't understand, if you can see things like that so clearly, why you dislike them so much.'

'I don't dislike them, Zel, I just ... I just think that at heart, they're self-promoters.'

'Oh, but it's not that simple, surely. They're NOT really like you, are they? You're ... you fit into the world so easily, so comfortably. You're not ... not an outsider.'

'An outsider! You should use your imagination. When I went off to school I was a pimply, undersized country boy, with a broad accent, and wearing all the wrong clothes—you think I don't know what it feels like to be an outsider? Maybe, Zel, you should try a bit harder to see what's under the surface of things.'

'What about Douglas, then? He's older, a teacher—he's been published. Surely what he's doing—surely that's *real*?'

He drew deeply on his cigarette, shrugged. 'Yeah. Douglas is something else, Zel. I wouldn't class him with the other blokes.'

'Then why are you so rude whenever he's around?'

'I just don't like him, Zel.'

'Why? What's not to like?'

He flicked the cigarette, ground it out with his heel and scowled, 'Zel, if you can't work out why I don't like Douglas Grant ...'

He is maddening and I wish he'd keep away from me if he really thinks I am such a drip.

December 22nd

Douglas is visiting an old friend in Melbourne. 'Will you think of me?' I asked, rather pathetically, before he rode off. 'I'll write,' he said. He's been gone almost a week and there hasn't been any mail yet.

Life is dull dull dull.

December 27th

Christmas over, thank God.
    No letter.

January 2nd, 1963

Two weeks and still no letter.
    Lonely at night. Cannot bring myself to go out or even to read. Spent New Year's Eve alone with only my sketchbook for company. Application due for the National next month, but haven't got the heart.

January 15th

No word—he said he would be gone a week, but it has been almost a month now. I tried phoning his flatmate, but Jonah said he hasn't heard either. 'He probably just got caught up,' he said. 'You know what it's like when you meet up with an old flame after so many years,' and then, recalling who it was he was talking to, he added quickly, 'but she's married now, with a couple of kids, I think.'
    Douglas hadn't told me he was visiting an old flame—but then I suppose I didn't really ask.

January 21st

At work Row asked me if I was ill. 'You look terrible, Zel. So washed out.' And then, direct as always: 'Has your lover dumped you, darling?' I must have looked as taken aback as I felt, and she purred, 'Well, it was written all over you these past few months. You've started to look like—well, you looked like a woman all of a sudden. The kind of woman a man might want to take to bed. But, now, well ... Right now you look rather like a ghost.'

A ghost. How right she is. I can feel myself disappearing, becoming transparent, translucent.

I am beginning to think that I feel solid only around him, as if only he is able to carve the lines around me, and fill me—like a master colourist—with life. The rest of the time I feel flimsy and unfixed, as impermanent and ill-defined as any preparatory sketch—and just as easily crumpled and discarded. Is this what love is <u>meant</u> to be, I wonder? D, I am certain, needs no one, and nothing, exterior to himself. He can colour himself in, and in whatever shade he chooses.

Still no letter.

February 13th

No letter.

March 4th

A phone call from Margot. The baby was born last December—a little girl—and was adopted out almost immediately. She wants to come back here to live as they're happy to take her back at the florist's—her parents told them that she had pneumonia and has had a long, slow convalescence—and she thinks it would be best to get back to as normal a life as possible. She says she is her old self—and that she is completely over Dave and the baby and everything and just wants to go on as if nothing ever happened. Poor girl. I said of course she could come.

March 9th

D back. He did not call me, but I phoned the flat and he answered. He says he's sorry he didn't write, but just got caught up. Went from Melbourne across to Adelaide with some old mates from school. Completely, utterly cold. As if I was the most distant of acquaintances. He said that he's busy writing—he is sailing for England in two months and the manuscript is due, but that maybe we could meet one night next week if I'd like.

If I'd like? *If I'd like?*

March 15th

There just isn't any point, he says, in me looking to him to be The One. It's not that he doesn't love me, he does, he insists, it's just that he's not ready for any of that, maybe he never will be— settling down, getting married, starting a family. And nor, he adds, should I be either. Didn't I know that there was no greater enemy to art than the domestic life—that a settled life, a mortgage, children, would require a regular income, which would mean an end to everything that he, and that I, surely, hold dear? He is ambitious, he says, and wants to make his name: maybe in art, but more likely as a critic. There's the book, and his pieces are getting easier and easier to place. The world is beginning to sit up and take notice of Douglas Grant, and it wouldn't make any sense, it would be career suicide, for him to go tying himself down to any one place, any one person.

And don't, please, expect him to remain faithful, he says, as <u>he</u> will not, but neither has he any expectation that I should remain faithful to him. We should have no claim on one another—or on anyone else for that matter. The more experience I have, he says, the better I will understand the world, and the better my art will be. Which is the only thing, he adds, that matters, isn't it Zel? Art.

So. This is what he wants. This is how we stand. How I fall.

March 18th

Margot arrived yesterday. She looks different; seems different. She's lost weight and had her hair cut short and seems far older somehow, and weary, her movements and even her voice quieter, slower, far less certain. She's taken up smoking. I made a meal for the two of us—set the table properly—put flowers around the place to brighten things up. After we ate we sat together, talking, drinking wine. When I asked her about everything she'd been through she said she didn't want to think about it—not just yet. That it was best to forget it all, to regard it as just one small unfortunate chapter—and to put it behind her and get on with the rest of her life. I asked if she'd heard from Dave, and she gave this terrible smile—a smile that didn't light up any part of her—and a bitter laugh. She'd heard, she said, that he was back in Australia, but that was all she knew. And all she cared to know, really. There wasn't even a little part of her that was still interested in Dave—or in men for that matter ...

Then she lit a cigarette, changed the subject. 'You look different, Zel,' she said, 'what's been going on in your life?'

I couldn't help it—I began to sob and sob and sob and when I managed to stop, I told her everything: how I'd found him, Douglas, the love of my life, how I'd imagined that it would be forever, was certain that he felt the same way about me too; how we'd spent those months, spent every moment with one another; how he'd gone away; how I'd spent all that time waiting; and how it had all changed, how he'd changed, almost overnight, and that it seemed already to be over, that my life was over ...

Margot listened without saying a word, passed me a hanky, poured more wine, patted my hand. She gave another hard little smile, crossed her arms, and then sounding rather like the Margot of old, said, briskly, 'There's no such thing, Zel.'

'No such thing as what?'

'As the love of your life. There's women and there's men. They each want something different from the other—and most women are after something that doesn't even exist. Love doesn't come into it.'

'Oh, but surely ...'

'Oh, Zel. You're such an innocent. I've been thinking about this a lot—seriously—I've had nine months to do nothing much else. If you ask me, it's just a story invented to keep us warm at night; to keep us happy, hopeful.'

It was hard to argue with her after all she's been through, so I said nothing. We sat in silence for a few minutes, and just as I moved to clear away the plates she leant over to me, her eyes suddenly bright.

'Zel. If you want him—for whatever reason, and I won't even bother to ask you what that might be—we both know it's nothing you'll ever be able to explain to yourself, much less to anyone else. But if you really want him, there's no point in sitting around moaning and weeping, and waiting for him to come back, waiting for him to realise just how much you mean to him, how much he needs you. Because, believe me, he never will.' She drummed her fingers on the table, thinking. 'I suspect that what a girl like you needs, what every girl needs, is a plan. A strategy. You need to be armed.'

April 2nd

Jonah only let me into the flat—reluctantly—when it became clear that I wasn't going to leave without making a scene. He looked nervously up the hall towards Douglas's bedroom and then shrugged, 'Well, go on then.'

I knocked briskly and entered without waiting for a response. Douglas was lying on his bed, reading, and he looked up at me coldly, without surprise or pleasure. 'Zel,' he said expressionlessly, 'long time no see.'

I wanted to cry—I could barely bring myself to speak, but somehow I managed.

'I've got something I want to show you.' I said, amazed that I sounded so cool, so businesslike. There was some lesson to be learnt here—and somehow, without any effort, I was learning it.

He raised one eyebrow. 'Well?'

I walked over to his desk and unclipped the portfolio, slid the prints out, one by one, then laid them down carefully, side by side—on the desk, the floor, even the end of his bed, and Douglas was captive, stranded in a sea of my work. There were fourteen prints all up; 16 by 16 squares, some coloured, some black and white. Every single one depicted the two of us—Douglas and I—making love. And in every print, in a blatant imitation of the Japanese Shunga—our enlarged and swollen genitals featured prominently.

When I'd finished laying them out, I stood silent, waiting, while Douglas inched cautiously around the room—studying each print, picking some up to study the detail more closely, standing back from others. Finally he turned to me. 'They're good, Zelda. I think, maybe,' he swallowed, 'I think maybe they're brilliant.'

I didn't say anything.

'They're rather—graphic. Very earthy, Zel.' His cool seemed to have deserted him, there was a slight tremor in his voice.

'Yes.'

He moved towards me, smiled, flicked me gently on the cheek.

'I've missed you,' he said softly, as if it had only just occurred to him.

I moved away, began stowing the pictures back in the folder.

'Do you want ...' he hesitated, swallowed again. 'How about a drink, Zelda?'

I was armed. I kept my head down, buckled up my folder. I declined the invitation.

But then he was standing close behind me and I felt his breath warm on the back of my neck. He took a handful of my hair, twisted it and pulled back gently, whispered in my ear, 'Come on, Zel. Or we can stay in if you want. Stay here.'

And I could feel my armour shattering, breaking into a thousand pieces. I stood trembling, stripped bare, defenceless. And every piece, every part of me—his.

May 22nd

D has gone. 'Good luck with it,' he said, giving me a friendly hug before he embarked. 'Maybe I'll see you if you make it to the National.'

I noticed that bitchy girl from the tech, Kelly—standing in the small crowd of well-wishers. Douglas's farewell to her was just as breezy. She was pale, her eyes were red-rimmed from weeping, her face puffy. We looked at one another, and looked quickly away.

He has made no promises to write. Nothing.

August 29th

I have this recurring nightmare: in it I am in bed dreaming that Douglas has left, and I have discovered I am pregnant with his child. And in the dream within the dream, I sob, and tear my hair and wail like an animal, and wish for death to take me. But then, still in the dream, I wake up—and Douglas is lying warm and solid beside me, and there is no baby, and I turn and sob my distress, my relief, and he pulls me to him, comforts me. 'It's okay, Zel,' he murmurs. 'It's okay darling. Everything's all right. I'm here, I'm here, I'll always be here.'

And then I wake up—and the nightmare is real.

September 24th

Margot has guessed. She thinks that I should tell Richard, in fact she has threatened to tell him herself if I do not. She says he is the one person in the world who can be trusted to help me, who will know what to do. She thinks I am right though to keep it from Douglas. There'd be no point. He's made his terms clear from the start.

September 27th

Richard says that I am too far gone for any procedure—that no decent doctor would risk it now. He has offered to marry me. I have accepted his offer.

October 13th

I have burnt the Shunga prints. Every one. As I watched I felt my heart curl and blacken and turn to ash.

October 27th

Poor Richard. I can see now what it is I have done to him—he loves me, I think, as I have loved, as I still love, Douglas. Richard is so certain there is some hope for him, thinks that eventually he will, through the force of his own devotion, make me love him. But love—this crushing, burning, tearing, all-consuming longing—only has one object. If there were some way I could transfer what I feel, I would, in an instant. If only there was a remedy: a pill, a potion, a charm, a spell. But it's no good—it can't be changed, can't be moved. And it's like a mountain of grief weighing me down—I am crushed under the weight of it. There is barely a moment when my thoughts run otherwise. And all the while I'm aware of how unutterably indescribably hideously selfish this grief has made me—there is barely any space in me for anyone else. And this growing, this burgeoning—surely it's not real, surely it's a physical manifestation of my grief, of the sick hopelessness that's inside me. It cannot be a life, surely—what hideous being will spring from this despair, this sorrow?

Oh God, what a start to a new life. What a welcome into the world.

Canst thou not minister to a mind diseased,
Pluck from the memory a rooted sorrow,
Raze out the written troubles of the brain,
And with some sweet oblivious antidote
Cleanse the stuffed bosom of that perilous stuff
Which weighs upon the heart

November 9th, 1963   Wedding day

Mrs Richard Howatt. Zelda Howatt. It has such a strange sound. And what a strange day. Me—sick as a dog, with barely enough energy to smile even for the photos. And looking dreadful—I could barely face myself in the mirror. And could barely face Richard—how glad I was to be wearing a veil for most of the ceremony.

Poor Richard. How could I agree to this? It is cruelty, torture for both of us. I am tied to a man I don't love, and he is tied to a woman—bearing a child that isn't his—who has no love for him.

The wedding breakfast was even more dreadful than I'd imagined. Jules and Paul were so painful, so stiff and formal. Jules's disapproval, her disappointment—though she likes Richard well enough—so achingly obvious. Paul was not so bad, but as always, his only concern was with trying to keep Jules happy. We've only told Richard's parents about the baby, though everyone will know soon enough. Miraculously, other than a thickening around my middle—which I managed to disguise with an empire-line dress and some strategic draping of my veil—there's still no obvious sign. I've been so miserably nauseous that I've actually lost weight for the first time ever. Richard's mother, though she hasn't said as much, is appalled by the shotgun nature of the wedding. She was all sweetness and light on the surface, but I could feel the deadly iciness of her dislike every time she glanced my way—though she bared her fangs frequently in her snakelike version of a smile. His father, Dr Howatt, or Dad, as he wants me to call him (at which Mrs Howatt positively blenched), is a lovely man, though. He seems thrilled by the prospect of a grandchild—even if it's arriving a little 'early'—and pleased to welcome me into their clan, as he put it. But Richard has told me that he's just been diagnosed with pancreatic cancer, and knows—he's a doctor, so of course he knows—that he probably doesn't have long.

It was a mistake to keep the breakfast so small. The presence of a few friends might have lightened the atmosphere a little—found myself wishing for Margot, even Rowanna. What a lonely cold affair it was. And a great mistake to have caved in to Jules's request that I invite Annie (though I got my way over Clive and the dreadful children). She found me alone for a moment at the table and made a great show of sitting down beside me—taking my hands, kissing my cheek, then like the bad fairy at the christening, she made it clear (not in so many words of course—she is far too clever for that) that what I was doing was a great mistake. She prefaced her remarks with her usual disclaimer; that she had given me up and had thus forgone her right to any influence, any opinion, but she had seen my work, a few prints at the Blandish Gallery, and had been surprised. And impressed. And the next thing she heard, here I was getting married ... to that lovely boy, a medical student, so respectable, darling Zel, what a pity his mother is SUCH an old bitch, you'll have some fun with her dear, though I don't suppose you'll be moving out there will you? Oh, you will? He's dying? Oh, dear. How sad. And on and on and on—with a carefully placed barb here about Ed, and then a jab about the Steeles, and then an entire artillery launched against the stupidity of country people in general. All leading up to her final comment: that she was glad I'd made the prudent decision—and had chosen sensibly: a REAL life, with a good man, and some financial security, and no doubt (looking me up and down—she knows, I'm certain) a family soon enough. It was just too hard—this with a dramatic self-pitying sigh—the life of art, and not one she'd recommend to anyone—and certainly not her own daughter.

I had to excuse myself and run to the bathroom to throw up.

Too much champagne, I told them when I emerged, still pale and shaking. Too much cheer.

February 18th 1964

I am punch-drunk, deliciously, deliriously in love. I had thought it impossible, had thought I would be filled only with loathing for this little kicking fiend, bloodsucker, nauseator, oblivious snatcher of my soul, my future, my life. Had accommodated her so reluctantly, then fought so hard against her arrival, resisted her coming, through all those desperate hours of pain and dread—until, still so oddly unexpected, she arrived, emerged, pink and furious, into this world.

She is a mass of contradictions: so perfect; so fragile. Fully mine; already her own person. Wholly known, she is a mystery.

I would—surely I just did—walk over broken glass, hot coals, molten lava for her.

A miracle.

RUTH

Salty pauses in the doorway as he passes by with a ladder.

'You okay, Roo?'

Am I okay? I open my mouth to say something noncommittal, reassuring, but nothing comes out.

'Jesus.' He leans the ladder against the outside wall. Walks over to the table and crouches down beside me. He picks up the notebook I've been reading and flicks through the pages, frowning. 'Some bad shit here, eh? Some stuff you'd rather not know?'

Again I try to speak, but somehow it's impossible. What can I say?

The world has cracked and shifted. I'm Alice down the rabbit hole, shrunk and drowning in my own tears. But this is no dream to wake up from; no book whose pages I can close. This is it. This is real.

I begin to tremble. Salty touches my shoulder, briefly feels the side of my face, then takes my hands, rubs them gently between his. 'Listen, mate, you're freezing. You haven't fallen over and bumped your head or something, have you? You look like you're in shock.'

I shake my head. But it's an enormous effort. His words feel like they're coming from miles away.

Salty hunts around the loungeroom and comes back with one of Granny's crocheted throws, which he drapes around my shoulders. He kneels down beside me again. 'Have you eaten?' He doesn't wait for an answer. 'I'll just go into the kitchen and get you something, eh. How does that sound?'

'Great.' My voice is just a croak. Barely. 'Thanks.'

'Ruth,' his voice tinged with anxiety, 'you don't think maybe—you sure you don't need a doctor?'

I swallow, make an effort to sound as normal as possible. 'No. No, I'm okay, Salty. Really. Just a bit—shocked—and maybe I *am* hungry. I probably just need to eat something. Really.'

'You sure?'

I nod.

'Well,' a grin, 'you're the doc.'

He still looks worried, but goes. I watch him leave the room, and even in this state I am still able to admire the contained power of his long unhurried stride.

By the time he returns with a tumbler of whisky and two ham sandwiches, I have myself under control again. Whatever had frozen me in shock has thawed slightly, and I'd found myself weeping—only briefly, but hard.

'Jesus.' Salty gives me a long, humorous look, shakes his head, then clears a space in the mess of notebooks for the food. 'Well, can't say you're one of those girls who looks good even when she cries. Guess you look a bit of a sight first thing in the morning too?'

I chomp on a sandwich. Talk through my mouthful. 'Thanks. You really know how to cheer a person up.'

'Well. I'll give anything a go. Once. So, is everything okay? You were as white as a sheet, mate. You're looking better now.' Then face straight, voice expressionless: 'Got a bit a colour anyway. I've always been partial to red.'

I throw a crust at his head. 'Oh, fuck off.'

He catches the crust, smirks. Then asks, his voice grave, 'It's not real bad news, I hope?'

'Not bad news. Not exactly.' I take a swig of the whisky. 'More a—a revelation.'

'A revelation, eh? Well, I hope it's one you can live with.' He pauses for a long moment, watching me, 'Maybe,' he adds cautiously, 'maybe it's not a real good idea—all this delving into the past. Into other people's lives.'

He has a point, but it's not one I really want to concede. 'But, Salty, the stuff in here,' I gesture towards the journals, 'it's about my life too.'

'Yeah, there's that. But what you've found out, is it worth knowing? I mean,' he breaks off, looks suddenly flustered, 'look, I'm sorry, it's none of my business, is it? It's just, well you looked really bad. You gave me a bit of a fright, actually,' self-consciously, 'I thought you might of had some sort of ... seizure or something.'

When he goes back to his painting, I stay in the surgery, reluctant to move. I reread parts of the diary: my mother's pregnancy, the report of my father's—Richard's—reaction, my birth, over and over, until I've almost learnt my mother's words by heart. I think about Salty's odd question: Is it worth knowing? I don't know the answer. I don't know its value—how can a price be put on knowing the truth?

I try hard not to think about what it means, what it *really* means to discover that my father's not my father, but there are certain things that immediately present themselves, that I can't avoid thinking about: that Andy isn't my full brother; that I share no blood with my Howatt relations; that a lifetime of accepted resemblances—physical, intellectual, dispositional—have all, in an instant, been rendered false, meaningless, imaginary. And then there's Dad. *Dad.* The knowledge—the *revelation*—is so huge, so immense, that it's almost impossible to take in; the very idea takes my breath away, sets my pulse racing, makes me giddy. *My father's not my father.* And looming over that, not really even beginning to sink in yet, is the unavoidable fact that someone else, someone I've never even met, *is.* My father. Oh, it's as if the ground beneath me has opened up. And I'm falling, falling, falling, down down down.

When Salty says he's going, I'm still sitting there, in the same position. He hovers outside the door, uncertain. 'Is there someone I can call, mate? Do you want me to get hold of Linda? Or your boyfriend—Chris, is it? Do you want me to give him a call? What about your brother? Maybe he could help?'

Oh God. My brother. What am I going to tell Andy? And Chris. For some reason the thought of telling Chris isn't at all comforting. The only person I really want—the only one who'd know what to say, who'd have the right answer, who'd be able to comfort me in any way is Dad. My dad. But he can't be reached, can he?

I blink back tears and smile blindly in Salty's direction. 'Oh, no, it's fine. I'll be fine, really I will. I don't think I could face talking to any of them at the moment. I'll get up and get something to eat in a minute ...'

'What if I get a Chinese, then, eh? I don't really have to be anywhere. A couple of beers—a bottle of wine?'

I accept his offer eagerly. I'm grateful for the offer of food and drink—but more than that, I'm grateful for the disinterested, undemanding company he'll provide. Right now I don't really want to be left here alone.

We get smashed. Correction: I get smashed. I drink the bottle of wine that he's brought, then down a couple of his beers, then open a bottle of Laphraoig that I find in the loungeroom sideboard. I feel guilty, opening it, knowing what Dad would say—it's bad enough that I opened his good whisky, but how much worse that I contaminated it with lemonade. I'm so pissed that I start smoking. It's a practice that, as a doctor, I abhor, and energetically advocate against, but tonight I go back to a long-kicked habit, and smoke the rollies that Salty patiently makes for me. I'm a responsible smoker, though, and insist that we smoke outside—I wouldn't want to give the new paint job a nicotine tinge, I explain to a bemused Salty, or impregnate the walls with the fumes.

'Do you really think you should be doing this, Roo? What about lung cancer?' he asks.

'Well, there've been studies done and these—rollies—are much better for you. There's less tar, less additives—the incidence is much lower.'

'That's bullshit,' he says, his hand cupped around the match as he lights me up.

'Yep, it's bullshit. They're all killers.'

'Ah well, s'pose we've all gotta go sometime ...'

This sort of fatalism usually drives me wild—but I can see that he's winding me up, and for once I don't take the bait—and don't say anything more. Just draw in deeply and exhale in his direction.

He laughs. 'Glad to see you're feeling a bit better, mate.'

'Truth is, mate,' I reply, 'Right now I'm not feeling much at all. My father wasn't really my father.' The confidence comes unbidden, blurted out between mouthfuls of whisky.

Salty pauses mid-gulp and puts his beer down on the table. He looks stuck for words, and I'm perversely pleased to have shaken him out of his characteristic calm. He clears his throat.

'Eh?'

'My mother—she was pregnant to another bloke before she married Dad.'

'Shit. Did your old man know?'

'Yep.'

'And you never had—you had no idea?'

'No. None. Not an inkling.'

'*Shi-it*,' he drawls again. 'I s'pose this'll change things.'

'Yes I s'pose it will.' I tailor my answer to echo his own understatement.

He takes a swig of his drink, says slowly, 'But the difference is only in your head y'know, Ruth. It doesn't really have to change things.'

'You don't think it might be a bit more complicated than that?'

'Nah. I don't, mate. You can make it whatever you want to make it. If there's one thing I've learned it's that some things are only as big as you make them.'

'You can't really think it's that simple? It's a pretty big deal isn't it? Suddenly finding out that your father isn't—wasn't—really your father?'

'Well, I'd say it's about as shattering as finding out that your child is someone else's—that the child you've always accepted as your own, isn't.'

I assume that he's talking about my dad. 'Yes, but Dad always knew. They only got married *because* Mum was pregnant.' And for the first time it occurs to me that Dad had had to live with this knowledge—that I was not his daughter—all my life. Wonderingly: 'He never said anything. He never let on ...'

Salty clears his throat. 'Actually, I didn't mean your dad. I was thinking of myself.'

'What do you mean?'

'I've always wondered ...' he pauses, clears his throat, starts again: 'Rebecca, my eldest daughter—she came early. The first I heard about it, Sheryl said she was already five months gone. But then the baby came two months early. Only there was no way she was a premmie. The doctor—it was your dad—never said anything, not to me anyway, but the midwives—y'know how women talk—all said she was full term. She was seven pounds three. Pretty average ...'

'So? Women get their dates wrong all the time.'

'The thing was—I was away at the crucial time.'

'Well maybe she was a bit early ...'

'No mate, I'd been away for four months. You probably won't remember, but I went to Sydney at the end of year eleven—it was some sort of city/country exchange programme. Anyway, even if she was a few weeks early, which is all it could've been, Rebecca must've been conceived during that time. I *couldn't* be her father. It took me a while to figure it out. Years. It honestly never occurred to me that Sheryl had been sleeping around. And I was young and sort of bewildered by the whole thing, everyone telling me what I ought to do, how I'd ruined me life. And by the time I worked it out, I actually didn't think it was such a huge tragedy. I really really dug Sheryl.' He gave a slightly embarrassed smile. 'I was kinda happy that we'd have to, you know, have to stay together. Mum probably tried to tell me after Beck was born—she'da known right off, but I wouldn't have listened.'

'Oh.' I'm not quite sure how I should respond. 'Well, you know it's easy enough to find this stuff out now. A paternity test; DNA ...'

He cut me off. 'Thing is, Ruth, I don't really *want* to know. I'm Beck's dad and she's my daughter and whether or not it's my blood running through her veins doesn't make any difference. I wouldn't love her any less or love her any different.'

Suddenly I see what he's getting at. 'So when you worked it out you didn't let it change things?'

He shrugs. 'It doesn't have to change things—not if you don't let it.'

'But what about Rebecca?'

'What about Rebecca?'

'What if she finds out?'

'What are you getting at?'

'Salty, it's not just your problem; it's not just your life. Don't you think she might want to know? That she has a right to know?'

'What'd be the point, mate? She's happy enough as it is. Why would I want to complicate things?'

'But life is just that ... Life *is* complicated. You can't just ignore things that don't fit in.'

'Why not? If nobody knows it's broken what's the point of fixing it?'

'There are all sorts of things—*Jesus*—there are heritable diseases, avoidable conditions, predispositions to certain cancers, diabetes ... Oh, God, Salty, the ramifications are endless.'

He's unconvinced, rolls another cigarette. 'Oh, come on. We've survived without knowing all that stuff for a long time. What's the bet that half the kids in the maternity ward at any given time don't belong to the blokes who think they're the fathers?'

'But it's the *truth*—surely it's always better to know the truth?'

'Well, you could answer that question, Roo.' He gives me a grin. 'What do you reckon? Is it better?'

It's a question I can't answer. Not yet.

We're still sitting outside at midnight, though now in companionable silence, and we're still drinking. I'm on my fourth Laphraoig—which I've decided to drink straight in deference to my father, and have insisted that Salty has a finger too, which he downs quickly, grimacing. It's a work day tomorrow, he reminds me, and he needs to get home, to get to bed.

'Have the day off,' I say airily, 'but don't go yet. Have another drink.'

'D'you want me to stay over, Roo?' He asks the question diffidently. I'd probably have asked him if he hadn't asked me, and I accept his offer eagerly. I'd rather there was someone here. I stand up, swaying, 'Come on then, let's make up the spare bed.'

Salty takes hold of my shoulder with a firm hand, steadying me, then steers me back to the chair and pushes me down gently. 'Don't worry about it Ruth. I've got a sleeping bag out in the ute—never go anywhere without it. I'll just bunk down on the loungeroom floor. I'm gunna hit the sack shortly. It's meant to be another stinker tomorrow and I want to get some of the outdoors stuff done early on.'

'Come on; just one more drink,' I plead. I slop more whisky into his glass before he can decline, and add another finger to my own.

'Well,' he grins and lifts his drink in a mock salute, 'you're the boss, mate. Just as long as you don't dock me pay.'

I watch him as he drinks, suddenly mesmerised by the unconscious grace of his every movement—the strong fingers so careful around the heavy crystal, the latent power of his sinewy brown arms, the working of his jaw, his neck, as he swallows. 'Would you do something else for me, Salty?' The words are out before I can stop them—really before I've thought about what it is I'm going to ask.

'D'you want another rollie?'

I almost say yes, for what I want is so outrageous—is the most outrageous suggestion I've made to anyone for a long time—but I take a deep breath: 'I want you to sleep with me.'

His expression doesn't change, his eyelids barely flicker, but he draws deeply on his cigarette.

After a moment, his voice deliberate, unhurried, 'Well. I don't like to turn down such a generous offer, but don't you think you might just be a little under the weather, Roo? Don't you think you might regret this in the morning?' He pauses, gives a slow smile, 'And no offence, Ruth, but I'm not sure that ... well, I'm a bit confused. Generally when a girl wants to go to bed with a bloke—there are all sorts of signals ...'

I take a deep breath, interrupt.

'I don't want sex,' I tell him bluntly. 'I just want you to sleep beside me. I don't want to lie there alone.'

'Well, I don't ...' He looks mildly stricken. 'What if we both bunk down in the loungeroom?'

'*Please.*' I want to hear someone else breathe beside me. I want to feel warm alive flesh beside me—a body full of life and energy, even sleeping energy. Evidence that I exist, even if I'm not the me I thought I was. Suddenly my head is clear, and just this once I'd rather it wasn't.

'Please, Salty.'

I lie on one side of the bed wearing an old full-length nightgown—as modestly clad as a heroine from a Victorian romance. Salty has showered and wears a funny old pair of cotton pyjamas that once belonged to Dad and are several inches too short. I giggle at the picture we make—like two awkwardly polite middle-aged virgins on their wedding night. For the first ten minutes or so we lie stiffly on either side of the mattress in the dark room, facing outwards, careful not to turn or jiggle or accidentally touch one another. But inevitably, as we slide into sleep, there's a meeting. It's just a brush of foot against leg to begin with—followed by a swift retreat, murmured apologies. A moment later we turn simultaneously into the middle of the mattress—and there's a dip, we both roll down, our shoulders brush, my breast grazes his chest. Our whisky breaths mingle, lips touch. Then somehow—without a word having been spoken, and consent being neither sought nor given—we are a tangle of sweating limbs. Our fucking is hard, hot, fast, furious. And mindless—just what the doctor ordered.

And then down down down I go into stupefied, dreamless sleep; held gently by a virtual stranger in the centre of my dead father's bed.

Chris is the first person on my mind when I wake the next morning, though not for the reasons he probably should be. Salty is still sleeping heavily, his long body curled beside me. Asleep his face is different: he looks forlorn—his lips turned down at the corners, his forehead creased. All the wry laughter that's never far from the surface in the daylight hours, so much a part of him, is completely absent. It's a good face—not exactly handsome, but strong—the kind of face that seems to get better as it ages. The jaw square, cheekbones defined—unlike Chris, whose once cherubic good looks have gradually given way to an ill-defined puffiness. His body, too, is as unlike Chris's as it's possible to be. Where Chris is soft and pale, his chest and body virtually hairless, Salty is lean and rangy and muscular—his skin dark, his chest covered in coarse hair. It occurs to me that Salty's is a body that has been used, has been called upon to function as the human body was built to function, to engage in hard physical labour. While Chris—a solicitor, who has worked for years in an office, and spends a large portion of his life seated at a desk—barely requires a body. Watching Salty now, defenceless in slumber, but the latent power still evident, there seems some essential, some almost *moral* difference between the two men. As a doctor, I know that all the external signs of health can mean precisely nothing and that Salty's body might harbour some disease, some hidden malfunction—especially given his smoking habit—that there are no guarantees. I watch him now, his breath slowed, eyelids flickering, and run my finger down his face, follow the strong creases that run down his cheeks—creases most typically seen on Greek men—and he stirs, his eyes flutter open, widen when he sees me. He sits up and leans back against the bed head, closes his eyes again.

'Shit.' Eyes still closed, but grinning widely. 'Did we really ...?'

'Oh, yes. We did.'

'Shi-it, eh?'

'Well, no. Not shit. It was pretty good actually—from what I can remember, anyway. I'd give it a nine.'

'Only a nine ...? I'd have given it an eleven, myself. Twelve if you hadn't ...'

'Shhh.' I press my fingers against his mouth. 'Shut up.' I trace the creases again. He sighs again.

'Are you Greek, Salty?'

'Eh?'

'Your face. These lines, your jaw. Your skin. The way your eyes are so deepset. All the, um, body hair. You have this look—I always call it a Greek fisherman look ...'

'Funny you should say that, my pop was half-Greek—Dad's dad. Dunno 'bout the fisherman bit, though.'

'But Gatton's not a Greek name is it?'

'Nah—it was the usual thing. The Greek bloke—Maroulis?— was already married, and had a family. He ran a greengrocer's in Grafton. My great-gran worked there, she was only young, sixteen or so, and they had an affair, she got pregnant ... It was a bit of a scandal, evidently. Her family were a pretty respectable bunch, churchy types, Methodists. Anyway, it was all kept hush hush, and Pop was raised by his grandma. She, Prudence, his real mum, eventually got married and moved away to Dubbo, raised another family. Then when her mum died, poor old Pop was still a kid, only twelve. Nobody wanted him and the old lady didn't provide for him in the will, and the uncles and aunties had him put into one of those boys' homes. Dad always reckoned it stuffed his old man up completely. He never got over it, poor bloke. He followed his mum out west when he grew up, but she wouldn't have anything to do with him. Her husband was a bank manager or something, and he didn't want it to get known about town, I guess. My grandad had a bugger of a life, really. The Depression; the war; he married my bitch of a nan—then dropped dead at fifty-six. He was a nice fella, from what I remember. But, you know, he was sad underneath. Really sad.' He pauses. 'Well, you would be, wouldn't you? Your mother not wanting you. You'd be sad all your life. There'd be no getting over it.'

I don't want to hear any more. I slide down on the pillow again, run my finger along his arm, following the prominent muscles from his elbow to his shoulder and then down across his torso.

'Hmmm. Triceps, deltoid, biceps, pectoralis major, latissimus dorsi all in perfect working order.' I give his buttocks a squeeze. 'And a very nice gluteus maximus, too ... Has anyone ever told you that you're a really fine physical specimen, Salty?'

'Well, not in such—er—clinical terms, no, mate.'

'And all completely natural. Achieved through hard physical labour. All those city professionals—people like me—who spend hours at the gym—and a bloke like you gets this body because you use it the way you were meant to ...'

Salty slides down to face me. 'I don't want to disappoint you, mate, I know you think you've discovered some uncorrupted natural man or something—but I have to confess to spending a fair few hours working out in gyms myself over the years. I spent a couple of years in the ring, too, when I was much younger.'

'Oh.' I'm embarrassed to have been so easily caught out in my Arcadian fantasy—but only slightly.

'But some things do come natural. Some of my attributes.' He takes my hand, guides it further down his trunk.

'Oh, yes?'

'Well, there's this for instance ...'

We stop talking.

Salty nudges me awake. 'What about your boyfriend?'

I move closer to him, feign sleep.

'Ruth?' he pulls his arm out from under me, gives me a gentle shake.

'His name's Chris, isn't it? What about Chris?'

I don't want to think about Chris. I don't want to think.

I sigh and try to roll away from him, but he rolls me back, effortlessly, so that I'm pinned directly beneath him, face to face. I squeeze my eyes shut like a recalcitrant toddler.

'Ruth,' he shakes me again.

'Well, what about him?' I open my eyes, blink up at his worried face.

'Well, it doesn't seem right.'

'Of course it doesn't, Salty. Because it isn't right.'

'So ...'

'So what?'

'Well, how do we make it right? I don't as a rule sleep with other blokes' women.'

'No. And I don't, as a rule, sleep with other blokes.'

'So where do we go from here, mate?'

'I don't know that I want to go anywhere. I'm perfectly happy right here, for now. Can we just not?'

'Not what?'

'Think. Worry. Get up.'

For a moment he looks as if he's going to argue, to press the point, but then his face relaxes. He stretches his arms above his head. 'Well, I really should get up and get to work, shortly. The boss is a bloody old bitch, a real whip-cracker ...'

'Oh no.' I groan. 'Just stay here. I need sleep. My head. Please Salty.' I give a pathetic little whimper. 'Please?'

'Righto, mate.' He sinks back down beside me. Pulls me close. 'You sleep.'

I sleep for another few hours and then stay in bed for the remainder of the day. Salty gets up while I'm asleep and puts a sign on the surgery door, explaining my absence. He brings me tea and serves me a lunch made up of bits and pieces he's scavenged from the rather rudimentary stock—last night's leftovers, a toasted cheese sandwich—and still somehow manages to get in a full day's work. He is tiling the bathroom—a job he freely admits to hating—and I listen with guilty pleasure—I should be helping grout—to his frequent curses.

I lie there thinking, not of this complication with Salty, but of what I discovered yesterday. There is no way to escape the fact that the diaries have changed my own life—immensely, irrevocably. My relationship with my father was never intense, both of us being reserved, somewhat detached and unemotional, but my regard for him—and his for me—was fundamental to my development, to my sense of who I was. I always was—and no doubt Andy would concur—a bit of a daddy's girl. Of course I know enough now about psychology to understand that this identification was probably some sort of defence mechanism; a natural reaction to my mother's death. Many girls who lose their mothers at an early age will idealise them—model themselves on their memories of her, try their best to become the sort of person they imagine she would have wanted them to be. Others, angry—however irrationally—at what they perceive as their mother's abandonment, head in the opposite direction. After all, why identify with the mother who didn't love her own children enough to stay and nurture them? What sort of a role model could she ever provide?

I spent my childhood working hard to be as unlike my mother as I could be. I ignored any attempt by either my father or my stepmother Judy, or as we grew up, even Andy, to get me to take any more than the most superficial interest in anything of an artistic nature, and had fiercely disdained any remotely creative activity—art, music, drama, literature. Before Mum died I'd excelled in all subjects, I was a natural reader and a confident writer, and had a precocious talent for copying and sketching and painting, but later on, after her death, these pursuits came to seem frivolous somehow. Instead I laboured at those subjects that interested my father—and that I knew were necessary if I were to become a doctor—even though I had no real aptitude for maths or science. I was bright, and I did well—but I knew I had no natural facility: I had to work hard. Even in my primary school reports the teachers were bemused by my efforts: 'Ruth is a bright, co-operative, tenacious and hardworking student in most areas, but makes little effort, and has a very dismissive attitude towards those subjects that do not interest her, though I am confident that she would excel in all areas were she so inclined.'

My father said little about this stubborn disinclination to extend my narrow range of interests and my marks in high school maths and science were high enough for it not to become an issue. But at university, I suddenly had to struggle to keep up. I needed tutoring in chemistry the entire duration of the degree, and though my father never questioned my need for such assistance, he did ask, once or twice, whether I was quite certain that I wanted to go into general practice. 'You're a clever girl, Ruthie—but the life of a GP isn't always the easiest—there are so many other things you could do.' But he left it alone when I showed no interest in changing directions—when he saw that I was determined to proceed along this safe, predictable course. By the time I was thirty-five I'd achieved everything I'd set out to accomplish. A medical degree, several years of work overseas, a general practice in the suburbs, occasional teaching stints, a secure relationship. Wasn't I established, financially secure, happily partnered?

But now, confronted by this dizzying new knowledge, what do all my former aspirations amount to? Suddenly it's clear that however hard I've worked to smooth out my own story, there are other stories, other lives crowding in on mine from all directions: bending it here, pushing it there—pressing it into quite a different shape to the one I've been trying to fashion.

It seems I'm no longer simply Dr Ruth Howatt, daughter of Richard and Zelda. And if I'm not that person anymore, then who am I?

I could be anyone.

I don't pick up the diary again until late that night. Salty buys take-away—fish and chips from the Greek cafe this time—and I put together a salad using the greens and late-season tomatoes I've discovered growing amongst the weeds in Dad's neglected kitchen garden. We share a bottle of white, we eat, make love, half-watch a movie, make love again. Even though we go to bed late, tired, I toss and turn for a long while, until eventually I give up and retrieve the journal I put down so dazedly the day before.

I've given up worrying about the darkness of the story seeping into me. I've been drawn in as far as I can go—my mother's words have already settled into every part of me, every bone, every cell—and the night will make no difference.

'Have you ever heard of Douglas Grant?'

'Eh?' Salty's voice is thick with sleep, 'what's up?'

'No, it's nothing really ... I just wondered whether you'd ever heard of Douglas Grant, Salty? He's an art critic, a biographer. He's Australian originally, but he lives in South America somewhere I think. Argentina? Chile? Brazil? He did some big documentary in the eighties—a series on world art. Oh God, I can't remember what it was called, *A World of Change*—something like that ... And he wrote a bio of my grandmother.'

'Can't say you're ringing any bells, Ruth ...'

It occurs to me that there's a copy of Annie's biography here. I pull the blankets off and slide out of bed. Salty sits up, startled.

'What're you doing, woman?'

'Hold on.' It should be a hopeless quest: there are bookshelves in every room of the house—and none of the books are in any particular order—so really it could be anywhere, but there it is, instantly discovered, unmistakable in its midnight-blue cover, in the shelves of my father's room.

This Savage Calling: The Art and Life of Annie Swift.

It is a book I'm more than familiar with. I can remember coming across the volume when I was about thirteen, looking for something to read on a wet winter's day, and had rushed out to Dad, almost crowing with excitement. Wasn't this woman, this Annie Swift, my grandmother? Imagine, a book about my own grandmother—what a remarkable discovery. Dad had let me read the book, but had prefaced my reading with a conversation about the contents, warning that I should be cautious, that biographies were tricky things, and that not everything in the book would be true—after all, it was only one person's interpretation of another—and was therefore fallible, however well-researched. Still, I can remember that first avid reading so well—I skipped most of the art criticism, which was of little interest, but true or not, Grant's evocation of Annie's life and her wilful, capricious nature had been entirely compelling.

Up until then Annie had been almost absent from my family mythology. Dad barely mentioned her, and it was only ever Granny who brought her into the conversation, and then it was always disapprovingly, dismissively, and always as the unnatural mother who'd so callously abandoned her infant daughter, my mother; an abandonment which had, Granny somehow managed to insinuate (despite my father's obvious distaste for the topic, and his frequent attempts to derail her well-worn conversational track), ruined my mother's life and somehow led to her early death. Reading the book I'd felt slightly guilty, mildly disturbed by the sympathy and understanding Grant managed to elicit. It seemed a terrible betrayal of my dead mother to think of Annie as a real person, with real feelings and experiences, happinesses and disappointments. It felt somehow transgressive to see her as she saw herself, or as others saw her, rather than as the two-dimensional witch whose story I had only ever considered as a footnote—a fundamental one, to be sure—to my mother's.

And Grant's biography was the first time I'd heard anything about the young Ed. Oh, I knew all about him of course; by the time I was in my teens he was the venerable old man of Australian art—and I'd actually met him once or twice during his occasional trips to Boolah—visits that had all the pomp and ceremony of a royal visit: the return of the Wild Colonial Boy— but he'd seemed no more real, no more connected to me, than Santa Claus.

Since then there had been a vast amount of literature written about Ed, about Annie, and about my mother, and I'd learnt to read such histories more critically—finally understanding that the interests and expectations and ideological position of the author frequently take precedence over the subject. But that first biography I'd read without any reservations, and enjoyed in a very uncomplicated way. (Typically though, Andy's response to the book had been quite different—much darker. He'd read the book several times, and had obsessed over it as only an adolescent can. He'd mulled over certain passages, certain events, studied all the photographs—of the woman, not the work—hunting for resemblances, likenesses. He'd brooded over it for a long time, he confided later, and felt vaguely—and entirely irrationally—ripped off: why hadn't he been given the chance to get to know this vivid brilliant woman, his grandmother?)

But tonight my interest is not in the story contained within the covers of the familiar volume. Instead I turn straight to the inside back sleeve. There he is: the biographer, Douglas Grant—I do some quick calculations—in his late thirties. It's an almost comically clichéd seventies portrait: the heavy (permed, surely) frizz of hair, the absurdly wide sidelevers, the regulation black skivvy, the self-conscious artiness of the bottom-lip Gauloise, the eyes half-shut against the smoke, the sardonic tilt of his head. There was no doubt he was a handsome man—aquiline features, dark brooding eyes, and from what I can see of his body, broad shouldered, solid—but his small, slightly pouting lips give his face an oddly feminine cast, a femininity further accentuated by the small dark mole—a beauty spot, really—by the side of his mouth.

I slide back between the sheets and hand the book to Salty.

'This is him. Douglas Grant.'

He looks at the picture.

'Jesus.'

He traces the side of my face with his finger. Down from my forehead, along my nose, over my cheekbone, pausing at the little dark mole that sits at the right hand corner of my mouth.

ZELDA

Extract from the author's preface to
***Hansel and Gretel: a story without words*,**
published by Bunyip Press, 1966.

After my Grandma Steele's funeral I took out the old volume of Grimm that she had given me years before, thinking I would read a story to my baby daughter, Ruth, later that day—though she was really far too young for such a tale, being barely twelve months old. I found that I was once again mesmerised, inescapably caught up in the Grimms' spare but compelling storytelling, illuminated so beautifully by Arthur Rackham's illustrations. The starkness, the simplicity, the logic of the metaphors ... the way they need no explanation, no augmentation or commentary. The way even the youngest child will take something precious from the tales, even before they can fully comprehend the narrative.

My initial idea was that I would illustrate the stories, but on gazing once again on the perfection of Rackham's illustrations, decided that there would be little point. Why attempt to better the master ... But my interest persisted, in fact I became quite obsessed, spent hours sketching scenes, experimenting ... but with no clear direction, no sense of where this would lead me. And then one day my husband arrived home from a trip to Sydney with a pile of books he'd picked up from a second-hand shop in the city. Knowing of my keen interest in comic books, two slender volumes in particular had caught his eye: *Madman's Drum*, by the American artist Lynd Ward, and *Destiny*, by the German expressionist Otto Nuckel. Remarkable productions, dating from the 1930s, they weren't comics, but wordless novels, adult picture books wherein serious novel-length narratives were related entirely through consecutive woodblock prints, and without any text whatsoever.

They were a revelation, an inspiration—and at last I had a direction. I would translate these familiar tales into pictures in their entirety. Not illustrations, but wordless renditions—scene by scene—moment by moment—rather like a sequence of old-time silent movie stills. This first work took some time: it took me many months to find a style that captured my own artistic vision without distorting the integrity of the original folk tale. The *Hansel and Gretel* you find here *is* Grimms' *Hansel and Gretel*—but told visually. I hope both children and adults will get as much pleasure from this pictorial retelling as I did from its creation.

Zelda Steele. Boolah, 1966.

November 17th 1967

A letter from Margot today. She's back from her travels, and was pleased to find my long letter waiting for her. She says she would love to visit, and will once she has worked out how she is to live. She is staying with her parents for now, but cannot do this indefinitely—though it is tempting. She is thinking of going into nursing. Though she's probably a bit long in the tooth to be taking orders from some old biddy, she needs the money— and some direction. She is blunt as always: she is so pleased, she writes, to hear that my life is heading in such positive directions, she had never really expected that Richard and I would find such pleasure together, had really expected disaster, not contentment—after such a strange, lopsided beginning. And the fact that I am pregnant again fills her with a terrible envy ... she says that for the first time in years she has thought of Dave.

She has bought copies of the three books, was going to give them as gifts to her little nieces, Alan's children, but once she 'read' them found herself quite fascinated and cannot give them up. And anyway the witch is far too terrifying for a child, surely. Where, she asks, do these pictures come from??? I would tell her if only I knew myself.

I had not realised that my letter spoke of contentment. I am so used to painting a bright surface over everything, of trying to convince everyone else that I am doing exactly what I want to do, that I think I have somehow managed to overlook the fact that I am, in fact, content—and far far happier than I had expected.

Margot says it sounds as if I have finally managed to fall for Richard. I wonder if this is true? I love him, there's no doubt of that—but it is such a muted, such a calm, affection, and perhaps based too much in gratitude. It cannot be compared to what I felt (what I feel?) for D. Or perhaps—though I cannot even now bear to think it—*that* was just a fantasy.

April 5th 1968

A call from Jules. Annie is sick, is dying. A cancer discovered just a few months ago—too late—already its rot is in every part of her: brain, liver, lungs. Annie had not told anyone—not even Jules, none of the children. Did not want her last few months spoilt by sadness, false hope. 'Typical of Annie,' says Jules, 'always so brave, so gutsy. She faces everything head on, without flinching.' She is in a hospice in Newport (Jules and Paul have arranged it for her, of course. It's one of the best, and the least they can do). Death is coming quickly—a week or two at most and Annie has told Jules that she would like to see me. The other two girls, Nesta and Eve, are travelling in India—they can't be contacted—and Annie insists that she does not want poor Troy to see her like this—he's away at school, is in the middle of exams—and they have not told him of the severity, do not want him to know until it is all over. Such an irony, Jules sighs, that it's her going first, and not Clive, when he's been so ill all these years. He's useless, in hospital again himself, his lungs this time—and Annie the strong one. I've barely known her to have a cold, Jules said.

'Why does she want to see me?' I am bewildered, a strange cold has crept into my bones. 'I haven't seen Annie for—well it must be almost five years now ... not since the wedding.' My lips are suddenly stiff, my voice has frozen, I feel as if I have shards of ice in my throat.

'I don't know, Zel. Clive called Paul. I haven't actually been to see her ...' her voice trails off and I know that Jules *won't* see her—that death is the one thing she won't face, can't face. I straighten up, breathe in, feel strong, feel powerful. Know that I can face this head on, without flinching.

I write down the address, tell Jules that I will go, that I will arrange something, no, she's not to worry, Cynthia will help Richard with the children, it would be too much trouble to bring them, and I'll be there as soon as I can—a plane tomorrow, the next day, Monday at the latest. That I'll stay while ever Annie needs me. However long.

I call Richard, he is sympathetic, and immediately concerned for me. 'Do you want me to come home, darling? Are you okay? Are you alright with the children? I can have Mum or Judy pick them up if you need some time.'

But I'm fine. I don't need help. I make the reservations—there's a flight tomorrow. I even call Cynthia myself. She is pleased to help, she says slowly, of course I know that I can call her anytime I need help with the children. It's no trouble, no trouble at all, she can rearrange the bridge meeting, miss golf, and no doubt the hospital committee will survive her absence, but why do I feel I should go rushing off at this woman's whim—she doesn't quite understand. She pauses. 'It's not like you owe her anything, Zelda,' she says coolly. 'You barely know her.'

'She's my mother.' I'm shocked by her attitude, though God knows by now I shouldn't be shocked by anything that Richard's mother says.

'She gave birth to you, dear. That's not the same as being your mother. I'd have thought that having your own you'd understand that there's a whole lot more involved in being a mother than merely giving birth.'

'She's still my mother.' My voice is stiff again, but this time with rage. 'She's dying. She's said she wants to see me.'

'Yes, and what about *your* children, while you're away? Andy's not even properly weaned is he?'

'She needs me.'

'Zelda, dear ...'

I hang up without saying good-bye.

RUTH

When children are fortunate enough to have constant access to both their parents in an intact marriage I imagine that their parents' separate existence is considered to be of little consequence. Oh, no doubt there are occasional periods when the mystery of their parents' past crosses their mind: what on earth they saw in each other, what they were like when they were in their teens, their twenties, were they ever really in love—*ugh*—unimaginable. But it's unremarkable, a given, and so easily taken for granted when parents are together, for better or worse, muddling their way through life together.

But for me, and I think for many children of dead and separated parents, unravelling the mystery of that previous relationship—so irrevocably over—can become something of a preoccupation. Anyway, there was certainly a period in my own life where the reconstruction of my parents' lives became an obsession. For some months during early adolescence, I pestered everyone I knew, everyone who was ever involved—family friends, my grandmother, local shopkeepers, even poor Judy (who remained patient and open and never showed any signs of irritation despite my self-centred lack of tact) for information about my mother and father's relationship. I mooched over pictures of the two of them together: as students, on their wedding day; candid snaps taken at parties, picnics, family get-togethers. I studied pictures of the three of us together, of Dad and me and my so vividly alive mother, and then when Andy came along, the four of us—not just trying to recall the captured moments, though that was always a factor, but to find clues about *how* my parents were. It wasn't only the big things that fascinated me—not just romantic love and all its icky ramifications—what

I wanted was the minutiae, the everyday, the inconsequential, the forgotten. The small transactions that constitute a life just as cogently as the more clearly significant moments. I wanted to know how they might share a joke, for instance, or argue about a chore that needed doing, or bitch about the bad behaviour of a mutual friend. I wanted to know how they shared their life, and I was avid for information—for any information. What I really wanted, of course, was to be there again, in the past, but this time with an adult consciousness, and aware of all that was coming, all that I was destined to lose.

But this detail was almost impossible to come by. It seemed that the only things that people recalled—the only things they were able to share, anyway—were the big moments, the public moments. And in their stories my mother was always kept quite separate from my father, from everyone—like some sort of celestial being, shining, solitary—as if death had somehow managed to enshroud her past as well as her future. Oh, there were all the expected anecdotes: how happy she had been on her wedding day; what a beautiful mother she was; how much she loved the two of us; how patient she was; how she was always so full of fun things to do—painting, drawing, trips to the river, surely you remember those tadpoles you raised to frogs? And those enormous murals your mother drew on the lounge-room wall for you to colour in with chalk—they were the talk of the town! It was as if she had always acted alone, as a single entity, and not part of the team—even if it was a dysfunctional team—that other kids' parents seemed to belong to.

When I changed tack and asked, outright, what they were like together, my mother and father, there would be a startled pause, and then: oh, they were like most young couples—they were terribly in love, they were a lot of fun. They were so lovely with you children, such natural parents, and so on and so on. But were they—and here I would become slightly embarrassed, but still press on—were they In Love? (And this, of course, is the one thing that adolescents who live with both their parents—with parents who are still sexual beings, quite determinedly DON'T want to know.) Why, yes, would come the answer, as inevitable as if it had been scripted—they just *adored* one another. Even after the separation. It was only ever a temporary thing ... just a misunderstanding. Why, your parents lived for one another—and for you children of course. And then, always, the impossible question quivering there between us: if they lived for one another, if they lived for us, then why, why, is she dead?

The cause of my mother's death had been another 'misunderstanding'.

I'd first heard about my mother's suicide late, when I was sixteen. I was in my fourth year of high school when the first biography of my mother—written by an American art academic—was published. My father had sat Andy and me down and told us of its existence. He'd been expecting it for some time, he said, as our mother's reputation had increased exponentially over the decade since her death. Her collected works—*Grimm Tales by Steele*—had been published around the world, and were already into their umpteenth edition, and her posthumous earnings—her literary estate administered by Paul Holland—had made us considerably wealthy. Over the years Dad had received copies of scholarly papers and the odd newspaper article written about her, but a year or two ago had begun to receive numerous requests for interviews, all of which he politely declined.

Once the book reached Boolah, Dad warned us, there would be a great deal of salacious gossip. He hadn't yet read it, but he'd heard reports, and it was likely that many of the incidents reported in the book would be exaggerated, or misinterpreted, or just plain untrue, and we were to come straight to him or Judy or even Granny, if ever we needed to. 'It's not that I think you can't look after yourselves,' he directed this dry comment to me specifically, 'but you need to be prepared. This is a small town—everybody knows everyone, along with their history—and there's going to be gossip. There'll be plenty of people—children as well as adults—who'll have something to say.' Dad told us to be on the lookout for inquisitive strangers, too, as there could be journalists about; he'd already had a number of calls from newspapers, requesting interviews. Our response should be that we knew nothing about any of the information contained in the book, and that they were to give our Dad or Judy a call if there were any questions. Needless to say, my father went on, he wouldn't be buying the book and he would prefer that we didn't read it either. 'Let's just wait till this whole thing has blown over,' he'd said, 'and then maybe we'll take a look.'

But of course it wasn't so simple—our straightforward deflection simply had no effect on certain people, well-meaning adults as well as less well-meaning and occasionally vindictive teenagers. I managed, though, to maintain my cool, ignoring the hastily discontinued conversations, remaining politely noncommittal in the face of enthusiastic questioning, until one particular incident. It was a Friday lunchtime and I was standing in the ridiculously long school canteen queue when Shane Steele, a distant cousin, a year younger than me and with a reputation as a nasty little thug, sneaked up from behind and dug me in the back with his elbow. 'I read that your dad and your stepmother killed your real mum,' he whispered wetly in my ear. 'They were having an affair. What a prick your dad must be. My mum says she always suspected something—and she's never been to his practice since. She reckons that Judy Monahan was a real slut—even if she was always up herself.'

I let him finish his spiel before I rammed my fist hard into the soft space just above his balls, and he lurched away, coughing, winded. 'Fuck off, shithead,' I hissed. 'Your *mum* says *Judy*'s a slut ...?' I gave a loud snigger, raised my voice to make sure everyone could hear me clearly. 'I think you'd better watch what you're saying there, Cuz. There're some things I could tell about your mum—though why would I bother when her number's scrawled on every phone booth in town? She reckons Judy's a slut? It's a case of the pot calling the kettle black, isn't it?' Not a word of what I said was true, I'd barely ever spoken to his poor mother, and really knew nothing about her. But it worked. 'Yeah, righto.' Shane backed away slowly, his hands held protectively in front of him. 'No need to make a big deal out of it. I was only repeating what I heard.' He gave a halfhearted smirk. 'But like the book said,' he added, just as he took flight, 'it was no wonder your mum killed herself.'

I suppose I won that round: I'd managed to save my own face while publicly ramming Shane's into the slimy evidence of his own cesspit mind, and that was the end of the matter at school. If any other parents or students had bought or read the biography—or had any opinion whatsoever on the contents, there was no one game enough to mention it. But Shane's nasty remarks had given me an alternative vision of my parents' relationship—and more importantly, the events surrounding my mother's death—that was disturbing, to say the least.

I had very little memory of the actual events themselves—I was, after all, only eight, and Andy not yet four. But the story that we'd been told (and it must have been very early on, because I have no memory of being 'told'—rather seem to have always known) was that my mother had drowned accidentally. My parents had been separated for some months by that stage, and my mother had bought herself a small cottage on the outskirts of town by the river, where we lived with her during the week, and according to the familiar history, things were looking positive for our parents, there was some talk of a reconciliation. It was a Friday night, and as usual, we were spending the night at Dad's, and for some unknown reason—though there was some evidence that despite warnings she had made a practice of these solitary nocturnal swims and rambles—Mum had gone for a walk along the river, either in the middle of the night, or early in the morning, and she had somehow stumbled and fallen and tragically drowned. She was missing for several days before her body was found several miles downstream by a shocked farmer.

So I'd never even considered suicide. Why would I? I'd never had any reason to doubt this story—it all fitted so neatly. My mother's life was clearly, undeniably tragic, and her death by misadventure, as it was termed, just as things were set to improve, seemed to fit the pattern of necessity. But immediately Shane whispered the word *suicide*, my tenderly nurtured picture of my mother's final moments rapidly dissolved. Oh, God—what had I imagined? My pretty young mama tripping along the banks of a deceptively benign Darling, picking wildflowers, singing folk songs, obliviously cheerful, only to be taken by a sudden wave? The absurdity of such a scenario was suddenly all too clear. How naive, how unutterably stupid was I? That night, lying in bed, I pondered for the very first time the strangeness of that death in the river: my mother had grown up by the ocean, she was a strong swimmer. In fact it was the one physical activity she'd really enjoyed. Transplanted far from her beloved ocean, she'd had to find a replacement for the body surfing that she so sorely missed, and had taken up water-skiing, which had been all the rage out here. As unlikely as it seems, she'd been a natural: we have scores of photographs of mum skiing barefoot in the wake of Roly Ward's speedboat, her long blonde hair spread out behind her, her face alight with laughter, one arm raised in exuberant triumph. Considering her complete ease in the water, the notion of her drowning during a midnight or early morning stroll seemed increasingly unlikely, and the likelihood of her death being by her own hand increasingly possible. But how could I find out? It wasn't something I could ask my father directly—it would mean accusing him and Judy, and virtually everyone I knew, of lying.

The next day I wagged school and paid a visit to the public library instead. The librarian—Enid Marsh, who was an old school friend of Judy's—looked slightly shocked to see me. Not, I realised almost immediately, because I was quite blatantly truanting, but because she was sitting at the loans counter reading what I guessed to be my mother's biography. 'Hello there, Mrs Marsh,' I chirped, and then as casually as I could, asked:

'What's that you're reading?' She swallowed and quickly thrust the book under the counter. 'Oh, it's nothing, Ruth dear,' she smiled nervously, 'It's just an old book, nothing special.' She licked her lips, pressed on, 'You gave me a terrible fright, Ruth, I have to admit. I really shouldn't sit here reading when there's so much work waiting to be done. All these new books to cat-alogue.' She sighed and stood up, carefully straightening her skirt. Composed now, she gave me a bright professional smile. 'Now, how can I help you, dear?' A frown replaced her smile as she realised the time, the day of the week, 'And shouldn't you be at—'

I interrupted. 'Mrs Marsh, that book you were just reading—it's that book about my mother, isn't it?'

She sighed. 'Well, yes. I'm afraid it is.' She twisted her hands guiltily. 'She was such a lovely woman, Ruth. And such an art-ist ...' She gave a sad little sigh. 'Really, it was such a loss—her dying so young when she had so much ahead of her.' Then, enthusiastically, 'She was practically a genius, you know dear, and a book like this—well it's a real tribute. I know it must be hard,' she sighed again and made a vague gesture towards me. 'I know it must be difficult when it's someone you loved ... read-ing about them like that—it must be,' lips pursed, head cocked to one side, 'it must be terribly shocking.'

'But I was only very young when she died,' I reminded her gently, 'so it's probably not as terrible for me as you'd imagine.' I paused briefly, 'And not at all shocking when I haven't actually seen the book itself.'

'Oh, so you haven't ...?'

'So, here I am. At the library. I knew you'd have a copy.'

'Well, I ordered two as it happens,' she beamed, 'I knew there'd be something of a demand in town. It's not very often we get written about out here—there aren't too many Boolah celebrities, well, other than your Grandpa of course, and you know there's even been articles about your mum in the Syd-ney newspapers. If you'd like a copy you can have this one,' she groped under the desk for the volume she'd been reading. 'It's catalogued and covered and ready for borrowing.' She held the book out to me enthusiastically, but then pulled it back abruptly just as I reached out to claim it.

'Oh. But Ruth, your father ... Are you sure Dr Howatt wants you to ...?'

'Oh, he has the book ordered,' came my blithe reply, 'but it hasn't arrived yet. I just couldn't bear the wait.'

I went immediately to the contents, turned to the chapter titled 'Final Days' and flipped through the pages until I found the relevant passages.

'Why did my mother kill herself?'

I asked the question at the dinner table. I couldn't help myself, blurted it out, disconcertingly belch-like, as soon as I sat down. Judy, who was dishing out the peas, froze mid-serve, my father choked on his beer, Andy stared at me in disbelief.

'Why, darling, what makes you ask such a thing?' Remarkably, Judy's voice was steady, as was her hand.

'It's that bloody book,' my father growled. 'I knew something like this would happen.' He shook his head, sucked in his cheeks. A vein started throbbing near his temple.

'Dad?'

'Not now, Ruth.'

'But Dad, surely this is—'

'Can we just finish dinner, darlings?' Judy intervened. 'It'd be a real pity to spoil such a lovely meal with an argument. Perhaps when we've had dessert, Richard,' she added with her imperturbable calm, all the while spooning generous dollops of mashed potato onto our plates, 'you and Ruth might have a little talk.'

We walked all the way down to the river without either of us uttering a word. I crouched down at the water's edge, and dangled my fingers in the freezing winter current, while Dad stood leaning up against a redgum and finished his cigarette, then threw the butt into the river and lit another, still not speaking.

I was the first to break the silence, impatient now. 'Well? Did she commit suicide or didn't she?' My fingers were hurting, the water was so cold, but somehow the pain seemed appropriate.

'Your mother left no suicide note, Roo, and so though the coroner came to the conclusion that her death may well have been at her own hand, it may also have been an accident—as we've always told you.' Dad's words were measured, his face impassive.

'I've already read that much in the biography, Dad.'

'I thought I asked you not to—'

I rolled my eyes, 'Oh come *on*, Dad: it's a book about my mother. My *mother*. How on earth could you expect me to *not* read it? Especially when everyone else in town seems to have a copy. So, yeah, I've read that much of it—and the biographer seems to have come to the conclusion that it *was* suicide. And she interviewed a whole lot of other people, even if you wouldn't talk to her.'

'Jesus.'

'So what do you think, Dad? What do you think really happened?' My fingers were pleasantly numb now, so I plunged my hand a little deeper, felt the ache move up to my wrist. 'Can you tell me what really happened?'

He didn't say anything at all for a few minutes, stood smoking, gazing out blindly into the water.

'I saw your mother the day she died. She was working, you were at school and she'd dropped Andy off at Gran's that morning. It was a Friday, so Gran was to drop you both back to me once I'd finished work. Anyway, I called over to see her mid-morning—I wanted to talk to her privately, without you kids around.'

'What about?'

'Well,' he looked down at the rushing water, cleared his throat. 'It was about arranging a divorce, actually.'

'A divorce? But even the biography says that you were thinking of getting back together ...'

'We'd been separated for almost two years by then—and I suddenly knew there was no point in waiting anymore, that she didn't ... that she was never going to come back. Her work was in demand—three books had been published, another three had been contracted, she was establishing ... something of a reputation—and she was content, settled. She was the happiest I'd ever seen her, Roo.'

'And so—you thought this was a good time to discuss divorce, Dad? Why?'

'Well, the thing is ... I didn't actually end up discussing it. You see ...' He lit another cigarette, his hand shaking, 'It's very difficult to tell you this, darling, but Ruth, your mum hadn't really ever loved me—not ever—'

'Not ever? But she married you, didn't she?' I was bewildered by this unexpected revelation.

'But there'd been another man, darling, before me. A man she'd never got over, who played with her, dumped her. She was heartbroken. We'd been good friends, and I'd been in love with her for years. I think you'd say she married me on the rebound.'

'God, Dad.' I felt as if I was stranded in some sort of temporal labyrinth, with no way of knowing where the tangled skein of the past was leading.

'Anyway, to get to the point. By then Judy had worked as my practice nurse and receptionist for a few years. I'd known her all my life, and she'd been very kind to us when Zel and I first split up—she'd stay over when I was on call ...' he trailed off, looking away from my no doubt hard, judgemental adolescent eyes.

'So, you and Judy were having an affair?'

'No, Ruth, we weren't. We hadn't actually, there wasn't anything, not yet ... but I could feel that things were beginning between us and I wanted to ... well, I didn't want anything to happen while I was still legally married to your mother. I didn't want to drag Judy into anything sordid. It was just before the family law changed and divorce could be a pretty nasty business.'

This legal digression was lost on me. 'And so then what? You told Mum and she killed herself!'

'No, no. The thing is, Roo, that in the end I didn't even speak to her.'

'Eh?'

'I went there intending to talk to her about it—and I got as far as her workshop. I could just see her through the studio window—but she didn't see me ...'

'What do you mean? What happened.'

'Oh, Roo.' He rubs his eyes, tiredly. 'In the end, I just couldn't. She looked so happy, so content, so busy, and so much more focused than I'd seen her—so much in her element—that I couldn't bear to ... to spoil it.' He gave a sad smile. 'And to be honest, I was a coward, too. I didn't actually *want* to get divorced—and at that moment, looking at her, I just couldn't do it. I realised that I would do almost anything to have her back.'

'But what about Judy? Were you just going to dump her? I don't understand.'

'It was so very complicated, darling. It probably sounds silly now, but there wasn't actually anything solid between Judy and me, it had all been rather tentative. I was still married—a respectable family man, after all—but even so, I'd determined to go back and talk to Judy that night—to tell her the truth, to confess that I still loved your mother and always would.'

'And so what happened?'

'I went back to the surgery, and of course was busy all the rest of the day, and then, just on teatime—Liz Barclay went into labour—you know Samantha Barclay? She decided to come along three weeks early and it was a long, difficult birth—poor little thing got stuck—and so I had to leave you with Judy while I delivered her. I was at the hospital all evening and didn't get the opportunity to say anything to anyone.'

'So the rumour that Mummy saw you and Judy together at home?'

'Is complete claptrap—wishful thinking, perhaps. But your mother did come to the house that night, though—that much is true.'

'She came?'

'Yes, she came. She knocked on the door, it was past ten, Judy was half asleep, she remembers being embarrassed that she was in her night-gown. Anyway, she explained to Zelda where I was, asked her if she wanted to come in, to wait. But she didn't.'

'Was there any sign, Dad? Was she distressed? Drunk?'

'There was nothing, darling. Judy said she looked as if she might have been crying, her eyes were a little puffy, but apart from that Judy thought she seemed quite normal. Very calm and composed.'

'And what happened then—she just took off?'

'She said it didn't matter, that whatever it was that she wanted to tell me could wait until the morning. That she'd head home, see me tomorrow.'

'And then?'

'That's the last anyone saw her, darling. Judy was the last person to have seen her alive—in her house with her children. And even though there was nothing, absolutely *nothing* going on between us at that stage—well, people have wicked imaginations. And of course in retrospect, it was foolish of me ... I've read the biography, you know, and I know the stance some of these critics have taken—I've seen what they've made of Clever Elsie and of Judy being there ... But you have to realise that it's impossible, Ruth. Those woodcuts were finished long before this—there's no way she could have planned them as some sort of coded suicide note. She'd started on *Elsie* long before she died ...'

'But why?' I was puzzled. 'I don't understand ... I mean I can't imagine that you would do something so silly—in a small town—you must have realised, surely, how suspicious it would look, a separated man having another woman over to stay?'

'Well, yes of course—I should have been far more careful, should have thought about gossip—but darling, that's the problem when you're quite innocent, you can't believe anyone would ever consider otherwise.'

A sudden thought: 'Why was Judy there? Why didn't we just stay at Granny's? Or couldn't *she* have stayed with us at home?'

'Roo, come on, you know Mum—it was Friday night.'

'Oh, God. Bridge.'

His smile was brief, bitter. 'You know, I actually rang her just as she was leaving, just as soon as I got word that I was needed, but she wasn't ... er ... helpful.'

'What about Mummy—didn't you ring her?'

'Of course, I rang her first, but she wasn't answering, and I thought ... Well, I don't know what I thought—that she was out, or working. I suppose I could have driven over, but there really wasn't time. And anyway I really hated to bother her when you were staying with me. I hated to disrupt her.

'So I only rang Judy when I'd exhausted all the other possibilities. And Judy came of course. She couldn't know what she was letting herself in for, could she? There's no way that we could know what was to come. Any of us.'

ZELDA

April 20th 1968

What had you hoped for? Some final reassurance of her love? An apology, an admission of guilt? Or perhaps even an admission that she has never loved you? Something big. Some final reconciliation—or conflagration. Something to mark the occasion. But what you never expected was this: the commonplace requests—for water, for oxygen, for help sitting, for pillows. Her eyes dim, unfocused. Polite strangers: you could have been anyone, you realise. Then on your second day's vigil, the quiet slide from sleep to unconsciousness. And that night a faint sign of resistance, her expression changes, and you think you see consciousness, panic, she labours to breathe. You call for the nurse, and while you wait, grip her hand, but there is nothing, the pressure is not returned. She's gone, without any acknowledgement, without a word.

You would have liked a word—had imagined final words, imagined her calling out. But who would she call for? Clive? Her own mother? Her brother? Nesta? Eve? Your father?

You?

RUTH

How could she do it when she knew the pain of abandonment herself, how could she bequeath the same anguish to us, to her beloved children? How could she not know that to a child, death represents the most profound abandonment. Or was her own pain so great that it simply obliterated every other emotion: love, pity, passion, compassion, even fear? Oh, I understand that she was, that she must have been, depressed, and over the years I've read all the books, attended the seminars, talked to the specialists—and have seen it up close in my patients. I know about depression.

But somehow I can't remember her displaying any of the usual symptoms. Though what eight-year-old—still in that blessed state of egocentric obliviousness—would? What I remember about my mother was that she loved us, that nearly everything she did was about us and for us. But then perhaps all children believe this about their mothers—that they're the centre of her world. And believe it even more keenly, as some sort of compensation for her absence, when she's gone.

ZELDA

August 1968

Lately you find yourself petrified, as if you have had a spell cast upon you by some wicked witch: you have become the sleeping beauty, or been turned to stone, a statue. You will be doing something—some everlasting never-ending task—washing dishes, clothes, scrubbing the floor, dicing potatoes, it could be anything—but suddenly you stick, stop, stutter like a malfunctioning cartoon robot. For a moment you cannot remember what it is you are doing, why you are doing it, where you are, even who you are. And then the child is calling you, she may have been calling for hours, even days, you would not know, how would you? *Mummy*, she cries, *Mummy, wipe my bottom Mummy Mummy Mummy* and someone waves a magic wand and you are free, you can do what you have to do: wipe the bottom, wash the hands, praise smile cuddle; and then the baby wakes, cries, you feed him, change his nappy, park him in the pram outside while you hang out bring in make lunch read stories shop clean cook iron bath bed stories lullabies kiss on forehead *hug me more hug sleep well darlings sleep well don't let the bed bugs bite.* Oh, you can move, yes: legs arms mouth, they're all in good working order, but you move through your life as if it belongs to someone else.

You ask your husband what this is. You try to explain, you are worried, you feel out of sorts, strange, as if you're not quite here. He listens carefully, but his answer is too glib, too easy. Oh, it's probably just that you're not getting enough sleep, he says—it's usual for young mothers. It's nothing to worry about. He takes your blood pressure, listens to your heartbeat, checks your eyes your ears your skin your tongue. Or perhaps you're lacking something: iron zinc calcium vitamin B4; he gives you pills, a tonic. He even makes an effort to help—he clears up after dinner, washes the dishes, runs a bath, reads the bedtime story. But it makes no difference. Maybe, he says carefully, you need to get out more, some outside interest, a mothers' group, the CWA ...? You just nod. Yes, perhaps. Adds gently, without emphasis: Perhaps you should get back to your work.

Outside in the shed are your tools—cutters, inks, roller, paints—gathering dust. They are the sleeping beauties, aren't they? As impossible for you to reach as if they're imprisoned in an impenetrable tower of thorns. They lie waiting for your kiss to bring them to life. But you do not think about them. What is the point?

You go on. Every day you do what has to be done. But you're not there, are you?

Where have you gone?

January 1969

She says to you—this pretty little blonde woman, the pharmacist's wife, with her hair just so and her voice pitched perfectly and her impeccable face-paint and her figure with its curves in all the right places—she tells you that your little books are just lovely, she has bought every one and her children just adore them and then she says how terribly clever you must be, how she admires a woman who has such a hobby, who can retain some interest beyond the family, though of course it must be kept in perspective, in balance, but a little *dabble* in the arts, she says to you with her kindly smile, her pearly little teeth just showing over her pale pink Coty lips, never hurt anyone. She has, she confides, always had a teeny bit of artistic talent herself, her drawings are rather nice, and perhaps you could come for coffee one day, see what you think, perhaps give her some advice. She thought perhaps it would be *fun* to do a children's book, something to occupy her spare time ... You stand gaping like a fool, unsure of what to say, what she wants you to say, you feel like an absurdly costumed clown being interviewed by the queen. And you would like—oh yes, confess it, tell the truth— you would like to spit at her, to see her lose her blank assurance, her elegant poise; instead, inevitably, you do the expected jiggle and juggle, and finally, your painted smile wide, you take up her offer of cake and conversation, trill: 'Oh yes oh how lovely oh how simply jolly that would be.'

July 1969

You try. Every day, when the children have their sleep, you take out your sketchbook, your charcoals, your pencils, your pastels. Start with a still life. You set up a simple tableau: a cup, a brush, a spoon, a rattle. Open to a blank page. Make a mark. And then another. One more and you pull the paper from the book, tear it into a hundred pieces. Rubbish. You start again, and then again and again. By the time Ruth wanders out, rubbing her eyes, ready for the afternoon, you're surrounded by a sea of white. Your life's work, life's blood, nothing but confetti.

March 1970

A dreadful fight with Richard. It's past seven. You're trying to make dinner for the two of you, but the children are still up, un- washed, not yet ready for bed; Andy crying, overtired. Richard, unable to comfort him, carries him to the kitchen, squalling. Holds him out to you: I think the boy needs his mum, Zelda. Mildly enough, smiling. But it's the last straw. You throw down the frying pan, yell something—what, you can't remember, but it's nothing new, nothing you haven't said a hundred, a thou- sand times before. The shape of the conflict is completely regu- lar, known, rehearsed until you have honed it to perfection; it's a work of art, almost. The argument moves from one predictable moment to the next—now he is shouting that you don't have to do so much, that he doesn't expect anything, that you know he will do anything anything anything—'We can get a cleaner in, a cook, a nanny; you can work all day on your book, or lie in bed, do whatever the fuck you want. Anything. If only you will be content, be happy'—and by now both the children are screaming. Andy red-faced and squirming in Richard's arms, Ruth hysterical, marching around the house with her hands over her ears ... And it is at this moment that the smooth predictable shape changes, now that you find you have somehow moved below the surface into deeper darker murkier waters—unfamiliar depths where all the deadly grasping weeds of your anger lie, waiting waiting to grab at you, to pull you both under. You are saying that there is no way you can be happy—not with him, that it's impossible, that it's always been impossible, it was a mistake from the beginning. You have tried, God knows you have tried, but you cannot cannot cannot do it anymore, it is not what a marriage should be, it is all a sham and you are sick of the sight of him, of the guilt, that his touch makes your skin crawl, there has only ever been one man—

You stop there. Silence. Even the children are quiet. Richard bends to pick up the frying pan with his free hand and when he moves past you to put it back on the stove you can see how pale his face is, how set, and when he looks up at you briefly, how cold his eyes are, how indifferent his gaze. You did not know, could not imagine that coldness from Richard.

'I think I should go, Ruth.' His voice quiet, expressionless.

'Now?' you say stupidly.

'I think you've made it quite clear what you feel about me. That you don't want me here.'

You want to say that you're sorry, that you didn't mean it—but it's too late, it's gone way beyond sorry.

You take the baby from him. He walks out of the kitchen without another word. Leaves the house without a backward glance.

This is what you wanted, isn't it?

Isn't it?

RUTH

I was, of course, in no way responsible for my mother's death, but in a way that I recognise now as being characteristic of those children whose parents divorce, the child of a dead parent can't help but feel, however irrationally, responsible. Once I'd found out about her suicide the feeling of responsibility was more intense, naturally, but long before that, I'd felt that I'd played a significant role in my mother's death. That I was somehow culpable. I secretly believed that if I'd behaved better, if I hadn't made her angry so frequently, if I hadn't whinged, hadn't been defiant, sulky, sneaky, whatever—she'd still be here. And perhaps, I can remember thinking desperately, perhaps if I changed, if I could manage somehow to be always good—if I kept my bedroom clean, picked up after myself, never teased Andy, never asked for an extra helping of ice cream after dinner, washed my hair without complaint, kept my school uniform clean—perhaps then, surely then, my mother would come back. She'd threatened to run away once or twice in my hearing—what mother hasn't, half jokingly, expressed such a desire? *Right, that's it, I've had enough. I'm going. You can all look after yourselves*—and of course it means nothing when they don't go, when the threat remains empty. But when the threat's carried out and they actually go, when it seems they really *have* had enough—there's no way of avoiding the feeling that something, surely, could have been done to stop them leaving. And that there must be some way to bring them back.

My mother doesn't say too much about it in the diary—but I know I didn't make it easy for her. I can remember hating her work, hating the way it took her away from us; I hated the way it meant that she wasn't available to me, not in body, not in spirit. Dad was different: when he wasn't at the surgery he was completely present—every part of him. There was no drifting off into contemplation of a line that needed resolution, a gouge that had been dug too deep—when Dad was home he was really there, with you 100 per cent and nowhere else. You wanted a question answered and Dad would answer, and not *in a minute*—now.

Mum's workshop was a forbidden room. Oh, I was allowed in every now and then, but as a rule the door was kept locked and she never worked in there when we were around, but only on the weekends when Dad had us, and occasionally at night, while we slept. If ever I woke up while she was working and stumbled out to the garage in search of her, she was always careful to close the door before leading me back to bed. Her workshop was a secret world, not just the exotic and intriguing tools of her trade—the knives and inks and blocks and paper, the old press in the corner—but the more mundane items of furniture, the scored and battered workbench, the easel, the high timber stools. Everything here seemed even more remote and mysterious than the instruments and fittings in my father's surgery: his stethoscope, thermometer, the magical paddle-pop sticks, all laid out neatly on the gleaming metal trolley, the wind-up hospital bed that I begged to be allowed to sleep in, the natty little corner sink with its own liquid soap dispenser.

But on the evening of my eighth birthday—and this is one of my last memories of my mother, still strangely sharp—my mother took me into her studio. There, laid on her tall workbench, was a parcel, wrapped in my favourite red cellophane paper, and tied with a giant pink ribbon. She'd already given me my 'proper' birthday present—the Crissy doll that I'd wanted so badly. She was a beautiful doll with flowing auburn hair that you could grow or shrink by turning a little plastic knob on her back, cleverly concealed beneath her lacy orange shift, and in the few hours of the day I'd spent dressing and undressing her, shortening and then lengthening her hair, I'd managed already to break one shoe, lose a button off the dress and create a great, impossible-to-comb-out knot at the back of the doll's head. Anyway, when I saw the parcel, I can remember the feeling of great relief that tomorrow, when I woke up, it wouldn't be to the stomach-sinking realisation that I'd ruined my long-awaited birthday present—here was another!

'Now this is a special present, Ruth,' she said as she sat me up at the table, on the highest stool. 'It's a present for a big girl, not a baby, so it's not a toy,' but somehow her words didn't sink in, and I pulled off the ribbon, tore the wrapping (oh, that satisfying cellophane crunch!) in a frenzy of excitement, expecting what, I wonder now? A Sindy doll to add to my collection, or some new furniture for my dollhouse, perhaps? I can still feel the terrible pang when the wrappings were shed and the contents of the parcel were revealed: a box of cutting implements, a bottle of black ink, a baren, an ink roller and a small piece of grey lino. 'I thought, maybe, you'd like to come out here with me sometime, Roo,' my mother said, oblivious to my scalding disappointment. 'Don't you think it'll be fun?' I don't remember what I said, or whether I answered, but I do know that I slid off the stool and left the room without the present, and without saying thank you.

The contents of the parcel were on the end of my bed when I woke up. I gathered them together and jammed them at the very back of my underwear drawer. That day I went off to Dad's for our usual weekend visit, and I had Daddy and Granny's gifts to open—another doll, rollerskates, a party dress—and was happily distracted.

A few weeks later my mother was dead. For a long while I forgot all about her unwanted gift, and by the time I remembered, by the time I wanted those tools, nobody knew where they were.

ZELDA

June 1970

You decide that it is silly for you to remain here—it is crazy for you and the children to remain when Richard has to come back every day, anyway, for the surgery. You think you will sell the terrace in Sydney, use the money to buy a small place, your own place, somewhere in Boolah. You discuss this with R. You stand in the surgery with the door closed fast against the patients in the waiting room—knowing the rumours, avid for gossip—and Judy, who remains calmly and politely uninterested. You stand back from the desk, arms folded, explain what you're going to do, how it will work. The children can stay with you during the week, then come back home, come back here to Richard on the weekends. It's too difficult for Richard to find a house *and* a new surgery. Much easier, and much better for the patients for him to stay here. Richard sits slumped at his desk, his face grim. 'Well, you've obviously got it all sorted out, Zel.' He shrugs, resigned to whatever you want. 'Do whatever you think's best.' He picks up a file; scribbles a note, doesn't look up when you leave.

July 1970

In town shopping, visiting the bank, your solicitor, you can feel the eyes watching you, hear the conversations pause as you walk past, only to be resumed in a whisper. You're a scarlet woman, a bolter. You're obviously the guilty party and Richard, poor Dr Howatt, just as obviously the one wronged. He chose the wrong filly, no doubt about that. One woman, the wife of another young doctor—you'd been friendly enough before, had them to dinner, been skiing together—pointedly crosses the road to avoid you. Do you care? You can remember on your visit to Comebella all those years ago you confided to Ed that you enjoyed the feeling of being known; of having a history, a firm connection. How much fun it was, on your visit to town, to be stopped by an absolute stranger in the street and asked whether you were the Steeles' grand-daughter they'd heard was up to stay; to have it commented upon that you had a look of your grandma, your grandpa, of your father, of this or that cousin—the Steele eyes, Steele mouth. You felt real, solid, connected. A part of something. And you remember Ed had told you that there was a part of him that loved that too—and had never ceased to miss it—that feeling of belonging. But to beware: it could turn bad very quickly, could change overnight. One day the fact that everyone knows you, and that everyone knows your business, could be destructive. They can turn on you in seconds, like ravenous animals ... Never turn your back, he said, but you didn't believe him, back then.

August 1970

You find a place at the western edge of town, by the river. It is a modern house—red brick and symmetrical, but you like the way everything is clean, new, without the accumulated dirt and wear of history and time. Most importantly, there is a Breeze-Air in the loungeroom and both bedrooms, and it is on a small acreage, with the river flowing through the back paddock. There is no front garden to speak of—there is more red dirt than lawn, and there are only a few straggling gums planted here and there. The outlook from the road is saltbush-strewn flat earth that stretches to the horizon and the place would be utterly depressing if it didn't back onto a beautiful stretch of the water. The river is only a few hundred yards from the back fence: the bank steep and lined with willows, the water deep and fast. There's a popular swimming spot—a sandy stretch ironically known as 'Bondi beach'—a short walk away.

The house has only two bedrooms, but there's a sunny north-facing sunroom you can make a playroom, and a garage that can be easily converted to a workshop. The terrace in the Cross should fetch just a little more than you need, and Paul has said he will give you any small amount you might need if it falls short—though the agent is certain that this won't be necessary.

September 1970

Paul and Jules have said very little about the separation. Paul is quietly sympathetic, of course, not questioning any of your decisions, but Jules—well, you can hear her impatience down the line, you can hear that she is itching to say, 'I told you so. What did you mean, burying yourself in that awful place with a GP husband for God's sake, and saddling yourself with two brats in the process,' but all she actually says, with a gentle, suffering, sigh, is: 'Don't you think perhaps it might be simpler, easier, Zel, just to come back to Sydney? We could find you a lovely little house, a beach cottage in Avalon—or anywhere you like. It would be so much better for your work,' she says, 'to be back in a *real* place, where things happen, and to be closer to us, closer to family ... and we could probably find someone to help out if you need it—a nanny for a few hours a day, perhaps'—but at this point you interrupt and tell her that you are perfectly happy here in Boolah, that you need to be here, that the children need both their parents, and that—well, that you and Richard are working things out. This isn't permanent, you just need some space, some time.

She snorts.

'I would think that buying a house—a house apart from your husband—is a sign of permanence, Zelda. And what will you be living on, dear, without the rent from the terrace?'

You have been expecting this question, have a reply at the ready: 'Well, Richard will have to give me a small allowance for the children, it's only right, and he's agreed to a reasonable amount—and if I can get another book done quickly ... I've told you Bunyip Books want anything I can give them—and there's a chance that they'll sell them in the States, and evidently Faber's interested in the UK.'

She snorts again. 'Oh Zel, don't go down that path—you know you can't expect to make any sort of a living from these kiddies' books. And all the time and effort you have to put into it. What about your art—your *real* art I mean? I'd thought before all this ... before you married Richard ... you were so close to establishing some sort of reputation. I thought that you'd keep on with the printing. Not this nonsense. When are you *ever* going to get serious?'

'And since when, Jules'—your cheeks hot—'did serious art ever pay? At least with the books I can depend on some income. I have two children to raise—and I don't see you offering any help. My books are serious, Jules: art doesn't really get more serious than this.'

You don't wait for her reply. You have to go; the children are waiting for their dinner, you'll ring her back, you say before disconnecting. But you don't.

November 1970

Always at the back of your mind, this fear that your work isn't about you at all, that all you have done, all you will do, has been done to show them: Paul and Jules; Ed and Annie. To show them what you can do. To show them who you are.

But mostly, you want to show her. Annie. Your mother. To prove yourself once and for all as worthy. Even now, even when she's dead, gone, you want to reach beyond the grave, beyond the silence—you want her to see, to acknowledge, to regret.

Yes—more than anything, you want her to regret what it was that she gave up. You.

RUTH

I have three of my grandmother's pictures. Two of them are significant works—part of the Water Dreaming series she began in the late fifties—valuable, instantly recognisable as hers. Rendered in her signature blue-green Quink, her characteristic 'molten' figures, with their grotesquely swollen heads and fluid bodies, provide a surreal counter to the almost scientific detail of the beachscape itself: the sandcastles, crabs, pippies, the elegant trails of bubble-weed, all so precisely delineated. The effect is disturbing, unsettling; typical of her oeuvre.

But it's the third picture that I love best. It is only fifteen inches square, black charcoal on cheap paper that's yellowed over time. It's a sentimental sketch, a simple, swiftly drawn portrait of a baby's solemn face. The child is perhaps six months old, with a tangled mop of curls, dimpled cheeks, eyes wide, the first tooth just pushing through. I'm not sure whether it's ever been catalogued—it's certainly not a picture that has ever been exhibited, or received any sort of public appraisal; it is not mentioned in the biography.

The picture isn't signed as they generally are—*Annie Swift* printed boldly in the top right-hand corner. Instead, on the back, there's a note in a casual scrawl: *Baby, December 1945*. And then her initials, AS. There's no mention made that it's a sketch of the artist's own baby—her daughter—my mother—Zelda.

ZELDA

January 1971

Lately, you find that certain scenes from your mother's life seem more vivid to you than scenes from your own. Indeed, sometimes your own past seems so sketchy, so pale, when compared to Annie's, that you wonder whether you really exist in the way other people exist. Other people seem so solid, so certain in their own skin. There is one incident you recall, during your last visit to Sydney—you are out shopping and smile at a passing woman, just an ordinary woman, middle-aged, young, it doesn't matter—but her expression doesn't change; she looks through you, past you, moves on without responding. It is nothing, nothing, but you are filled with a sudden terrible dread. You stand stock-still there in the middle of the busy city footpath for a moment, panicked. You pinch yourself to see if you are awake. You take an inventory: arms, hands, fingers, legs, feet—you can see and feel all the body parts that you should be able to, but this does not re-assure you. You find a shopfront. Search for your reflection. For a moment you are confused—you are expecting a small, dark, laughing girl, but all you see is a tall pale woman, not young, dressed badly, long mouth dragged down. Not Annie. You. Zelda.

You remember a few moments of your babyhood. Just images, really. The brilliant blue of the sea, hot golden sand; a bright yellow ball on a green lawn. A man with a beard—Ed?—lifts you high, high, higher ... A seat covered in striped red silk; you stroke it, follow the weave of the fabric down and around, back again. A woman's face, red-lipped, smiling. The face turns toward you for an instant, then away. A curtain of fine dark hair. Your mother.

You remember a visit. You are five, maybe six, and *she* is coming for lunch. There are preparations in the kitchen, in the dining room, in the garden. Everyone is so busy. They keep moving you out of the way. Telling you to sit here, go there; to wait. *Later, later.* Then they are busy preparing you. You're given a quick bath, dried roughly, carefully dressed. Your pale hair is brushed, then pulled and twisted into two damp plaits. Jules explains that your mama is visiting. You do not really remember her—your mama—there are photographs and you know what she looks like from these, and you have been told over and over about her. But she remains like a bedside story; a princess in a fairytale. Thoughts of your mama bring some sort of association with pain—you vaguely remember crying, shouting, trying to hold on to her, being plucked away—so perhaps she more closely resembles a fairytale witch: you imagine nails like talons, a mouth that breathes fire. Your mama. Jules evens up the red bow at the end of each plait, regards you for a moment, then abruptly, uncharacteristically, pulls you close. She sighs and murmurs above your head, you can only just make out what she's saying, and it makes no sense: *Sometimes love can't solve everything. Sometimes it makes things worse.* Her chin is sharp on the top of your skull, her smell cloying and you wriggle impatiently out of her clasp. Jules is smiling, but her eyes are bright with tears. You turn away so that you don't have to see.

When your mama finally arrives she is more beautiful than a princess in a fairytale though she does not have golden hair—it is cropped, curly, dark—and instead of a long velvet gown she is wearing pants. There is a man with her: Clive. No Prince Charming, Clive seems almost elderly—frail, bald, he wheezes loudly, and shuffles about with the aid of a stick. And there is a baby; your mama has a baby. *This is your little sister, Zelda*, she says, kneeling down and presenting her to you as if she's making some sort of offering. *Your baby sister. Nesta.* The baby is thin and wrinkled and hairy—fine dark hair that seems to grow all the way down to her eyebrows. She smells dirty, sour, like milk left out overnight. You stand there blankly. You don't know what you are meant to say, to do. Your mama brushes your cheek with her red lips and stands up. She says something, but you're not listening, are busy scrubbing your cheek. Jules says gently, *Zel darling, your mama just wants to know if you'd like to nurse the baby, nurse Nesta?* You shake your head. You do not.

After lunch the adults stay at the table drinking and talking and you watch slyly from the little table in the corner, where you sit drawing pictures of castles and princesses with long golden hair and knights in armour slaying dragons. You watch your mama. You see how even though she is laughing and talking with the rest, she is always looking at Nesta. That she will laugh at something that is being said, but still all her attention is held by that little wrinkled bundle. Every now and then your mama will brush her face against the baby, or her lips. Sometimes she holds the baby's face up to hers and breathes her in. It is impossible not to notice that almost every moment she is stroking, tickling, touching Nesta. She passed the baby to Clive while she ate her lunch, but hurried through the meal so she could have her back again. You notice that your mama doesn't look your way. Not once.

You want to make her life into a story. You think that if you can do this you can explain it to yourself—that this will explain not just her life but your own. That somehow it will make it all clear and you can put it all behind you. *Behind you*—it's a lovely image. As if the past can be sloughed off; shed like a skin. As if it isn't somehow inside you, intrinsic, inescapable, as vital an organ as the heart or the lungs. And like any organ, it's prone to disease, to infection, to metastasis: the past is as capable of killing you as any tumour.

You have some evidence of her life—enough evidence to piece the important parts together. You have all the frequently repeated stories: the stuff of legend, your larger-than-life, practically mythological mother. You have anecdotes—some of them really just throwaway comments—but seized by you, avid, desperate for any sort of contact, any sort of connection, however tenuous. So much information seized and stored away. And then there are the letters sent to Jules, or Jewel as your mother always called her, that were passed on to you at your mother's death.

Mostly though, you imagine. Oh, soon enough you won't have to imagine. You have heard that He has finally finished her biography, that he's already contracted to a publisher; that the book contains Scandalous Revelations, that it's bound to be a bestseller, make her reputation; confirm his. That story, HIS version of her, will be available to you just as it is available to anyone who cares to know. A part of the Public Record. Authorised History. Yours will be different; yours will be imagined. But for all that, you know it will be more real. More true.

You imagine her at the beginning. A baby. Just born. Her tiny crumpled face. Eyes squeezed shut against the light. Dark hair slicked with her mother's blood. Her mother. You could keep going back. But you won't. Begin here. Begin.

ANNIE

She is a bright little thing. Bright as a button. Sharp as a tack. Quick. Small and dark and curious. A whirlwind. Her own mother can't keep up. She is sitting up at five months, crawling at seven, walking at ten, then running. Once she can run she never walks anywhere. And with language, too, she is fast. She says her first word at six months: *Want*. Surely this is apocryphal?—but her mother swears that this first verb was enunciated clearly and deliberately by her demanding tot. *Want*.

From the first Annie is suspicious of the grown-up world; wary of adults. She is not one of those little girls who basks in the attention of her elders; nor is she the type who remains on the periphery, silent, observant, circumspect, listening to everything. There is no benign interaction with adults: adults are the enemy. She is an expert in negotiating their world, in manipulating it to suit her purposes (an extra cake; an outing; ways of getting this or going there). Her siblings are the enemy too. Purveyors of censure, of disapproval, they are on the side of authority, loyal emissaries of their mother. She is nothing like them. Her older sister Alice is compliant, content. A loving daughter. *Alice is such a good girl*, says her mother, smiling and patting her tidy curls fondly. Her brother, Norm, is a good boy: quiet, agreeable, affectionate. Almost ten years older than Annie, he is busy with his own life, can afford to good-humouredly ignore her; Alice, though, only four years her senior, is bewildered. *You'll be best friends one day*, her mother had said when Annie was newly born, the longed-for baby sister. *You look after her, Alice, and one day you'll be best friends*. Alice tries her hardest, but by the time Annie starts school, the two girls are openly hostile. Every opportunity she has to humiliate or cause her sister physical pain, Annie takes. She pushes, pinches, punches. She sabotages games, destroys toys. Alice—slower than her sister, but patient, vigilant—takes a bitter pleasure in spying on her sister, noting her misdemeanours, and ensuring that Annie is regularly caught, first by their mother, then, at school, by teachers. *Dobber*, Annie hisses, but Alice knows it's justice.

Annie's always getting into scrapes. Climbing out to the furthest branches of the trees. Going higher than any of the boys. Falling out. She learns to swim early and spends as much time as she can on the beach. She is always being ordered back in closer to shore by the guards. She breaks an arm in the surf; twice she has to be rescued, dragged out by a rip. She is not afraid of anything. *Annie is a worry*, her mother sighs, frequently, her brow creased with anxiety. *A real worry.*

Older, she is more than a worry. She is *trouble*. Teachers complain. Annie is rude; Annie is insolent. On occasion Annie is violent. She is frequently absent from school without excuse—the truant officer demands an explanation that her shamed mother cannot give. By the time she is fourteen there have been incidents in several shops. A silk scarf. A compact. A set of tortoiseshell combs. Things are paid for, replaced, hushed up. Respectable mothers discourage their daughters from keeping company with her, but there are always other girls, followers, keen to admire her, to flatter her, to do her bidding.

Soon enough, sooner than anyone could imagine, there are boys. Seeking her out, walking her home, calling for her. Then there are the boys who don't call. There are late nights. Flights from the window. Nights when she doesn't come home.

She is thrown out of her private girls' school at fifteen—she has hit someone, broken her nose—and this is the last straw. She will be thrown out of home, too, her mother says, if she doesn't find a job and quick smart. Her mother is at her wits' end. A widow, she has worked hard for her children, for *all* her children, and the serpent's tooth bites sharp and deep. She has always been self-sacrificing in the face of immeasurable difficulties. She has tried, and only God knows how hard, has tried to understand, to guide, but to no avail. She loves her daughter, but Annie is so difficult, so demanding. She is too much for her. She is a bad girl. (But this is not the story that Annie herself tells. *That old bitch*, she will say. *Had it in for me from the beginning. Don't know what I did to deserve it.* What she remembers is shouting, hair pulling, slaps, being locked in her room. Sometimes in the cellar. Her sister, Alice, was a toadying little bitch and her brother a pompous fool. They were all, she insisted, against her from the beginning. She didn't know what it was that she'd done. She thought perhaps she was a changeling. Hoped.)

Annie is saved by her Aunt Lucille—her dead father's youngest sister. Lucille is Young and Modern. She works in a commercial design studio where she draws advertisements for hats, clothes, cigarettes. The studio needs trainees, unindentured, and Annie is taken on. The pay is low—daylight robbery really, only 7/6 a week. She has never displayed any observable skill or interest in drawing or in artistic expression of any kind, but it seems she is not without talent and learns quickly. The job is in the city, too far to travel from home, so she flats in Newtown with her fast, platinum-blonde aunt. It is the late nineteen-thirties, and a war is looming in Europe. But not in Annie's consciousness; not yet. The only thing looming is her future; vast, unimaginable, limitless.

There is a boy at the studio. There is always a boy. He is a designer, a commercial artist who has recently completed his indentureship at the studio. He walks with a swagger that none of the other boys possesses. Not a boy—a man. He is as quick and clever and as wild as she. Nights he goes to art school. He is an artist.

Perhaps this is the point where the story really begins. Her story. Their story.

Your story.

Annie stands in front of the mirror in the ladies'—momentarily displeased with her reflection. She reddens her lips, pinches her cheeks, eyes her hair critically, then unpins it, brushes it out, fluffs the curls with her fingers. She smiles at her reflection, satisfied now. She's good-looking, there's no denying that: springy dark curls, bright eyes, lips wide and full, clear skin tanned golden from hours in the surf. Her body is small, compact but curvy—a pocket Venus. She isn't vain, not precisely—though when the day comes, as it will, when age and time reveal their claws, she will cling ferociously, desperately, to the remnants of her looks. But right now she takes her beauty as her due, knows how to use it to her advantage, as a weapon to get what she wants.

She waits outside in the hallway until he comes out, the cigarette dangling between her fingers her pretext for being away from her desk. They have not been properly introduced, have never even exchanged a word, but she knows his name, has made it her business to know: Edward Steele. Ed. She knows very little else about him—someone has told her that he's a country boy but there's nothing to indicate this—nothing of the rustic or the bumpkin about him. Oh, there are some essential things she's well aware of, a few things she's observed: he's tall, wide-shouldered, thin, but powerful looking. His hair is a tawny brown, his skin is lightly freckled, he has a square jaw, straight white teeth, laughing blue eyes. Annie has been watching his movements: she knows that he always gets into the studio just on time, never early; that he leaves on the dot. She knows that he always takes his afternoon break promptly at 2.30—he delivers his drafts to old Merewether, then wanders into the hallway for a smoke. So she knows that despite his relative youth he's already a creature of habit; knows that she can use this to her advantage, makes a plan, takes her time.

'Oh God, this is hopeless'—Annie plays the old trick, fumbling with the matchbook, bending the match awkwardly against the flint, gives an impatient sigh. Then softly: 'Do you think you could light me?' He saunters over, smiling faintly, leans in to light the cigarette, set loosely between her lips now, and she—just like the sultry heroine in countless black and white movies (that's how you're imagining this scene: the two close together in profile—is it Bogart and Bergman?—*Casablanca* comes later, doesn't it—but no matter—this is how you imagine it: in black and white, no background music, the shadows looming against a stark background)—she rests her hand loosely over his, leans close, her breast almost, almost, brushing his arm. Lit, she moves back again, exhales, blowing the smoke above their heads, while he lights his own, then leans against the wall, his eyes on her, watching. Waiting. (You think perhaps he's been anticipating this moment, has seen the looks she gives him whenever he passes through her office, has heard the whispered questions, the giggling, the desperate shushing as he passes by again on his way out. He's wondering what he's got himself into; what to do next.)

'So,' Annie's voice is low, husky, even this single drawled syllable is loaded—suffused with suggestion, possibility.

'So,' he throws the word back at her—a hard flat monosyllable—and leaves it at that, still watching her, eyes narrow in the smoky hallway.

She's slightly put out; his response isn't quite what she expected. There should be a certain inflection—a question that must be answered—but he's left her with no place to go; instead of prolonging the conversation, he's ended it. She's uncertain momentarily—maybe he's not interested, perhaps she's overplayed her hand, read the situation wrongly—but then she catches the glimmer of the smile he's working hard to contain. (You can imagine your father even at this young age—twenty-one, twenty-two—already a cool customer. He'd read a minx like your mother effortlessly. He'd have to see that she was playing a part. He couldn't fail to be aware of the filmic qualities of this scenario—the way she's standing, one hand in her pocket, head tilted, her oh-so-studied, oh-so-casual exhalations. Maybe he's determined that the scene should be played out another way, that she should dance to his tune for a while.)

They smoke in silence—she drooping slightly now, some-what petulant, he seeming perfectly at ease. Annie tosses her butt into the trough. 'D'you want another?' he offers her his pack, and she takes one coolly enough, says: 'Why not.' Another dead end. He moves close again to light her up, and this time she keeps her hand well clear of his, holds her body still, distant, but when the cigarette's alight he stays where he is. He is a little too close, and she can feel the body heat, smell the print-room smell of turpentine, ink, overlaid with something else, something indefinable, but recognisably masculine.

'Do you like art?'

'Art?' She's confused. This isn't in the script. She gropes for an answer.

'D'you mean ... paintings and drawings and things? Well, yes. I should say I do. Doesn't everyone?'

'Paintings and drawings and things,' he mimics her, his voice light and high. He gives a wide grin, his lean face breaking into interesting angles.

'Christ, girl ...'

'Well, what do you mean, then?' Her voice is sharp with anger.

'Well.' He considers a moment, shrugs. 'I guess I do mean paintings and drawings and things ...'

'So?' she raises her eyebrows, her composure quickly recovered.

'So.' He laughs aloud at the irony of the conversational cycle—here they are back where they started—but now she's got him on the back foot, somehow.

'So. I'm going to an exhibition after work—it's my own work, actually—mine and a friend's—and then out for drinks. And I just thought, well, seeing as you like "drawing and paintings and things", that you might like to come.'

'Mmmm. I don't know.' She hesitates, leans back, closes her eyes as if thinking hard—she's not quite ready to let this encounter go its own way, that wouldn't do. Not yet.

'It's your work, you say. Are you any good?'

'A genius, actually.' A statement: dry, unironic, unhesitating.

Her eyes widen. 'Right. You're a genius.' Now it's her turn to laugh. 'A certifiable loon, more like.'

He gives in; gives her what she wants. 'Actually—even if you don't ... even if you've no interest whatsoever—I'd still ... I'd like you to come.' He's no good at this, at playing a part—it requires too much effort and he's happiest, most himself, when he's being forthright, honest.

She drops her cigarette, gives a soft slow smile.

'I'll meet you,' she says, 'after work.' She doesn't wait for a reply, turns her back on him and heads back into the drafting room.

She can feel his eyes on her and knows that he's taking in all that she's offering—the rustle of her silk-clad legs against her skirt, the soft click clack of her heels, the easy swaying of her hips, the shoulders squared, the head held high, the dark hair with its casual swing. She can see him, a brooding Clark Gable to her sultry Joan Crawford, lighting another cigarette. She wonders whether he even knows her name. It's not important—after all, he will. He will.

She had expected—she doesn't quite know what. She has only ever been to an art gallery on school visits—and that was the National Gallery—the grand edifice, the monumental space, the gilt frames, the muffled footsteps, the voices hushed and reverential. And the paintings themselves—if not recognisable, at least memorable, and a few works at least—the Lindsays, Streetons, Roberts, McCubbins—familiar. She can remember her delight at finding a particular familiar, an old favourite, exhibited there. Her mother had a large reproduction of Poynter's *Visit of the Queen of Sheba to King Solomon* displayed in pride of place above their fireplace, and it was a great thrill—like some sort of personal communication—to discover it, so huge, so sumptuous, hung right there in the gallery in all its original neo-classical splendour.

So she had expected something else: certainly not this cramped dark space.

Annie had met him as agreed. She had been twenty minutes late (of course!) and Ed had been impatient, indifferent to her not-terribly-sincere apology, had hurried her along unfamiliar back streets, through narrow lanes crammed with run-down terraces, dusty streets populated by kids playing cricket barefoot. They had walked for what had seemed miles—speaking only sporadically at first and then, after he had replied brusquely and in the negative to her request that they take a cab, a tram, anything—not at all. She hadn't dressed for such an expedition—why would she?—and her heels were a little too high, her skirt a bit too tight, her shirt too close around the neck. She practically had to run to keep up with his long strides. She could feel herself reddening—with anger as much as exertion—what sort of a man was he to expect such a thing, this long tramp through this wilderness of slums?, and would have gladly turned back had she had any idea of where they were. But eventually, just as dusk was settling, they'd arrived. Arrived where? She still didn't know. They paused outside the doorway of what must have once been a corner shop, and Ed had straightened his tie, smoothed his hair, offered her a cigarette, which she coldly refused, then lit one for himself. They stood awkwardly on the pavement, Ed studiously ignoring Annie's pointed glare, her muttered complaints, until he ground his cigarette into the gutter. 'Come on then.' He grabbed her hand and pulled her through the doorway. It was not the hushed, well-lit, whitewashed space of her imagination, but a dark hallway opening to a dim cavern-like room, a room thronged with talking, smoking, drinking people, young, ill-dressed students in the main, all gathered in tight-knit groups, talking loudly, passionately, gesticulating wildly.

It takes her only a moment—barely a moment—to make some sense of what is going on. She might be unfamiliar with these particular people, this particular milieu, but Annie is expert in quickly dissecting a social scene, any social scene; has a highly calibrated sense of which way is up, so to speak, so all she needs are just those few seconds before entering to observe that all the groups are gathered at specific areas of the room, that the focal points of the conversations—and arguments, she would guess from the vehemence of some of the participants— are the artworks. The works themselves, numerous and diverse: sketches, oil-paintings, pastels, watercolours—are displayed higgledy-piggledy around the room, some framed and hung properly, others propped against the wall, leaning at dangerous angles with what can only be a contrived randomness.

She has no way of judging the artwork, though she can see that there's none of the glamour surrounding the *Queen of Sheba* in the work displayed here—no classical grandeur, no gilt; and the room itself is dark and dank and uninviting. But she is quick to judge the room's inhabitants, that's easy—the people are shabby, unappealing, there is an unmistakable air of poverty, of down-at-heelness—and, what's worse, a type of stolid earnestness that she cannot bear. Look: see that pale girl with spectacles, her laddered stockings sagging, her dress—which is not so bad itself, not the latest fashion, but not irredeemable either—worn without any sense of style, any attention to detail. It's as if she doesn't know, and doesn't care to know, about such things. The girl is speaking loudly—her voice a tiresome ee-ore—to a man of indeterminate age, or no, he's young, perhaps not even twenty, but the mistake is understandable, he holds a pipe—ugh!—and already there's a bald patch at the back of his crown. He slouches, narrow-shouldered, weedy, and nods—solemn, ponderous, intense—taking whatever the ghastly girl is saying so seriously, giving it a weight, a significance it surely doesn't deserve.

So she recognises instantly, instinctively, that there is nothing, and no one, of any interest to her, here—and Annie has resolved to say something cutting to her negligent escort, damn the consequences, *how dare he bring her to such a place!*—when she becomes aware that the crowd has suddenly quietened, that

there's a feeling of excitement, of anticipation in the room—
and that it's directed towards the two of them, still poised to
enter. More precisely, they're all—inconceivable as it may be
to her (this rude, raw boy?)—waiting for Ed. She turns to him,
bemused, a wry comment at the ready, but when she sees him
the words dissolve in her mouth. For just one moment his lean
face is transformed by an expression of wild triumph, almost
exultation, an expression that's so quickly concealed, replaced
by his customary dry calm, that she can't be sure that she really
saw anything. But now, for some reason she can never explain
to her own satisfaction, her irritation, her messed hair, grimy
face, aching feet, they're all forgotten; she has no intention of
leaving, no desire to be anywhere else but here.

Years later, asked to recall when it was that she was first seized
by the creative impulse that was to become such a driving force
in her life, she would choose not her first tentative attempts, nor
her first successful exhibition, no, she would fix on this specific
moment, the moment of entering that dark and shabby room.

And now he raises an eyebrow, she nods; he takes her arm,
ushers her before him—and with Ed grinning shyly behind
her, Annie enters the room. And from that moment she's a part
of it. And it's part of her.

She stays close to him that first night, stays close and quiet,
like a shadow. She realises almost instantly that her presence
barely registers. Other than a few thinly disguised attempts
by some of the women present to size her up, to place her, the
attention, the notice, is all for Ed. There's no doubt that he's
the bright and shining star in this particular firmament. It's the
art, she supposes. Half the works exhibited here tonight are
his—the other half belong to a bearded wild-eyed older man,
some sort of European, a Pole, a Slovak, she thinks, who is pretty soon roaring drunk and politely ignored. And even Annie
with her lack of artistic knowledge can see that his paintings
and sketches have a mysterious *something*. She can't understand
them—they don't correspond with any artworks she's ever seen

before, and don't often correspond with reality, but their stark simplicity provokes and holds her attention. The others assembled here are clearly in awe of the work. She hears snatches of their conversations—most of it is dry academic waffle that she can't understand, but what's clear is the admiration, adulation and, in some cases, reverence. And it's not just the art: there's something physically compelling about this man, so very different to the other men—unmistakably city men—in the room. She enjoys looking at him, watching him: the way he'll light a cigarette and then, overtaken by the conversation, let it dangle, unsmoked, from his bottom lip, his eyes narrowed to avoid the smoke. The casual way he rolls up his sleeves, revealing his sinewy forearms, artist's forearms, the golden hairs glinting. And the way he speaks, a little too slowly—as if he's considering every word—the slight country drawl. He's raw and tough and dangerous and she can see that the women all like him; she recognises the subtle signs: cheeks are pinker, chests push out a little, backs straighten, they stand a little closer than is really appropriate when they talk to him. But she's surprised that he seems just as popular among the men: voices are louder, deeper, there's more backslapping, and there's a subtle jostling to gather round him, to be in his presence.

He barely speaks to Annie all evening. The conversation revolves around his work, and art-school gossip—but she knows that his attention is never far away. He is considerate, lights her cigarettes, makes sure that her glass is filled with the rough red wine that seems to be the only drink available, and every now and then his eyes lock with hers, and he gives a sly smile as if he's laughing at himself even as he glories in all the attention. So she is happy to stay close by, knowing that her being there, being part of it means something, for whatever reason, to this man she still barely knows. To both of them.

Towards the end of the evening—she has been there almost two hours, is beginning to droop a little, is looking forward to the promised dinner—an older couple arrives. They provide quite a contrast to the rest of the assembled company; in their thirties rather than their twenties, they are neither impoverished students nor teachers. They are very obviously well-heeled. The woman, though not what Annie would regard as good looking—she is too old, too unadorned, her face too long—is nevertheless striking, dressed expensively and stylishly in a simple silvery sheath with a single strand of pearls around her neck. The man is darkly good looking—a thinner, darker Ronald Coleman—and like the woman he is dressed well—a little too well, in a style that most of the men she knows would scorn—a white dinner jacket, white shirt, a peacock-blue silk cummerbund around his slim waist. The couple are obviously on their way to a dinner engagement—the sort of dinner engagement that Annie has only ever dreamt about.

The woman rushes straight over to Ed, the tight circle that surrounds him dispersing mysteriously, while the man wanders over to a smaller group gathered around one of the paintings.

'Dear Edward, Eddie.' She kisses him on the cheek, takes his arm. Her voice is breathy, her accent cultivated: to Annie, she sounds English. 'We can't stay, you know that, we've promised to go to this do at the National,' she gives a slight moue of distaste, 'but we so wanted to see you here'—she waves her arm about vaguely, taking in their unsavoury surrounds—'with all your work around you. We were down earlier, of course—did you know we helped Wolinski hang them? I hope you're happy with the arrangement. Anyway, we just wanted to congratulate you. When we saw them all together this afternoon, I realised again ...' her eyes are bright suddenly, as if with tears, 'well, you know what I think already, Ed. They're magnificent!' She pauses to survey the room, only now taking in the crowded space. 'And we managed to get Eric Rogers to come, you know, that young art critic at the *Herald*. Paul talked him into bringing along a photographer, too—and, well, he was just astounded. He says there'll be a piece in Friday's paper. And he said, that if word gets about,' her eyes widen dramatically, 'you might even get a visit from the police.'

Ed splutters at this. 'God Jules, I can't imagine they'll be interested in anything we've got down here.'

Her companion, who has moved close enough to overhear their exchange, remarks dryly: 'I think the only vaguely suggestive work here is that cubist nude of Wolinski's—which you'd have to concede is barely recognisably human. And I'd defy anyone to confidently describe Ed's subjects, let alone find anything indecent—what looks like a breast is just as likely to turn out to be a garbage bin. I imagine the only people who'll find anything terribly objectionable here are the worthies we're off to dinner with now.'

The two men greet each other, the older man pulling the younger to him for a second in a brief, fatherly hug. The woman sighs and rolls her eyes theatrically, moves away to examine one of the paintings. Annie, at a loss suddenly, wanders over to stand beside her, trying hard to think of something clever, something significant to say, for some way to make herself known to this glamorous creature, who is just the sort of woman one would expect—would hope!—to meet at an art exhibition. And her name—so sparklingly appropriate, perhaps she's misheard, misunderstood: Jewel. 'They're just marvellous, aren't they,' the woman looks away from the painting for a moment, speaks in a hushed voice. 'I've been to all the major European galleries, I've seen the works of the old masters, and the new—and I'm not, I'm really not exaggerating when I say that standing in front of one of Ed's works—well—it gives me the same feeling as when I stand in front of a Rembrandt, or a Cézanne. Spiritual, almost divine.' She gives a little shudder, and turns back to the painting. Annie tries hard, but she can't suppress the giggle that this comment provokes. It's too absurd—the work they're considering seems particularly slight, undistinguished, looks to her like nothing more than a half dozen wavy black lines on a pale blue background. Hardly a master work. And hardly worth trembling before. The woman turns back to her in surprise, 'I'm sorry. Are you laughing at me? I hadn't realised I'd said anything the least bit funny.'

Annie is giggling openly now. She takes a deep breath, tries to calm herself, mortified, but is unable to control the bubbling laughter. 'Oh dear. I am sorry, I really am, it's just that ...'

She's saved by Ed, who's somehow there beside her, 'It's just that this painting's been hung upside down.' He takes it down, expertly rearranges the wire at the back, re-hangs.

'Look here, you silly bastards,' Ed stands back, arms folded, his face a picture of satisfaction, 'Now, *that's* a masterpiece.' He nudges Annie gently in the ribs, 'That should wipe that big fat smile off your face, girly.'

The painting's subject is still no clearer, the painting seems no more impressive, but she's grateful for this intervention. She arranges her face into the appropriately solemn expression. 'It's the work of a genius,' she says, not believing a word of it. 'No doubt about that.'

When they finally stumble out into the night she's drunk so much of the red wine, and on an empty stomach, that she's barely capable of walking to the end of the block, let alone all the way home. Ed—who's not much better—whips off his coat and makes her a comfortable seat in the gutter while he runs to the nearest crossroad to whistle down a taxi.

In the cab she leans against him, rests her head against his chest, pulls his arm around her. 'So where are we going, genius boy?' Her voice is slurred, sleepy. 'You said you were going to take me out to dinner—but I think it might be a bit late for that.'

'I guess I should just get you home, then. Whereabouts do you live?'

Annie gives her address.

Despite her sodden state, she can hear the disappointment in his voice—knows that he'd like this night of triumph to go on a little bit longer; knows exactly which direction he'd like it to take. She says nothing, yet, just sighs and snuggles a little bit closer. She's not quite ready to end the night either. She gives him a little hint: slides her hand over his; moves it down to her knee, up under her skirt, then nudges it a little, releases her grip. He is hesitant without her guidance, but she nestles even closer and his hand moves further, just slightly, but far enough, of its own volition.

'Why don't we,' she speaks now, her voice soft, but all the sleepiness, all the slurring suddenly gone, 'why don't we both go back to my place?' She lets her fingers climb, teasingly, playfully, along his thigh. 'I live with my aunt, but she won't mind.'

'Sounds good,' Ed's voice crackles, he swallows, gives a small moan. 'Why not.' Then, inexplicably, he's pushing her away from him gently, and sitting up, straightening his tie.

He clears his throat. 'There's just one little problem.' He's sitting primly, all larking abruptly at an end.

'What sort of a problem?' She imagines a waiting landlady, a mother, a wife. Nothing that can't be easily overcome or just as easily ignored.

'It's just that I don't ...'

'What?' She's impatient to resume, squirms across the seat.

'I don't even know your name.'

You know what's going to happen next, don't you?

It should be pointed out, however, that in 1938, the year Ed and Annie first met, nice girls didn't have sex before marriage— and good boys didn't expect them to. Not without certain iron-clad guarantees, parents consulted, rings bought, date set, cake on order. But Annie was never a nice girl, was she? She never even pretended to be. Ed'll have learnt more than her name by the end of the evening. They'll pay off the taxi driver, stumble up the stairs to Lucille's flat, creep through the dark hallway into Annie's bedroom, close the door quietly ... And it's probably just as well to leave this scene here, now. To pull a curtain across. Avert your gaze. There are limits, even to the imagination; and these *are* your parents, after all.

What do they say to one another, during those first days and nights that they spend together? It's hard to imagine, hard to recall really, what lovers ever say to one another during those first moments, first days. And it's as much physical as spoken—lives given and told as much by touch and feel, by the body's give and take, as by actual words. What's said is simultaneously banal and profound—and doesn't bear repeating. The story of their two young lives; their hopes and fears and dreams and aspirations.

Annie will have told Ed the story of her upbringing: you can imagine her telling the tale, the quicksilver wit, the cruel but clever mimicry of her mother, of the stolid Norman and obedient Alice. She'll tell of her mother's despair over the teenage Annie's appearance: her indecently seamed stockings, her oxblood-coloured lips, her long scarlet fingernails, enamelled toes, drawn-on eyebrows, the dresses that were no longer demure: 'Oh, Annie, Annie,' (Annie would do a fair interpretation of her mother's too-carefully rounded vowels, her pursed lips). 'It's just so terribly common; it's not *naice*.' She'll have told the story, too, her eyes wide, glittering with unshed tears, of her father and his thwarted musical genius. He'd been a bright boy and after the war had trained for the law, worked as a suburban solicitor, but what he'd wanted most was to be a musician. He had played the violin, and had a voice—he was a tenor—'like an angel,' sighed Annie, though in truth she could barely remember him singing. But his wife had (and here she is perhaps embellishing, or even repeating something that her aunt, no ally of her mother, has told her), his wife—ambitious, unimaginative, grasping—had destroyed all his dreams, had insisted that he concentrate on his business, give up any musical ambitions, and had, of course, driven him—an alcoholic, a gambler, a hollow wreck of a man by then—to an early grave. Oh, how Annie had loved him, her old man, and how different her life would have been if only he had lived.

Ed will have told her the uncomplicated story of his life so far: he's a country boy, brought up in the outback, on a station 100 miles northwest of a small town called Boolah. Ed's artistic talent had been evident from an early age—an unlooked-for aptitude in a family as dry and worn as the land they tended. He had resisted all claims on him to take over his father's work, had left that thankless hard graft to his brother, and escaped to Sydney—not quite with his parents' blessing, but with their resigned acceptance. The apprenticeship at Cartwright's studio had been arranged by an art teacher who'd seen his drawings at a local exhibition, and for the past five years he'd done little else but work and paint—attending art classes at night—and had won numerous prizes, and been shown in several joint exhibitions. But his greatest stroke of luck, as he sees it, was his meeting the Hollands—Jules and Paul—the couple who'd arrived late at the gallery. He was only eighteen, the rawest bumpkin imaginable, he tells Annie modestly, when he first met Jules and Paul. They'd championed him from the first, and every opportunity since had been provided by them. They were like surrogate parents, he said, no, more like fairy godparents— they were unbelievably wealthy, he told her, and poured much of that wealth into supporting their favoured artists, buying their work, promoting them, arranging exhibitions, supplying contacts. They even had a studio, built especially on their acre- age at Avalon, to accommodate impecunious artists like him, for months at a time. He tells her names that she doesn't rec- ognise now, but will, one day—Prescott, Boyle, Frane, Rayson, Tebbut, Wilson—they'd all had the benefit of time at Holland House as it was called—and from the loans and stipends that the Hollands granted, much like the artistic patrons of Europe. The Hollands had introduced Ed to a world he'd never imag- ined—not just the world of art, but the world of literature, of philosophy, the world of the intellect. They had opened up the universe in ways he had never anticipated, never foreseen.

Eventually Annie switches off—shuts him up with her hands, with her mouth. She wants Ed's focus back on her. She has listened long enough; has heard all she wants to hear, knows all she needs to know. Enough, for now.

He takes her up to Avalon to visit Jules and Paul just a few weeks after the exhibition. They've spent practically every night together since then. Ed has only been back to his Surry Hills room for his clothes and materials, Annie's Aunt Lucille—having her own fish to fry—being quite unconcerned by his overnight stays. They take no notice of office gossip; walk to and from work together, eat their lunch in one another's company, visit galleries, pubs, attend the rowdy meetings of the newly formed Modern Art Society together. Annie is introduced to all his mates—an interesting if motley assortment of the usual bohemian types: aspiring artists, poets, philosophers, musicians, the odd journalist. They're not the sort of people Annie's used to associating with, but she very quickly finds herself in her element among them. They appreciate all the characteristics that have, previously, caused her trouble, made her unpopular. She feels at home, comfortable, somehow, amongst these larrikin men at the margins of polite society, and they return her approbation, admiring Annie's quick wit, her sometimes vicious humour, her frank observations, her loudly voiced—and frequently wrongheaded—convictions, her obvious delight in her own appeal. Though these are overwhelmingly masculine gatherings, occasionally the men will be accompanied by a woman. Sometimes they're whores who don't take too much notice of Annie, who is nevertheless fascinated by them, but every now and then a respectable girl will join them at their regular table—an insistent fiancée, or one of the more pushy female students—and almost immediately Annie will feel the ooze of disapproval, the ill-disguised antagonism. She has no idea what she does to provoke such a reaction from women, but she can never resist the impulse to make matters worse, to lead the other woman right up to the brink of battle.

So she's prepared, when Ed takes her down to visit the Hollands, to encounter more such hostility. She's met Jules before, of course, and guesses that laughing at Ed's work wasn't really the most auspicious beginning to a long and fruitful friendship, but surprisingly, that's all been forgotten—or perhaps forgiven. Jules doesn't mention their previous encounter and greets Annie warmly, with a friendly hug, as if they're old friends. She links her arm through Annie's, taking her on a tour of the house, showing her the cottage, the carefully tended kitchen garden, while the men conduct some sort of business in Paul's office.

Annie's impressed by the stone house—just as she was impressed by the sleek luxury of the Daimler, just as she was impressed by Paul's expert driving, his extreme courteousness, his urbane conversation; just as she's impressed now by Jules's expensively simple crepe pantsuit, the eclectic mix of antique and ultra-moderne furniture, the casual untidiness of the stylish home. She's had no experience, really, of people with money. There'd been one or two girls at her school, but their riches had been somewhat crude, nouveau—and most of the other students had been stolidly middle class. There'd been none of this ease, this expectation of excellence, this elusive element of distinction that she can feel, that she can almost smell, practically taste. There are generations of money here. The Hollands are unselfconscious, unapologetic about their status, but not flashy or snobbish, or, God help them, pretentious. She imagines them as the sort of people who have never experienced anything—possessions or people—considered second-rate, or even ordinary.

She's impressed too by the hospitality and generosity of the older couple: when they sit down to lunch and Annie compliments Jules on one of the dishes, a veal ragout, Jules is up straight away, donning her spectacles, locating a pencil, a notebook, laboriously writing the recipe out for her—with no thought as to this kind act being a complete waste of time, as Annie can scarcely boil an egg. When Ed professes an interest in reading T.S. Eliot's *The Waste Land*, Paul insists that he take his copy, a first edition, which is a collector's item, already valuable. They are so enthusiastic, so set on sharing everything, not just material possessions, their home, food, wine, belongings; but their knowledge, their ideas, their passions.

Most of the conversation at the table revolves around Ed's art: despite its insalubrious location, the recent exhibition has been a minor success. It had been reviewed scathingly in several newspapers, but was given a glowing report in the prestigious *Australian Art* journal, with Ed being hailed as the Sydney avant-garde's bright shiny hope—an antipodean Cézanne who will provide a necessary bridge between modern artists and the academy. More than half of the works have been sold, with two taken by the National, and Jules and Paul have decided that they will purchase the rest—no, not because they are trying to help him out, Jules pats his hand reassuringly, but because they just know, they are certain that the work will one day be priceless. Ultimately the purchase will be as great a benefit to them as to Ed himself. And of course, he has exhibition rights—whenever, wherever he needs them, they're his. Ed has already discussed all this with Paul, earlier, and Paul has written him a cheque for the total—a substantial sum, enough for Ed to think about leaving his job at the studio—but even more than the money he is pleased to have his success, evidence of his growing reputation, alluded to in Annie's still vaguely sceptical presence.

So there's a toast—with very good champagne—to Ed's continued success; to the future, and Annie feels herself to be included, warmly incorporated into their predictions and prognostications of greater things to come, and part of a circle of like-minded, exceptional beings. She knows that in similar situations—thrown in the deep end into a milieu she has no real understanding of, amongst her 'betters', to be crude, she could just as easily have felt resentful, felt her ignorance and inferiority keenly and spiked her conversation accordingly, but somehow, here, now, with these people, she feels herself expanding, as if to fill their expectations. Initially she stays quiet, smiles and listens, laughs at the appropriate moment, but soon enough she finds herself contributing to the conversation: when they talk about art her comments are intelligent, admitting her lack of knowledge gracefully, but remaining open, inquisitive; and when the topic switches to literature and then politics she finds herself genuinely interested and eager to understand what's being discussed. And in her characteristic way, she's soaking it all up quickly—she'll read the books they're recommending, take an interest in what's going on around her, she'll view the world differently, try and see the world the way *they* see it. She wants to be like them; to be a part of their world, to *be* them.

Annie and Jules are in the kitchen, clearing up, making coffee, while the two men sit out on the patio with port and cigars.

'So Annie,' Jules scrapes the plates carefully into a bucket beside the sink, piles them ready for washing, 'Ed says you work at Cartwright's with him. Are you one of the ... er ... secretaries?'

'Oh, God no.' Annie laughs, 'I'd be a rotten secretary. I'm in the art room.'

'No. Somehow I can't imagine you in a typing pool.' Jules pauses in her scraping, looks at Annie consideringly and for longer than Annie, setting out cups and spoons on a tray, finds comfortable.

'You're far too pretty for typing. And far too clever. All the other girls would hate you.'

Annie's not quite sure whether she should be flattered or insulted, isn't sure how to reply, but the other woman asks brusquely before she can formulate an answer: 'Have you any talent?'

'Any talent?'

'Well, you're in the art room—so surely you must be able to draw a *little*.'

'Oh. Well, it's all very basic ...' she flounders, 'and really it's just copying—and sometimes tracing—so you don't need any actual talent. Really,' she adds modestly, 'any twelve-year-old could do it just as well as most of us.'

Jules laughs at this. 'And you're not so far away from being twelve yourself, are you dear?'

'What do you mean?' Annie quickly provides herself with several additional years. 'I'm almost twenty-one.'

Jules appears to take her at her word. 'Goodness. Twenty-one. You barely look sixteen.' Sighs. 'I must be getting old. Everyone under thirty looks like a child.'

Now it's Annie's turn to be confused, 'But surely you're not so terribly old. How old are you?'

'Oh, disgracefully old, Annie dear. Ancient.' She hobbles theatrically to the coffee bubbling on the stove, says with a quaver in her voice, 'I'm about to turn forty, you know.'

'Oh, dear.' Annie nods seriously, 'yes, I can understand your worry. That is quite ancient.' She takes in Jules's appalled expression, adds, her eyes wide, innocent, 'but I'd never have guessed—you don't look a day older than, oh, thirty-eight. Really.' She grins.

'Oh.' They're both laughing now. 'Ed warned us that you were quite wicked. And I suppose I should have realised when you were so scathing of Ed's painting that you weren't some starry-eyed art student.'

Annie tries to deflect the conversation, 'No, I'm certainly not starry-eyed, but I'm not really so scathing ...'

But there's no need, Jules has embarked on her own conversational tangent, and interrupts: 'You know, I had my doubts. When I first saw you I thought you were just—well to be honest, Annie, I thought you were just some tart that Ed had picked up. Pretty enough, but dumb. And I wouldn't have blamed him. Men like Ed sometimes need women like you, like that, I mean. As a foil, I suppose, or to be perfectly frank, just for the sexual release. Artistic vision goes hand in hand with an extraordinarily strong sexual drive, in my experience. But I can see—watching you both today, that there's something more, isn't there? There's something big between the two of you—something *real*?'

Annie is shocked, can only nod.

'Well, I don't know if it's what I would have chosen at this early point in Ed's career—it's probably the last thing, the worst thing, right now. For Ed to be tied down, hemmed in in any way, I mean. But I don't get to choose, do I?' She smiles then and Annie is not sure whether it's a friendly smile, or grim, resigned, pained—it's always hard to tell with Jules. 'But I do think we're going to be friends, Annie,' she takes Annie's hand, then pulls her close, lowers her voice, 'good friends. I don't think, if we're to help Ed fulfil his potential, his destiny, that we'll have any choice.'

It's only later, insomniac beside a snoring Ed, that Annie stops to wonder why these people have so much say over Ed, why they're so concerned. She wonders whether it's a little strange, wonders whether they might not be a little mad, wonders whether Ed himself has thought deeply into what he's accepting along with their money, their patronage. What they'll expect in return for helping him to fulfil his glorious potential, *his destiny*. His soul? There's no such thing as a free meal, her mother always says, and for once Annie thinks she's probably right.

But she's excited, nonetheless, about her part in all this—that she's even being considered a part of this golden being's manifest destiny. It'll be a little while yet before Annie starts to consider herself as a being with a destiny that's quite distinct from Ed's. As a being entitled to her own.

She complains about the way he draws her.

Annie's been sitting naked on her dusty bedroom floor, a sheet draped around one shoulder, but not so that it's hiding anything. It's just to add some additional interest along the diagonal, and to keep her back warm. She's been holding the awkward position for what seems like hours. Finally, though, she has had enough.

'Okay. That's it, Ed.' She ignores his protests, his requests for just five more minutes and stands up, winding the sheet around her like an Indian sari. She wafts over to see what he's sketched. Her eyes widen at the sight of it, and she pulls the sketchbook out of his hands, appalled by what he's done.

'Oh, Ed. It's awful.' She turns it this way and that, peers closely at the page, then moves it away, squinting. 'It doesn't look like anything. It certainly doesn't look like me. What on earth are you trying to do?'

Ed pulls the book back. Speaks through gritted teeth.

'Listen. I keep explaining that I'm not drawing *you*. You have to understand that it's not supposed to be an exact representation. It's your form I'm after.'

She rolls her eyes, 'I know what my form is, Ed, and this is not it. My form has arms, legs, a head, breasts, an arse ...'

'I don't mean that—it's not the actual parts, but more the essence of your physical being ... It's not about what you look like—it's ...'

'Oh, for God's sake.' She pulls the charcoal from his fingers, puts it between her teeth, and starts unbuttoning his fly. 'Annie. Really, I'm not in the right state ...' but there's nothing erotic in the way she's pulling on his trousers, and now she's begun on his shirt.

'Annie?' His state, heedless of her intentions, has changed rather dramatically.

'Listen, genius. I've had more than enough of this. You get your daks off and sit over there. No, you're not leaving them on—you can take everything off. Like me. Now *you* pose—do exactly as I tell you. And I'll draw you.'

It's no masterpiece—she never claims that, though she treasures this sketch—in fact it's nothing special to look at, merely a rather laboured charcoal drawing on butcher's paper. An almost recognisable young Ed, looking vaguely miserable, no doubt highly embarrassed to be captured like this—forced into a position that no man (and no self-respecting artiste!) would ever assume voluntarily. Naked and vulnerable, sitting spread-eagled, one hand (intentionally blurred—so difficult to get those digits right) holding his erect (and very precisely delineated) cock, the other clenched atop his hairy thigh. It's all a little out of kilter, the perspective skewed, the proportions not quite right, the chiaroscuro (so despised by Ed) slightly overdone.

Annie had thought she would achieve nothing more significant than the tedious copying and drafting that she does at work, but this work is different, alive somehow, and she hands it over to Ed with a flourish, her cheeks pink, eyes bright. It's raw, but it's lively, vital, and it's not bad for a first attempt—and Ed (once he recovers his composure) is the first to concede it. Annie might not be brilliant—but she's got *something*.

You wonder, now, what Ed's initial reaction really was. Legend has it that it was Ed who discovered, encouraged, and nurtured Annie's talent—that he recognised Annie's artistic potential almost immediately. That he encouraged her to enrol in those notorious night classes run by the infamous Clarrie Howe; that she was his constant—and vocal and contentious and divisive—companion at every meeting of the Modern Art Society; that he directed her first experimental works; that he was as essential to her receiving the recognition she so craved, as he was to her development.

Ed's legendary generosity towards Annie is made all the more poignant by knowledge of her later betrayal. But surely this story of his fostering of her talent, his unstinting promotion of her artistic career, is rather too convenient—and you wonder whether it might not be a post-betrayal invention. You wonder if Ed wasn't, in fact, rather disappointed to find that this wild un-selfconscious girl was, after all, not so different to the hordes of art-school girls he already knew; a little put out to discover that she too had latent creative powers, that she might one day have artistic aspirations (if not ability) to equal his, that perhaps she wasn't content to be just his girl. Perhaps he thought it was a bit of a nuisance: after all, women were meant to be muses, models, providers of sustenance, succour, sex—what fellow wants to battle his girl over paint, canvas, studio space, reputation?

But perhaps you should give him some latitude, a little credit for disinterested generosity. It's too easy to forget, isn't it, the heady but straightforward affection that exists only at the very beginning of a love affair? Before the doubts, the deceptions, the bitterness, the inglorious denouement. Perhaps Ed was excited by the thought of this girl being able to fully share in his life of art—to think that he'd at last found a partner who might one day share, or at least understand, his scarcely articulated, most cherished dreams. A soulmate. Perhaps when he looked at that crude drawing he felt simple uncomplicated pleasure, unadulterated by envy, the conviction that he'd found the one: that together they could, they would, set forth and conquer the world.

They marry early in 1940. Neither family is invited to the wedding. Annie's mother has visited once, has called into the Newtown flat six months earlier—unexpected and unwelcome. This will be one of the last times Annie ever sees her mother.

It is late on a Sunday morning, past eleven and Annie is still in bed. She's alone, fortunately, when Lucille taps on her bedroom door and then opens it without waiting for a response.

'Annie,' she calls softly, as Annie, face still rosy with sleep, turns towards her. 'Annie, you'd better get up, lovey. It's Maud. It's your mum. She wants to talk to you.'

'Mum?' Annie wonders whether her previously pleasant dream has moved into nightmare territory. 'Here?'

'Yes.' Lucille is mouthing words that Annie just can't quite make out, gesturing frantically, looking wildly around the room. 'What? What's wrong?' She thinks it must be bad news—there's been an accident, someone has died—she feels a fluttering, then, nothing. If her Mum has bad news it won't be about Ed, will it? It could be Alice or Norm, she supposes, but is shocked to find her heart rate settle. 'What is it, Cill? Don't stand there having kittens—just come in and tell me.'

Her aunt looks quickly behind her, then slips in through the door, closes it carefully. Hisses: 'She's found out, somehow, about Ed. She's, well, she's furious. She's been here for fifteen minutes, trying to get me to let her into your room. She's convinced he's in here, now. And she's been threatening to call the police—reckons I'm running a brothel—says she would never have entrusted me with your moral well-being if she'd known I was a—well a whore, basically.' She pulls Annie's silk dressing gown off the back of the door. 'Listen, get this on, and I'll let her in.' She tosses it over to Annie, who's sitting stunned, one leg dangling over the side of the bed, uncertain what to do next. 'Sorry, darl, but it's the only thing that'll satisfy her. There's nothing here of his, is there? Nothing of Ed's? You'll catch it—we'll both catch it—if there is.'

Annie gets up, scouts the room for incriminating evidence. She shoves a pair of Ed's trousers into her wardrobe, a shirt, then thinks for a moment and pulls them back out again, her face breaking into a smile. She drapes the shirt over a chair, positions it carefully. Throws the trousers on the floor. She gets down on her hands and knees, finds a pair of Ed's shoes, his socks, pushes them conspicuously into view. Rummages on the desk, finds his tie, slings it over the bedhead. She retrieves a couple of discarded pencil sketches that Ed has done of her, nudes, and arranges them so that they can be clearly seen from the door.

Annie takes off her slip, puts on the gown, but ties it loosely so that she's showing an indecent amount of cleavage, her naked thighs. She messes her hair, disarranges the bedclothes. She lights a cigarette and sits on the bed. She composes herself for a moment then grins at her bemused aunt, motions to Lucille to open the door. Lucille swings the door back, goes to sing out, but Annie's mother is standing there already, her black patent leather handbag clutched tight and held close to her chest, lips pursed in disapproval.

'Mother,' Annie accompanies her drawled greeting with a slow exhalation of cigarette smoke. 'What an early bird you are. Out before lunch on a Sunday. Why don't you come in?' Lucille takes the opportunity, slides out the door, squeezes past her gorgonic sister-in-law without meeting her eyes.

Her mother gazes around the room, taking it all in: the man's clothes, the stained and rumpled bedclothes, her daughter's déshabillé. 'You get yourself decent, miss, and I'll speak to you in the loungeroom. And you can put that disgusting thing out.' She goes to turn away, but Annie stops her.

'Mother. Mum. It seems to have escaped your notice, but this is my home, not yours. If you want to speak to me you can do it on my terms, not yours. Come in here, and sit down.' She pats the bed beside her, notes with pleasure her mother's look of revulsion, her obvious disgust.

'I will *not* enter that room.' Her mother's lips barely move. 'You come out here, young lady. You do as you're told.'

'There's no point, Mum,' Annie's voice is as breezy as she can make it; she might be discussing the weather, a trip to the seaside. She gives a friendly smile, holds out her hand. 'Why don't you come over here and chat. We have so much to talk about, you and I.' She gives her mother a sly wink, pats the bed again invitingly. 'Two women of the world.'

Her mother's face is pale, her hands are shaking. She seems to be shrinking.

'I had never ever thought to see … my own daughter. No better than a common whore.' She pauses, takes a breath. 'Well, don't you think you can come running back to me when it all turns bad, Annie Swift.' She clears her throat. 'From now on in you're nothing to me. Nothing.' She turns, heads back down the hallway, brushing past Lucille without any acknowledgement. She opens the door, steps through, stops, turns back. Then, standing straight, her voice loud and clear, vowels rounded, clearly enunciated: 'Your poor dear father, poor poor Herbert. He'll be turning in his grave. His baby daughter,' her voice breaks, 'a whore.'

She doesn't wait for a response, exits, slamming the door hard.

Annie moves suddenly, takes hold of the nearest solid object, a green glazed vase of tulips that she was sketching the week before. She's down the hall, fast as a whip, wrenches open the door, runs out onto the landing. Her mother is clipping down the stairs at a furious pace. Annie stands at the top of the staircase, takes aim, and throws the vase as hard as she can, just missing her target, but spraying her horrified mother with stagnant water and half-dead flowers. 'You bitch,' she yells. 'You cow. Don't you dare. Don't you dare bring Daddy into this. And you know what—I'd rather be a whore any day, than a fucking murderer like you.'

So, at the wedding, there's no family. Annie hasn't bothered about Alice and Norm, she knows she'll have been written out of their dreary lives too—Alice plainer than ever, married to a suburban schoolteacher ten years her senior, pregnant with her second child, Norm still and forever his mother's good boy—living at home, balding, insufferably complacent. Ed has not informed his parents or siblings of his impending nuptials, either, hasn't yet told them of Annie's existence. He's rarely in contact with them, has seen his parents only twice since he left home. Oh, he sends a postcard occasionally, with a brief un-informative message scrawled in pencil—*Dear Mum and Dad, everything's good here, they're working me hard at the studio. Guess you'll be in the thick of the shearing soon. All best, Ed.*

What are the stories you've heard about their marriage? That like so many of their generation, fearing what the war would bring, they'd married quickly, without too much thought or preparation. Only a few blurred snaps survive, but you know them well. There's one of the four of them, standing together outside the central registry office. Annie and Ed, looking ab-surdly young, in the centre, Jules and Paul on either side. Annie is clutching an already wilting bunch of chrysanthemums, her dark brown hair uncharacteristically neat, those wide oxblood lips curved with a child's unqualified delight. But Annie is un-mistakably a woman: the dress has been cut to follow the curves of her hips, to accentuate the small waist, to reveal a little more of that pert bosom than is strictly modest. And there's the way she's leaning ever-so-deliberately against her new husband, as if claiming him: she's a woman all right. Ed looks slightly self-conscious, but regardless, handsome, happy. Proud.

It's only six months since war was declared but already it's begun to bite in little ways: already there are shortages, and even essential items are suddenly difficult to find and discouragingly expensive. Everything's makeshift; done on the cheap. Annie's dress has been recycled from some old figured silk curtains that belonged to Jules; her hat is one she's worn for years, the felt brushed, made more exotic with some strategically placed feathers. Ed's suit is an old one of Paul's—a little tight across the shoulders, the arms slightly too short; his shoes are just his ancient work boots, polished, the spatters of paint carefully scraped and blacked.

Jules, regardless of any shortages, rationing, is as always beautifully turned out. There's nothing makeshift about her outfit, not a hair out of place, not a wrinkle in her simple crepe dress. Her shoes look new, her slim ankles accentuated by the extreme arch of the sole. These forties shoes (you recall dressing up in them as a child—you have a dim recollection of clacking about, feeling deliciously, perilously tall) always look slightly clumsy to you—a little Minnie Mouse, too solid, too heavy— but they're the latest thing, no doubt, and they're considerably more elegant, even you can tell this, than the shoes that Annie's wearing, with their sturdier heels, their scuffed toes. You wonder whether it was deliberate—Jules attempting to outdo the bride—but surely not, surely it's just the way it works. The monied always look better. Jules and Paul look the million pounds that they're worth; Ed and Annie—well, you don't see the money oozing off Annie and Ed, but what they have, what you see shimmering all about them, like a haze, like an aura, something that Jules and Paul can't have for all the money in the world, is their youth.

What fun it must have been to be Annie, then. Young, ambitious, feeling the intoxicating rush of early success, the heady burgeoning of reciprocated lust, love, whatever—of all the endless endless endless possibilities before her. Her unquenchable sense of entitlement. Her certainty that she will never ever be ordinary, be like them—ordinary people—caught up in the pointless round of day-to-day existence. No, her life will be different—larger, better—she has stepped outside the banal existence that she's seen offered, and she's not—ever—going to step back in.

But you, writing it all down in the future. You can see it differently: you may be writing a beginning, but you can't avoid it—you know where it's going to end. You wish you could somehow call out to her—to them—sound a warning. About what exactly, though? About time, about the way even seemingly limitless love can end, about the way ambition will eventually erode affection, about how, one day, all that was once so significant, once imperative, becomes as dust, as ashes? You can see the tragic end of it all—you know what's looming, what's ahead of them. Not the war—although that's hardship enough certainly, and they'll both be touched, like everyone else they'll be changed forever by the events of the next five years or so— but beyond that they have their own individual measure of hardship to survive: indifference, betrayal, abandonment, loneliness, death … it's there already, inevitable. It's already written, if only they knew—their future, your future, silently playing its perfect counterpoint to their present.

You know. But even if you could somehow warn them, they wouldn't listen, would they?

So, they're married. And for a while, for a short while, life goes on as before. Or as much as it can. Despite all their best efforts to dissuade him, Ed joins up. Paul knows a few 'high ups' in the ministry, is sure he could find him an agreeable civilian position, but his brother Albert joins the AIF, as do most of his old mates from Boolah, and Ed joins up before any strings can be pulled. Paul must know a few high ups in the AIF, too, because for some reason, Ed is pulled out of the unit he's been assigned to, just days before they're due to embark, much to his chagrin, and is sent up north, and put to work in an armaments store.

Jules can't persuade Annie to move in with them—she can have the cottage all to herself, they say, but Annie can't be shifted. The city's too exciting right now, and Avalon seems like the back of beyond; why, she may as well move out to Boolah! Anyway, her work at Cartwright's studio has been deemed essential; the studio has been co-opted by the war ministry, and they churn out posters and advice booklets and various bits of propaganda. Annie's missing Ed, of course, but most of the young women she knows are in the same boat, their men elsewhere. Somehow they manage to have their own fun, regardless. There's always something on somewhere—a dance to go to, a fundraiser, a dinner, an exhibition, and they're almost too busy to worry. Annie's still drawing, too, going to classes when she can—she can't get hold of any paints or canvases and doesn't really have time, but butcher's paper is still available, and Annie's often to be found, the centre of a gaggle of fascinated bystanders, cigarette in the corner of her mouth, sketching her impressions in charcoal, or sometimes in confident blue ink brushstrokes. She can't resist giving these works away to their subjects when requested, so very few survive. Eventually, as the war grinds on, Jules and Paul, feeling too removed from the centre, from the action, buy a row of Kings Cross terraces and move into one for the interim—offering Annie and Ed the second bedroom, for no rent, an offer that Annie somewhat reluctantly accepts.

Here's the story that Jules tells: it is during the war, when Annie is living with them. Ed is somewhere in the Territory, Jules and Paul are satisfied that their boy is well out of the way of danger. And this is when Jules and Annie's friendship really blossoms. It's a friendship that becomes, later, almost mythical. Paul's away much of the time too—working in intelligence, his work so hush-hush that even Jules doesn't know much about what he's doing—only that he's away a lot, travelling a week here, two weeks there, busy, important, making a contribution.

And so they're pretty much alone, the two of them, and thrown into one another's company, tentative and somewhat reluctant at first, they soon get to know one another well. They get so close that for just a little while they mean everything to one another—it's like a love affair in a way. They are closer even than sisters: unlike sisters, who grow up thinking that they know one another, they have to start from scratch.

Jules teaches Annie, little barbarian that she is, to cook. Every night they prepare something special with the available ingredients, their wartime allowance of food augmented by vegetables from their tiny kitchen garden; they set the table in the front room and share a bottle of wine from the cellar with their meal. Night after night in the dark, a ritual, they'd sit with just a candle or two, talking until late. They share their secrets, their disappointments, their desires. They tell each other everything.

They're sitting there in the front room, the room they've designated the dining room, that sort of formality still being appreciated. It's only early—just past seven—but already they're ever-so-slightly sloshed. They've eaten, but only lightly—an omelette, some cheese, tomato and onion doused in salt and white vinegar—Annie's favourite. It's not all that dark outside, it's early summer, but the room has been darkened according to the brownout regulations—sheets of heavy cardboard have been taped over the once pretty bay-window and the room is dim and close, lit by a single flickering candle. By all rights it should be claustrophobic, depressing—the cheap deal table, the rickety chairs that don't match, the gingham curtains valiantly attempting cheer, the general dinginess of the room—it's the sort of setting that might be used on stage or film for some dreary domestic family drama. But the two main players are not the types generally favoured by such fare: one young, rounded, darkly attractive, hair short and tousled, dark weary circles under her eye, leans back casually, her stockings pulled down, feet up on the chair opposite. The other, older, tall, angular, her dark blonde hair netted tidily, sits across from her, her cigarette burning away in the ashtray—reading aloud from a small book. It's a cosy scene, a scene set for confidences.

The younger woman listens intently as the older woman reads:

Beware of the literary spirit, which so often causes paint-
ing to deviate from its true path—the concrete study of na-
ture—to lose itself in intangible speculations ...

Literature expresses itself by abstractions, whereas
painting, by means of drawing and colour, gives concrete
shape to sensations and perceptions. One is neither too
scrupulous, nor too sincere, nor too submissive to nature,
but one is more or less master of one's model and, above all,
of the means of expression.

Get to the heart of what is before you and continue to
express yourself as logically as possible.

At this point the younger woman interrupts. 'Oh, yes, that's it, Jewel. That's the part. Ed and I had this *huge*, this ding-dong row about that sentence. I told him that last passage you read—that bit about getting to the heart of what is before you and expressing yourself logically, I told him it was utter nonsense. That it wasn't logical, that it made no sense when you tried to sort out what he's actually saying, what the words really mean. It means nothing. I quite understand—at least I think I do—what he's saying before that,' a light frown puckers her forehead, 'about the difference between art and literature, that's quite clear, but the next bit—what *is* he actually saying? When you get down to it he's not saying anything is he? It's really just the most complete flummery, don't you think? Anyway, I said this to Ed and he just about throttled me. He told me I was a fool, a philistine, that I didn't know the first thing about art, that I didn't have a creative bone in my body—and what Cézanne was saying there was the truest thing in that whole passage, and that I was just proving Cézanne's whole bloody point!' She sounds slightly indignant, but her mouth twitches with suppressed laughter, as if she's simultaneously appalled and amused by the memory.

The older woman is rereading the passage slowly and carefully.

'Well, I think I see what you mean, Annie. It's not quite as clear as it could be, is it? Perhaps it's a little ambiguous, a bit vague,' she adds doubtfully, 'but then it is only a letter.'

But Annie's not listening. 'Actually, it was more than a ding-dong row, Jules ... you remember those black eyes I had—I told you I opened a kitchen cupboard, hit my nose?'

Jules looks up at her quickly, her long face serious. 'Did Ed do that? Did he hit you?'

'Well, it wasn't quite that straightforward,' she sees the other's sceptical expression. 'No, really, Jules, he didn't punch me, it wasn't quite that drastic.'

'Well, what was it? Two black eyes seems pretty drastic to me, however, er, considerately administered.'

'Well, it all just got pretty wild, out of hand. We'd drunk two bottles of red between us, and we were talking—and arguing. I remember him telling me that I had no right to question any word that a man—a genius—like Cézanne had ever uttered—that basically Cézanne's shit had more art in it than anything I would ever be able to contribute.'

'Good grief. How unpleasant.'

'Anyway, I saw red, then—and said some terrible things.'

'What sort of things?'

'Oh, that he was a second-rate poseur, with delusions of grandeur, that he was a laughing-stock—that he wouldn't know real art if it fell on him—how would a boy from the outback have a clue of anything of that sort ... Anyway, you can imagine.'

'Yes,' Jules says wryly. 'I can.'

'So he tried very hard, poor fellow, but I just kept goading him, and I came closer and closer, until I was virtually shouting into his face,' she swallows, 'and eventually he, well, he grabbed me by the hair, and then pushed my face down against the table. Too hard. I hit my nose,' she looks up, embarrassed, rueful, 'and it started to bleed all over the place. It was ages, ages, before it stopped. And there was so much mess ... Ugh.' She shudders. 'Anyway, it frightened him, and then when my eyes went black—well, he was utterly ashamed.' She pauses. 'And I was frightened.'

Jules looks slightly sceptical, 'Oh, but, Annie, you have to admit ...'

'Oh, no—I wasn't afraid of him, of Ed. Not for a moment. But I was afraid—of myself—of what it was I wanted. You know, it was almost as if I *wanted* him to hit me.'

'Why ever would you want that? Why would anyone?' Jules is repelled, but nonetheless fascinated.

'I don't know Jules. I've been thinking about it a lot, since. And I really don't know. But I do know that when he finally lost his temper, when he put his fingers around the back of my neck, when he ground my face into the table, I was glad. In some horrible way I enjoyed it. I wanted it. And then I wanted more. And I was disappointed. I wanted him to take it further.' She shrugs, 'It's probably nothing. We were just drunk.'

There's a silence between the two women, not uncomfortable, but protracted. Jules tops up their glasses, Annie lights up a cigarette which they pass back and forth between them. Jules clears her throat. 'Maybe,' she drawls, 'Maybe it's just that you ...'

But Annie interrupts, says in a rush: 'Actually, I *do* know what it is, Jules. It's because he doesn't see me. I know that sounds awful, and I know he's wonderful and brave and intelligent and handsome and a bloody genius, and I know that half the women he knows, including you, would do anything to have him—'

Jules looks affronted, 'Oh, Annie, that's not true, I'm just very fond ...' but Annie waves her assurance away.

'No, it is true. I've always known it—and really it doesn't matter. Your secret's safe with me. But the thing is, Jules, you don't know him, not really. And I do. And he's got no space in him, not for anyone else, not really. He doesn't need anyone. Oh, I don't mean he doesn't love me—I'm sure he loves me in his own way. And I'm absolutely certain, as certain as a woman can be, that he'd be faithful. The thing is—I don't care. In some way I'd rather that he was unfaithful. All he really cares about is his art—everything else is just peripheral. Love, me, you, Paul, his friends, his family, we're not at the core of who he is. And that's what I wanted, Jules—I wanted to be at the centre, to make him really see me, *really* see me—even if that meant making him hate me. But you know,' she shrugs, gives a hard little laugh, 'it didn't make any difference. He gave himself a fright, we made up, but still, really, I could have been anyone—I'm just a release, a physical need satisfied. Other than that ...' she shrugs again.

'Oh, darling, I'm sure that's not true,' Jules takes her hand, strokes her arm with gentle fingers.

'No, it is. It's the truth. And I don't think it's something I can live with.'

'What do you mean?' For the first time Jules sounds startled, shocked. 'You can't leave him, Annie, just like that. It'll, well, it'll destroy him.'

'Hah!' her voice scornful. 'Don't believe that, Jules.'

'But what about *your* art, Annie? You're just getting somewhere. Doesn't that have its ... its consolations?'

'Art as consolation.' Annie sounds thoughtful. 'That's a funny way to describe it, don't you think, Jules? Nobody'd ever suggest that to Ed, would they? No, I don't think consolation's my thing, Jules. Art has to be a passion, surely, not a consolation.'

'You know darling, what you're feeling is perfectly normal. After a period all marriages feel like this—a little empty, a little flat—as if they've lost all their meaning. But you're so fortunate, Annie, you're both young and healthy, and ... well, there'll be children soon enough ...'

'Jules,' Annie is staring at her friend, astounded. 'You're not telling me that I should be having children as some sort of replacement for Ed's affection?'

'No. Yes. Oh, you're so young, Annie—you don't know what it's like to face the fact that you'll never—never be a mother.'

Jules's eyes well with tears, but Annie doesn't notice, says hotly: 'Young or not, Jules, I can tell you now that being a mother isn't one of my dreams. And I certainly don't want it as some sort of booby prize ...'

'Oh, but that's not ...'

'Jules, darling, I know you mean well, but ... I'm not going to miss out. I don't want consolation. I want life.'

So far you have had to rely on story and where that fails, imagination. But there are some scenes that you don't need to imagine: she has left proof, evidence, in writing. Letters. You're glad—these are the scenes you would never have wanted to write, that you would prefer not to have to think about, think *into*, too hard. They provide the part of the story that is most significant—and where, for you, the story ends. But you can leave this part to her—let her tell it herself, let her tell it her own way. In her own words.

July 3rd, 1945
Dearest Jewel,
Thank you for all the beautiful bits and bobs for the baby—
and for your visit which meant so much. They will let me
out of the hospital next week they say—the weakness from
the haemorrhaging should have passed. It is so silly, I am
as weak as a cat and all the other women here seem to be
up and about (which the matron here insists on) only a day
or two after the birth just as if nothing had ever happened
which seems ludicrous to me, as I have never experienced
ANYTHING as awful as that—had never even imagined
anything could be so dreadful. You should consider yourself
extremely lucky, dear J, that you will never have to under-
go such an ordeal—though I know you do not consider it a
matter of good fortune, believe me my dear it is. You can en-
joy all the pleasures of being a woman with a man without
ever fearing the consequences which are not, let me speak
bluntly here, so good. At the end of the nine months—I can-
not believe I have suffered the entire time!—of feeling seasick
and miserable all day (they say morning sickness, but it is
an all-day misery, truly without a moment's respite) and

then twenty-eight hours of the most complete and utter agony—I do not know why they didn't etherise me as I have heard it's quite common—but the matron here is a hard bitch, childless and no doubt certain that there is something character building in it. All that Jewel—for THIS. They had said that all would be well when the baby came, that it would all be worth it—and for most women perhaps it is. Or perhaps they are just not honest. But for me—nothing. No great surge of maternal love or instinct. Just the thought of this endless responsibility which I am not ready for. Just this mess of constant feeding, crying, changing ... I have not dared say a word of this to the nurses here (though thank God for them—if it were left up to me I'm afraid the poor infant would be in strife) or Ed—who is quite sentimental over the whole thing (good then, let him take care of her!) and certainly not to Mum, who visits every day (all is forgiven, for now!)—but I am sure she knows, I can see it in her expression—the way she is loath to hand over the baby for me to feed, and would do it herself if she could. My lack of proper maternal feeling for this baby is just one more way in which she can prove that I am a failure. But this is something I don't understand—this judgement from Mum, who as far as I can tell has never felt any maternal passion towards me, and if there is some terrible coldness at the heart of me it has to have come from her.

I am sorry to burden you with this, dear Jewel. I hope that you and Paul are well and happy—I cannot wait to see you both and only wish we could go back to those fun and carefree days—days that I did not appreciate, of course. It seems that one never does know when one is happy.

With all my love,
Your,
Annie

PS We have finally decided on a name. Ed has agreed to Zelda—reluctantly I might add. He favours the most dreary names: Jennifer, Susan, Barbara, Beverly, none of which I can stomach seeing that every second child you meet bears one of these names. So she is Zelda Caroline— for Ed's mum—Steele.

August 10th, 1945
Dear Jewel,
This morning the bath water I had prepared for the baby was too hot, so hot that I scalded her—and Ed had to take her to the hospital as there was nothing I could do to soothe her. She screamed and screamed and screamed and then I was screaming too, it was all I could do not to throw her out the window to stop the bloody row. I know how awful it must sound, but sometimes it seems a tragedy that she was ever born. I was not meant to be a mother dear J, and it is spoiling everything in my life right now. I can hardly bear to talk to Ed nor he to me even though he is only here for a few days' leave and when he has gone I know that I will be desperate to see him again and full of terrible fear that I will never see my poor boy again and that I will be stuck here forever with Zel and that I will never draw or paint or find that which I know is in me—IS ME—and what a loss. To not have lived the life that you know you could have lived. Oh, J. I do not think that I can take much more. I think sometimes that I should take her to Mum's, only that would be a cruelty I could not bear to inflict on any soul—perhaps I should wrap her up and leave her at the church door … she could not have a worse time of it even in an orphanage, I think. Only Ed would kill me, it is his daughter and that means something to him though it does not seem to mean that he will ever do anything for her or help me in any way that would count. For instance, take her out in a pram for an hour or so, or go to her in the middle of the night. He likes

to make sketches of her—he has done a good one of the two of us asleep—we look so peaceful, a perfect mother-and-baby pair, but it is all tosh with none of the real horror of the thing—the all-day feeding, the nappies, the washing and no sleep & not a minute of time to myself. It is like some terrible nightmare there's no waking up from. If I were to paint the landscape of my soul right now—if there was ever time for such luxury—it would resemble Hieronymus Bosch.

At a visit to the baby clinic last week (you see I do on occasion do the things I should) the other waiting mothers—all so neat and tidy and their hair done and collars starched—looked at me as if I was slightly mad when I said something about this whole thing being so difficult, why hadn't we been warned, that I would much much rather have had a puppy. They turned away disapproving as you can imagine and clutched their babies to them as if I was the bad witch at the christening, about to mutter my curse. This is how they keep us down, I said, what good are we, what changes can we make, what ripples in their murky waters if we are enslaved by this? They looked at me as if I were mad, but it is they who are mad, I think. I have tried to make a sketch, tried to capture their stunned complacency, but have not had time or opportunity to make anything more than the barest scratchings. There is just NO TIME, Jules, and yet somehow the days are endless.

You will have had more than enough of this whingeing I've no doubt so will stop now & thank you very much for the cheque and the beautiful little cardigan which the baby of course does not appreciate but that I do ... I hope that your garden is coming back to life after your long absence—I'm afraid I have not been able to do anything here, but the cabbages you and I put in last year have miraculously returned.
Your,
Annie

January 14th, 1946
Dear Ed,
It is no good. We—you and I—are no good. There are no recriminations from me—it is nothing you have done, and nothing you can fix, either. I know that you will have felt this coming for some time, that whatever it was that was between us is over, is only a stale memory of love, which is not something that will sustain us in the years ahead. I cannot explain what it is that has soured—it is not something that I can easily pinpoint—but I think that it is something in me, Ed, dear, that there is something in me that wants more than to be merely your wife, & mother of your child, which is the fate that I know will befall me if I do not do something now, before it is too late, before we have grown accustomed, and perhaps adapted to the blankness that is growing between us, which is what we have seen happen to so many people, and is not any way for a human to live a life—the REAL life that we have always said is the only LIFE WORTH LIVING. It will not be so hard now to start again, we are both young and still have our lives ahead of us. I wish you all the best and will always treasure the wonderful times that we had together and for all that you have shown and taught me which is more valuable than I can ever express.

With affection
Annie.

PS I have taken the baby to Jules and Paul.

PPS I am sorry but I have taken all your savings from the box at the bottom of your sock drawer. There was probably not so much as you thought as I have had to use it for expenses over the past few months.

January 18th, 1946
My darling Jewel,
I am truly sorry that I did not—I could not—stay to ex-
plain properly, and grateful that you took the baby with-
out question or hesitation. I could not have made any
explanation then, and even now it's difficult to put the—
desperation—of it all into words. Because the situation is
desperate—it could not really be worse—though perhaps
you will not think so. Perhaps you will think my actions
extreme and selfish, but all I can tell you is that it is neces-
sary for me to get away if I am to live and I cannot really
live if things continue the way they have been.

Oh, Jewel, for a while it seemed as if I was PART of
something bigger. To be young, to be beautiful, to have tal-
ent!—to be part of a movement of like-minded individuals.
It was as if my life was so full of possibilities. As if what I
did—who I was—might actually MEAN something in the
larger scheme. I was convinced I had found the way out of
what MOST women settle for. The lack of money, the un-
certainty of the future, none of it mattered. And then all of
a sudden I am <u>a mother</u>. Housebound. Ugly. Frumpy. Mis-
erable. Pathetic. Alone. In thrall to this being who I cannot
seem to love as I should. And Ed—Ed dashes in and out
of here when he's on leave. A cursory peck on the cheek, a
pat on the rump, I could be a sack of potatoes for all the in-
terest he shows in me. Oh, there's the occasional guilty 'do
you want to come? Oh, but I suppose you can't really—the
baby ...'

It is as if I have been transported to another life. I may
as well be that housewife in the suburbs that I despise.
How am I different to her? I worry about money endlessly:
where once I could have stayed calm about having only 10
bob to last the week, now I am wringing my hands, wor-
rying about food, nagging at Ed ... I agonise over what to
make for dinner, how to get stains out of the carpet, how

to get the nappies dry, what to do about odours ... it's as if I am slowly sinking in the water, Jewel, just occasionally making it to the top for a gulp of air—to a sort of memory of what LIFE IS, what life CAN BE—should be—and then down down down I go again. And each time the surfacing gets harder and harder, requires a greater and greater feat of will, kicking and turning and fighting against the undertow. What I fear most is that as the memory grows fainter and fainter, eventually I will just give in to it and go under, relieved that I don't have to struggle any more, that I can just sink into this blessed oblivion—give into this siren song of domesticity—which I know will be—for me anyway—a type of death.

I am with Clive at Sutherland—though you have probably guessed this. I do not think I could bear to be without him for even a moment when we have only just discovered what it is we can be together—which is something great I think, not just as individuals getting on with our lives, but as Artists in the purest sense. We can teach and learn from each other in a way that I NEVER could with Ed. It is not that he is a bad man or that I do not love him—he is as good a fellow as ever was, you do not need to remind me of that, & I will always love him as a good man, but for me he is somehow stifling which is a hard thing to explain and maybe I cannot. There is not anything that I can properly put words to—he is generous and patient and loving, but somehow, everything that is worst in me wells up when we're together. And it is much the same with Zelda. However I try I cannot find it in me to feel maternal toward her ... It is not her but me and I only resent all the time that I am expected to give, that she requires, & there is no compensation from that mad love I have been told that a mother feels, should feel, and that I do not. I feel like a picture all out of perspective with no centre, a canvas with no balance. I had thought that it was just the feeding, but even though she is weaned there is no change. I am angry most of the day that she takes so much of me and I wish her asleep (and sometimes worse) so that I can work.

And Z is such an odd baby—I do not know what I really mean by that as I suppose all babies are odd, with their strange unfocused gaze and their unfathomable desires. But she is so foreign to me. You know when a woman has a miscarriage and the doctors talk about an incompatible foetus due to their blood type, in these cases there is something intrinsic to the child that cannot survive with such a mother—the source of its life will prove its death—well, I sometimes feel something similar has occurred between me and Zelda. I suppose there's the look of her which is all wrong—she is so pale, so hairless, and those cool hard blue eyes, so much like my mother's, I think sometimes—so judgemental—they see me so clearly and do not like what they see. And she is so sensitive—sometimes I think that my very touch is painful to her—she shrieks just as if I have burned her. We are such opposites—did you know that her birthday is the winter solstice, and mine the summer? It could not be clearer—it is as if we were fated to repel one another.

She is according to all accounts a good little baby—regular & content—& I do not think she will cause YOU too much grief. Anyway, I am sure that Ed will rescue you as soon as he can. And in the meantime, thank you from my heart.

My love and gratitude to you and to Paul, too,
Annie xxx

June 12th, 1946
Dear Jules,
Well it is up to you my dear to do what you think best. There is no going back for me—it would be better all round

if there was to be a complete break. I can see no sense in my having what you call regular contact visits with the child, it will be too painful and confusing for her, surely. And if Ed really doesn't want her, or doesn't feel he can supply the 'stable, secure home life' as he puts it that she needs, then yes, I think that it probably is best if we make the adoption formal. Though I am never going to change my mind and claim her as my own, I can see that it would be clearer both for you and the child. Also if you wish to as you say settle money on her. You can give her more—and I don't just mean in a material sense—than either me or Ed ever could, you know that. Love comes easier to you, Jules, you are lucky that you have escaped the burning driving force of art that consumes everything else. And Miss Zelda Holland will be a fortunate child indeed—everything that is the best, and all that artistic talent to be nurtured. Who knows, perhaps we have borne a prodigy, a genius with all the best of us in her—you will be the best person to encourage and direct all that talent so that at least something good may have come from Ed & me.

I hope that Paul is as set on this as you—that he does not see Z as cuckoo in the nest so to speak, as I know some men would have a problem with a child not their own taking up so much of their wife's attention—and even when they are their own. But I suspect that as always he will be with you 100 per cent. You are fortunate, Jules, to have a man so faithfully love you. I do believe you could be unfaithful a thousand times and still he would love you. Clive is not so easy going, I am afraid he is frantically jealous and nights when I am working he becomes quite serious, questioning where I have been and why I am away at this time or that. This is only a small fault though and made worse of course by his condition and our current isolation and the fact that he cannot work much at the moment, but I am sure this will all improve and we are in general and most of the time deliriously happy.

Thank you again for the money—it helps.
All my love,
Annie

PS. Good news. We have just found out that Clive's Aunt Louisa has died (oh how cruel and selfish this sounds— hers was a sad life by all accounts) & she has left him a house at The Entrance! We can move up there or sell but are thinking that we will perhaps make the move—it is just the place, C says. Only across the road from the surf beach & a decent weatherboard cottage as he recalls. We are to travel up next week to see if it will do. It will be far less trouble than selling & anyway we would not get the sort of money we need to buy elsewhere. It could not be any more of a wilderness than here anyway.

RUTH

Though they were legally our grandparents, Andy and I spent very little time with Jules and Paul as children—even when my mother was alive. It seems that once she'd married Dad and moved out to Boolah, Zelda had wanted as little to do with her old life as possible. Oh, there were letters and the occasional phone call between them and parcels on birthdays and at Christmas time, but they were hardly a meaningful presence in our lives. While they'd been relieved to see her settled, and they both seemed to be fond enough of Dad, the Hollands had serious reservations about her living in Boolah—the back of beyond, as Jules always referred to it—and Jules could never understand why Dad stayed on after Grandpa's death. On Sydney trips we'd usually stay with Dad's aunt, Lorna, who lived in Manly, rather than with Jules and Paul, whose cottage was never big enough to accommodate us comfortably, and who were far too busy running the gallery by then to be bothered with small children. We'd be left with Lorna, who was sweet and rather vague. She had a television and a wonderful stash of sweets and could always be persuaded to let me stay up and watch something completely inappropriate.

Jules and Paul had visited Boolah once or twice. I have some dim memories and fading Kodachrome snaps of a Christmas visit just a few months before my parents separated. Other than a vague recollection of being given a very special book as a Christmas present—a valuable first edition of *Snugglepot & Cuddlepie*, which Jules said was far too precious for me to actually read, but was instead to be put away until I was older, I can't recall much of that visit, but even in the photographs the strain is obvious. In every shot, Jules, though she's as immaculately turned out as ever, remarkably youthful and elegant, looks awkward and uncomfortable. There's one shot of her nursing a mud-covered toddler—Andy—on her knee (though you couldn't really call it nursing, it's more a feat of balancing, as she has him pushed as far forward as possible) and the look on her face is one of almost comical distaste. And there's a photo of Paul looking ludicrously out of place in a picture taken at a riverside skiing barbecue. Paul, smiling stiffly, dressed nattily even in old age—he was in his mid-seventies by then—his only concession to the heat and the season an open-necked shirt, surrounded by a bunch of young men, Dad's mates, all in varying degrees of undress and inebriation. There's a single photograph of the four of them together which must have been taken at this same event—my mother flanked by Jules and Paul, her arms around them, Dad a little to the side. Their smiles seem forced, and they all look vaguely unhappy, as if they'd rather be anywhere else.

Their last visit to Boolah was for Mum's funeral, but all I recall of that was running outside to greet them when they arrived with an enquiry as to presents, and being upset when they bewilderedly confessed to having arrived empty-handed. So many people had brought Andy and me little gifts, to keep us occupied, I suppose, or as some sort of consolation, and I can remember being shocked and disappointed that they, my so-called grandparents, hadn't bothered. It seems odd, looking back now with an adult perspective, but during those first few weeks after Mum's death, the toys were much more tangible, much more real, than my mother's absence. The toys made it seem like we were celebrating an extra Christmas, an early birthday. I had no idea what was going on, no real understanding. How could I know that when people told me that Mummy was never coming back, they were telling me the truth: Mummy really wasn't coming back, not ever.

After that visit I could count on one hand the number of times I saw Jules and Paul before they died, both of heart failure and within months of one another, during the late eighties. And each time I saw them I'd been amazed by the elderly couple's continued insistence on formality, their painful self-imposed distance. They were kind and politely interested in our doings, but it seemed to me then that they existed in a world of their own—one not peopled by such ordinary folk as us. Jules, in particular, seemed to have very little to say to the members of our rowdy busy family—involved in sports and caught up in local business—and they doubtless found us rustic, provincial, very dull. I think that Andy may have given them some vague pleasure, some slight hope of the persistence of artistic inheritance and aspiration, and I can remember Jules commenting on his physical resemblance to Annie, and noticing, even when he was still only a little boy, his rapier wit, his quicksilver temperament. I suspect she would have felt some sort of satisfaction in his career—a performer rather than the longed-for artist—but still he was connected, in his way, to those ever-sought Higher Things.

ZELDA

January 1971

Now, finally you are ready, able to make a start. You have the workshop as you need it—you have had the walls lined, another Breeze-Air installed, the tilting garage front replaced with glass sliding doors. The cement floor is covered with cheap honan matting, and you've had electrics put in, decent lighting. You discovered two old high-school science-lab benches going cheap, with matching stools. It has cost a pretty penny—it has taken all the residual money from the sale of the terrace—but it's necessary, if you are to get on with the next book. If you are to make a start. There will be no more working in the kitchen—there is a necessary line drawn now between your work and your life—which, when the children are home, is as it must be. You look back longingly, sometimes, to the days when work and life—art and life—blended seamlessly, days when you could rise, spend an hour or two on a print, then stop for a meal, start again. Days when there was nothing else and no one else nagging at the peripheries. No weight, no other responsibilities. But those days are merely a chimera, aren't they, a fantasy of a non-existent lost past? In reality you know there never has been such a time, unclouded by any other troubles or obligations.

But you do recall days when the burden of housekeeping didn't lie so heavily on your conscience, days when the keeping of a home wasn't of particular consideration. In the terrace you simply didn't care, there was no one else to see, and it didn't matter. Now, even if the children are at Richard's there is still washing to do, and mending, and ironing, clearing out the fridge, or filling up the pantry in preparation for the week ahead. And then what of all the maintenance: the dusting, mopping, vacuuming, the cleaning of the windowsills, the fly screens, and the windows themselves, brushing down spider's webs that appear as if by some fairy magic—instantly sagging, heavy with red dust—in every corner of the house. And then there are the unseen things—the mess that's accumulating stealthily, in places you've never even thought about: the gutters, the filters of the washing machine, the Breeze-Air, on top of the cupboards, in the bottom of drawers, the dust of dead insects caught in the limbo between window and screen. And there's the garden. It is in a sorry state—the bare patches of red earth extending, the roses that you enthusiastically planted when you first arrived needing to be watered, pruned, the impossibly luxuriant weeds that threaten to overtake, to choke the life out of every last living plant. It is frightening even to contemplate doing what you know must be done. You wonder sometimes whether it's worth it—whether it might be easier to give up, to just give in.

If you could afford it you would employ someone to see to these tasks, to restore and maintain order. You had never really thought about it before, but how carefree they must have been, those wealthy Victorian and Edwardian women who, with a guilt-free insouciance that's impossible now, employed others—an entire staff—to tend their home and their children, to control the chaos that increasingly threatens to engulf everything. To keep these privileged beings free to pursue their Higher Callings. There had always been domestic 'helps' at Jules and Paul's—hardworking women who you're ashamed to say you would be hard-pressed naming: they were constantly changing, an undifferentiated mass—but how much they must have done, how they must have made Jules's life one of relative ease.

Some days you ignore these duties—leave last night's dishes, ignore the washing, some days you even leave your bed unmade—and these are inevitably those days when someone will call in: Mrs O'Malley from up the road for instance, who'll drop in with a little cake, 'thought you might enjoy it while the kiddies are away, dear. Thought you might be lonely, that you'd enjoy a cuppa tea, a bit of a chat.' She'll look around avidly, her disapproval barely disguised, secretly delighting in your very obvious shortcomings. You can imagine her reporting back to your mother-in-law: past two and last night's dishes still unwashed in the sink; the loungeroom in a terrible state, books everywhere, piles of ironing to be done and the wash not brought in yet though it was obviously dry, a glimpse of the bedroom—the bed not made, and I'm certain it was a man's shirt I saw lying there on the floor. And dear Zelda—well I hate to bring it up, but she was dressed very oddly, her hands covered in ink, and I'm not sure that her hair had been done. You know I'd be very surprised if she'd bathed ... Poor Dr Howatt—I know that you think that he's well out of this—but those dear little kiddies, how they must be suffering. Not, of course, that I have anything against her in that regard, I'm sure she's a responsible little mother ... Must give her the benefit of the doubt though, maybe it was a bad day, maybe she needs to let go when the children are away (the cat will play, ha ha). Stands to reason, I suppose. I'd have liked a day to myself every now and then, when I think back. Wouldn't we all ...

But it's a start—and you find that it's working, that at least two days a week, you're working again, things are beginning to happen. It's beginning to feel real, to feel a part of you again, this work. The garage has become a workshop: coils of timber shavings litter the floor, you love the crunch as you step on them; the fragrant tang of the cut cherry is becoming familiar again. All around there is evidence of your industry: work drying, plates abandoned, prints half done, sheets of rice paper tossed and crumpled. Your hands are permanently stained with ink ... There's no rush of excitement or apprehension when you walk in—instead it's a muted, quiet pleasure. You are working again, and though you have not found any real direction—nothing is settled yet—you're confident you will.

February 1971

Ruth asks for more from the Grimm storybook, and for once she scorns the old familiars. She wants something new. She chooses one that you don't recall having read before, *Clever Elsie*. Ruth giggles madly, of course, at Elsie's silliness—and she IS absurd: stranded, howling, terrified—contemplating a disaster that has happened in her own imagination. And the further absurdity, the way they are all carried along in the river of her fears. And then to fall asleep instead of working. It makes you laugh, knowing that this is what most people here think you are doing. Snoozing and dreaming. Wasting your time. *Scandalous.* And yet the end is quite terrifying and sad, rather like Andersen's *Red Shoes*—the punishment is so cruel, and far outweighs poor Elsie's crime.

You had thought you might move on from Grimm to mythology, Greek tales, the Celts, perhaps, but for some reason Elsie strikes you as being the ideal story. Each scene so easily, so perfectly (now, at least, in your mind!) visualised. You are imagining doing half a dozen coloured blocks—for the key images—rather than merely hand-tinting the finished prints, and leaving the others black and white. The idea is daunting: you have had very little practice in this technique, but the greater clarity, the greater depth of colour; the symbolic possibilities that are opened up ... it's irresistible.

CLEVER ELSIE

There was once a man who had a daughter who was called Clever Elsie. And when she had grown up her father said, 'We will get her married.' 'Yes,' said the mother, 'if only any one would come who would have her.' At length a man came from a distance and wooed her, who was called Hans; but he stipulated that Clever Elsie should be really wise. 'Oh,' said the father, 'she's sharp enough;' and the mother said, 'Oh, she can see the wind coming up the street, and hear the flies coughing.' 'Well,' said Hans, 'if she is not really wise, I won't have her.' When they were sitting at dinner and had eaten, the mother said, 'Elsie, go into the cellar and fetch some beer.' Then Clever Elsie took the pitcher from the wall, went into the cellar, and tapped the lid briskly as she went that the time might not appear long. When she was below she fetched herself a chair, and set it before the barrel so that she had no need to stoop, and did not hurt her back or do herself any unexpected injury. Then she placed the can before her, and turned the tap, and while the beer was running she would not let her eyes be idle, but looked up at the wall, and after much peering here and there, saw a pickaxe exactly above her, which the masons had accidentally left there.

Then Clever Elsie began to weep and said, 'If I get Hans, and we have a child, and he grows big, and we send him into the cellar here to draw beer, then the pickaxe will fall on his head and kill him.' Then she sat and wept and screamed with all the strength of her body, over the misfortune which lay before her. Those upstairs waited for the drink, but Clever Elsie still did not come. Then the woman said to the servant, 'Just go down into the cellar and see where Elsie is.' The maid went and found her sitting in front of the barrel, screaming loudly. 'Elsie, why weepest thou?' asked the maid. 'Ah,' she answered, 'have I not reason to weep? If I get Hans, and we have a child, and he grows big, and has to draw beer here, the pickaxe will perhaps fall on his head, and kill him.' Then said the maid, 'What a clever Elsie we have!' and sat down beside her and began loudly to weep over the misfortune. After a while, as the maid did not come back, and those upstairs were thirsty for the beer, the man said to the boy, 'Just go down into the cellar and see where Elsie and the girl are.' The boy went down, and there sat Clever Elsie and the girl both weeping together. Then he asked, 'Why are ye weeping?' 'Ah,' said Elsie, 'have I not reason to weep? If I get Hans, and we have a child, and he grows big, and has to draw beer here, the pickaxe will fall on his head and kill him.' Then said the boy, 'What a clever Elsie we have!' and sat down by her, and likewise began to howl loudly. Upstairs they waited for the boy, but as he still did not return, the man said to the woman, 'Just go down into the cellar and see where Elsie is!' The woman went down, and found all three in the midst of their lamentations, and inquired what was the cause; then Elsie told her also that her future child was to be killed by the pickaxe, when it grew big and had to draw beer, and the pickaxe fell down. Then said the mother likewise, 'What a clever Elsie we have!' and sat down and wept with them. The man upstairs waited a short time, but as his wife did not come back and his thirst grew ever greater, he said, 'I must go into the cellar myself and see where Elsie is.' But when he got into the cellar, and they were all sitting together crying, and he heard the reason, and that Elsie's child was the cause, and that Elsie might perhaps bring one into the world some day, and that it might be killed by the pickaxe, if it should happen to be sitting beneath it, drawing beer just at the very time when it fell down, he cried, 'Oh, what a clever Elsie!' and sat down, and likewise wept with them. The bridegroom stayed upstairs alone for a long time; then as no one would come back he thought, 'They must be waiting for me below; I too must go there and see what they are about.' When he got down, five of them were sitting screaming and lamenting quite piteously, each out-doing the other. 'What misfortune has happened then?' asked he. 'Ah, dear Hans,' said Elsie, 'if we marry each other and have a child, and he is big, and we perhaps send him here to draw something to drink, then the pickaxe which has been left up there might dash his brains out if it were to fall down, so have we not reason to weep?' 'Come,' said Hans, 'more understanding than this is not need-ed for my household, as thou art such a clever Elsie, I will have thee,' and he seized her hand, took her upstairs with him, and married her.

After Hans had had her some time, he said, 'Wife, I am going out to work and earn some money for us; go into the field and cut the corn that we may have some bread.' 'Yes, dear Hans, I will do that.' After Hans had gone away, she cooked herself some good broth and took it into the field with her. When she came to the field she said to herself, 'What shall I do; shall I shear first, or shall I eat first? Oh, I will eat first.' Then she emptied her basin of broth, and when she was fully satisfied, she once more said, 'What shall I do? Shall I shear first, or shall I sleep first? I will sleep first.' Then she lay down among the corn and fell asleep. Hans had been at home for a long time, but Elsie did not come; then said he, 'What a Clever Elsie I have; she is so indus-trious that she does not even come home to eat.' As, however, she still stayed away, and it was evening, Hans went out to see what she had cut, but nothing was cut, and she was lying among the corn asleep. Then Hans hastened home and brought a fowler's net with little bells and hung it round about her, and she still went on sleeping. Then he ran home, shut the house-door, and sat down in his chair and worked. At length, when it was quite dark, Clever Elsie awoke and when she got up there was a jingling all round about her, and the bells rang at each step which she took. Then she was alarmed, and became uncer-tain whether she really was Clever Elsie or not, and said, 'Is it I, or is it not I?' But she knew not what answer to make to this, and stood for a time in doubt; at length she thought, 'I will go home and ask if it be I, or if it be not I, they will be sure to know.' She ran to the door of her own house, but it was shut; then she knocked at the window and cried, 'Hans, is Elsie within?' 'Yes,' answered Hans, 'she is within.' Hereupon she was terrified, and said, 'Ah, heavens! Then it is not I,' and went to another door; but when the people heard the jingling of the bells they would not open it, and she could get in nowhere. Then she ran out of the village, and no one has seen her since.

Since that first biography in the early eighties, there have been two more biographies and several critical studies of Zelda's work. These books have made their authors' reputations—have provided tenure in art academies and universities. They are the authorities. It is difficult to know what Zelda would have made of it all—she would, I think, be amazed. Posthumously my mother, a humble children's book illustrator, has a reputation that is as big, if not bigger than the reputations of either of her parents—which is something she never expected or, I'd guess, wanted.

Despite all the assurances of professional detachment, objectivity, there has never been an estate-authorised study, and over the years all of us (Dad, Judy, Andy, Jules and Paul) had refused countless requests for interviews, opinions, invitations to discuss Zelda's life and work. 'I know nothing,' comes my stock reply, 'I was only a kid. There's nothing I can tell you.'

The scholars are always disappointed by our lack of sympathy—our strict maintenance of silence: but as Judy used to say when we were kids: what do they expect? A medal or a Davy Crockett hat?

In each of the biographies, and in almost every word that has been written about her by either journalists or academics, it is the story of my mother's suicide that drives the narrative. The tragedy of her death informs every aspect of her life and work. It's as if her death was some sort of cancer, undiagnosed, but eating away at her from childhood, gradually infecting everything.

A good ten essays, along with a handful of book chapters, have been written on the connection—the nexus—between my mother's life and death and her final Grimm woodblock—*Clever Elsie*. None can resist reading the tale—or the tale as retold in my mother's prints—as if it provided a clear metaphor, an allegory almost, of her life. I'm not saying that there are no such metaphors in her work. Her concern with the fate of abandoned and stolen children is clear in her initial choice of stories: Hansel and Gretel, Rapunzel, her strange rendering of Rumpelstiltskin, where the queen is no innocent, but a voluntary spinner of straw, a gold-digger, ruthlessly giving up her child to further her ambition, pursue her desires. And I wouldn't really like to deny that, even if only subconsciously, the stories did represent her own feelings of abandonment. But the common critique of *Elsie* goes beyond that, into the realms of the absurd and the grotesque, with the suggestion that it was a coded suicide note.

I cannot help wondering if my mother's fame is as much a matter of coincidence—a collision of serendipitous events—as anything else. My mother died right at the beginning of the sexual revolution: in truth her work stood outside the new paradigm, being highly idiosyncratic, but was almost immediately appropriated by and for the feminist cause. The suicide of such a prodigiously talented, but fatally frustrated, tragically burdened, female artist, coming as it did just as the women's movement really took off in the early seventies—made her an almost perfect martyr to the cause of oppressed women everywhere, her death glibly and oh-so-conveniently attributed to her position as wife, as mother—passive, subject, and always always wronged.

She would probably be affronted—or perhaps amused—to find herself a poster girl of feminism. She was never one for gangs and groups, never part of a scene. In her diaries, there's a clear sense of the injustice of her situation as a wife, of the difficulties inherent in the maternal position, but this isn't manifest—or not without what I would call a fairly imaginative critique—in the work. She wasn't trying to accomplish anything, represent anything above and beyond the work itself. Not yet anyway. There's no telling what would have happened over the course of the next twenty or so years, had she been granted that additional time.

It's impossible to know what she would have made of feminism itself: how she would have reacted to the consciousness-raising sessions, the women's groups, that I've been told sprang up around Boolah just a few years after her death, when news of the sexual revolution finally made it into that bastion of CWA respectability. Perhaps she'd have been barefoot and bra-less, defiantly growing her underarm hair, tasting her menstrual blood and discovering her clitoris; exchanging tales of oppression and repression, looking for means of escape. But perhaps not.

It's true that her work is remarkable, no one doubts that, but without the romance of her tragic life and death I doubt she would ever have become the Zelda Steele so beloved of the academics and theorists; the Zelda Steele of mythology.

ZELDA

February 1971

You will never, even if you live to be a hundred, get used to the heat. You notice that most people, those who have grown up in Boolah, seem oblivious. You were amazed, your first summer here, to see Richard dress every day, regardless of temperature, in a long-sleeved shirt and long trousers, and even by the end of the day he would still manage to look cooler than you in your sleeveless shifts, with your bare feet. The relentless summer sunshine, the airlessness, the long long days and even longer nights—some days you are driven crazy by it. There have been weeks—the temperature never dropping below forty degrees—when all you have managed to do is lie on the bathroom floor, not moving a muscle. You would be happy to lie there from dawn until dusk, but of course this is not possible with two small children who somehow, miraculously, barely notice that they live inside an oven and are able to keep going going going all the long red-hot flyblown days. On these days you do not think of working—all you can think of is the crazy heat—there is no escape from it. You try making loads of ice to keep cool but the freezer cannot keep up with the demand, and the overworked Breeze-Air makes no difference, producing only long wheezing gusts of hot wet air. There is no point having a bath or showering; the tank water is hot. The only source of relief is the river. During the day it is too hot to walk the children down through the paddock, but in the late afternoon, when the sun begins its slow orange descent, you and the children follow the bank until you reach Bondi, and there, while Ruth and Andy paddle happily, you find the deeper water and sink down until you're cool, calm, able to think again.

Sometimes at night when sleep eludes you, you lock the house carefully and wander down with a torch. Richard has warned you a thousand times that the river is dangerous: that even the seeming calm of the shallows is deceptive, that there are hidden currents, logs and weeds that can snare you, pull you under, but you are careful, swim only at the little beach that you're so familiar with during the daylight hours. You lie flat on your back, float, careful not to put your face under the water. You know you are being irresponsible and foolish, that the hidden dangers of the daytime are multiplied in the dark, and that you'll never see the log that's heading your way, or the dead cow, until it's too late. But right now you need this—this enveloping black, this weightlessness. You wish you could stay this way forever, floating silently in the slow current, invisible even to yourself.

One night you realise you have drifted further downstream than usual, you swim to where you imagine the bank should be, but it's gone, the river has widened impossibly. You turn, swim across the suddenly powerful current, in what you hope is the opposite direction, but still you cannot find the silty bottom anywhere. You try hard not to panic at this endless black depthlessness, and you know enough about drowning not to, but it is difficult to stop the fear rising. For the first time the river seems treacherous, the dangers that you have been warned about omnipresent, imminent: you imagine a branch flowing along with the current, barging into you, knocking you out. The weeds that tickle your feet—previously delicate and pliable, benign—are suddenly stiff and unyielding, malevolently tugging at your ankles; and then, then you imagine great monsters in the depths—hungry crocs and sharks that have been supernaturally transported, or some undiscovered water-beast that has spent lonely millennia in the nameless depths, waiting for this moment, for you.

Oh, and how your heart is pounding, how quick, how shallow, your breathing has become, how weak, how desperate your stroke. And just as you begin to flounder, to gasp in water with every other breath, to give in to the fast flowing pull of the current, just as you imagine yourself sinking, lost, your feet find the bottom. You follow the gentle rise in, scramble up the steep bank and sit panting beside the rushing water. It takes you half an hour to calm yourself down, to orient yourself—you can see the town lights behind you, so you assume you are on your side of the river. It takes another half hour to find your way home, panicking now about the children: what if Andy has woken, has fallen from his cot—or Ruth, you see her awake and terrified, wandering the house, crying out for you—or worse, happily playing with knives, matches, climbing the bench to the medicine cabinet or somehow managing to get to the rat poison you keep on top of the fridge ...

April 1971

You are surprised by how lonely it is at night, when they're finally in bed, finally asleep, the kitchen and living room set to rights, and surprised even more at how much you miss Richard. You had thought that it would be a relief, to not have the persistent, nagging feeling of not being enough, of not wanting enough, of not being available in the way a wife should be, and yes, it's true that that has gone. But alone on the couch, too tired to work, another interminable evening ahead, nights when you try hard not to blot things out the easy way with a glass, two glasses, three, then six; sitting alone then, you think how pleasant it would be to lean back against him, to listen to his stories about the day, to have his comments on the work you have, despite everything, managed to complete, on this or that idea, on what the letter from the publisher said. To have his reassurance, his confidence when you've had a bad day: the smack that Ruth did not deserve, the ruined biscuits, the soiled Grandma-knitted jumper you could not bring yourself to hand-wash, but instead threw fecklessly into the garbage. And how pleasant to be able to share the good things, too: the funny dance steps that Andy attempted; Ruth's remarkable elephant-shaped pie; the serious way Andy grips your face and looks hard into your eyes before kissing you wetly on the lips. How hard it is not to have anyone to share these things with. Or not anyone—Richard. You have taken to writing little notes to remind you; tell Richard about Andy's alphabet, tell Richard about Ruth's nightmare, tell Richard ...

August 1971

You remember Richard, exasperated by something you'd said years ago before you were married, claiming that you nurtured this feeling of being an outsider—of not fitting in, you and your friends. But you know that for you, at least, it's not true. You've never wanted it; and you certainly never encouraged it. You can remember even as a young girl at Helicon, watching how easily most of the other girls managed to fit in—even those who appeared outwardly defiant, rebellious—you could see that they didn't have to work hard, didn't have to make an effort, just to be themselves. You knew they felt comfortable, secure in their own skin. You wonder whether other people get this consciousness of themselves from their families, their homes. You can remember as a child having a clear sense that even at home you were only a guest—not unwelcome, but you just knew that Jules and Paul were waiting for you to grow up, waiting for you leave home, so that their real life, their previous life, could be resumed. There was no unkindness, not even, if you're honest, any real absence of affection, but there was a certain lack of ease, a feeling that both of them were perpetually on their guard, and the relationship between the three of you never really evolved beyond a cautious, polite esteem. The three of you were in no way similar to the tight little family unit that Margot, for instance, belonged to, and you had no access to that nutritive sac of family support—endless, unqualified, taken-for-granted—that you'd glimpsed in other people's lives.

Now, and perhaps because of this, there is this smallness in you—it's almost physical, like a hard little stone of need, of meanness, of envy—this sense of your own inconsequence that always makes itself felt when you are confronted by stories of other people's happy childhoods—their loving parents, grandparents, the fun they had, the closeness, the wholeness of their family ... How you would like to embrace their happiness, their complacency, but instead you feel yourself tighten, prickle up, resist. You worry sometimes that one day you will react like this with your own children—that they will expand, bloom under your maternal sunshine, but that you will somehow come to resent them for their willing acceptance of all you give them. You want them to grow up without all this hardness in them, to have the sense of themselves as important, capacious, large—but you want them to know too, that they're lucky, and to be prepared.

Some days it stuns you—their completeness. They're so little, so young, and yet already you can see, you're sure, parts of their adult personality so clearly. Ruth, so stolid, so serious, so eager to be helpful, to please—and yet with that remarkable stubbornness that rears its head every now and then, when she really doesn't want to do something, or really wants something—it catches you off guard, every time. And you've watched her with other children—she's quiet, watchful, rarely the centre of attention or directing the game, but she's not timid. You've seen her push a little girl back, quite matter-of-factly, without histrionics, just giving what she gets. In this she's nothing like you, you're certain; in fact she reminds you, oddly enough, of Richard. Even Richard's mother remarks on Ruth's similarity to him as a child. And there are certainly some surface resemblances; they both have pale skin, thick brown hair, thick-lashed eyes, full lips. It's said so frequently: *Ruth takes after her father*, that you've begun to think it too—and you have to pull yourself up, remind yourself that she's not, in fact, her father's daughter. You can see the similarity to Douglas, it's unmistakable, once known—the square solid body, the dark blue eyes, the strong nose, the mole by the side of her mouth. You'd rather not be reminded, really, but he's there with you always, in every glimpse of your daughter. Odd, how her physical resemblance makes you think fondly of him, without anger, without pain.

Andy is another matter. He's the image of your mother in so many ways. He's small, dark, quick. Even at this young age you can recognise that restlessness—the way he's never still, never silent. He has Annie's reckless full-throated laugh—and her flair for drama. You and Richard have marvelled at his ability to mimic, to tell a story, a narrative, clearly and confidently and coherently before most children can even string together much more than a simple sentence. He's a charmer, quixotic, merry. But there's a darker side too, that you glimpse every now and then. The quick, vicious temper—Ruth still has a scar on her finger where he bit her hard enough to need stitches. And he's a self-dramatiser. Sulking, yelling, threatening to leave home, slamming his bedroom door. At three. You hate to imagine what he'll be like as a teenager. You're surprised by Cynthia's attitude—you'd have thought she'd have taken a set against Andy, with his resemblance to Annie, but it's Andy who she adores. *Granny's little man* she calls him, besotted. He takes after my brother, Charles, she insists—Charles, a hero, a fighter pilot, gunned down over the Pacific during the war, by all accounts he'd been a handsome scoundrel. You can't really make out the resemblance in the photographs, but you're happy to agree.

You can see already that Andy won't be taking the easy route, that he's a complicator rather than a simplifier, that he somehow wants the dramatic, the dark, but Ruth is not as clear. Somehow, for all her compliance, her good behaviour, there's something else, something you can't put your finger on, can't get to. Something withheld, you think, even from herself.

But both of them—both already so much themselves, with their futures before them, already mapped out. Already written. It gives you a pain in the heart, a shortness of breath, thinking about that vast relentless future unwinding ahead of them, a future that you can't necessarily save them from. You do all you can to keep them safe, guide them, help them overcome all the obstacles of their childhood, and then—blam!—there's all the messy incoherence of their own lives, their unknown, unknowable futures.

It strikes you now that even the best-planned life is nothing more than a tangle, a muddle—only every now and then are a few threads pulled clear of the snarl. A cool day, a meal enjoyed with friends, happy antics of children, laughter, a kind word. Companionship. Such small things, you think, but all we can hope for, perhaps, to shore ourselves against the encroaching chaos.

You wonder again at your particular muddle. A mess largely of your own making. You wonder at what you have done; why you have done it. You wish it could be undone. That things could be unsaid. That the spool of time could be untangled, reeled in. That you could go back back back.

You wish that you could go home.

November 1971

Ruth is lying on a mattress in the workshop: it's late at night, and she's been home all day, ill, feverish, a sore throat. She is watching you, dreamily, sucking on her thumb as she still does occasionally, stroking Tedna's worn ear (compulsively, unconsciously). 'Mummy,' she calls softly, 'What's the new book going to be called?'

'It's *Clever Elsie*. Remember I read you the story?'

But it was a long time ago, more than a year, and Ruth doesn't remember, shakes her head blankly. You start to tell her the story, but she's not interested in that. Interrupts: 'Is it almost finished?'

'What?' You are distracted, trying to concentrate, cutting a block for the pinks on the second-last page—Elsie's cape, her shoes, some small delicate flowers, a bird's wing. Symbols of her much disdained dreaminess and lack of resolution. Fiddly bits.

'Have you got much more to do?'

'No—a few more blocks. Only a few more pages. I should be finished soon, I think.'

You haven't stopped to think of it, haven't let yourself consider the end, have just hurled yourself toward it—but it's true. You're almost finished; almost there. A little knot of anxiety—so low-grade, so constant that you've barely even noticed it—begins to unfurl.

Ruth's face, heavy-eyed and pale, brightens a little.

'Really. And then is that *all*?'

'What do you mean?'

'Will that be it then? You won't have to make any more books?'

'Well no ... it doesn't work like that, Roo.'

'Well, how many more?'

'Oh, I don't know.' You see a lifetime of work stretching before you, endless, inexorable. Does it fill you with joy or horror? You suspect both simultaneously. You calculate the working years left: if you can do a book a year, or at the very least every two years, it's twenty, maybe more. 'About ten or so,' you tell her, keeping it simple.

'Ten? Really?' From her downcast expression, Ruth sees only the horror. 'Do you really have to do ten more? Can't you just do five? Can't you stop?'

'Why, darling?' You slide off the stool, sit beside her. 'What's wrong?'

'It's just that,' her voice is plaintive, her eyes wide, 'you don't ever play with us when you're doing a book. You just ignore us.' Her voice quavers, with a seven-year-old's righteous indignation.

'Oh, that's not true,' you say crossly, 'I only ever do it when you're in bed, or at Daddy's ... and anyway you like them, don't you?'

'Yes, of course I like them, it's not that.'

'Well, what is it?'

'It's just that even when you're not *actually* working ... you still don't have time. To do anything else. You're always thinking about it … Sometimes I think you're not *actually* here.' She gives a pathetic little cough, wipes tired red-rimmed eyes, holds out her arms to you.

You gather her up and murmur sweet nothings as she drifts towards sleep. By the time you tuck her up in bed it's too late to start cutting again, you're too tired and anyway have somehow lost the impetus. You wonder if what she says is true. Wonder if you're doing something terrible to your children—working.

Wonder whether it's true that you're not really here. Wonder where you are.

January 1972

A dream. You and Richard are in the surgery talking about Andy and Ruth—you are telling him how worried you are about Ruth in particular—that this last month she has refused to sleep, that she has cried every night for him and says she will NOT sleep until she sees him. No matter what you say, no matter what promise you make, she won't sleep, wills herself awake all night. You are exhausted, you tell him, you cannot cope, you have not slept yourself. There must be something, some treatment—a course of medicine, a pill, an injection that will cure this. He shakes his head, perplexed. Then goes to his bookshelf, browses through a magazine. He comes back, still carrying the magazine, but it has unaccountably become a large blue hospital pillow, which he puts down on his examination table. Then he helps you climb up—you are wearing a hospital gown, tied wrongly, so that you are exposed at the front, but for some reason you do not care. Richard plumps up the pillow and helps you to lie down, and then climbs up himself and stretches out beside you. He is wearing a long white artist's smock which he somehow pulls up to cover the two of you: it goes right over your heads, enclosing you completely. This is the only known cure, he says. Sleep, he says, and you close your eyes, comforted, content, knowing that when you wake up it will all be better.

RUTH

On Sunday afternoon while Salty is sleeping off the effects of a beery lunch I take my mobile out into the garden and dial my Sydney number. The phone is answered almost immediately, and I know before I even hear his voice that it's Lewis, can see him bounding to the phone, as he always does, always so hopeful, so eager to connect with a new person. 'It's me, Lewis. Roo. How are you?' I have slipped into using my old name so easily, but it's a name that's never been used by either Lewis or Chris. But Lewis doesn't seem to notice, burbles away brightly about the concert for refugees that his father's planning on taking him to next weekend, John Butler will be there and maybe even Silverchair, and Jack and Oscar his two best mates from school are coming too and then staying for a sleepover.

I interrupt. 'That sounds fantastic, darling. I wonder if I can just have a quick word with your dad?'

'Yep. No worries. I'll just get him.' I realise when he goes that that's probably the first time I've ever called him darling. I've kept my distance so scrupulously, have always worked hard to maintain strict boundaries in our relationship, a strategy that I always felt worked well—for all three of us—but now I feel a terrible sadness momentarily, wondering if what I'm about to do will have a greater impact than I've imagined. But then Chris is there, on the line and I steel myself to do what I know needs doing.

We haven't spoken for more than a week, but even so his greeting is distant, distracted: 'Hey, Ruth. How are things?' I am his lover, we've shared our lives for more than five years—and yet somehow I've never really noticed it before, this impersonal politeness. There's no hint of longing, of missing, of wanting, of desire. Oh, I've read enough guff about the inarticulacy of men, their inability to express their emotions, the difficulties that they have expressing their needs, and I don't doubt it, am happy to give them the benefit of the doubt, reduce my expectations in line with their capacities, but this confirms my decision: this impersonal, one-size-fits-all salutation seems somehow representative of our entire relationship. The apparent intimacy—the hollowness at the centre. Maybe Chris deserves something bigger, something more real than I could ever offer him, anyway. Maybe we both need to stop skating over the surface; need instead to feel the sting and burn of the cold current that swirls beneath the ice. The thought is enough to dispel my guilt momentarily, to harden my resolve. I come straight out with it, don't beat around the bush or try to honey it up.

'Chris. I don't think I'm going to come back.'

'Oh.' There's silence for a moment, then he repeats what I've just said, slowly, as if to himself. 'You're not coming back.' I can imagine him standing there, his hand fossicking in his hair, brushing it back as he does when he's thinking, the frown of mild puzzlement, his bottom lip pushed out into a funny cartoon pout. 'Um. Do you mean you're not coming back to Sydney, to work ... or to me?' Another pause.

'Though I guess you mean all of that, don't you?'

'Yes. I'm sorry. This is a shock, I know. But Chris—it's a shock to me too. I didn't realise—I mean I've just realised how distant we are. Really. From one another.'

'Distant. Yes.' He gives a hollow little laugh. 'You're in Boolah and I'm in Sydney. It's almost a thousand kilometres, isn't it?'

'Oh, Chris. I don't mean just physically—I mean,' I hesitate, wince as I say the word, 'emotionally.'

'Right. Emotionally. Okay.' He clears his throat. His voice suddenly brisk, businesslike. 'So you're not coming back. Not ever.'

'I don't think—I mean ... Well, obviously I'll have to get things, sell the practice, I suppose. But no. I'm not.'

'You're not coming back. Just like that.' He clears his throat again. 'So.'

'I don't think we're ... going anywhere.' I finish lamely.

There's another painful silence, and then a great whoosh of breath surges down the line—a gasp, a sigh, a sob.

Chris, his voice faint, halting, quavering: 'I can't talk any more, Ruth. I'll call. Later.' He hangs up.

We always think we know each other, don't we? We try so hard to get what the other person's about—spend so much time and effort analysing this action, that conversation—because that's all we have, that's all that's available to us, all we're given. But sometimes I really think we may as well give up, stop trying. Sometimes, most times, it seems that however hard we try, however deeply we care, we never manage to work them out. Just when we think we've put our finger on it—the essence—the meaning, the one thing that makes this or that person tick, we're proved wrong. And anyway, it's such arrogance, isn't it—thinking that we can understand each other, see into the heart of another—when our own motives, our own desires, are never certain, and never explicable. Not even to ourselves.

ZELDA

March 12th 1972

A perfect morning. You take Ruth to school, then drop Andy off at Cynthia's. She will collect Ruth in the afternoon, take them both to Richard's in the evening. You have only a final block to grave, and then to print, and the work will be complete. It is a simple scene, this last, and should be finished quickly. It's been done in negative, so only the lines need to be carved out, rather than the surrounding space. A picture of poor silly Elsie's face, gazing longingly through a window. Cynthia is civil for once; almost friendly. 'Hope you get some good work done, Zelda,' she smiles, 'and don't worry about the children. I'll get them over to Richard's tonight.' Andy runs inside without even a backward glance, without waving, bursting with excitement: Granny will take him down the street, will buy him a milkshake, will let him watch *Sesame Street* and *Play School* twice in one day. You're forgotten in an instant, which is exactly what you want, isn't it?

At home you are straight into your work. The day stretches out in blissful endlessness: without the children here you can work all night if you want; you need not stop, not for meals, not for anything. It feels—it feels like freedom, or it should, but there it is, that faint tug, that ache, real as hunger, of missing them even as you exult in being alone. You start, and soon you are lost in the carving; lost in the rhythm and pulse of the cutting; the scraping; the lines and whorls; the fruity tang of the timber as you cut into it. The excitement as the figure takes shape, the story opens up. Then closes. There's nothing like it.

You stop for the mail. You are expecting—you are always expecting, hoping for—a letter from your publisher, news of an overseas sale, a cheque. But there's nothing from them. Only the phone bill and a parcel. A parcel that obviously contains a book, large, weighty, substantial. You turn it over, excited—what can it be? You haven't anything ordered. It could be a gift from your publisher perhaps, but there's no sign on the brown paper wrapping, no return address. You cut through the string, tear open the paper. There's a familiar picture adorning the jacket: your mother's most famous seascape—the naked man outstretched, prone, the seashell beside him, suggestively genital in its soft curling vulnerability. The title, emblazoned, bold: *This Savage Calling: The Art and Life of Annie Swift.* And the author's name, unmistakable. Douglas Grant.

You have been warned that publication was imminent, but still you feel slightly sick. Turn the book over—and there is Annie's face, that small photograph you know so well. Annie in her early twenties, just before your conception, at the height of her beauty, her hair cropped—boyish, bold, daring at the time, but suiting her perfectly—revealing that famed bone structure, the wide lips curved with laughter, eyes half-closed, the sprinkling of freckles that only accentuates her youth. Beautiful Annie. You feel the familiar heart squeeze at the sight of her. You open the book to look at the inside back sleeve. And there he is. Douglas. He is beautiful too. Older than you remember, but still with that wild Irish look—the dark eyes, his thin lips still with that sardonic turn despite the cigarette in the corner of his mouth. His hair is longer than you remember, and he sports fashionable sideburns, but there's no grey—though knowing Douglas's vanity, that might not be completely natural. His expression solemn and scholarly. Dressed in arty black. You snap the book shut. Your hands are shaking and you are damp with perspiration, though the day is relatively cool. You want to put the book down. You want to throw it—but it will not be put down, will not leave your hands. You do not know how long it is that you stand there petrified. Your whole body is shaking and you can feel the burn as the bile rises and you only just make it to the sink.

You go into the bathroom and look at yourself in the mirror. You are puffy, pale; your eyes red-rimmed. *You look like a white rabbit, Zel.* Your hair is a mess. You can hardly bear to look, but you try to put it all to rights. Splash water on your face, then scrub it dry, trying to put some colour into your cheeks. But now you look feverish, ill, your cheeks burning, eyes red. You pull the brush through your hair, tie it back into a ponytail. Pull it out. Scrape it back with a comb. You find an old lipstick, but somehow your lips have disappeared and you make a mess above and below. You line your eyes with kohl—oh, this is an improvement! See, you are alive. You do exist. You look at yourself again. There are stray hairs on your upper lip, your eyebrows are a mess, prickling through all over the place, you really should ... But you don't. You take a deep breath, stand for a moment, steadying yourself, readying yourself.

You go back to the kitchen and make a pot of tea. Get biscuits, three Monte Carlos on a bright blue plate. They look so pretty, you wish you could capture the prettiness, the innocence of them. You sit down at the table, pour. Two sugars, why not three, you might need them. Milk. You take a sip, with a steady hand. You pick up the book. Open to the back pages first—the index. You're there, of course: a scant five entries: iv; 85; 89; 120; 226.

But you can't look up the references. Not yet.

Instead, you find the photographs. There are three photographic sections, evenly separating the narrative. The first section, in the usual way of biographies, features portraits of Annie's family, your family. Her Swift grandparents—Mary and Horace, newly arrived from Ireland. Grandfather Horace has a long white prophet's beard, dark, hollowed-out eyes; his wife, Mary, is slight, grim, already worn-looking in her thirties. The next photograph is of your grandparents on their wedding day. Maud, smiling happily, looks unbearably hopeful. Her new husband, the soon-to-be-extinguished Herbert, his face composed, but his eyes bright, twinkling, humorous. Annie's eyes. A photograph of the three fatherless children: Norm, Alice and little Annie. Annie, already a gorgeous child, poses for the camera, face uplifted, sunny, her irrepressible nature apparent even in this static image: despite her diminutive stature, a fairy child, tiny, somehow she takes up most of the space in the frame, her sullen mousy older sister pushed to one side; Norm, solid and impassive even at ten, stands behind the girls. You flick forwards to a shot of a young Annie and Ed, taken mid-stride on George Street. They are looking at one another and not the camera, and it looks as if they are moving fast—as if they are going places, as if nothing and no one will stop them. Ed is in uniform, the photograph is dated October 1944. You would have been conceived—just. You flick forwards again, to the last page of that first section, to a snapshot of mother and child. The baby—you—is six months old, pale, hairless, plump. She—you—regards the camera from her position on her mother's hip, slung casually, as disregarded as a sack of potatoes, while the mother—Annie—gestures, cigarette in hand, engaged in animated conversation with an equally animated Jules. The caption beneath reads: 'Annie (holding baby Zelda, six months) and Julia Holland. December 1945.'

How fitting, you think, to be parenthetically attached to your mother.

You turn to the first page. Start reading.

You are halfway through the preface when you realise something: Douglas has been your mother's lover. You do not know how it is that you know this—he hasn't actually said as much—but there is something, and no doubt it is only something you could pick up—something so intimate, so proprietary in his tone, as if he is saying: *I know you.* You recall it so well from when you were with him. And suddenly this—the preface, the book—seems like a message from him, from them both, to you—the proof of their double, inexplicable, unforgivable, betrayal. You cannot read any more—will never read any more. You close the book. Put it on the table and leave the room. You light a cigarette. Fill a tumbler with whisky. Drink it quickly, pour another. You pace from room to room, smoking, leaving a trail of ash. You don't know how you will endure this; you don't know that it's endurable.

You try hard not to think of it: of the details. You remember a brief meeting at the gallery, Annie delivering some new work, preparing for a joint exhibition, soon after you'd met Douglas. The introduction made by you: ever so proudly. Your man. Such a man. So handsome. So impressive. So charming. And you're pleased, for once, that Annie is your mother. She looks gorgeous, and you hope some of her glamour will rub off on you. You remember your mother's raised eyebrows. 'Mr Grant? A friend of yours, Zel? Oh, your teacher. A critic as well. My. And still so young. Goodness, I'm honoured.' The outstretched hand. 'Yes, perhaps I have read some of your little articles—oh, *The Times*. Well, no, possibly not. To be perfectly honest I try to avoid art criticism as much as I can.' A challenge, thrown out, politely ignored. And that's the last you recall of them together. What happened? How could you have missed the spark of interest, the quick intake of breath, the lingering handshake. But then why would you have noticed? Your own eyes were too full of stars, your own breath too rapid, your own heart beating too quickly, too loudly. Your lover, here! Yes! Yours! You wouldn't have noticed a Wynyard bus careening through the plate glass windows until it was too late. But you'd have noticed a phone number written down, a card given, an invitation? Surely.

Perhaps they met again during the exhibition night itself. You cannot recall Douglas being there, you would have been too busy, too frantic, the gallery crowded with people, the artists themselves, potential buyers, critics; you would probably have asked him not to come. But perhaps he called in anyway, dropped in early before a class, left before you'd even realised he'd arrived.

It had been an exhibition of women's art: *A Woman's Work*, Georgia had somewhat prosaically styled it. Ten Sydney artists had been asked to show, a rather scornful Annie, in her first exhibition for several years, among them. She had had little time for her own work over the last few years. With Clive sick again, she had to take a daytime job at a local commercial studio, drawing advertisements for small businesses, and several nights a week taught life drawing at the local tech. Occasionally, when she managed to sell something, she would buy materials, and work on weekends. Her nights off.

You can remember seeing her standing a little to one side that night, somehow excluded from the buzz and the excitement, and it suddenly occurs to you that Annie was the odd one out amongst these other artists, well-to-do matrons from the North Shore, the Eastern Suburbs. You imagine now that she must have despised them a little—busy, clever, self-important—even as she admired their work and envied their lives. Oh, she'd have recognised their talent, there was little of the dilettante about any of them, and she'd have had to concede that the best of their work was probably technically superior to much of hers. But their easy acceptance of their own insignificance would have irked her: the way they made it clear that there was no need for them to compete, to be ambitious, to push themselves forwards, to make themselves a success not only critically but commercially. They had, some of them, substantial incomes from husbands, parents, were comfortably middle class, and would have had no experience of the world that Annie herself inhabited, where money was always scarce, where penury was a reality and grasping poverty only one pay-cheque away. With no idea of their privilege, they were free to do their best, always, to follow whatever instinct they needed to follow. There was never any need for them to leave their cosy domesticated academic circle, to enter brazenly into the cruel and dirty world of commerce. No need, in short, for them to make a living.

You can almost feel how Annie's heart would have twisted when a woman in a Dior suit—a writer for the women's page of some city newspaper—wandered up to her small selection. You can imagine her watching the woman desperately, waiting for her reaction, trying to read her expression, her gestures, and the terrible pang when the woman moved away, moved on without lingering over any particular work, or making any notes in her conspicuously displayed notebook. What is there to single out her work, anyway? There was no luxuriating in these latest paintings—only a rush to finish, to let it go before she was really happy; and then to live with the knowledge that her best work would never be done, that despite her best intentions she had again sold herself short. Compromised. She can remember saying once, that to her, Art was Life, and she had meant it. It had been like breathing, and every breath was a delight. Now, though, that early delight had gone—each blank page, each canvas, only an argument to be won—a battle—a means to an end. Now she can only wonder if there's any way back to that pure state—where it is only the work itself that matters, and not its reception, what it's worth.

Perhaps she was standing there, contemplating all this, when Douglas walked in off the street. Slightly impatient, knowing he would be late for his ladies, but too curious to stay away. He would have seen Annie immediately, noticed the faintly bitter smile on that still beautiful face. You can imagine him realising that you were nowhere to be seen, moving quickly to her side. It would have taken only a few moments—you know exactly how many. He would have expertly admired her paintings, added perhaps some brazen flattery, and then his *coup de grâce*: 'This book I'm writing on Australian art? I'd really like to interview you. Maybe devote a chapter?' Annie's smile would have lost all its bitterness, she'd have felt buoyed, confident, young again. Her life suddenly full of possibility. And then a meeting—an assignation arranged instantly, surreptitiously. *I hope you have some etchings to show me ...*

You try hard not to imagine them together, alone, but it's almost impossible: you know exactly how he would be; how he would cup Annie's elbow in that particular way as they walked together. She would have felt the pulse of his energy, his desire, even in that first inconsequential touch. The way he'd look into her eyes as he lit her cigarette, or filled her wine glass—she would have wondered, vaguely, how he managed not to overfill or miss the rim completely. He would have made the first tentative advance, you're certain of that—what would it have been, you wonder? The backs of hands meeting as if accidentally, then turning, gripping, or perhaps a chaste goodbye kiss that became a lingering farewell, moving downward, from cheek to lips, from lips to throat, from throat to breasts—you know that path of his so well—and then the rest of it—the pushing, the gasping, the murmur deep and deeper in his throat, the breathless sticky collapse—oh, God, you can almost feel it. But it's not you, is it, and you thank God for this: that it's not you crushed, pinned down forever beneath the weight of his arrogance, his vanity. It's your mother.

Suddenly, and it catches you unawares, the whole thing strikes you as unbearably absurd. Vain middle-aged Annie. Annie, fast losing confidence in her artistic abilities, but still so sure of her sexual allure, taken in by the smooth, the charmingly unprincipled Douglas Grant. Thinking that he must adore her, that she is irresistible, even to a man not yet in his thirties—and her daughter's lover no less—a young man on the rise, going places. Never thinking, not for a moment, that it's all a calculated act—that Douglas would have had this in mind, that whatever she told him in the heat of the moment would be stored away. That he would think, even as he ran his fingers down her body, even as he told her he was bewitched, that she was a veritable goddess, that he was speechless, struck dumb by her beauty, her talent, even then, it would be there. This thought: that she could be useful. If not now, one day.

This was never a part of your story. This changes everything. You will have to go back, revise her past; revise your own.

RUTH

Already I'm almost sixteen years older, have lived sixteen years past the sum of time allotted my mother.

Before reading the diaries, I'd often wondered what this really meant, wondered how far beyond my mother's experience I'd actually come, how well I'd 'used' those additional years. By the time my mother died she'd married and separated, borne two children, produced numerous paintings, sketches, prints, and published four books. Posthumously she'd managed to secure a reputation as one of the world's great children's illustrators. Even in her short time she'd lived a life that seemed far above and beyond my secure, routine existence. It had been hard not to conclude that despite its truncated span, Mum had lived more fully—a bigger, darker, heavier, more substantial life than I could ever hope for. From my end of her narrative—a narrative half-imagined, fleshed out by others' stories, their embellished memories, the simplified, condensed versions provided by detached biographers—it seemed that there had been no coasting. No waiting. That no moment of her life had been wasted or forgotten—that her life was made up only of hugely significant moments, all leading to the ultimate realisation of her artistic vision, and then inevitably, culminating in her tragic end.

But her diaries tell quite another story. Grant had said that he hoped the diaries would contain information on my mother's work, that light would be shed on the ideas behind the woodblocks—light that would be invaluable to critical studies of the work—but there's very little of that nature. They're the diaries of a young girl, of a young woman in love, of a wife, a mother—this is the only life she really writes about. The work—the work is something else, it belongs to some other part of her.

The diaries are full of the same small moments that make up all our lives, and there's a certain satisfaction in this for me, as her daughter, and some relief. Sure, my mother's life—the trajectory of her completed life—was dramatic, but her real life, her lived life, was full of the ordinary, the banal, too. The slow dull days of adolescence; the boredom, frustration, bafflement, irritation with the adult world. And then the confusion of her early adulthood—of wanting, of waiting, of not knowing what direction to turn. There were plenty of wasted days here, and nights spent sweating on the future, willing it to come, willing it to be revealed as if it was always just waiting there, finished, complete.

Like everyone else, I'd always thought that her suicide was not only inevitable, but a fitting conclusion to her life.

But in the end it was death that chose her, wasn't it? Like most people, my mother had had no say in the matter or the manner of her going—the choice had been made for her.

And what do I feel? It's hard to know right now. There's no calm centre from which to take a reading, but I think what I feel is a terrible terrible sadness. My mother should have lived. I should have had a mother.

I tell Salty of my decision later that afternoon. We're finishing off a section of the hallway; I'm carefully applying the thick enamel paint to the skirtings, while Salty tackles the picture rails—though rather more efficiently.

I tell him that I'm going to contact Grant. That I'll go to wherever it is he lives, that I'll take the diaries with me and let him read them, let him discover who I am. I don't know yet whether I'll let him use them in any way; after all, other than the fact that he's my father, I don't really know all that much about him—about who he is now, anyway. I don't ask Salty for his opinion and he doesn't give one. After a while, still painting, he says without taking his eyes from the wall: 'You're a game girl, you know that, Dr Howatt. You've got a bloody nerve.'

'*Gwani*, as Linda'd say.'

'Whadda you think your old man'd think?'

'I really don't know.' I stand up slowly, stretch my legs. 'Maybe he'd be pleased—maybe he'd think that I'm doing the right thing. The risky thing, I mean. I think that Dad'd say that I've been a Clever Elsie for far too long.'

'What do you mean, a Clever Elsie?'

'I'll come back, though,' I say, deliberately avoiding answering his question. 'I've decided to stay, to move back. I'm going to set up the surgery properly. Full time.'

It feels so strange, saying this. Once I'd wanted so badly to escape, been so desperate. Once it had seemed that it was only away from Boolah, away from the kind knowing eyes, that I would succeed in remaking—or was it making?—myself. Now, back after so many years, it's as if I'm undergoing that same process, but in reverse.

'Well good for you, Roo. I've only got a few more days work left here. And then I think I'll head off.'

'Oh.' I try to keep on smiling, but it's an effort I can't quite manage.

'I've been thinking,' he looks up from his painting again, 'of doing a bit of travelling, actually. Mum's pretty well settled, and I've got a little nest egg saved. I might just use it to see a bit of the world.'

'Oh.' I swallow. 'Well—that sounds—'

'Always wanted to go to South America. Maybe we can meet up somewhere, eh? Have a drink?'

I take in his words, and a weight that I barely realised had settled, lifts. I am surprised by my own pleasure in this—another unexpected turn, another possibility.

'Why not,' I say.

ZELDA

March 12th 1972

It is late. It's past ten, but I drive to Richard's—drive home. It seems suddenly urgent that I see him. I want to speak to him honestly for once, to tell him that I think we should try again, not just for the children, but because it is what I want. I am prepared to beg if necessary. But Richard's not there—Judy answers the door in her night-gown, sleepily apologetic, slightly embarrassed. He's been called to the hospital, a delivery, she's minding the children. Would I like to come in, to wait? Though it might be a while. It doesn't matter, I tell her. It'll keep. I'll see him tomorrow.

It's too hot to sleep, and too late now to bother. I'll go for a walk, a swim.

ACKNOWLEDGEMENTS

For their many and varied contributions—without which this novel would never have been written—my grateful thanks are due to the following:

Deborah Beck, Winifred Belmont, Anna Crago, Meredith Curnow, Jessica Dettmann, Rebecca James, Nelsyn Kelly, Andi Kocher, Shari Kocher, Pippa Masson, Sophie Masson, Sharon Noble, Cathy Parker, Felicity Plunkett, Michael Sharkey, Darren Shepherd, Sam Shepherd, Jane Sloan, Bruce White, Liz and Mari of the LWC Inc., and of course—as ever—my family.